Carmen Reid is the author of the bestselling novels *Three In A Bed, Did The Earth Move?, How Was It For You?* and *Up All Night*. Her new novel is *The Personal Shopper*. After working as a journalist in London she moved to Glasgow, Scotland where she looks after one husband, two children, a puppy, three goldfish and writes almost all the rest of the time.

You can drop her a line at www.carmenreid.com

D1081004

www.**transworldbooks**.co.uk

HOW WAS IT FOR YOU?

Carmen Reid

CORGI BOOKS

TRANSWORLD PUBLISHERS
61-63 Uxbridge Road, London W5 5SA
a division of The Random House Group Ltd
www.transworldbooks.co.uk

HOW WAS IT FOR YOU?
A CORGI BOOK : 9780552155830

First publication in Great Britain
Corgi edition published 2004
Corgi edition reissued 2007

A CIP catalogue record for this book
is available from the British Library.

Addresses for Random House Group Ltd companies outside
the UK can be found at: www.randomhouse.co.uk
The Random House Group Ltd Reg. No. 954009.

The Random House Group Limited supports The Forest
Stewardship Council (FSC®), the leading international forest
certification organisation. Our books carrying the FSC label are
printed on FSC® certified paper. FSC is the only forest certification
scheme endorsed by the leading environmental organisations,
including Greenpeace. Our paper procurement policy can be
found at www.randomhouse.co.uk/environment

Typeset in 11/12pt Palatino by
Falcon Oast Graphic Art Ltd.
Printed and bound by CPI Group (UK) Ltd, Croydon, CR0 4YY.

4 6 8 10 9 7 5

For my 100 per cent organic,
totally additive-free parents
With much love

Acknowledgements

Many, many thanks to:

Über-agent, Darley Anderson and his team, who always see the bigger picture and take care of it.

My editor, Diana Beaumont – so inspired, encouraging and calming.

The brilliant people at Transworld, because writing may be a solo job, but a book is truly a team effort (and I have the best team!).

My friends and family – all woefully neglected this very busy past year.

The vital support system: Caroline, Debbie and most especially, Thomas Quinn, who hopefully knows that I couldn't do this without endless cups of tea, boxes of peppermint chewing gum, the occasional 'creative' tantrum . . . and him.

Chapter One

'I'm 34 years old and I'm shooting up in a nursery. This is ridiculous,' Pamela told herself with almost a smile, as she prised open the plastic case with pretty fingernails, slid her skirt up and jabbed the pre-loaded syringe into her bare leg.

It used to be difficult, used to make her feel squeamish, faint even. But now, no problem at all, she was quite the expert, stabbing the needle in up to the hilt, feeling the cool flush under her skin.

She was so absorbed with the injection, she hadn't noticed the trip-tripping high heels of her current client in the hall. Sadie Kingston-Jones, owner of a string of bijou boutiques and married to a nearly-millionaire, came into the half-finished room and watched her interior designer with fascination.

'I'll have whatever you're having,' Sadie shot out so loudly that Pamela just about fainted with surprise. Bad enough being caught injecting by the woman currently paying for your services, let alone having her think you're some kind of junkie.

'Sadie! You gave me a fright,' Pamela looked up, still rubbing her leg. 'It won't do you any good, it's purely medicinal.'

'Are you sure?' Sadie said striding towards her on spiked red heels. 'Because if it has any sort of sedative effect at all, I want some right now.'

Then, despite the red cheongsam, pulled screamingly tight over the monstrous bump of a twin pregnancy in its seventh month, Sadie wriggled down to sit beside her on the floor and gave a sigh so loud, so deep, it was almost a moan.

'This is complete fucking hell. I am never, ever getting the decorators in again . . . in my entire life. That includes you, darling. And I mean it.'

'Oh dear,' Pamela replied carefully.

'I have four men digging up my bathroom, you and yours fussing about up here, a cleaner, a nanny and a PA downstairs, all constantly needing my attention. I'm going to go mad! And I can't even have a cigarette. Bloody babies.' She put a hand on each side of the bump rising like a red space hopper from her lap. 'Just one more, that was all I agreed to. But oh no, I have to land myself with twins, don't I?'

They surveyed the emerging room: smooth pale pink and green walls, curved wooden shelves which wrapped round the space in an ever-ascending staircase, the newly made window seat, still unpainted. It was going to be adorable.

Pamela's mobile began to ring. Sadie watched her check the number and brace herself with a deep breath before answering.

'Sheila, hello.' She put a smile into her voice which wasn't on her face. A pretty face, pale with dark eyes, and darker hair, much more delicate than her figure, all Italianate boobs, curves and hips threatening to spill from her fussily fashionable jersey dress.

'Right ... But don't you ...? Well ... what I ...' Pamela was obviously not going to be allowed to tell the person on the other end of the line very much. Far too much of a nice girl, Pamela, Sadie could tell. A sort of head-girlie, people pleaser; she clocked the wedding and engagement ring and guessed at a steady, happy marriage made earlyish, to a similarly nice guy, maybe in the parish church, watched by two sets of proud parents; a Home Counties girl, she was sure. Children? Not yet, but they were definitely on the agenda. This woman spent all day designing nurseries, for goodness sake. But then again, what did she know? She'd only met Pamela a handful of times and people were constantly surprising.

Pamela ended the conversation and put her phone down.

'Who was that?' Sadie asked.

'My boss.' Pamela said this very evenly, but not quite nicely.

'Sheila Farrington! She's a bitch from hell, isn't

11

she?' Sadie brought her fingers to her lips and breathed in, then out between them, a virtual cigarette.

'Well . . . I wouldn't . . .'

'Of course you wouldn't,' Sadie smiled at her. 'You are her loyal and hard-working right-hand woman and I'm sure your reward awaits you . . . in heaven.'

Pamela laughed shyly at this and dared to say: 'I've been working for her for three years now. I'm used to her. But the plan is still to go freelance one day . . . move out of town . . . a bigger house in the countryside. All that.'

'Oh yes,' Sadie knew. 'All that. Going freelance – moving out of town – we're all dreaming about that, aren't we? Waiting for the next promotion . . . for our house to be worth just that little bit more. But hardly anyone does it, you know. We all just grind on. You've got to live in the present, make what you've got right here lovely,' she lectured, doing the breathing through her fingers thing again. 'That's why I brought you in, to make my home in the here and now . . . lovely . . . Eventually, once you've finished pulling it to bits and making my life hell!' Glossy smile at this.

'Anyway, what do you want to live in the countryside for?' she added. 'Nothing ever happens out there. No good shops or parties, you can't even buy nice food.'

Pamela laughed. 'What do you mean?'

'It's true,' Sadie insisted. 'When we were in Cornwall last summer, the village shops only sold frozen pizzas, plastic ham and tins of beans.

There's no focaccia or Starbucks or Parma ham or even a fresh vegetable out there in the country-side, you know.'

'Of course there's no Starbucks, isn't that the point?' Pamela was a little outraged at this dissing of her dream of rural bliss.

'Believe me, you only realize how spoilt we are when you go out there. There's no nipping round the corner to buy lipstick, or even tampons. No, from now on, we're only holidaying in other major international cities. If you want greenery and open space, go to a park.'

Pamela, laughter sparking in her eyes, bit her tongue. Sadie was highly pregnant, highly stressed and she didn't really want to argue with her anyway.

'So, what are you injecting yourself with?' Sadie picked up the syringe case, wanting a fresh topic. 'Are you diabetic?'

'Well, er . . .' Pamela Carr. Once a 15-a-day smoker, who'd been a bit square about drugs, who'd only occasionally had a joint at the week-end, who'd once slipped an E and hated every moment of it, who'd only rubbed coke onto her gums on an exceptional night out. Pamela's new drug of choice was expensive, loaded with side effects, available on prescription only and designed not to make her happy or high or mellow or morose. This drug, which she injected into herself several times a day at certain times of the year, was designed to make her pregnant. She'd been doing this for five years now and it was still awkward to explain.

Especially now that she was carving out a new niche for herself at West London Interiors in nursery design. She knew exactly how bizarre it was, that couples at all the best addresses should be calling on her – oestrogen and progesterone junkie, weekly attendee of the St Francis Hospital IVF support group – to design new rooms for their children.

But maybe her longing, her passionate need for a baby, was what made her so good at her job. No detail was too much trouble. She was super-careful, super-caring, super-cautious about the precious rooms for these precious babies. Only non-toxic, milk-based wall paints, linseed treated wood for the floors, Swedish oiled planks for the shelving, organic German cottons for the curtains, for the ties around the beds and the cots. Reclaimed maple and cherry for the cupboards, chests of drawers, window-seat toy boxes. Everything was double-checked, cross-referenced and she could quote all the latest research linking MDF fumes to asthma, varnish vapours and new carpeting to cot death.

It was, of course, spectacularly expensive, but parents trusted her. And she did a great job, made the rooms jaunty, childish, with all sorts of tiny little user-friendly ideas dreamed up during the countless hours of research spent with her four-year old niece and two-year old nephew. Acres of shelving, little canvas toy hammocks above toddler beds for all the cuddly toys who couldn't be squeezed into bed, child-high wooden pegs dotted round the rooms for

14

dressing gowns, satchels, art aprons, pyjamas. Changing tables which folded out then disappeared back into walls, night light holders, aromatherapy oil diffusers, canopy curtains which could be opened out into a tent, then undone and tucked away again. Beds built waist high with cosy dens underneath. Smooth beach pebbles tied to the end of the light pulls and specially chosen plants on the windowsill to suck toxins from the air.

Nothing over-designed: no beds shaped like cars or trains, everything pared down and simple, versatile. She thought it best to let children invent, imagine for themselves.

'I'm doing IVF,' she told Sadie, who cringed inwardly at her insensitive bump, at all the complaints she'd made about it, all the moans about varicose veins, piles, expense and inconvenience. Shit.

'I'm sorry,' Sadie said. 'That must be very hard.'

'Oh, not really–' and this wasn't all lie – 'I'm used to it now. We've been doing it for five years. Trying different things. Amazing what you get used to.'

And it was.

She was currently preparing herself for another go. Hopes in neutral, neither up nor down. Trying to prepare herself physically for the hormonal rollercoaster, for the medical interference, somehow reining her thoughts in, not allowing herself to speculate on the outcome. That, she had learned, was the only way to go on.

Because nothing had been so crushingly

15

disappointing as their first IVF attempt and the fact that it didn't work.

She and Dave had been 'trying' for two years then. All their married life, from when it was still sweet and funny to have sex by the calendar and then a few more times a week, just for luck.

The love and the hope in the silly routines they had back then.

'Honey, I'm home.'

'Honey, I'm ovulating.' Cue wife emerging from bedroom in silk négligé.

'Is there a thermometer in your pocket or are you just pleased to see me?'

'I've been eating oysters ... Tonight is your lucky night.'

But eventually, endless trying and endless disappointment made it a grind ... so to speak.

'Oh no ... we don't have to have sex tonight, do we?' Dave woken from the sofa, the remote removed from his hand, the empty crisp bowl taken from the top of his stomach.

She'd suspected for a long time that something was wrong and hadn't even bothered with the NHS waiting list. It was straight to St Claire's, the private hospital, double-checked on the internet, with the highest success rating and fees to match.

Of course, since then, they'd changed hospitals twice – as you do when you're on the IVF fairground, because someone somewhere else has always got a better ride, with different games, big dippers of hope and despair, no promises, no guarantee and certainly no money back. It was as big a part of her life now as her work and her marriage. Her family and her old friends knew about it. Her new friends, well, they were all made at the St Francis support group, so they *shared*.

But the first time.

It had seemed such an obvious, fixable problem. Dave's sperm count was low and her hormone levels were shaky.

'Think of it as pre-pre-menopausal,' the consultant had explained, but all she'd taken in was the word 'menopausal' and the first inklings of fear had prickled her.

'But I'm only 29!'

'Very early stages,' the doctor had assured her.

And he made it sound so blindingly simple: her eggs would be harvested, Dave's sperm washed, spun and selected, the embryos would be popped back into her hormonally primed body and *voilà* – pregnancy.

Three embryos were implanted and Pamela had gone home happy-hearted, pencilled round the due date, planned her maternity leave and debated with herself when she would be ready to go back to it all, post-baby.

She felt different, she told Dave over breakfast every morning, expecting the sickness to set in any moment now. God! What if they actually got twins?! Triplets!! That was the magical IVF prize. You waited and waited for a baby and then, just like buses, two – sometimes even three – came along at once.

17

She was granted two weeks of this happiness and then she took the test and it was negative. Pamela was so surprised, she immediately wanted a second one.

The second test was negative too and several days later they went for a debriefing with the doctor.

'Why hasn't it worked?' She was bewildered; had done everything, every tiny little thing requested of her to the letter. To no avail.

'I'm afraid, most of the time, it doesn't work out,' the nurse had told her gently once their time listening to the doctor's spiel was over. Out in the corridor, underneath the wall of success-story baby photographs, Pamela had cracked open and cried miserably, noisily, so the nurse had ushered her and Dave into a little room which, judging by the stack of magazines and videos, was the sperm collection facility.

Over the years, they had lurched on from try to try, from one hospital to another. Getting to know a whole lot of other tryers on the way. People who'd done St Claire's and St Francis and were moving to the Lister. People who'd done the Lister and St Claire's, Hammersmith and were now at St Francis.

All kinds of combinations. All chasing something new ... the latest this ... swapping hopes and fears, all kinds of tips and research nuggets with each other whenever they had the chance.

'My sister suggested the Foresight programme, you know, where you give up alcohol, smoking, tea, coffee, sugar and E numbers for six months and you have to get your hair tested to see which heavy metals you're polluted with and which minerals you need to take.'

Pamela had listened to it wearily at the last support group. She'd heard it all before. She'd tried it as well and so far, it hadn't worked. But just to make sure, just to cover all her bases, she always ate well, attempted to avoid the forbidden foods. Before every 'try' she totally cut out every bloody fun thing she had ever enjoyed, from wine to wine gums, and hoped that it would help.

But when the tests came back negative, or when she was just feeling down about it all, she took it out in food. Cinema-sized bags of Revels, party packs of Mars Bars, the entire Thornton's Continental Selection. Blamed her weight gain on the drugs, but really knew in her heart it was the unhappiness.

'No, I can't do tonight, big day at the hospital tomorrow,' Pamela reminded her friend Alex on the mobile.

'Tomorrow? Sorry, I forgot. Sorry . . . stupid of me,' Alex apologized. 'Are you going to be OK? I don't know how you cope, I really don't. All that rummaging around . . .'

'Don't remind me!' Pamela tried to block out the flash of stirrups, pipettes and tubing, the usual cast of thousands looking on from over their surgical masks. 'I don't know what I'd do if I didn't do this,' she added. That was the plain, unvarnished truth. The IVF game, it was now for her above all a way of coping. A way of keeping very busy, very focused until she was finally ready to deal with her infertility.

Somewhere way at the back of her mind she knew this. But she pulled back, concentrated her thoughts on the day ahead of her.

'I'm thinking of you. OK. I really, really hope it works for you,' Alex told her, 'And it might, Pam, it's . . .'

'I know, it's different this time,' she interrupted. She didn't want to hear the words out loud right now.

She had wondered if it was a mistake to confide such a thing even to Alex, but the stress had been so much. There had to be someone she could confide in, someone to share it with.

After five years of trying to make a Pamela and Dave child, they had finally abandoned that hope. Tomorrow was the first attempt at Plan B: making a child that was part Pamela and part anonymous donor sperm.

Chapter Two

Alex. Where would Pamela be without Alex? Her latest and almost immediately closest friend because she'd needed someone different, someone who didn't know her as Dave's wife, Sheila's henchwoman or an IVF patient. Alex let her be, made her laugh raucously, allowed her to forget all the other things, at least for a while.

They had met over a year ago in a secondhand shop in east London. Not a junk shop, the kind of shop where design classic stacking chairs fight for space with Swedish light fittings and 1970s 'groovy baby, groovy' sideboards.

A tall, red-brown-haired, strikingly dressed woman seemed to be lingering over all the same things that Pamela admired: the big black glossy vases, the ebony leather armchair, the enormous charcoal fur rug. 'I'm going through a very black phase right now. Gothic meets Japanese,' the woman had volunteered as they took turns to stroke the rug and sigh over the price.

'Me too,' Pamela had told her. 'Mine's a Fred Astaire does *Breakfast at Tiffany's* kind of thing.'

The woman had replied: 'Cream walls, black sofas, cigarette-holders? Oh yes, I know where you're coming from.'

So conversation had broken out quite naturally, and the 'what do you do?'s and 'where do you do them?'s had revealed that Alex was a professional 'sourcer'.

'A dealer, really.' Alex had smiled and her accent which Pamela had taken a moment to place as mildly Scottish, had broken into pure Del Boy: 'What can I do ya for? Some lovely 1960s plastic tablecloths ... genuine kitsch for the kitchen.'

Her lifetime's work was hunting great stuff down, from all over the place and selling it on to collectors, designers, stylists, whoever was interested.

So, of course, her eyes had taken on a slightly professional gleam when Pamela told her she was an interior designer, who did offices and corporate lobbies but also a lot of high-class nurseries.

'Oh, I'm always coming across great kids' stuff,' Alex had enthused. 'Little French day beds, coloured lanterns, old school desks and I've hardly got anyone to flog them off to. We must swap details.'

She had undone the gold clasp of an antique crocodile handbag and brought out an engraved silver cardholder, while Pamela scrabbled in her bag for paper to write on.

*'Because you still haven't found
What you're looking for.'
Alex Finisterre*

The card also gave a mobile number and email address. 'I'm quite pleased with it,' Alex had commented. 'But it does make me think of U2, which is unfortunate.'

'Finisterre? What a beautiful name,' was Pamela's response.

'The ends of the earth. It's quite appropriate, really.' Alex left it at that. So Pamela wasn't sure if she meant she'd made the name up or not.

'Well, I'd love to hook up some time. Do lunch, see your portfolio, find things for you,' Alex had said, putting the paper with Pamela's details into her bag, 'Great to meet you.'

She'd squeezed Pamela's hand and exited the shop, with a swoosh of outrageously bright turquoise afghan coat and waft of woody-rose perfume.

A few weeks later there had been a call with the offer of a lunchtime sandwich and the chance to take a look at some 'amazing children's quilts'.

'I'm not being a heavy saleswoman, honest,' Alex had assured her. 'Just come for the chat, it would be nice to see you.'

It would be nice to see you. Pamela had realized how long it was since she'd made a new friend; well, apart from the IVF support group. But it would be good to know someone away from all that.

Alex turned out to live in a block of red-brick

flats, just streets away from east London's epicentre of cool, Hoxton.

Cool, but still inner-city grubby. Pamela rang the bell and waited, watching the wind gust plastic bags and crisp packets down the street while three boys half-heartedly kicked a football round a small, tarred car park opposite.

'Hello, you found it OK then?' Alex had pulled open the heavy metal and glass front door and ushered her in.

They climbed four flights of stairs to a front door painted turquoise blue and baby pink.

'Never be boring,' was Alex's explanation.

Then they were inside a small but perfectly formed sitting room/kitchenette filled, as Pamela had expected, with all sorts of wonderful things: dainty crystal chandeliers, engraved glass vases, a pile of books with leather covers in sugared almond colours, antique crockery, a battered studded cream leather sofa swathed in small, shorn lambskins. Impossible not to wander round and look and touch, just like in a shop. In fact Pamela wondered how Alex lived around all these things. They took up all the space. The few chairs were piled with stuff; so were the table and sideboard. She stood in the centre of the room, unsure where else to put herself.

'Such gorgeous things,' she'd said.

'*Everything* is for sale,' Alex had told her from the draining board where she was shaking the water from a rose trellised teapot. 'If you love something, let me know.'

'Tea?' she'd asked. 'Don't take your coat off,

we'll go out and sit on the terrace. There's more room out there. Oh, but look at the quilts first and I'll knock us up some food. Is there anything you don't eat?' She'd poked her head round the corner of the half-wall which divided her kitchen from the living space.

Technically, there was a great list of things Pamela didn't, at that time, eat or drink but suddenly she couldn't be bothered with it all. 'What are we having?' she'd asked instead.

'Bacon butties, brown sauce, a proper salad and red wine, stuff the tea.'

Should she worry if the bread and bacon were organic? Whether or not the salad was unsprayed? Brown sauce was toxic stuff that was definitely off her menu ... let alone wine. She hadn't touched a drop for four months. But she was ravenously hungry and brown-sauced bacon butties sounded unimaginably fantastic.

'Perfect,' she heard herself reply.

'The quilts are in the cardboard box on the sofa. Dig them out. They're from a car boot sale in Essex. I get fantastic stuff in Essex, it must be Britain's clear out your clutter capital or something.'

Pamela opened the flaps of the box and brought out an armful of fabric. She had expected something antique, faded and delicate. But this was a single-bed-sized quilt home-made from jumbled, brightly coloured off-cuts. She could see nylon turquoise and brown patches, polyester purple, yellow chintz, bits of taffeta, all mixed into a crazy hotchpotch then sewn onto a heavy cream bedspread.

Her immediate reaction was 'yuk', but she threw it over Alex's sofa and brought out the other two.

They were just as bad.

'Aren't they fantastic?' Alex popped her head round the wall again.

'Hmmmm.'

'No, I agree. You'll need a moment to adjust. But I'm thinking a mainly white room, splashes of primary colour here and there and three wee beds with these quilts.'

She was right, it would probably be stunning.

'Just imagine the Essex gran who cut up all her old polyester summer dresses and stitched them together into these for her grandchildren,' Alex added, mouth full of something. 'They probably loved them, but I bet their mum had a fit!'

Pamela laughed at this.

'Well, they were £30 the lot, so if you fancy them, that's the price. I never profit from a first deal, but don't worry, I'll rook you the next time. Right, the terrace.'

Alex slung on her afghan and opened the big window-door at the end of the sitting room.

The terrace was only slightly less jumbled than the sitting room. Alex appeared to have just taken delivery of an assortment of large terracotta pots.

'These are great,' Pamela commented.

'Twenty quid a shot,' was her hostess's reply, followed by a wry: 'Don't worry, you'll get used to me.'

They were sizing each other up as they sat down to the big platefuls of food and even bigger tumblers of wine on the terrace. It was light grey and chilly out there, with a view of rooftops, TV aerials, and washing lines strung out over balconies, but they pulled their coats around them and Pamela soon found the wine was heating her stomach like a fire. How had she managed four months – four whole months – without this?

She thought Alex was intriguing: messy, a little studenty, chaotic, but obviously so enthused by what she did and, as the trace lines on her pale skin revealed, much older than her clothes, crop-fringed reddish hair and silver trainers might have suggested.

Alex saw a dark-haired, reserved, maybe slightly shy, maybe slightly careful woman, dressed almost entirely in black but whose very funky green buckled bag and matching green boots hinted at something more interesting.

'Do you always wear black?' Alex had dared.

'Oh . . .' Pamela said, a little knocked off guard, 'I've put on weight and I suppose I do that black cover-up thing. I hadn't realized how bad I'd got.' She was in another big black coat, tied tightly with a belt.

'Are you married?' Alex had asked, although she had noticed the little gold and diamond combo.

'Ah ha,' Pamela had managed from the depths of a bacon sandwich almost religious in its perfection.

'Kids?'

So casual, nothing but polite interest meant by it, but this question kicked Pamela in the stomach, brought a slight gasp to her throat every time. So hard to get the answer right.

A casual 'no' wouldn't do, because it implied she didn't have them and it was no big deal.

A 'sadly, no' invoked too much sympathy from strangers. So she had now refined her answer to: 'Not yet, we're still trying.' Followed by a question to swiftly change the subject.

She tried this out on Alex. The follow-up being: 'You live on your own, do you?'

'Yes. That's obvious, isn't it? No-one else would put up with this amount of mess. But I *don't have cats*,' she said with emphasis, 'I want you to know that. I am not one of those lone forty-somethings with a cat-child! Have more wine,' she had commanded, dangling the bottle dangerously over the tumblers on the wrecked metal table.

'No, no, I can't. My head's already reeling.' Pamela had put her fingers over the glass and wouldn't be persuaded.

So that was how the friendship started and since then it had been cemented with many more glasses of wine out there on the terrace, and regular weekend junk shop and car boot sale scavenging trips.

Finally, a few months in, Pamela had wanted to explain to her new friend her regular hospital trips, her yo-yo-ing weight, her unpredictable

28

moods and the great big knot of unhappiness inside her which she didn't think was ever going to be untied.

They were driving home with a car full of treasures from a day trip to Hastings when Alex, who'd long suspected what was going on, asked how long Pamela had been 'trying'.

'Four years. We've done five IVF cycles. Not the slightest sniff of pregnancy.' Her voice had remained neutral. 'Dave has a very low sperm count and apparently I'm sub-fertile ... pre-menopausal.'

'I'm so sorry,' had been Alex's response.

'I'm absolutely desperate for a baby,' Pamela had added, straight arms on the wheel, eyes fixed, unblinkingly to the road. 'I'm beginning to think I'll do anything, I almost don't want to see my brother's kids any more because I'm going to snatch them ... eat them up. I'm starving for a baby. I can't explain it any other way.' There was a big, wrenching sound after this, somewhere between a sob and a choked cough. Car still gunning down the dual carriageway at 70 m.p.h.

'I'm so sorry. I'm sorry I've brought it up now. Do you want to stop for a moment?' Alex was slightly concerned about the safety of this conversation.

'No, no. I'll be fine. I don't cry about it. Can't cry.' Pamela's eyes still fixed firmly ahead.

'Why the hell not?'

'Because I've cried enough. And I worry that if I start, I'm never going to stop. I'm going to be upset about this till the day I die.'

A long moment of silence passed between them. Alex looked out of the side windows at the hedges and fields whizzing past.

'Anyway, there's another go coming up in three months' time. The odds are better now. Twenty per cent of cycles work. We've already done five, so maybe this will be the one.'

'What about you?' Pamela asked now. 'Don't you think you would like children?' – the unspoken 'And haven't you left it a bit bloody late?' acknowledged by both of them.

'Well . . .' and Alex knew how unfortunate this was going to sound now, 'I'm from a family of five children. Have I told you that before? And . . . I know I've lived away from home for twenty years or so, but I'm still grateful for the peace and quiet. I'm sorry. That must sound odd to you. I don't know . . . I like babies. I love little children. But having this person to be responsible for . . . for the rest of my life . . . It's a bit selfish probably, but I'm just not up for it.' She shrugged her shoulders lightly. 'So there you go. We're a very odd couple then. Reminds me of that grace: "Some could eat, but have no meat. Some have meat but cannae eat." '

Pamela managed a smile.

Chapter Three

Pamela woke much earlier than she needed to, still tired from yet another restless night. Enviously, she turned to watch her husband fast asleep beside her. David Carr, a good person, nice guy, who wheezed slightly as he slept, was no longer quite as good-looking to her as she'd once found him. His once wild, curly blond hair had been tamed into a short, thinning crop and he was so stressed out with work right now, he was even skinnier than usual.

His clothes actually hung off him, which seemed faintly ridiculous for someone in their late thirties. But she didn't feel angry with him about it, she felt sorry. Like her, he was busy, busy with work and had the added stress of a long commute and a job with the NHS.

He was part of a trust management team. A career that had once looked so promising, altruistic even, but now was bound up in cut-throat politics, in-fighting, futility. He loathed it, was drained by it. All he had energy for when he got home was watering his plants, then slumping onto the sofa with beer and Pringles. He was an addict of the reality escape programmes: 'Birmingham family move to rural Greece', 'Mancunians build French fishing lake', that kind of thing. His dissatisfaction with life was one of the things that kept her awake at night. Once in a while he talked about 'getting away from it all', but then, didn't everyone? And as Sadie had warned ... who did? And was it any better out there?

They'd been married for seven years now and been together for five years before that, since she was 22. Was this how marriage went? Or was it their fault? Had they let everything get a bit stale? Because she couldn't deny how *wildly* they'd once been in love.

Whole-weekends-in-bed-together *love*, love-letter *love*, meeting-him-at-the-door-naked *love*, driving cross-country through the night to be with each other *love*, soulmate *love*. Where did it go? How had it so slowly, step by tiny step, changed from that to this?

From wanting to *die* for someone ... to wanting to *kill* them for leaving a towel, *yet again*, in a damp heap on the bedroom floor.

But then when they'd met, they'd been *artists*, art school romantics. Love and all the great romantic gestures had come so much more easily back then, when love was new and they felt like the first people who'd ever fallen into it.

Her third-year class had shared a life drawing

lesson with the fourth-years. Throughout the afternoon, she'd found her eyes wandering up over the top of her paper to the wiry blond guy beside the window, utterly absorbed, sunlight setting his frizz of curls alight. She hadn't been able to tear her gaze from the pale face, the oh so intense eyes. To her sensitive, art school soul, he had looked like a warrior angel Gabriel.

OK, so it was maybe just the tiniest of disappointments to find out that the angel Gabriel's name was actually Dave and he was from the Midlands. But Dave from the Midlands turned out to have as truly poetic a soul as she'd wanted back then. He'd sent her sketches he'd made of her secretly, pinned illustrated poems to her bedsit door, and when he'd won her over, he'd dared to talk of undying love.

They were inseparable, fascinated, dressed in each other's clothes, had even the tiniest things in common. They went on a penniless hitch-hiking holiday to sketch their way round France and Spain, somehow surviving on bread, cheese, chocolate and wine.

Both sets of parents had looked on with a mixture of awe and anxiety: Dave's parents liked her; Pamela's loved him. All worried it would end horribly, but secretly hoped that it wouldn't, that maybe this fledgling couple might realize what a perfect match they had made so young.

Dave had graduated first and spent a year in Liverpool waiting for Pamela to finish her degree. He painted all day long – paintings that no-one wanted to exhibit, no-one wanted to buy – and worked in a supermarket, stacking shelves at night. By the time she'd graduated, it had got to him. He'd enrolled on a hospital management course, desperate for a 'proper' job, something he could do to make a difference. And she'd decided to retrain in interior design.

Another year of grinding, grown-up student poverty followed and the romance of being poor wore off in their tiny flat full of damp, beans on toast, vegetable stew, a one pint limit at the pub.

They chased hard for jobs in London, then rented somewhere as expensive as they could now afford to begin their 'real' jobs in the 'real' world. The world which owned them not from nine till six, as they'd imagined – 'we can still paint in the evenings' – but from 7 a.m. till the moment they fell into bed. Way too tired to ever lift the lid on the boxes and tubes of dried-out, hardened watercolours and acrylics. There had once been so much romance: a marriage proposal by poem, a candlelit wedding . . . where had it gone?

Somewhere in the back of a wardrobe, unlooked at for years, was the book Dave had made her as a wedding present. It was full of the paintings, drawings and stories which detailed how they'd met, how they'd fallen in love and the way he hoped their life together would be. They never even mentioned the book now, because the reality of their marriage was turning out so dismally different.

34

An added irritant for Pamela was the happy perfection of her parents' marriage. They had never admitted to 'difficulties' of any kind, so she had never asked them for advice. Anyway, they always assumed that Pamela and Dave were *fine* and they devoted their energy to Pamela's younger brother, Ted, and his on-off-up-down-hot-cold relationship with Liz, the mother of his two children.

'You know, Ted and Liz remind me a lot of Simon and me at that age,' her mother had told her recently. *Simon*. She never referred to her husband as 'your dad'.

'They have that "zing" . . . that special buzz.'

Oh yes, Pamela knew all about that buzz. The buzz which had begun so many years ago when daring American trainee art teacher Helen had set eyes on dashing English entrepreneur, flash-wheeled Simon.

Buzz . . . buzz . . . buzz: the lock on her parents' bedroom door, Christmas presents of see-through nighties, antique copies of the Kama Sutra . . . Helen, 61 next year, usually wore stockings, suspenders and silk underwear. Her father sported a trim goatee, which her mother, *her mother*, claimed to find '*very pleasure-enhancing*'!

The two had taken Pamela out for a candlelit dinner on her 12th birthday to talk her through more sex ed than she'd ever wanted. They'd insisted boyfriends stay over. In general, much as she loved them, and she really did, she'd found them the most embarrassing parents in the world and it was hardly surprising that she preferred romance, poems and soulmates.

'You and Dave are different,' her mother had added, sipping at her tall glass of lime and soda, smoothing the sleeves of her silky kaftan. 'You two are much more . . . fraternal.'

Pamela hadn't liked the sound of that at all. Fraternal? Yuck! What was that supposed to mean? They were passionless best friends? Ouch.

But where was the zing? she couldn't help wondering as she watched her husband wheezing in his sleep.

Had the zing well and truly zung?

No. No, she told herself. It was just all this stress – work, the IVF. If only they could just get pregnant, get on with all the plans they'd made for themselves and their children, things would be like they once were.

She decided it was time to get up and make a pot of revolting decaffeinated Earl Grey tea.

When Dave finally appeared in the kitchen, she had already showered, dressed and breakfasted. She'd put on a wash and made her work calls. His hair was on end, his chin razor-scraped and he had on a T-shirt and sagging at the knee chinos.

'Can't you wear a shirt? You look so much nicer in shirts,' she wheedled.

'But I'm more comfortable in this,' he said defiantly. 'I'll put a jacket on top.'

'Oh all right.' She was only too aware that they hadn't even said good morning yet and already there were the makings of a fresh row in the air.

'You look lovely,' he told her. Diversion tactics. As if that excused him from looking like a mess. He kissed her forehead and started hunting about for bowl, spoon and cereal boxes.

'Are you nervous?' he asked as he sat down at the table beside her.

'A bit.' She ching-chinged her nails against her third cup of tea. 'I just want it to work. We've tried so hard . . . we're trying so hard. Don't we deserve a bit of a break by now?'

Dave stroked her arm. There was nothing left to say that they hadn't already said to each other.

We'll get there . . . You never know, this could be the one . . . We'll work something out . . . Where there's a will, there's a way.

Over the years, they'd tried out all the responses, all kinds of comfort. And now there was just silence.

They knew the odds – small every time – and they knew the pain of it. Grieving for something that has never been. A little death died again week in, week out, month in, month out. Every pram passed in the street, every bundle in a papoose, every giggle overheard, all the tears they would never be needed to comfort.

Without children, life was so grown-up. She saw the difference every time she went to visit Ted.

His home was filled up with four-year-old Martha and two-year-old Jim, plastic toys, Lego, things that barked, quacked and squeaked. It was noisy, full of laughter, shouts and shrieks.

Ted and his family spent weekends at the park,

in the sandpit and swimming pool, whereas she and Dave did pubs, long lunches and the cinema. They read lots, whereas Ted claimed he didn't even have time to watch TV any more.

There was a big fork in the road. People with kids and people without. She and Dave were on the grown-up, calm, sophisticated road, but it was by mistake. They'd missed the turning. It was all wrong.

All this churning about in her head as she searched the big white flat for the things she needed and prepared to set off for another 'go' at the hospital.

Chapter Four

'Mr Pennes?'

The clipboard the nurse was holding was shaking slightly, Pamela noticed.

'Mr Pennez?' the nurse tried again. But there was no response from the small gathering in the waiting room today.

'Pinnez?' she offered, a blush spreading across her cheeks.

Silence, all heads turned expectantly now.

'Oh . . . *Penis*?' a heavily accented voice volunteered, loudly but with total nonchalance. 'Penis? That's me.'

The man, smartly dressed in a dark suit, sauntered over and followed the nurse through the double doors. Her shoulders were definitely shaking with suppressed laughter now.

'Did he say . . . ?' Dave began, but Pamela silenced him with a dig in the ribs. If everyone else in the waiting room could cope with this without dissolving into giggles, so could she.

'Maybe he's the sperm donor,' Dave whispered and then it was no use, Pamela was overwhelmed with the need to laugh.

She jumped from her seat and rushed towards the toilet door. After she'd slammed it shut, she let go, honked with laughter, tears jumping from her eyes.

She dabbed at her face with a dampened paper towel, aware that this was not normal behaviour. She was caught in the vaguely hysterical, emotional whirlpool between laughing and crying because this was so bizarre. In under an hour, she was going to be implanted with three embryos – half hers, half an anonymous donor's. Maybe they were Mr Penis's. She'd never know.

It made her feel like a dairy cow. All those bony cow bottoms lined up in a row for the Artificial Insemination man. She'd seen the TV programmes.

Of course she and Dave had talked it through over and over again and he'd insisted that it was fine, not going to be a problem at all. If there was a baby, it didn't have to be biologically his, so long as it was emotionally his. So he'd said. He'd almost had to talk her into this. She was the one who worried that it was too weird . . . another man's sperm. Dave was always so good at implantation time. Could make soothing, mildly funny jokes which took the edge off the medical procedure, all legs up in the air, probing and horrible.

In the past, their eyes had held and they'd agreed, somehow, to try and think about making

40

love, think about all the best times, not let the doctors get in the way of this trying to make a baby.

But would it be different this time? She was about to go through the most medicalized, sanitized version of having sex with someone else while her husband watched and held her hand.

Dr Rosen patted the top of her head.

'Just lie still now, try and relax. Think happy thoughts.' His eyes creased, so behind his paper mask, he was smiling at her.

Relax.

Not.

She tucked a finger up her sleeve so she could touch the wool dolly her niece had given to her as a lucky mascot for today and began her baby prayer. The one no-one else knew about, not even Dave.

It was a grown-up version of the one she'd done at the dentist's when she was small: 'Dear God, if I don't have any fillings, I promise I will brush my teeth twice a day and never eat sweets again. I promise.'

It was ridiculous to pray, she argued with herself now, lying on the crinkly plastic-backed sheet over the hospital couch, *willing* these embryos to implant.

She didn't believe in God, did she? Not the one she'd learned about at church and school, anyway. She believed vaguely in something, thought of herself as 'spiritual' but 'God' was a convenient way to put it when she went through air turbulence or right now, when she needed to pray and plea-bargain.

'God, please, please, let me get pregnant. Please. If I have a baby I promise, I'll be the best mother ever. I'll never get tired or angry or grumpy with this baby. I'll never shout at it, or keep it up late, or feed it anything other than organic food. In fact, it will only wear those organic cotton clothes and biodegradable, bleach-free nappies and be *so* happy. Have the happiest childhood ever, the perfect childhood. Just please, please let me be pregnant. Please.'

A kaleidoscope of images of her fantasy baby filled her mind. A baby in a bright red knitted cardigan, in a blue gnome hat, a baby pulling daisies from the lawn, drooling, trying to decide if they should be tasted. A baby sleeping heavy and warm in her arms. She could never picture a face, but saw the details – the closed eyelashes, tiny knuckles and nails. Lucky, lucky parents. Lucky, lucky.

She wanted this so much.

Two tears squeezed out from her eyes and slipped down into her ears. Dave gently brushed away the one hanging like a pearl from her ear-lobe. They were alone in the room now.

'I'm sorry,' he said. 'I'd do anything to make this work. You know that, don't you?'

She nodded, not taking her eyes from the ceiling. She didn't dare to look at him, couldn't bear to see the pain in his face. It was almost too much to carry on under the weight of her own hurt. She couldn't deal with his as well.

*　*　*

They didn't say much on the tube journey and then the walk home. Through the shopping mall, out on to the high street and along the quiet residential roads. They spoke about the weather, about food in the fridge for supper, but then he caught up her hand and squeezed it tightly.

'Who knows, Pammy,' he said. 'Maybe this will work. I really hope it does, for both of us. Maybe this will be the one.'

But it wasn't.

She already knew she wasn't pregnant before the bleeding started, but periods were increasingly hard to handle. When this one finally arrived she was already developing a bad head cold, so she switched off her phone, crawled back into bed and dared to hide from Sheila, work and the world.

Head aching, nose streaming, she lay in bed and allowed herself to cry and cry until her eyes felt scratchily dry and uncomfortable to blink. Her head whirled with the 'what ifs'. What if they had another go and it worked? What if it didn't? What if they didn't try again? What if they split up and she met someone who already had children? What if Dave did?

What if she tried for *one moment* to stop thinking about all this?

It was almost lunchtime when she surfaced from her bed and went down to the kitchen. She made a honey, hot water and lemon drink, then decided to slug some of Dave's prized single malt whisky into it. Several sips down, she felt a little better and it occurred to her to phone Francesca from the support group.

Fran worked from home, was due to have another try round about the same time, was probably sitting on her sofa right now either waiting to go in or worrying about the result, or even, like Pamela, trying to cope with the fallout of another failure.

She rang the number and waited for the pick-up without the other possibility entering her head.

'Fran? Hello, it's Pamela. How is it going?'

'Oh, Pamela. Hello! How are you?'

They didn't spend long on the preliminaries. Fran immediately wanted to know about Pamela's latest attempt. When Pamela told her the news, she sounded so sad and sympathetic, Pamela had to take a quick sip of toddy to steady herself.

'How about you?' Pamela asked.

'Em . . .' There was a long pause which Pamela took to be Fran bracing herself to share her own disappointment.

'I'm not sure how to tell you this . . .' came the hesitant voice at the other end. 'It's very early, way too early to know what will happen . . .'

'Oh my God,' was Pamela's breathy interruption.

'I'm pregnant,' Fran said but not in an enthusiastic, jubilant 'congratulate me' sort of way. Fran knew just how fragile a thing this was, as many of the women in the group had had mis-carriages. She also knew exactly how awful it was for Pamela to hear right now. 'I'm so sorry,' Fran added.

'Don't be silly,' Pamela managed. 'It's very exciting. I'm so happy for you.' She wished this was true, but all she felt was an overwhelming burn of jealousy. 'You've got a really good chance, Fran—' She tried her hardest to sound pleased. 'It could happen.'

'I know.' Fran was almost whispering, as if talking out loud about this pregnancy might jinx it. 'Long way to go.'

'Well, good luck, we're all thinking of you.' Pamela hoped Fran couldn't hear the catch in her voice as she said this. 'Are you coming to the meeting next week?'

'I don't know . . . I might have something else on.'

The meetings when someone pregnant attended had been so obviously painful that there was now a tacit agreement that during their often short-lived pregnancies, members stayed away.

'Loads of luck – from us all,' Pamela said.

Fran thanked her and then said something about a ring at the door, which they both knew wasn't true, but Pamela was grateful because she really wasn't going to be able to stop herself crying out loud for another moment.

She put the phone down and buried her face in the sofa cushions. There wasn't going to be any change. That was the worst thing. She was faced

45

with endless more of the same: more of not being pregnant, more 'trying', more rowing with Dave, more hating her boss, more of Dave hating his job. More . . . more . . . more of this unending rut.

It was always Saturday mornings when the trouble started. Maybe because it was the first time in the week when they had time to be together, time to start talking. Monday to Friday was a blur of working late, and dinner could often pass relatively pleasantly, catching up with the day's events. Then they could watch TV until they were almost asleep, crawl to the bathroom and into bed where they would kiss each other good night with exaggerated yawns. Then Dave would sleep and Pamela would begin her nightly worry vigil, working through the worries one by one until she fell into a sleep peppered with wakings, trips to the bathroom, even cups of camomile tea.

But Saturday morning was when the tension surfaced, took in a big lungful of air and roared around the house.

Dave would come down from bed after 11 a.m. to find her on the sofa in the already tidied sitting room, drinking tea, all ready to row with him. Well, that's how it felt.

Seemingly bland 'What do you think we should do today?' type questions and niggles about 'Oh I can't be bothered going there' would escalate rapidly into: 'You can never be bothered!' . . . 'Why is that always such a chore for you?'

And on to: 'Fine, I'll go on my own, then. That's probably what you wanted.'

'Don't know why we do things together anyway, we never enjoy it.' Erupting in: 'Especially sex.'

'Sex! When did we last have sex? Oh guess what, I can't remember.'

'I'm going through some difficult things.'

'Oh *you* are, are you? Just you. What the hell do you think I'm going through then?'

Until someone stormed out and there was crying, shouting, things being thrown, fury hurtling about the flat. They could not go on like this. They both knew it. They were wearing each other out. Being at home was like being on high alert, all the time. Using the marital radar to pick out the nuances in the simplest of questions.

'What shall we have for dinner tonight?'

'Why are you asking me? I haven't had a chance to shop. I thought you were getting something.'

'Why didn't you phone me? You can't just assume I'll get the food.'

'I wasn't assuming . . .'

Too late . . . petty argument number 6,378 was already up off the ground and gathering speed.

'You never . . .'

'I'm always the one who . . .'

'Why can't we ever . . .'

'This is such a waste of . . .'

'I've had it up to here . . .'

At the heart of it all was the increasingly unresolved way forward. She wanted to try more donor sperm IVF. He now wanted them to have a break from the medical merry-go-round and at least think about moving in a different direction. Consider adoption ... consider alternative medicine ... consider coming to terms with life without children.

'The longer we keep doing IVF, the longer we're putting everything else off,' he would argue. 'We're getting older and older. It'll be too late to try anything else. We'll be too old to adopt by the time we get to the top of the register.'

'But we haven't given the donor IVF a chance,' she would plead. 'We've only done it once. You have to stack up the odds a bit better than that. Two more goes would be more realistic. We could be just months away from a baby if we sign up and do it again.'

'Well, maybe you're right, but even the doctor said you have to have a rest,' he told her. 'You're in a state! You're just not yourself any more and God alone knows what the drugs are doing to you in the long term. You need to get well again. And anyway ...' he moved on to his foremost concern: 'we're not going to be together for much longer if we carry on like this. But maybe that's what you want?' Anger rising in his voice now. 'It's just the baby at any cost, isn't it? You don't care what this is doing to your health, our relationship ... I won't even mention our bank balance.'

Worst of all was the Saturday conversation which had begun quite amiably with Dave asking her if she was feeling better, if she was ready to talk. They had managed to begin quite calmly, only to watch the vicious genie spiral up out of the bottle, out of control.

'What shall we do next, huh? Just what shall we do next?' She had folded her arms across her chest and stepped towards him.

'We can't do this,' he'd answered. 'We can't keep doing this. We're fucked, we can hardly bear to be in the same room together.'

The words *This is your fault, this is all your bloody fault*, were choking Pamela. She was desperate to scream them at him, but up till now, she'd held back. Up till now, it was mainly *his* sperm, but *their* problem. This time it was all her fault. His sperm hadn't even been involved.

'We should have done donor sperm from the outset,' he'd accused. 'We've wasted all this time, all this money and still no result.'

'I did the other stuff for you!' She couldn't stop the scream now. 'I did it for you. I thought it had to be your child too, or else it would never work between us.'

'See! You haven't got any faith in us any more.' He was still seated, but shouting now. 'Why are you endlessly tidying up and getting rid of things? The flat looks like we're about to move out. Just face it. You have no faith in us.' With every one of those final six words, he smacked his hand hard on the low table in front of him.

For the first time in her life, Pamela understood what it was to see red. She started to run, easily clearing the coffee table, and leapt on him, eyes closed, punching his neck, his shoulders, pulling his hair, whatever she could get hold of, as hard as she could.

He wrestled for her hands and for several moments they grappled, Pamela furiously trying to free her arms, hitting him in the face with an elbow as she did, Dave yanking hard at her arms, burning the bare skin on her wrists.

And just as suddenly as it had appeared, her fury evaporated. She collapsed against him and began to weep. This was pathetic, downright tragic . . . and where did they go from here?

Just where, exactly?

Chapter Five

'We're all off to sunny Spain . . . Y, *viva España*.'

This was Alex's way of saying hello at 6.50 in the morning in grey and grimy Heathrow.

It was all her idea, of course. Well, wasn't it always? A 'working trip' to Barcelona, so they could cruise the cool furniture shops, meet some designers, hang round a salesroom or two and generally have a totally tax-deductible mini break.

Alex was much more glamorous than usual. The turquoise blue afghan had been replaced with a vintage pink and silver dress coat slung over silky trousers and high-heeled boots.

'Now, you did bring your heels, didn't you?' Alex asked her as they queued to check in. 'Because you need to know that all the women in Barcelona, every single bloody one of them, will be more beautiful, more groomed, more fabulously dressed than us. But this is not going to bother us, because we are *British*. We are allowed to be eccentric, one-off and totally unique, but most importantly, we are going to be TALLER.'

Comfortably cocooned in the aeroplane, they had a late breakfast and a very early mini bottle of white wine *each*.

'Isn't nine o'clock just a tiny bit early to be drinking?' Pamela scolded.

'Ten o'clock Spanish time. Think of it that way, a pre-aperitif,' Alex had assured her, filling up their clear plastic glasses and badgering the hostess for ice.

Nothing goes to the head like cold white wine in the dehydration of a plane. Pamela could feel her brain numbing as it soaked the drink up like a sponge.

'Very many good-looking men in the city we're going to,' Alex was telling her. 'I mean, I know you're not allowed to touch, but absolutely no harm in looking, absolutely no harm at all. You just wait and see.'

It had struck Pamela before that Alex approached men the way she approached her work. She was always on the lookout for genuine ones, always sourcing 'real finds', but she never seemed to hang onto them for long and was always more than happy to pass them on to a good home.

Pamela had asked Alex about it often: didn't she want to find someone just for her? Someone to keep? Someone to lurve?

But Alex's views were typically forthright. She didn't want children and therefore she didn't need a long-term relationship thing either.

They'd discussed the not wanting children bit very hard over several different conversations, Pamela trying to drag every little reason out of her friend, trying to come to an understanding of how someone quite casually couldn't want the one thing in the world she was desperate to have.

'I don't want children. I want money, occasional sex, cigarettes, to keep my figure and more wine, please,' Alex had told her. 'And I don't care who knows it.'

In a more serious vein, she'd said that her four brothers and sisters and a tribe of nephews and nieces was plenty.

'They're all domesticated up to their ears and it's lovely to visit them once in a while, just like it was lovely to grow up in our big, noisy household, but it's even nicer to have my own place, peace and quiet. I'm a natural spinster, a born maiden aunt . . . a wannabe hermit. That's me. And,' she would confide once in a while, 'my sister, Moira, who has three, keeps telling me that if I don't want children with all my heart then I shouldn't do it because it is the hardest job in the world. No pay, no overtime, no holidays. I mean lots of perks, of course . . . lots of lovely perks—' and here she almost sounded a little bit wistful – 'but there you go. Hardest job in the world.'

It was completely logical to Alex that if you didn't want kids then why would you want a man hanging about you for the rest of your days?

'Women only put up with men over the long term because they are their children's dads. I swear to God, there is no other reason. Why else would you let these saggy-underpanted, woolly sock-wearing, snore in their sleep creatures stay? You just wouldn't. Moira's husband leaves his toenail clippings on the bedroom floor! He can't be bothered to have sex when a wank or a blow job would do instead. Why would you put up with that?'

Pamela had pretended to look shocked. But had also realized with a sinking feeling that her marriage was racing in this direction.

'Don't you think in the future that wanting to live with someone else for the rest of your life will be seen as a bit strange? It'll be classed as an addiction and you'll be able to get treatment for it,' Alex had offered.

'Oh for goodness sake,' Pamela had snorted. 'What about parents for little children? Or are you going to have them farmed off to boarding nurseries as soon as they're weaned?'

'No. They'll make a special exception for them, I suppose, but there will be so few children left by then. I mean, who will be willing to do that? Spend all that money and all that time creating dysfunctional little skateboarding net heads, who will turn against you as soon as they've outgrown their Start-rites? Life is too short.'

'Oh God, you're being so depressing. Is that what you think parenting is like? And anyway, if none of us have children any more, who's going to pay for your pension?'

'Now, you know perfectly well how seriously I take my pension.'

And this was true. Sometimes Pamela thought the only thing Alex spent money on was her pension. It was affectionately known as 'the Shirley Conran Fund' because, as Alex put it: 'I too want to live in Monaco, have enormous silicone boobs and a toyboy when I hit my mid-fifties.'

When they arrived in Barcelona, they were amazed to find that it was already early summer. Much warmer than Pamela had expected. Such eye-wincingly bright sunlight that Alex slapped on 'vintage' (i.e. car boot sale) mirrored shades and Pamela peeled off her raincoat, feeling over-dressed in her all-boring black.

In their cool hotel room, with tiled floor and slatted blinds, they changed into lighter clothes, then went out in search of a café table to plan how to fill up the days, both bringing out magazine clippings, address lists, shops tracked down on the internet.

To Pamela it felt good – warming, thawing and different – just to sit still, sip at tiny, heart-belting coffees and watch all these gorgeous brown people walk past.

'We just can't do summer dressing like this, can we?' she thought out loud, looking at her woefully white legs flash between her black skirt and shoes.

'No, we can't.' And Alex gave a nod at a woman striding towards them. She was in a khaki linen safari suit, sleeveless, with knee-length shorts ironed into rigid stiffness. On her deeply tanned bare feet she wore suede leopard-skin pumps, and her dark, gelled-back hair was tied into a ponytail with a leopardskin scarf. Gold-rimmed sunglasses and a supple brown bag with just a hint of leopard detailing completed the look.

She was so pulled together, so perfectly chic and accessorized, it made Pamela want to rush out to buy matching shoes and bags, fake tan, hair gel . . . decent sunglasses for once . . .

'Don't even think about copying,' Alex warned. 'This is high-level continental dressing; we cannot even *dream* about going there. Khaki is disastrous on pale skin . . . linen wilts in the damp . . . we have no idea how to put scarves in our hair without turning into Gypsy Rose Lee, we know not the slightest thing about complex accessorizing. We are British: the only options open to us are to look cool, to look classic or to look a mess.'

'Why is that, though?' Pamela whined, knowing exactly which category she was in despite spending way too heavily on fashionable labels. 'Why can't we even begin to get it?'

'They have no school uniforms.' Alex was warming to her topic. 'These women have been co-ordinating and eye-lining since primary three. We don't stand a chance. Plus there's still the whole Catholic, marry young, have babies, keep your man happy vibe going on here as well.'

'Ha . . .' Pamela saw a beautiful mama in a strappy red sundress and matching heels pass, pushing a double buggy with baby and toddler just a year or so apart. 'Who knows,' she said. 'Maybe they've got it right and we're the major cock-ups.'

Alex would have liked to utter a pithy 'speak for yourself', but her friend was too raw, too fragile. She could see the dark circles on Pamela's pale face, proof of how badly she'd been sleeping, could see the tiredness, the lack of energy, the grind of trying to act normally, go through the motions with this great weight of depression tied to her every moment of the day.

She wished she could do more, but there was nothing she could say to make this better and anyway Pamela didn't want to talk about it much. Alex suspected that the IVF ordeal was now bringing Pamela down, and her marriage along with her.

The least she'd been able to suggest was a few days' break, a few days in which Alex was determined to keep her friend busy, amused, preoccupied; give her a mental holiday.

So they wandered the streets, poking their noses into every shop, art gallery, museum and café that looked interesting. They ate platefuls of seafood, fish and tortilla, sank rough old Spanish Rioja and chilled sherry with ice, nibbled at fat olives dripping oil.

Pamela began to thaw in the warm April sun, heard herself laughing long and hard at some joke of Alex's, the sound taking her by surprise. It wasn't possible not to ache most of the time, especially in a place so filled with babies, children, burstingly pregnant mothers-to-be.

But maybe it was possible to laugh, really laugh, in spite of the ache. That alone made her feel a little better.

On their third night, they stayed out eating and touring the bars in the heart of the old town until after three in the morning, then meandered home, slightly too drunk, through the cobbled streets. When Pamela fell into her white bed in their shared white room, she closed her eyes and for the first time in months, sleep came straight away.

But she woke up in the strange room from a dream so intense, she cried in the half-asleep moments when it was beginning to fade and she was waking up to realize it wasn't true.

She had dreamed absolutely vividly that she was Spanish, that she had smooth racehorse brown limbs, looked good in khaki, was making a leisurely four-course feast for a film-star-handsome husband and their three golden-brown children.

That she too could twang her bikini in confidence on the beach, rinse off under the public showers, then change into an immaculate little white cotton outfit with crochet detailing. Comb through long brown hair with honey highlights. Be married to one of those men who looked good all summer, who suited pink and jade green polo shirts, who waxed and manicured his feet so they looked elegant in sandals, who carried a manbag and made it look suave.

She knew why she was crying about this. It was regret, yearning, for her own family, for long, carefree summers, a sense of belonging, happiness. A bronzed Spanish family sitting round a supper table conveyed all the things she didn't have. And desperately wanted. Only too late. That was how it felt. Too late.

She got up, passed Alex sleeping soundly in a tangle of sheets and went to the bathroom to wash her face and shower.

Under the warm water, she thought of Dave. Recently, the unthinkable was turning into a serious possibility: she and Dave could undo their marriage. She could leave him. She could box up all the things she'd carefully chosen for their married life and home together, dismantle the kitchen, sell the heavy wooden sleigh bed, divide out the cutlery, the crockery, neatly stack books into piles of his and hers. There weren't many joint things to squabble over. There had never been too many things in their flat and she had bought most of them. Dave had been in charge of acquiring CDs, DVDs. He could have the telly, the stereo, the computer, she decided. The marital hardware.

Maybe she would live in a tiny flat, like Alex, for a while, but really, she hoped she would find someone else, maybe a man with children of his own. A divorced dad, instant family. Maybe his wife could have died. No, too tragic. Left them to go abroad . . . never to be seen again. Oh for God's sake. Too ridiculous, she acknowledged.

In the back of Pamela's mind was the thought that, if she could start over, a future without her own child wouldn't be so bleak. Right now it felt that the worst thing in the world would be to have to stay with Dave and accept this childlessness. Live on and on with it and with him.

And didn't Alex have a point? That really, it was only children that held people together, over the long term?

There in the shower, surrounded on three sides by glittering white tiles, fat chrome lever taps, drenched by the 12-inch-wide showerhead, she dared to think about single life. Being single again for the first time in twelve years ... the chance to start at least a few things over.

Only images of Dave on holiday came into her mind. He didn't do summer well. He could still look good to her in a thick sweater or a suit, quality tailoring filling him out in all the right places, shoulder pads doing for him what his own posture never could. But in the heat, casually dressed, he was a disaster, all loose T-shirts and baggy shorts, thick factor 50 on his pale skin, and sandals revealing hairy feet. On holiday with him, she always felt ill at ease. As if she wasn't with Dave at all, but an annoyingly embarrassing younger brother; someone who thought wearing a baseball cap backwards 'to stop my neck getting burned' was OK.

The truth was, she had no energy for the big decision ahead. The 'would she?' or 'wouldn't she?' stay with him. Even on the days when she thought she did want to leave, making the bed was too much, so how would she deal with unmaking a marriage? So every day, the decision remained unmade, all the arguments raging round her head.

Probably she owed it to Dave to try therapy, couple counselling, but the thought of sharing all the agonizing, all the angry silences, the petty rows, was too hard.

Everything felt too hard. She knew from the group that most of them had been through all these things too. But 'working through it', 'talking it out', 'sharing' – she didn't want to. She wanted to stay here, in this hotel, in this city for as long as possible. Escape, run away. Maybe she could just rent out a room and live here. Not have to go back and pack up her belongings or face Dave and tell him she didn't want to do this any more. She could just phone him:

'Hello, it's me . . . Yes, I'm still in Barcelona. No . . . I'm not coming back. I'm going to stay.'

Rinsing off the last of the conditioner and soap, Pamela closed the conversation with herself, decided to try and not think about it for a few hours and reached over for one of the hotel's thick towels.

Alex was still sound asleep when she went back into the room, so she decided to dress and go down to breakfast alone.

She chose a big glass of orange juice along with coffee – hot, black and fully caffeinated – scrambled egg, toast and a fluffy croissant.

The breakfast room had floor to ceiling windows which opened out onto the hotel's lush green garden of a courtyard where some of the guests were seated. But it looked too bright for her out there, the tables, crockery and waiter's shirt all glared far too white in the strong sunlight for someone with a trace of unaccustomed hangover.

She was daydreaming, coffee cup in hand when she felt, like sunlight falling on her bare arm, the warmth of someone's stare. She looked up and saw, several tables away, a very attractive Spaniard looking at her over his coffee. When her gaze met his, he smiled, raised his cup slightly, then picked up his paper, a little self-consciously, and began to study it.

Just like the Spanish husband she'd dreamed about, he wore an immaculately ironed pink polo shirt and his dark hair was slicked back from his face. A soft sweater was draped over his shoulders and she was sure if she got closer he would smell of limes, coffee, bergamot and sun. She put him at around 40 and clocked his ringless fourth finger just as she saw that he was looking up at her again.

He smiled and she darted a snippet of smile back before looking down at her plate. She suspected this was why Barcelona women always looked so fantastic. It was such a flirtatious town. The air was full of unspoken compliments, sideways glances, longing looks, it was hard not to be drawn into it. In fact, wouldn't she actually love to be drawn into it?

She looked down at her sleeveless black top and the pale, un-toned upper arms sticking out of it, and felt dissatisfied.

Well, well, Pamela teased herself, if she was

going to run away from Dave and rent a room in Barcelona, she would have to improve the look, wouldn't she? Shape up. Wear ironed khaki and matching leopardskin.

But as Alex had warned, she wouldn't even know where to begin. Maybe shoes? A new handbag? But she was always buying those things. Nice shoes, good bag. They were a cop-out, too easy to get right. It was the in-between area – what to put with the boobs and the tummy, the curvaceous bum and thighs. Sex appeal oozed from everyone here. She had no idea how to do that. Her dress sense had gone from school uniform to art school uniform (ripped jeans and secondhand corduroy) to clever designer uniform (black knits, smart trousers, fashion items, Gap at the weekend). She had no idea how to do *sexy*.

Her breakfast had been slow and leisurely; already it was some time since the handsome Spaniard had finished and walked out past her table, sending another smile in her direction, which she had pretended not to notice. The last of the coffee in her cup was too cold to drink and as there was still no sign of Alex, Pamela decided to venture out on her own. There was a shop she had noticed on their trawls up and down the boulevards and she thought she might quite like to go in there, although she suspected this would require some courage on her part.

Looking into the shop's front window, she saw that this was true. All sorts of items of Barcelona chic were laid out in front of her: rich conker brown bags, ruffled linen clothes in rust, black and red. The mannequin was dressed in a stunning evening gown of burnished gold and brown.

She caught her reflection – black and white English frump – and wondered if she dared even cross the threshold.

'Oh for God's sake, it's a shop, not an IVF appointment,' she told herself, then pushed open the door, releasing the tring-a-ling bell.

A slim, chignoned, perfectly *maquillaged* woman looked up from a brochure on the counter and gave her a chilly smile.

'Hello,' Pamela said and smiled back.

'Can I help choo?' the heavy accent asked.

'I'm looking for . . .' and here her confidence faltered. For what, exactly? For a new life? For a Spanish husband? For a baby? For a way to come to terms with the pain in my head?

Her eyes fastened onto the racks and racks of clothes and momentarily, stupidly, she thought she was going to cry.

But she saw that the chilly smile had warmed a little and she managed: 'I'm looking for a new outfit, something nice. What do you have that would look good on me?'

'A dress?' the woman asked. 'To go out?'

'Yes,' Pamela told her, because really, she should go out more, there was nothing she needed a dress for particularly, but surely it would be a good thing to have?

The woman came out from behind the counter, so Pamela could see her rigidly pressed trousers and her carefully co-ordinating sandals, and stood right in front of her, sizing her up.

The top of the woman's head was level with Pamela's shoulder, and she was so bird-like and delicate that Pamela felt even more like a galumphing big frump.

This was just going to be humiliatingly awful. She imagined herself trying to squeeze into some tiny little Spanish suit with gold buttons.

The woman went to the rack and slowly began to scan the dresses, quickly flicking past the ones she didn't think would suit. Pamela wasn't asked to help in this search.

Soon she had five or so in her hands; she came back to Pamela and held them to her, hangers under her chin.

Carefully she appraised each one with a tilt of the head, little sigh and occasional 'hmmm'.

'I think thees good for choo,' she said finally and handed Pamela just one: a surprisingly dressy midnight blue taffeta and chiffon concoction.

'In here—' the woman pointed her to a little changing cubicle. 'Choo ask, I help with zeeep.'

In the changing room, Pamela hung the dress up and looked at it carefully before she began to undress.

The flared taffeta skirt was topped with a tight ruched chiffon bodice, wide shoulder straps and a chiffon scarf. It wasn't like anything else she had in her wardrobe at home. She couldn't think when she had ever worn a dress like this, or even tried one on. It was so . . . *feminine*. She usually stuck to straight, square, simple clothing in the hope that she was being minimal and elegant. But really, she had finally realized, she just looked dull.

When she'd pulled the dress on, she tugged at the zip, but it was obvious it wasn't going to do up. Looking in the mirror, she almost laughed. It was horrible. This was why she had no dresses like this in her cupboard at home: her arms looked ghastly and her boobs were spilling over the top like trapped puppies struggling to escape.

Obviously bird-woman was not going to be the shopping fairy godmother she had been hoping for.

She just wanted to whip the thing off and get out of there.

But bird-woman was at the other side of the curtain.

'How eees dress?'

Pamela stepped out into the shop to give her the full horror effect.

'Not good,' Pamela said.

'No, no, no, no,' bird-woman tutted, tilting her head to the side again, touching the gaping sides of the zip.

'We try again, no?' she asked and before Pamela could stop her, she began the flick, flack, flick through the laces, satins and silks and the holding up of dresses under Pamela's chin.

After five dresses had failed to look anything other than badly fitting, Pamela really wanted to go, but she could see bird-woman was only becoming more and more determined to find something that would work.

She was over at another rack now, with longer dresses, some swathed in cellophane, and she studied one dress long and hard before bringing it over. 'We try thees?' she asked.

And Pamela was back in the changing room, slithering a long creamy satin number out of its plastic wrapper.

She looked at it and wondered whether she should even bother. It was a Greek goddess dress, for God's sake, bound to cling to every bulge and roll. But awkwardly she pulled it down over her head and shoulders and let it drop to her ankles.

Then she took a deep breath, opened her eyes and looked in the mirror. The effect was surprising. The bumps didn't exactly disappear, but they were transformed into curves. Suddenly the most important things about her figure were the soft hint of cleavage under the draped neckline, her small waist and her delicate ankles; nothing else seemed to matter too much. The lined satin didn't cling too hard, it hugged, it caressed. And there were even little split bell-sleeves to disguise the arms.

She turned slowly to each side and looked long and hard at the back view. A cunning knot of fabric in the lower back made the most of the waist and disguised the rear.

It was unbelievably clever and flattering and best of all she felt comfortably elegant. She couldn't think of a single thing she'd wear it to, but it really would have to be bought. For whatever might come, she would be prepared. When she stepped from the changing room, bird-woman actually clapped her hands.

'Bravo, this is the one, no?' she informed rather than asked Pamela. 'Beautiful ... classical, no? Italiano,' she said and Pamela had a bad feeling about the price tag.

They both looked in the mirror to admire the dress from all angles and Pamela, totally committed now, tried to sound a little casual when she asked the price.

The woman told her with an expectant little smile.

Oh dear God. Euros, euros, of course. Well, that wasn't sooooo bad, was it? She did the maths, lopped a third off the figure and well ... for the perfect dress?

'I'll take it,' she told the bird.

'Chesss, choo must,' she agreed.

Paying was the wobbly moment. She saw the puddle of cream lying over the counter top and wondered if it was going to be one of those expensive follies that would hang all forlorn in a corner of the cupboard for the rest of its days, unworn, not because it wasn't beautiful, but because she didn't have anywhere to wear it.

She would *find* somewhere, she determined, handing over the card firmly.

Out in the street, bag, tissue paper and dress in hand, she wondered what Alex would think of it. On the walk back to the hotel, she passed the big, glossy display windows of a fabulous furniture shop and decided, what the hell, she'd go in there too.

She stalked round past the chaise-longues, the loungers, the maple tables and over to lighting. A great big sculptural chandelier made out of bulbs, milk bottles and scraps of paper was hanging down into the middle of the room and she stopped to look it over carefully.

'Fantastico, no?' a man hovering at her elbow asked. She didn't look round but agreed, eyes fixed on the light, trying to read the messages she could see now were scrawled over the paper.

'Are you in ziz business?' the man asked and she turned to see the polo-shirted, jumper-scarfed, very attractive Spaniard from the hotel's breakfast room.

'Oh, hello.' She couldn't believe how calmly this came out when she was feeling so stupidly flustered.

'Are choo a designer?' he asked with the chewy, caramel accent everyone in this city was using to hypnotize her. How else could she explain the wildly extravagant cream satin dress in a bag dangling from her wrist, a vivid dream about turning Spanish and now feeling caught in the headlamps of this man's warm stare?

'Interior designer, yes,' she answered, amazed at how calm this sounded. 'You too?'

'No, no. This is my shop. I have one in Madrid where I live and this is the new one.'

She took this in, but the most important thing was the way he said 'Madrith'.

'Are you from London?' he asked.

And when she said yes, he told her how much he loved London, loved the designers, dreamed of opening up a shop there. He named his favourite shops and sources and she knew them all.

'You have to meet my friend Alex,' she said, smiling. 'She knows all these amazing places.'

'There is a gallery opening in town tonight. Would choo like to come?' He was reaching into his back pocket for a card; when he handed it to her it was curved and slightly warm.

'Gallery is here,' he said and pointed to the address on the card, brushing past her hand as he did so. 'The party starts at 8 p.m., so come after ten.'

He smiled.

'Can I bring Alex? We're visiting Barcelona together.'

'Of course.'

'What's your name?' she asked, almost as an aside, as if it hardly mattered now.

'*Si*, of course, Xavier Garcia Majo.' He held out a hand she was almost frightened to take. What was she starting here? Where would this end? Xavier Garcia Majo . . . jumper draped over his shoulders like a cloak, fine-boned face, dark eyes fixed on hers. Perfectly sleek, perfectly groomed, he was like a prince, a glossy, minor European aristocrat, luring her into a world of gallery openings, champagne, expensive cars and adultery.

That was the word popping unbidden into Pamela's mind as she took the warm hand and allowed it to close around hers.

She imagined the small ad: Handsome Spanish prince available for champagne receptions, fast car rides, expensive shopping and adultery WLTM unhappily married Englishwoman or similar for discreet fun.

'Pamela Carr,' she said.

'A beautiful name,' he replied. Eyes not leaving hers, hand held tightly round hers.

'Take your time, look around,' he said, finally releasing her. 'I will see choo and choor friend tonight.'

She said goodbye and managed to drift slowly around the shop for a few more minutes, until her desire to rush out and run back to the hotel to confess all to Alex was too strong to resist.

But confess what? she thought as she hurried along the pavement. This was all entirely made up in her deluded little head.

Shop owner invites London interior designer to friend's gallery opening. So what! Just maybe, he was hoping she would buy a painting . . . not exactly planning a rush into a torrid extra-marital affair.

Alex was still in bed but now she was damp, showered, drinking coffee and tucking into a room service breakfast.

'Great,' was her verdict on being invited to the show. 'And how have you wangled this for us?'

'I was in this shop and got chatting to the owner, you know.' She thought she might give something away if she wasn't careful, so she changed tack, adding: 'It's you he wants to meet though, for your London address book.'

'I see . . . and what is this shiny bag I spy in your hand? Have you been out shopping without me? I hope you've done it properly. If I look in here and see something black and architecty from John Smedley, I'm going to be angry.'

Pamela opened the bag and unfolded the tissue-papered dress across the bed.

'I don't believe it,' Alex grinned. 'You're wearing it tonight, aren't you? It's all clear to me now. You've been chatted up by some hunky Spanish shop owner who has invited you to a party and you've rushed out and bought this dress.'

'No, I got the dress first. It's not what you think at all,' Pamela huffed.

'It's OK. I'm sorry,' Alex soothed. 'But you realize you'll need shoes? Absolutely nothing you have with you will do,' she added.

And casting a quick glance at the ankle boots and flat backless walking loafers, Pamela knew she was right.

'So, more shopping . . . Oh good,' Alex said and flicked back the sheet. 'Now I have a reason to get out of bed.'

Not having to be there till ten, they spent too much time getting ready and a little bit wine-high.

Fighting for mirror space, swapping mascara, trying out different lipsticks reminded Pamela of school.

'I'm a bit suspicious of you,' Alex told her, when Pamela was finally ready, looking totally unusual, in satin dress, the strappy heels Alex had made her buy, hair up, red lipstick, dark eyes: looking, in fact, quite delicious. Better than Alex had ever seen her look.

'Suspicious? Why?' Pamela was smiling.

'I'm just wondering who it is we are going to see tonight.'

'Last night I dreamed I was Spanish,' Pamela told her, deciding to ignore the hint. 'Can't you just let me pretend a bit?'

'OK, are we all set then?'

Alex was groovy, and totally London in her black trouser suit, lace bra and baseball boots.

It crossed Pamela's mind that they looked like a couple. Scary London lesbians, she thought, smiling, as Alex matter-of-factly took her arm and they stepped out of the hotel lobby into the warm night. Down busy pavements set with tables, chairs and everyone up, everyone out and about, some shops still open.

The gallery was wonderful. The party exactly the beautiful people's night out they had secretly been hoping for. Big, dramatic rooms hung with just one or two canvases, packed with people, and although Pamela was surreptitiously scanning for Xavier, there was no sign of him.

'What a brilliant place,' Alex was telling her as they sipped at the cloudy yellow cocktails pressed into their hands by passing waiters.

One of the rooms was part library, but Pamela had never seen bookshelves like this before. So perfectly neat, all alphabetized, all books by the same publisher placed together in the neatest, most perfect rows. 'I want my bookcase to look like that,' she told Alex.

'Me too, but it'll never happen. C'mon. Let's see the terrace.'

They walked up a scarily unbanistered, floating staircase and came out onto an airy terrace lit with rope lights and candles and graced with another shiny, champagne-decked bar.

The terrace was overlooked on two sides by tall, elegant buildings, framed with wrought iron balconies, which glowed with the light escaping from inside.

'Oh wow, why don't we do this more often?'

'Because we don't live in Barcelona?' Alex reminded her.

'London must be full of parties like this.'

'But no charming Spaniards to invite us.'

Right on cue, Xavier was by her side, gasping in admiration at the dress, kissing her and then introducing himself to Alex.

Which was just as well, because Pamela was momentarily stunned by the fierce Spanish kissing experience. His arm had pulled her in, then left, right, left, he'd pressed into each of her cheeks, lips close enough to cause a breeze as they passed. And he'd smelled just as she'd imagined, of lime and bergamot, of suntan oil and summer sex.

Sex . . . and now the word was there in her mind, all three letters of it. She was trying to listen to what he was telling them but s-e-x, s-e-x, was playing over and over again. He oozed it, she saw now, in his white linen suit, dark skin,

74

shirt unbuttoned one rung lower than anyone British would have dared. In the way his eyes lingered on her when she spoke. It took him just a little bit too long to move back to Alex with the conversation.

'I'll get more drinks, yes?' he offered, then plucked their glasses from their hands and turned barwards.

'This is him, yeah? Party fairy godfather?' Alex asked. 'Has he got the hots for you! Whooo smoking,' she teased, mercilessly adding: 'Would ya?'

'Would I what?'

'You know, would ya?'

'Alex, I'm married!' Pamela protested, but they both noted her omission of the word 'happily'.

Xavier was back with a sophisticated-looking couple in tow.

'Meet my friends, beautiful new friends from London,' he told the couple, waving an arm expansively, flicking a spray of champagne into the air.

And so the evening whirled on: meeting more guests, drinking champagne, more cloudy cocktails, touring the paintings with Xavier as an informed guide at their side.

Until, mid-heated conversation, another group invited the three of them on to another party just a few streets away.

'No, no,' Xavier protested. 'I was going to walk the tourists around town, show them the best parts of Barcelona by night.'

'Si, si, choo must do this,' one of the guests agreed. 'But later. Now we party.' Xavier asked which they would prefer and just as Alex said 'Party', Pamela said 'Walk about.'

So it was settled: the other guests would take Alex on with them into the social swirl and Xavier would escort Pamela round the town. He held out an arm for her to take and as she bade them all good night, she thought she saw a glint in Alex's eye that suddenly suggested this had been set up all along.

'So where to now?' she asked Xavier as they left the party and hit the noise and glamour of the night-time pavements.

'Everywhere!' He smiled and tucked her arm tightly in against his side.

Chapter Six

They walked through the night, past illuminated buildings decorated with coloured tiles, ornate carvings, balconies brimful of foliage. Everything seemed so lavish, so adorned. Even the paving slabs had flower designs pressed into them.

Down into the narrow streets of the old town they went, and all the time Xavier held her arm up against him, his fingers tightly locked into hers and although Pamela tried hard not to notice, it was making her breathless ... dizzy, almost. What did it mean? Did it mean anything at all? Everyone walking past them was arm in arm: teenage girls, middle-aged women, old men. Maybe it meant nothing at all.

But she was so awake, so fizzy, this was what it was like to *flirt*, to be *chemically* attracted to a man, to be so attracted that she wanted to bury her nose in his armpit, lick his sweat, delve into every secret, unseen crevice of him.

She was driving herself crazy; thought she really must be going insane.

'And look ... look at the curve on this—' He was pointing out a balcony to her, she really wanted to pay attention to the words, not just the full red-brown lips speaking them: 'Sweeping, graceful, beautiful, no?' With the word 'beautiful', he held her gaze and she was left wondering, like a ridiculous teenager, does he mean *me*? Does he think I'm beautiful too?

Because 'Does he want me?' was the question at the front of her mind. She was constantly evaluating every moment, making up long lists of arguments for and against. Debating inside her head like some frenzied prosecutor and defence counsel: 'He invited me out for a drink ... he invited Alex too. He's holding my hand ... it's a Barcelona thing, look, everyone is holding hands. Look at the way he's gazing at me ... maybe he's that kind of person. 'Well, go on then ... ask him if he's married,' the prosecutor demanded. 'See what he has to say about that.'

Because so far the conversation had been totally lofty: London, Spain, art, design, the party. Not a single personal detail had been shared between them.

Xavier picked out a café and guided Pamela to a small shiny-topped table, pulling back the chair for her to sit on. Then he saw the goosepimples on her arms and insisted on putting his suede jacket over her shoulders.

She couldn't help thinking how cherished, how cosseted it made her feel, all this Cary

Grant-like behaviour. You would practically tell men off for this in London, when actually it was lovely to be treated like this.

Xavier sat down and suggested espressos and cognac. The jacket around her was warm like an embrace, wafting leather and the scent of him.

She wanted to hear him talk, his rich voice and chunky accent pouring over her like caramel sauce.

'Caramelos,' the Spanish word for caramels, she got him to say over and over again.

He was laughing but complied.

'Caramelos . . . caramelos . . .' He lowered his voice to say it again and she moved her head closer to his.

'Caramelos . . .' He was almost at her ear and she dared to move closer.

'Caramelos,' he whispered against her lobe, choosing the moment to slide a hand onto her leg and pull her in.

He kissed her ear first and she felt as if an electric shock had been administered. She turned to kiss him back and their mouths pushed together, his tongue searching for hers.

Pamela had been utterly faithful to Dave for twelve years, so the shock of kissing, *tongue kissing*, someone new was almost too much to take in. And then they were talking again; Pamela so stunned, she even wondered if she had made it up – the kiss.

'Pa-me-la,' she heard him say. 'Lovely name.' And it was, the way he said it, like *caramela*.

'Are you married?' she asked him. She'd

wanted it to sound casual, but instead it came out bald. Bubbles popping, spell breaking, coaches turning to pumpkins . . .

He raised an eyebrow slightly, put his hand over hers and waited for a long moment before replying: 'Does it matter?'

'Well . . . yes! I think you'll find somewhere in the small print, you're not supposed to kiss other women.'

He waved his hand as if he were batting a fly out of the way.

'You are married too, yes?' he asked.

'Yes,' she said but didn't tell him Dave's name. That was the kind of callous harlot she was turning into by the second.

'Of course,' he said, then leaned over, put his hand at the back of her head and drew her in for another kiss.

'Dave,' she said in the daze of the aftermath. 'Someone called Dave. I mean, my someone is called Dave.'

She wondered if it was possible to have a heart attack induced by kissing. His hands were on her hips, moving up and down against the silky fabric. Stroking, persuading, making her feel more turned on, more breathless than she could ever remember.

She was going to drown here, slide under the table in a faint with longing for him.

'Is this hurting you?' he asked.

'No.'

'Is this hurting Dave?'

'No . . .' with a little less certainty.

'It's not hurting me or my wife. They are hundreds of miles away and we are just kissing. Like friends.'

Their lips touched again, slowly, softly. It wasn't true, she had never kissed any friend, ever, like this. But his words made her feel better.

When they finally broke off, she watched him gather up his glass and drain the last of the brandy from it. He took a smooth brown wallet from his inside pocket, put a note down on the saucer with the bill. Then pulling her close to him, he suggested they walk back to the hotel.

Xavier gripped her hand, folded her arm under his. Laughing, he pointed things out on the way, Pamela desperate for another kiss, just one more mouthful of him. Hoped maybe it would happen just once before the hotel, in the cover of darkness. They kept walking past dark doorways, narrow alleyways, and she prayed that he would pull her into one of them, put his hands all over her. Have her.

Began to think she was delusional and deranged. This charming, urbane man wasn't going to drag her into a dark corner for ravenous sex, and was that really what she wanted? *Really?*

Wasn't this just some charming grown-up fantasy he was spinning along with her? Two consenting adults on a harmless, flirtatious, wonderful night away from home. That was what he meant, wasn't it? With his 'not hurting' rules?

But what felt frightening was how much she wanted him. Desired him. Was turned on by his laugh, his smile, his warm grip on her arm, the rumple of his white shirt. Good grief!

She didn't think she loved Dave any more. There it was. The fact she had been denying to herself for so long.

Throughout their many years together, of course she had sometimes noticed other men, looked at them too long, thought about them too much, even dreamed about being with someone else, very occasionally, but this was hot Spanish flesh, pressed against her arm, kissing her on the lips, taking her back to her hotel. Someone she would strip off her dress for and make love to, if she dared . . . if he would let her.

She thought about his wife, picturing a glossy brunette in a pink dress, with cleavage and beautiful children. There wasn't a hope. She was obviously crazed. This was flirting, kissing and fun. There was probably a Spanish word for it. A 'when the cat's away' saying. And really, wasn't it so grown-up?

Her impression of Spaniards was that they seemed to be playing by such old-fashioned, chivalrous rules . . . and it worked! You married, had your children young, lived next door to your mother, then had your career. Your husband was a perfect gentleman who complimented other women and indulged in a little flirtation and mouth on mouth when he was away. Everyone was happy. The sun shone all summer long, you ate olive oil on your bread and tomatoes, never got fat and didn't peg it early with some horrible stress- and pollution-induced tumour.

They even went to church. It was all so 1950s, but modern, done with assurance and panache, she concluded. Just as Xavier swept her into the lobby and demanded both their room keys from the concierge.

Loudly, unembarrassed as they waited for the lift, he asked if she would like to see his room.

'It's on the sixth floor, with a wonderful view of the city.'

The doors opened and they stepped into the shiny metal lift before she'd made a reply.

When the doors closed, he smiled and at last kissed her again, pressing his mouth against hers, sliding hands against her breasts and then, the satin offering no resistance, down her dress.

'Oh,' she heard herself breathe into his ear.

The dress was so filmy he could move to the one tiny part of her which longed for him without a whisper of guilt.

The numbers stacked up as he touched her. Her eyes closed, Pamela leaned back against the cool wall and felt his mouth on her neck, her legs tensing involuntarily. Four . . . five . . . six . . . the lift lurched to a stop just as she shuddered against him. Her eyes pinged open with the doors.

He took her hand and led her out. He walked backwards so he could draw her towards his room without breaking their gaze. Maybe he knew her reluctance to be a bad person was going to surface any moment now.

'I should say good night,' she said at his door

and made an attempt to pull her arm out of his hand.

But he held onto it tightly and told her: 'It's OK. Just come and see the view.'

'No. I don't think I can.'

'OK, Pamela, *caramela* ... shall we say good night?' He touched her forehead, ran a finger over her lips and then smoothly, she would think later, very smoothly, just a little too practised, he kissed her, gathered her up with one arm, squeezing her against him as his other hand slipped the card into the door to pop the lock.

So with the kiss, she was spun gently into the room. Her eyes fixed on the spectacular view and when the door closed behind her, it closed on the great swarm of choices and feelings and fallout raging around in her head. She made the decision to leave all that out there on the other side just for now. Her dress slid to the floor and she let go.

Chapter Seven

For a long time Pamela lay in the bed awake, watching Xavier sleep beside her – deep brown limbs thrown carelessly over hers – and wishing that all this could be hers: living in Barcelona with this dream of a man . . . a man who looked good in white linen . . . a man who smelled and tasted wonderful and yet of himself. As if he'd absorbed mint, limes and suntan oil and was breathing, exuding them back.

She put a hand on his back and stroked the warm skin. He was extraordinarily appealing.

Much earlier on in the evening she had worried that Xavier was a serial philanderer who did this all the time and that she was just falling for a routine. And when he closed the door of his hotel room, she realized this was exactly what he was. And realized also how much she wanted it. Wanted a practised, deceitful man to get physical with. Saw how her sex life with Dave, with all the pregnancy issues hanging over it, had become so mentally complicated that even the slightest manoeuvre meant something else. It was a mine-field so difficult to negotiate, no wonder they preferred to turn off the lights, kiss chastely on the lips and try to fall asleep.

But this! He had been superb. The lean, brown body . . . sexy, persuasive whispers . . . condoms at the ready. He did this all the time. But she didn't feel used. Oh no. She'd taken advantage of him. Flirted, flirted, teased, made him work so hard to please her, to have her. There were stubble scratches all over her thighs to prove it.

Can the reality ever be as good as the fantasy? *Oh yes!* For at least one night, it can.

But she knew she didn't want to wake up with him in the morning, or for Alex to suspect any-thing either. So now it was time to go.

Pamela slipped out of the bed, retrieved dress, underwear and heels and scribbled just the words 'Good night, goodbye, Caramela x' on the hotel notepad beside the phone and left. Back to her own room, to the shock that it was 5.30 a.m. and to sinking shoulder-deep into hotel bubbles to replay the adventure in her mind.

She lay in the bath giggling, hardly able to believe what had happened. She felt extra-ordinary. She'd just had sex with a stranger, over and over again, and it had been wonderful, in-credible, ecstatic and yet terrible. Awesome. She wanted to laugh, wanted to shout, but that might wake Alex and she knew already that this was her very own delicious secret. No-one else would know about this. That was the rule, the marital infidelity code. We're all grown-ups having our fun. If everyone is grown-up and behaves, no-one needs to get hurt. Ever.

And for her this was entirely a one-off. It was in another country. And besides, the man was married.

There were some things you could tell your new best friend about – like the fact you'd been inseminated with an anonymous donor's sperm. But frantically hot sex in a hotel room with a Spanish design dealer – that was private. She wondered how often she would think about it . . . and also wondered, with a lot less giggling now, if she and Dave should call it a day. Maybe it was sensible. Maybe there was still time to find more Xaviers, to catch up on some of the experimental stuff she should have been having in her twenties and see what else was out there.

When she finally got out of the bath and dried herself, she felt sorry that the smell of her lover, bergamot, limes, sweat, muskiness, was washed away. *Lover!* Dave had once been a lover of a very different kind: young, romantic, poetic, the type of guy who'd always brought his soul to bed with him. Somehow they'd outgrown all that without moving on to something more adult . . . more sexy. And now it was as if they didn't know how to begin.

A bottle of Alex's body lotion stood at the edge of the bath. Pamela pumped out big, creamy handfuls of it and rubbed it over her soft, loved-up body. When she stroked round her breasts and her stomach, she forgave them a little. She had begun to so hate this body for stubbornly refusing to reproduce, but after tonight, she felt a little better. Tonight, she had remembered what else it could do. How sexy a very sexy man could find breasts, a rounded stomach, big handfuls of bum.

Creamed, soft and naked, she fell into her own bed at last and slept, slept and slept as if it was her last night on earth and there was no reason to get up ever again.

Alex's voice was in her dream before she heard it consciously.

'Hello, helloooo there. Wakey, wakey.'

When Pamela had broken the surface of sleep and struggled up into awake, she saw her friend sitting on the edge of her bed, armed with a bowl of coffee.

'It's our last day,' Alex said. 'I didn't think you'd want to miss all of it. It's lunchtime. Spanish lunchtime ... so that's quite a lie-in you've had ... Sooo?' She raised an eyebrow, gave a hint of a smile and asked, when her friend was upright with the sheet tucked round her and the coffee in her hands, 'How was your tour of Barcelona?'

'Very interesting,' Pamela managed as evenly as she could. The desire to dance about the room and shout: 'I got *laid*! By the most beautiful man! Like I've never been laid before!' was still there, was surely creeping like a grin across her face right this moment and Alex was going to guess ... and must not be allowed to know.

'He was charming, Xavier. I had a lovely evening.'

'Hmmm . . . and? And? Why were you not here when I got in at 4 a.m.?'

'Oh, we walked, we had coffee, drinks, more coffee, you know . . .'

'So nothing surprising . . . nothing unusual . . . nothing at all out of the ordinary to report?'

'No. Well . . . obviously I don't go swanning round Barcelona on the arm of Spanish male perfection every night of the week – but nothing like you're thinking,' she even managed to sound a little stern with this.

'Well, no, I don't mean . . .'

'He's happily married, to an actress,' Pamela lied and hoped that would be an end to it. 'Now, tell me all about the party.'

And as Alex did, Pamela got out of bed with the sheet still tightly clasped around her so that none of the bites, scratches and scrapes on her white skin were visible.

She only saw Xavier once again, on the following day, where she had first set eyes on him: in the breakfast bar. Although Alex was still upstairs packing, Pamela had decided she needed break-fast before the trip to the airport.

Sitting down with her plate and coffee cup, her eyes had flicked up and round the room, maybe in the hope of one last look, one last reminder of what she had enjoyed.

When she did see him, she felt a jolt of excited surprise. She loved the fact he was exactly the same: ironed polo shirt, pastel blue this time, navy sweater tied over his shoulders, sunglasses perched in his black hair. He was looking at the paper, and just as she was about to wave, call his name, do something to raise his brown eyes to hers, he looked up and saw her.

His smile was restrained and there was something about the curt nod he gave her that stopped her from calling out 'Good morning.'

She smiled back just as a petite dark-haired woman came up to his table with a cup of coffee and a plate of bread. She set them down before him and when he scowled and spoke to her, she took the plate of bread away again. It was obvious she wasn't one of the hotel waitresses. The woman was definitely his wife.

Xavier's wife came back with a plate of croissants this time and a glass of orange juice. He let her put these in front of him and began to eat as she went back to the buffet to get her own food.

When his wife returned again, she smiled and fussed over Xavier in such a babying way, Pamela thought she was about to tuck the napkin under his chin and spoon the food into him. It didn't seem to be helping. Xavier snapped grumpily at her and finally pulled the paper up in front of him as she was in mid-sentence.

Charming, Pamela thought. Not at all the suave, sophisticated gentleman she thought she had been with two nights ago. But it was strangely thrilling that this was a man whose mouth had been between her legs, yet now he was a total stranger to her. A man whose surname she didn't even remember, whose home address and telephone number she didn't know and never would.

She drained the last of the coffee from her cup, stood up and walked slowly, pointedly past their table, quite enjoying the sight of Xavier wrapping the paper just about round his head, clearly terrified she might be about to speak to him.

She was tempted to ruffle his hair as she walked past, but that would hardly be fair on his wife, who looked like a nice girl, who probably deserved much better than him, but who should have made a scene, got tough, got stroppy and threatened to walk out the very first time Xavier had expected her to wait on him like this.

It occurred to Pamela that it was probably a good idea to know how a man treats his wife before you cheat with him.

Chapter Eight

'Stop throwing the doll about, just *stop it*! *Now*! It's going to land on Manda's head!' Rosie glared in turn at her five- and seven-year-old sons, strapped into the back seat of the car, big cheeky smirks across their faces while their baby sister giggled wildly between them.

'Just try to be quiet for five seconds!' she shouted. 'Or my head is going to explode!' All three children shrieked with laughter at this, so with a resigned sigh she faced forwards again and tried to remember what the hell she was talking to her husband about.

'What was I saying?' she asked in exasperation.

'Erm . . .' He glanced at her from the wheel.

That was it. That really was it. He didn't bloody remember either. Absolutely no-one listened to a single thing she said. *Ever*. She was about to tell him what she thought of this when his mobile rang. Saved by the bloody bell.

She folded her arms tightly across her chest and huffed. She wasn't going to turn round and tell the boys yet again to shut up because Daddy was on the phone. Let him bloody well deal with it.

'OK ... right ... no problem,' he was saying, glancing into the rearview mirror in annoyance. Then, abruptly, he braked hard, thudded the Isuzu up onto the grassy verge and got out, slamming the door shut, so he could carry on his conversation in peace.

Rosie, deciding that she didn't want to get involved with the fourth round of dolly catch kicking off in the back seat, unbuckled her belt, opened the door and got out as well. When she closed the heavy black door behind her, the noise from the children stopped completely. Like magic.

She looked around and soaked up the moment of quiet. It was the first day of May to have real heat to it and she felt the warm touch of sun on her face and forearms. They had come to a stop halfway up one of the few gentle hills in the area and luscious green farmland rolled away into the distance, punctuated with bursts of trees and the odd farmhouse, crisscrossed with hedges and fences.

Rosie had lived in this corner of Norfolk all her life, but never tired of the views, the greenness, the open spaces and the pale glimmer where sky met sea in the distance. Just a moment or two of taking it in, noticing how well the crops were coming on this year and she felt restored. She heard Lachlan say goodbye, fold up his phone, and she turned to look at him over the high bonnet of the 4 x 4.

'Hello there,' she said with a smile. Looking at him in the sunshine, really looking, for the first time in days.

'Hello,' he answered back, their eyes meeting.

'Nice to see you,' she said. And it was a pleasure, her big, bull-necked, broad-shouldered hunk of husband. Still so Aussie despite all his years here, dark blond hair in a stumpy ponytail, Cuban-heeled work boots.

'Nice to hear you!' he replied, looking at her from beneath tanned brows scrunched together against the sun.

'The third one was your idea too, remember.'

'Yeah, I remember,' and there was that particularly teasing smile on his face which could still give her a thrill. She smiled her own particular smile back. 'And don't even think about giving me *that* look!' he warned.

'Why not?!'

'Because, before I know it, we'll have four!'

'Oh good God! No way! Never! You'd have to drug me.'

She tried to remember when they'd last made love. Was it last month? The month before that? February? Lachlan's birthday? Oh God, surely not? And she *still* hadn't gone to have her post-natal diaphragm re-fit and Manda was nearly two!

'I love you, really,' she said. As if that made up for it. She knew perfectly well their relationship

94

was currently completely overdrawn. If there was a love bank they'd be thousands of pounds beyond even the agreed early parenthood overdraft limit. They would have to try and do something about this, try and pay some tiny little bit of attention to each other, despite their three small children and the busy, busy farm.

'Can we go out?' he asked, maybe thinking the same sort of thing. 'A babysitter? We must know someone who could come and babysit.'

In her mind Rosie ran through the likely suspects. Mr and Mrs Portillo, the retired couple who lived on one of the farm's cottages, and quite frankly didn't like to be asked, although they sometimes grudgingly agreed, so long as the children were in bed and it wasn't going to be a late night. Or Tony, Lachlan's thirty-something psychopathic workman who also lived nearby. No, only in emergencies, although the boys loved him. There was Mrs Birbeck's daughter in town . . . but she would need a lift in and back home again . . .

'Why don't you sort it out?' she asked her husband because really, she couldn't accept one tiny more single thing to do. Or *crack*, that was going to be it. The camel's back would be well and truly buggered. Beyond anything a physio, an osteopath, or even a cranial-sacral osteopath (or was it cranial-whatsit-sacropath?) could do for it.

'OK,' he said.

She wondered in which decade she would hear back from him on that.

'We'd better go back in,' she said, nodding in the direction of the children.

'Once more unto the breach, commander,' he joked. But it didn't feel like so much of a joke when they opened the doors and found Willy and Pete fighting furiously over the dolly, pulling frantically at either end of it, while Manda screamed at full volume at the horrible tug-of-war taking place across her.

When some sort of calm was restored, with the aid of the squashed packet of biscuits Rosie dug out from the bottom of her sack of a handbag, and they were back on the road again, she suddenly remembered what she'd wanted to tell her husband.

'Harry and Ingrid,' she said, catching his attention. 'That was it . . . Harry and Ingrid are going to make the move. They've put their farm on the market.'

'Linden Lee?' he asked, unnecessarily because he knew it well. 'Where are they going?'

'They've had an offer accepted on the Dyer farm.'

'Nah! That's like 300 acres or something. Even Harry can't weed 300 acres.'

She knew exactly what her husband thought of Harry and his precious 50 acres of organic fruit and vegetables. Lachlan thought he and Ingrid were *barmy*, but despite that, they'd grown very close to the couple over the years.

'What the hell is he going to do with 300 acres? And how did he get the money for it?'

'He wants to start a beef herd and apparently

he's done so well at Linden Lee, the bank are happy to loan him.'

'Blimey. Organic beef?' Lachlan asked.

'Of course! He's even talking about a dairy herd in the future.'

The sound that came from Lachlan now quite closely resembled a 'humpf'.

'How do you know all this?' he asked.

'I met Mrs Campbell in town this morning and she was telling me. I mean, I know they've been talking about it for a while, but it looks like they've taken the plunge. We'll have to go round. Hear all about it.'

She hadn't seen Ingrid or Harry for weeks. What was the matter with her and Lachlan? They had to rekindle their social life, make some attempt to revive it, if rigor mortis hadn't set in totally.

'Well, Mrs Campbell.' Lachlan was shaking his head. 'She gets the wrong end of the stick once in a while.'

But Rosie believed it. Every time she went to Linden Lee, she marvelled at the neat rows, the glossy plants and Harry, Ingrid, their little kids and the two big dogs, out in rain or shine, picking, hoeing, planting, digging. Not like the farms round about: vast fields full of staggeringly dense rape, barley, wheat, or row upon row of uniform strawberries, like at their place, but empty. Sometimes a tractor, sometimes a combine, sometimes a sprayer gliding up and down, but apart from picking season, empty of people. At Linden Lee there was always someone on the land, farming.

Sentimental old nitwit, Lachlan would tell her. No money to be made that way. But then how much money were they making at their place? Until the summer's end when the strawberry money came in, they were pretty well broke. And when the money did come in, they would put their share away in the bank for that time in the future when they were definitely going to need it. They farmed land worth at least a million pounds, yes, but in reality it felt like they were flat, stony, no summer holiday, or even new summer outfits for the boys, broke.

'Wonder who'll buy Linden Lee?' Rosie mused.

'I wonder,' Lachlan echoed. But she had already lost his attention. He was gazing into the distance, worrying: worrying about rain, about irrigating, about hours of sunshine, about ripening times, about which varieties he'd planted, about supermarket orders. This was the busiest, most anxious time of year for them all.

Chapter Nine

When Pamela pulled up outside her flat in the taxi she'd treated herself to from Heathrow, she was surprised to see the sitting room lights on. Dave must have left them on when he went out to work this morning, she reasoned. Surely not burglars? was her next thought as she put the key into the mortice lock and found it open.

Then, as her second key unlocked the Yale, and she pushed the door open, Dave came out into the hallway to meet her.

'Hello!' She tried to look pleased, but really, she was taken aback. Why was he here? Why wasn't he at work? Allowing her some time to unpack, to settle down, to begin to think about how she felt about him now . . . now that she'd spent time away trying out the idea of leaving him . . . trying out more than just *the idea* of being with someone else. She had come back with one thing clear in her mind. There was going to be change. It would not carry on like this any longer.

She was going to leave Dave ... maybe ... or maybe they would move out of town ... or she would finally give up her job and freelance. All the things she kept thinking about doing. She would finally do something. No matter how scary it felt, or how Dave might argue against it.

'Hello,' he said and smiled broadly; came to hug her tightly, kiss her mouth, then pulled her in so his chin hooked over her shoulder. 'I've missed you.'

'Me too,' she said automatically, not liking the fact that it wasn't true. She dropped her bag and let her head rest on his shoulder as she put her arms around him. She felt his collarbone under her cheek, his hands on her back. He smelled like toast. This was her safe place. This was home. This was ... very confusing.

'You look well,' he said, looking into her face again. 'Have you had a good time?'

'It was great. So warm ... fantastic city ...' she wittered, taking off her coat and hanging it up on the hallway rack. 'Anyway, how are you?' She turned to face him. 'Are you working from home today?' she asked.

'Er ... well.'

As Pamela waited for his reply, she thought about how much she wanted a cup of tea. She hadn't had a cup of tea in all the time she'd been away, but now *craved* one.

'I've been told to take a fortnight off.'

'Really? Is there something big in the pipeline?' She was heading for the kitchen now with Dave following.

'Well, no, not at work. Well, there is something big in the pipeline . . . very big.'

She glanced up to see him scratching distractedly at the back of his head, looking round the room. Twitchy, she thought, very twitchy.

'But it's maybe . . . maybe not what you're thinking,' he said at last.

He sat down at the table, but then stood up again and began to shuffle through the pile of paperwork stacked behind the fruit bowl – which was piled high with fresh pears and apples, she noticed.

'Really?' she felt a wave of concern. 'So, what's this all about?'

He knew this was too soon. He hadn't meant to rush into this conversation as soon as she came in the door, he should have thought of some stalling tactic. But now it was too late. He would have to plough on.

'Well, apparently I'm stressed.' He gave a shrug. 'The Trust's doctor – and there are plenty of them, as you can imagine – has diagnosed me as officially stressed and signed me off for a fortnight.' He gave another shrug and a little laugh this time. 'It's almost quite funny. *Infertile? Worried about it? Going through repeated IVF treatments? Marriage falling apart? Never mind, have a fortnight off, that'll sort it.*'

He laughed again, a little too forcefully: 'A fortnight off. Yes, that'll really help me get out of this shit hole of a situation called my life.'

And then he sat down on one of the kitchen

chairs and faced her, awaiting some kind of response. Pamela was rooted to the spot, kettle in hand, horrified that she was hardly home and they were already having to do this to each other.

'Has something happened at work?' she asked, trying to stay calm, determined not to let this be a row already.

'Of course something's happened at work. Everything's happened at work.' Dave was still scratching his head and she was desperate to tell him to stop it, but clenched her teeth.

'I can't do this any more. It's a crap job, Pammy. I'm not going to do it any more.'

'I see.' She put the kettle down on the counter top, switched it on, concentrated on it in an effort to hold back the things she really wanted to say: Good grief! Let me sit down. Let me drink my bloody cup of tea. Don't wallop me round the head with all this . . . already!

'Do you want tea?' she asked, calmly, feeling anything but calm. Feeling guilty, feeling confused . . . feeling unable to deal with Dave and Dave's new problems right now.

'Yes, I'll have some tea.'

'So what's been going on?' She came over to him and put her hands on his shoulders.

'I'm not going to work there any more. And since I made the decision, it's been quite good fun really.'

'OK.' She didn't add more. She wanted to try and listen to him first.

'I can't take it seriously any more, it's a joke. They're all such pompous arses. All their stupid

102

little worries: who's in the next promotion round; who's been given which project, what funding and why. I can't be *bothered*. I'm not playing the game any more, Pammy, I'm not going to do it.'

'Dave, running three hospitals is hardly a game, is it?' She couldn't help herself. 'I mean, I can think of a lot of funnier games.'

'Oh it's a bloody hilarious game, believe me. But it's even more fun when you're not playing.'

She pulled up the chair next to his and sat down, putting a hand over the clenched fist on his knee.

'On Monday,' he went on, 'we had this big ring-fencing strategy meeting and at the end of an hour-long, completely dull load of meaningless waffle, that we all know is just entirely for show, because all the decisions we take will be re-taken for us further on down the line ... but anyway, at the end, Robert, "team co-ordinator" for the day, wanted to know if there were any questions. So you know what I did?' He was looking at her with a peculiar sort of earnestness that was more than worrying. 'I put up my hand and said: "Robert, global warming ... do you think about it a lot? You know, icebergs melting, devastating floods, irreversible climate change ... do you think about that at all?"

'It was hilarious! You should have seen his face! Not to mention everyone else around the table. Of course, he tried to dismiss me with "I don't think that's really relevant right now, David, I'm looking for questions pertinent to the agenda, thank you." But I kept at him. "Not relevant? I think it's a pretty major issue actually, I mean, our *planet* is being destroyed and here we are sitting about discussing this load of old crap, not thinking about the problem at all. Do you recycle? Is your home insulated as well as it should be? Do you buy organic? You're a father . . . don't you worry about this stuff?" '

'Jesus,' Pamela interrupted. She didn't want to hear more, had a horrible vision of the scene. Fifteen or so senior trust managers thinking about work, or golf, or maybe even lunch, and then right in front of them, quite out of the blue, one of their colleagues goes truly mad, right there, in the conference room!

'Global warming? You started to ask them about global warming?' She wanted to double-check.

'Well I've been thinking about it a lot.' He opened his fist and let her hand slip into his.

'Obviously.'

'We used to care so much about all that: we didn't have a car on principle, we had recycled, reclaimed, biodegradable everything, worried about it, tried to make a difference. Where the hell did our ethics go?'

She didn't like to answer the question. What was the answer? *Oh get real, Dave, no-one has time for that stuff? No-one can be bothered. It won't happen in our lifetime . . .*

'What about my nurseries?' she asked instead. 'At least I'm trying.'

'Yeah, but don't forget you still do the offices too, the plastic, foam, MDF, whatever.'

104

'I can't change all that myself.'

'That's everyone's answer though, isn't it? I can't change this myself. But if you don't believe one person can make a difference, what can you believe in?'

He fixed his eyes on hers. Pale blue, troubled, beyond tired. He looked exhausted. Maybe the company doctor was right: maybe Dave *was* going to well and truly crack up. She'd always thought she would reach the end of her tether first, but now he was the one signed off work, ranting about global warming, looking like he'd dropped a stone in weight in the five days she'd been gone.

'One child.' He hit her with now: 'Just one child. That's all I want. Just one . . . Is that too much to ask? One child to talk to, to teach, to read stories aloud to, to tuck up in bed at night, to do homework with . . . I want to tell my child about my mum and dad, who would have loved to have been grandparents.' A reluctant sob broke from him at that.

'Oh darling.' She put her arms around him, a tide of guilt flooding over her. She shouldn't have gone away, she definitely shouldn't have *cheated* on him . . . Jesus! What would happen if he somehow found out? In this state? The thought was making her feel sick and sweaty. She couldn't *leave* him. He was going to have a nervous breakdown. He needed her. He didn't have anyone else. They were in this mess together. Maybe they would only get out together. No-one else really knew how it was.

'We'll find a way forward—' But she broke off. The comforting platitudes didn't work for them any more. Maybe there was no solution. Maybe they were never going to feel better.

'Do you want to change jobs?' she asked instead.

'No. I'm leaving. I'm definitely leaving.' He lifted his head and squeezed at his eyes with his fingertips. She hadn't seen him cry since his father had died, over a year ago now, just two short years after they had buried his mother.

He got up and went to make the tea, which had been forgotten about.

'I'm leaving the Trust and I'm leaving NHS management. That's all I know right now. The rest is a bit vague. I just have this feeling that we have to do the things we've been putting on hold.' He didn't need to add 'waiting for the baby that might never come', because it was there, deadly obvious, between them.

'Have you thought about what you'd like to do next?' she asked, trying out the positive voice, trying to be open to suggestions. Although she couldn't yet shake the idea that if only she'd been born Spanish, life would have worked out just fine.

'Yeah, lots of thoughts . . . lots of ideas. But I'm very worried you're going to think I'm mad.' He wasn't so far off the mark there.

'Well . . . I have a pretty good job, you could take a chance on something new for a while if you really wanted to,' she offered.

'But you don't want to stay in your job either, do you?'

'Not ideally . . . but Dave, we can't both just jack it all in for some vague sort of idea! What are you thinking of anyway? D'you want to move out of town? D'you want to freelance? Can you be a freelance manager?'

Probably. Wasn't everyone freelance these days? Freelance plumber . . . freelance neurosurgeon – everyone except her and Dave, who kept saying they were going to do it . . . going to take the leap.

He set the cups on the table but told her to wait, he had something else to give her first.

'Close your eyes,' he instructed.

'Why?!' It was so unlike him to play any sort of game. Well, came the next thought. It was so unlike him *now*. He had once been a champion joker, game player, king of surprises. The kind of person who had once arranged secret weekends away, dressed up for Hallowe'en, sent flowers the day *after* her birthday 'in case you're feeling sad it's over'.

'It's nothing bad. Close your eyes.'

She did as he said.

'Open your mouth.'

'Are you sure?' she asked through gritted teeth.

'You'll like it, I promise.'

She opened her mouth and he put something soft and round inside. It was slightly warm. Fruit, she thought, which has been sitting out in the sunny kitchen. It was small and rounded with a slightly rough, gritty surface. She hadn't bitten down on it yet, but she sensed a flower-sweet scent moving from the back of her mouth up into her nostrils. She squeezed her tongue against the roof of her mouth, squashing the fruit, which she now realized was the most perfect strawberry. It melted, burst, *exploded* with flavour across her tongue, pips popping between her teeth. It was a taste so delicious and so nostalgic, she felt almost tearful. This was how a strawberry *tasted*, but she'd been eating those chilly, hard, shrink-wrapped impostors for so long now, she'd forgotten. *This* was a strawberry: the perfect balance of sweet, full, ripe with an undercurrent of tang. The just right place between soft and firm, between fleshy and gritty. It stirred long-buried memories of shy May sunshine, birthday parties, paddling pools, sponge cake, and a mouth crammed full of the first strawberries of the summer.

'That is amazing,' she told him, eyes flicking open when she'd tasted every last moment of flavour and let it slip down her throat. 'Regression therapy by fruit. Could be a whole new science. Did you grow it?' There were herbs and summer tomatoes in his windowboxes, so a strawberry plant wasn't a leap too far.

'I wish,' he laughed.

He held out a half-empty plastic punnet, and as she picked out another one, he said: 'Naturally grown, 100 per cent organic from Wiltshire.'

He was impatient to know if the fruit was having just one tiny bit of the effect on her that it had had on him. He'd bought the berries absent-mindedly from the chichi little deli down the street but just one mouthful had spun him surer than time travel to the back of a wooden tractor trailer bumping down dusty tracks, as he hitched a lift with the stacked, dripping crates of fruit to the wholesalers. Summer holidays on his uncle's farm. He didn't think any time since then had ever been as happy.

The strawberries had convinced him his idea wasn't so mad after all. He'd looked at the box: it was stamped with the name of a farmer, a farm and an address. See, someone had done this. Someone had ploughed up whatever else was growing on the land, planted row upon row of strawberry plants and waited and prayed. Now, the punnets were selling for the best price at his local deli.

There was a way.

'They're amazing,' Pamela was telling him. 'So . . . strawberry-ish! There isn't a better word.' She smiled at him and wondered what this was about. Weren't they supposed to be talking about what to do with the rest of their lives?

Dave paused. He was about to set his dream for the future in front of her and if she didn't get it, if she laughed, shrugged it off, told him not to be so stupid, he wouldn't be able to bear it.

'Pamela . . . what do you think about moving out of London?'

'I think it's probably a good idea at some point, but . . .'

'I've seen this place,' he interrupted her, not wanting to hear the 'buts' right now. He'd rehearsed them all himself.

'Yes . . .'

'It's quite big . . . it's very big. But it would be a business too. Pammy, this is what I really, really want to do.' She heard the earnestness in his voice, the seriousness.

'What?' she asked. She hadn't got this yet. 'What business?'

'I want to buy a farm. Well, it's a very small farm – a smallholding, technically.'

There, he'd said it and there was nothing else to do now but hold his breath and wait for her reaction.

'A farm?!' She tried not to sound as surprised as she felt. *A farm?? A farm??! What the hell did Dave know about farming?* 'What kind of farm?' It was the most neutral thing she could think of saying next.

'An organic fruit and vegetable farm. Very big growth forecast in the sector,' he added in the hope that a blast of analyst-speak would convince her that they should leave behind the city, their overpriced cubicle of a home, the screamingly frustrating tube journeys, the endless competition of life in London to move to rolling fields, wide open space, sky, a cavernous farmhouse . . .

'Let me show you something.' Dave went out of the kitchen and returned with a copy of *Smallholder's Weekly*.

'*Smallholder's Weekly*?' she couldn't help asking. She knew he'd had a farmer uncle he'd spent a lot of time working for when he was young, she knew he'd always wanted a big garden, to grow their own vegetables . . . one day . . . when they moved to their place in the countryside . . . but she couldn't help feeling that they'd missed a stage. How had it jumped to *Smallholder's Weekly* and buying a *farm*?

'I thought you wanted to be a painter, not a farmer?' she couldn't help asking.

He made no reply, just flipped the relevant pages open in front of her.

The pictures didn't really help: aerial shots of fields, the roof of a house and steadings, trees which looked like rounded bushes from this height. It was all green, but a uniform businessy green. Rows of things, neat fields, hedges, a straight road from the boundaries up to the farm buildings.

'This is Linden Lee,' Dave was telling her. 'A 50-acre farm which has been fully organic for three years. It's owned by Harry Taylor and his wife.'

'How do you know all this?' She wondered why she taking so long to understand what was going on.

'Because I've been speaking to his solicitor,' he said. 'Because I've expressed an interest in the place. Because I've arranged for us to go and see it on Saturday.'

'For us to see it?' she repeated. 'You want us to buy this farm?'

She picked the magazine up and scrutinized the page once more. This time she saw the asking price. Jesus Christ. The company doctor didn't have it right at all: this wasn't stress – this was insanity.

111

'Where is it?' She thought she should at least know that before she listed all the reasons why they couldn't do this.

'It's in Norfolk. North of Norwich.'

'So I wouldn't be able to commute? How is this even going to begin to work, Dave? What is this about? What are you thinking?' Pamela's voice was raised and she was on the very edge of shouting, but something in his face stopped her. He looked so desperate and so sad.

'I don't want you to commute,' he said, then picked her hand up and linked fingers with her. 'You hate working for WLI. What happened to the plan to set up on your own? Do projects at your own pace? This is your chance to do it. And anyway, I'll need you to help me run the farm.'

Run the farm . . .

She was pretty good at choosing paint shades, at sectioning a room with colour to make it look bigger, at *über*-creative shelving systems – but farming? What was that about? Driving tractors, ploughing . . . sowing . . . wellingtons.

She knew absolutely *nothing* about farming.

Chapter Ten

Very few relevant words passed between them on the long drive up to Linden Lee. Pamela was convinced this was not going to work, could never work, that Dave would see the farm, be overwhelmed by the sheer scale of the venture and realize what an idiotic idea this was.

Dave saw her set and serious face looking out at the landscape from the passenger seat and didn't want to risk a conversation.

He hoped she was at least approaching the place with an open mind. As he was trying to. He didn't want his enthusiasm to run away with him; he wanted to be realistic. Could they really do this? What kind of place would it be? He hadn't been on a farm since he was 22, for one last sad look around Ingleshaven before it was sold on his uncle's death. His uncle had left him a hefty chunk of the proceeds, which had been tied up in sensible investments along with the money he had inherited from his parents, but now he was ready to free it all up and jump, take the risk. He glanced over at Pamela again. Her face was giving off nothing beyond a sort of bored exasperation.

It took over three and a half hours before they were finally past the turn-offs for Norwich and on to the small dual carriageway that would lead them to the farm. They had a road map and a sheet of crinkly fax paper with Harry's careful, handwritten directions.

Grudgingly, Pamela admitted to herself how calm, green and empty the landscape had become. Vast mountains of white cloud were pushing up from the horizon into the blue sky and way in the distance, the land dropped off and fell into an endless pale blue of sea.

They passed the long-disused bodies of windmills looming over them and she played a game with herself: if the farm had one of those, she would consider it. She had a vague memory of wanting to live in a windmill . . . or a lighthouse. If the farm had cats, she'd consider it . . . or a view of the sea . . . if the house was really amazing . . . had 'potential'. If . . . if . . . if . . . Christ, she had no idea. A farm? What would they do all day? And they wouldn't know anyone. They'd be so alone, just the two of them, north of Norwich, with all their problems.

But then, her parents lived near Cambridge. That wasn't so far away. And commuting to London by train wasn't an impossibility. What would her parents think of this? Suddenly she longed for their opinion. But she'd decided not to tell anyone until she'd seen the place and she and Dave had reached decisions of their own.

'We head into the town, take the main road out, then the turn-off is the third on the left,' Dave said. They were approaching a charmless collection of modern houses leading to a small, grey high street and parade of shops. There was a café with a white plastic table and two chairs in the forecourt, a metal Cornetto sign so faded, she'd barely been able to make it out.

'Does that count as a turn-off?' Dave asked, as they passed an untarred dirt track leading up a small hill.

'Don't know,' Pamela answered. She was looking around in a rush, trying to figure this place out. Already trying to give herself reasons to like it or dislike it.

'Well, let's try up here.' They turned into a narrow unmarked road, which twisted and wound for several miles.

They were driving so slowly, she could look out at the dense hedgerow and try to remember the names of the flowers and bushes they were passing. That was hawthorn, the low trees were elders, the cow parsley was in full flower. She was pleased with how much she could recall. It seemed decades since she had looked, really looked, at wild flowers like this. Those were blackberry flowers, berries to pick in the autumn ... *Watch it*, she warned herself, we're not even going to begin to think about autumn.

Dave pulled the car sharply up onto the verge

as a green Land Rover sped past. A woman in the front seat waved cheerfully at them.

'Bloody hell, that was close,' he complained. But she saw that it wasn't really, there had been inches to spare between the cars, the driver probably knew every swing and dip in the road, and they were newcomers – visitors, she corrected herself.

'Can this be right? We've been on this road for ages.' His patience was wearing thin now: a long stressed-up drive and only more stress at the end of it. His thoughts flicked between excitement and the growing conviction that this would be the biggest embarrassment of his life with Pamela to date.

'Maybe we can ask someone?' she suggested, but as they'd only passed one speeding car in fifteen minutes, it didn't seem very likely. 'After this bend, we should be able to see what's ahead.'

They passed the curve, mounted a steep hill and came out from the tightly hedged road into an open view. She saw the working windmill, sails creaking slowly in the breeze just before her eyes caught the ornate metalwork sign, slightly lopsided, which pointed up a long white cement road to *Linden Lee*.

'This is it!' she said, not able to keep a hint of excitement out of her voice.

'Thank God for that.' Dave was hunched over the wheel in an acute whirl of anxiety.

They turned into the farm road, both aware of the futility of the flashing indicator when there wasn't another car around for miles, and drove towards the farmhouse and the cluster of big mottled grey stone steadings behind it. Pamela tried to work out what was growing in the fields on either side of the road – grass? Oats? And what was the white stuff? Whole fields of plants seemed to be growing under a white, fleecy blanket.

Even she could recognize the lusciousness of it. Not just the juicy green fields, even the grass verges were spilling on to the road, strewn with buttercups, scruffy ox-eye daisies and all sorts of wild flowers she couldn't name.

The farm was set on a gentle hill, with the farmhouse and outbuildings in the middle. Bright green, golden and fleecy fields sloped away above and below it.

They turned right into a crunching gravelled drive and pulled up outside the house. Before the car engine had been turned off, the back door opened and two black dogs shot out barking and wagging their tails fiercely. A broad, blond man came out after them calling them both to his side and waving at the car.

'Hello,' he said as Pamela swung open her door and landed herself with a lap full of dog.

'They're very friendly, won't do any harm,' the man she took to be Harry was telling her.

It seemed too rude to answer: 'No, but get them off, they're drooling all over my skirt,' so she pushed the two big dog faces off her knees and scrambled out of the car.

'Hello,' Harry repeated. Red-cheeked and straw hair on end, he was holding out his hand.

'Pam.' He shook her hand vigorously and then it was Dave's turn. 'Come in, come in, we're just having a bite, then we'll show you everything you want to see and more besides.' He gave them a wide grin, all wholesome, bulky guy, with an outdoorsy face, muscular shoulders and the checked shirt and baggy, beige cords Pamela realized she'd been expecting.

They followed him through the back door of the house and into a dark corridor, then into the bright jumble of a large, flowery kitchen, around which wafted the most gorgeous, edible smell of fresh bread.

'Just a bite' turned out to be a huge farmhouse table full of food. She was introduced to Harry's wife, Ingrid, and his two small blond children, Kitty and Jake; usually she would have been totally absorbed with them, but the food was such a distraction.

She and Dave were ushered to seats and served platefuls of chunky vegetable soup and slabs of bread. There was a butter dish on the table and plates of tomato salad, green salad and a hunk of ham lying with a knife casually slung alongside it. Harry leaned over, carved off a fat slice and sat down to smother it in relish from an unmarked jar.

'God, I'm sorry,' Ingrid fussed a bit, getting them matching plates, glasses and cutlery. 'We have no manners, we get so ravenously hungry out here. It's all the physical work – hard labour, that's what my husband has sentenced us to,' and she smiled fondly at him.

As the soup went down, Pamela allowed herself to look a little at the Heidi-healthy children sitting opposite her, sneaking peeks over their bowlfuls and giggling. They had messy curls, glowing cheeks, white teeth and pink tongues.

Blond and pretty Ingrid was every bit as wholesome-looking in her tight jeans and red T-shirt. Pamela felt pale, stodgy and just a bit grubby compared to them. They were like a farming family from a Swedish film or something, scarily perfect. Her overwhelming reaction was that she was *never* going to be like this. She was *never* going to be rosy-cheeked, outdoorsy, effortlessly producing home-made soup and children; she might as well get back in the car and go home now.

Harry was deep in talk about why they had to move now, because Kitty was about to start school and they wanted somewhere they'd be for the next ten years at least, somewhere big enough for a proper herd. They had an offer in on a place just seven miles away.

'Ridiculous to move house and fields and have all that upheaval, have to convert another farm to organic all over again, but we hope it'll be worth it in the long run.'

'So what are you growing this year?' Dave asked, which prompted a long explanation of all the different fields and their crops from Harry.

Ingrid wanted to know if Pamela had lived on a farm before.

'No, total farm virgin,' was Pamela's answer,

then she panicked that the word was unsuitable for five-year-old ears.

But Ingrid laughed. 'Me too. Kitty was tiny when he dragged me here kicking and screaming from York with his mad organic veg scheme, and I got pregnant with Jake about five minutes later, but I love it. I always liked gardening and growing things, and now I just do what I liked to do on a huge scale. Almost everything we eat, we've grown ourselves. Coffee?' she asked, and quickly added, 'not home-grown, I can assure you of that.'

Was that just the merest hint of Swedish accent? Pamela wondered, or was this whole blond, apple-cheeked thing getting to her? And why did Ingrid have to be nice and a bit funny and self-deprecating when Pamela really wanted to *hate* her?

'Has it been very hard work?' Pamela asked.

'Well, not really. Two years we spent with a big garden full of vegetables watching the grass grow, because the place was in conversion. The last three years have been very full on, growing, growing, trying out all kinds of different things, working out how to get rid of bugs and weeds without the nasty stuff, then trying to sell the produce. Because, guess what? Hardly anyone round here eats organic vegetables . . . or vegetables at all, as far as I can see. All these people living in this gorgeous countryside and they're trailing off to the supermarket every week to buy packet soup and microwavable lasagne . . .' It looked like she was working up to a bit of a stormer. But she caught her husband's eye and stopped with a smile.

'I'm sorry, I'm always going on about it, it's like a religion or something. Vegetable Eaters Anonymous, I need your help.'

'We actually sell most of the stuff to Norwich market and even New Covent Garden,' Harry explained. 'We do some veg box schemes as well. The organic oats and potatoes, they do really well. You can grow great big fields of them and they all get sold. Big demand for more. At the moment, we buy in loads of dung, because we only have a few cows, but when we have our herd, the crop rotation, manuring, fields in grass, will all begin to make much more sense.' Harry was warming to the topic and Dave was defrosting too. Pamela could see now how nervous he was, sure he'd look such an ignorant amateur. But after Harry had been chatting for half an hour, Dave dared to ask him if he'd known much about it when he started.

'Not a lot!' was Harry's disarming reply. 'I'm a farmer by the book. In fact, I'll even admit to you, if you don't tell anyone, that I'm doing an organic farming diploma by correspondence course right now. But you know, lots of books, lots of wacky experiments, we're learning as we go along, you'll soon get the hang of it, and we hardly seem to spend any money at all. No big supermarket bills, no big restaurant bills, no commuting fares, no keeping up with fashion—' he winked at his wife. 'Hardly any toys needed, even. The simple life.' He leaned back and beamed at them.

Ingrid brought over a plate with a wholemeal fruit loaf on it. 'I know how bad this looks,' she said to Pamela, setting the still warm cake right in front of her where it breathed spicy, inviting fumes. 'Like I spend all day chained to the Aga cooking and baking. I'm not a 1950s housewife, I promise. I just really like to cook and find I have the time for it since we moved here . . . and it's quicker to bake a cake than drive to the town to get one . . .' She stopped herself, smiled and added: 'Look, I'm going to stop apologizing for it. Just have a slice.'

See. Too nice. Too funny and yes, Ingrid was half-Swedish, it turned out.

When the coffee cups were drained and the last crumbs of cake had been wiped from the plates, it was time to tour.

'D'you want to do the house first, or the farm?' Harry asked.

As Pamela said, 'House,' Dave answered, 'Farm.'

'Pamela's an interior designer, so the house is quite important,' Dave explained, with a smile.

'Oh no! You're not!' Ingrid looked quite pained at this. 'I cannot cope with an interior designer going round the house! We had all sorts of plans, but . . . I'm not sure what happened. Pathetic. Come on then, might as well get this torture over with.'

'Honestly, I don't mind . . . the kitchen's lovely.' Pamela tried to put her at ease. In truth, the kitchen was the gaudiest, most early Eighties bit of hideousness she'd been in for years.

Matching brown sink, brown taps and brown cooker, orange wallpaper, yeuuurgh!

As she toured round she made encouraging noises, but, really, she was mentally changing everything. The house was large, but didn't have too many rooms. They were all on a generous scale: four big bedrooms, the luxury of a dedicated office . . . a dining room!

There was lots of brown, tired-out magnolia, patterned carpeting, patterned wallpaper and fiddly bits and pieces everywhere. It obviously wasn't Ingrid's doing, because most of the rooms looked worn and tatty, the curtains had faded long ago and the flowered sofas gaped at frayed holes on the arms. There were strange collections of things all about the house. Beside the downstairs fireplaces, towering stacks of newspapers and baskets of logs.

'The *Sunday Times*,' Ingrid explained. 'Lights the fire all week.'

In the small room which housed the washing machine and drier were rows and rows of clean jam jars, assorted sizes, stacks of plastic plant pots, balls of string.

But Pamela's professional eye took over and saw only the all-important basics: the big, 12-paned windows which let light flood into the spaces, the solid, flat walls, the wide spiralling stairs, the long cast iron bath, original sink and radiator in the bathroom.

She imagined acres of rustic sisal flooring, shades of palest pistachio, duck egg blue . . . Oh yes, a fantastic project.

Every window framed a view more beautiful than the last: the tall trees which sheltered the house, and from every room upstairs, miles of greenery and sky.

The bright light was the biggest surprise. She'd imagined a farmhouse of low ceilings and gloom; instead she saw now that the light streamed in from every direction because it was unchecked by any other buildings.

'I find I sort of follow the sun around,' Ingrid was explaining. 'Our bedroom and the kitchen are on the east, so we wake up to the early morning sunshine and have breakfast with it, then the office and sitting room are sunny all day long and in the evening, the children watch the sunset from their bath. I don't think I could have even told you in which direction my old house faced, but here it's inescapable. You notice all kinds of things much more. The trees turning yellow at the end of the summer, the new buds in spring. The dirt on the window panes! I just hope the new place is going to be as nice as this. It has a character all of its own. I'll be really sorry to go.'

'OK, farm time,' Harry said, when even the smallest storage corner and cupboard had been inspected. They trooped down the stairs through the kitchen and into the dark corridor where Dave and Pamela headed for the door but the Taylors peeled off into a pantry dedicated to coats, anoraks, overalls, scarves, hats, winter boots, welly boots, hiking boots, dirty boots . . . and came out five minutes later clad in wellingtons and light, muddy cagoules.

'We've got spares, if you want to change.' Ingrid pointed politely at the dainty, Spanish open-toed sandals on Pamela's feet.

'No, no, don't worry,' she insisted, slightly horrified at the thought of putting her bare feet into someone else's wellies.

So obviously, if they were going to move here, they would have to have a new wardrobe of outdoor clothes. Did they only come in grass green or navy blue? Pamela wondered, having seen the rack. Was there a reason for this? Were you not allowed to scare the horses, or make the bulls run after you? So many rules – a whole way of life she didn't think she knew the slightest thing about . . . and where did you even begin to ask?

Dave was thinking about more practical requirements, asking Harry about tools and machinery and what was included in the sale and what would be needed on top.

There was mention of rotovators, the cost but reusability of Agromesh. 'No substitute for a bit of manual hoeing though,' Harry was explaining. Not just new clothes – they would need to learn a whole new language, if they did this.

Outside, they walked past a low wooden and breeze block construction. 'What's that?' Dave asked.

'Oh it's absolutely fantastic.' Harry, with a fresh burst of enthusiasm, lifted the lid to reveal three paper bundles the colour of unbleached coffee filters and a dark brown tangle that – *Jesus*

Christl Pam jumped back from the box – was moving.

'Worms,' Harry told them, grinning. 'They eat Jake's nappies. Turn them into compost. Isn't that amazing? I mean, we use special biodegradable nappies, but I still find it brilliant. Nappy in at one end, compost out at the other. This is the future.' He knelt down and tugged at the bottom of the box, jerking out a tray lightly covered in brown earthy stuff.

'There's a liquid collector too—' he tapped a tin at the side of the box. 'I won't get that out . . . smells a bit, but it's worked wonders on the tomatoes.'

Pamela stepped further back from the wooden crate of horror. Worms which ate the baby's nappies and this connected somehow to the tomatoes they had just eaten for *lunch*??!

She couldn't do this. It was too much. She glanced at Dave and saw that even he looked a bit shaken by this revelation.

Harry put the lid down, wiped his hands off and smiled at them proudly.

'So, did you settle in here OK?' Pamela asked Ingrid, not wanting to think about composting worms for one moment longer. They both kept their eyes on the giggling children racing ahead to the gate in the hedge behind the house. The latch had been fixed up high where they couldn't reach it.

'I don't think it was any worse or any better than moving to a new town,' Ingrid replied after a pause in which she seemed to be gathering her thoughts. 'Some people are really friendly, want to know you; some aren't. There are as many social things to get involved with as you like, or then again, you can just close the gates at the bottom of the drive and be alone.'

Ingrid swung the latch, releasing her children out into the farmyard: 'Other farmers, they can be a bit tricky, though,' she was telling Pamela. 'It's the organic thing. Most of them don't get that, don't even want to know about it, think we're a bunch of freaky hippies or something. And I can understand that. I don't think all other farmers are bad, most are pretty good, have a healthy respect for "the land" and all that. But there are a few horrors.'

Jake tripped up and fell his length, landing face down screaming. Pamela watched as Ingrid picked him up quickly, dusted him down, but didn't fuss too much, just wiped his hands with hers, set him up in his wellies and sent him off again.

They toured the steadings and the old barns. So much detail, Harry keenly pointing it out: 'This is where they kept the straw so they could just roll it down the slope into the forecourt where the cows would be all winter . . . I'd like a horse, I like the idea of going back to ploughing a single furrow with a horse, but Ingrid won't have any of that. She's the organic technological forefront kind of girl. I want to grind my oats by waterwheel, she's into genetically modifying potatoes so they don't get blight . . . I mean, GM? She's practically the enemy.'

'Did you get the windmill working?' Dave wanted to know.

'Oh yeah, it's brilliant, isn't it? Took an entire winter but now I wouldn't want a farm without one. Have to get the one up at the new place going again. This one lights the entire steadings, you know.'

'That's four lightbulbs, Harry,' Ingrid nudged him. Obviously the woman who kept this slightly crazed man grounded.

They walked and walked all over the farm, down to the bottom boundary where overgrown wire fences and a lazy stream separated it from the neighbour's fields. And all the way up to the top of the hill from where they could see for miles in the clear, bright light.

All the time Harry and Ingrid talked, explained, showed off the results of their years of work.

'Always, always something to do. Something falls down just as you've finished patching something else up. It's a bit like owning an old house but on a huge scale,' Harry said as the top rail of the gate he was shutting came loose in his hand.

'Bugger.'

Burst of giggle from Kitty.

'Ooops.'

'Just wait till you have a herd of cows,' Ingrid warned him. 'We did try chickens,' she added, 'but cleaning the henhouse was horrendous, plus the chicken food attracted the dreaded R-A-T-S.' She spelled the word out with a shudder. 'So the hens had to go, in a kill fest which turned us vegetarian for weeks . . . chickens running about without their heads – they really do that – it was gruesome. Urrgh.'

Pamela had earth in her sandals, right in, wedged between her toes, small gritty bits underneath her soles. Now there was talk of rats and headless chickens. She had loved the views, and, yes, she had loved the house – but the fields with their big bushy vegetables and crops felt like a mystery she didn't know how to begin to unravel. You planted what? Where? When? How? And how did you make it grow? Whenever Dave was away, she struggled to keep the houseplants alive.

They had been out for over two hours and the children were tired and whiney. Was there anything else they wanted to see right now, or was it time to go in for tea? Harry wanted to know.

Tea was set out on the scruffy lawn in front of the house with big mugs, more slabs of fruit loaf, a huge bowl of strawberries and a jug of cream. 'Not ours,' Ingrid said as she set the bowl down on the table. 'There's a massive strawberry farm five miles away, run by Lachlan Murray and his wife Rosie, they supply M&S, Wimbledon, the Queen . . . No, she probably only eats Charles's home-grown ones. I don't really like to think too much about what they do to them, but they taste really good.'

'So strawberries grow well round here?' Dave asked.

'Oh yeah, it's sunny, pretty dry most summers,'

Harry threw in. 'The soil isn't too claggy. I've tried a few rows myself, but they were a bit small and mouldy. So, we eat Murray berries all summer. We've got raspberries though, but they're not ripe yet.'

Dave was eating his strawberries one by one, chewing thoughtfully.

Pamela heaped some onto her plate, beside the big slice of cake she now felt starving for. She put the berry in her mouth and bit down. Warm and sweet, as Ingrid said, it tasted good.

She looked up to see Dave watching her. Was he thinking about the other strawberries? she wondered. The ones which had brought them here. Was he hoping she could taste a difference?

'They're good,' she said, in a quiet voice, just for him. 'But the other ones were perfect.'

This seemed to please him.

It was Ingrid who floated the idea of dinner, wine, watching the sunset and staying over.

'You've such a long drive ahead of you. And such a big decision! Why don't you stay? Wander about the place on your own. See it again in the morning, drive over into town . . . see it all . . . try to imagine living here. When we came to look at this place, we stayed for nearly a week, the Hurleys thought they'd never get rid of us,' she added.

The offer was so warmly made, they were easily persuaded. Pamela thought of the cosy guest room Ingrid had at the back of the house with a small window and a giant puff of old-fashioned feather duvet on the bed.

'And don't worry, I have spare toothbrushes, pyjamas and things. You've got to get used to that in the country, people staying the night instead of driving home.'

Pamela walked beside Dave all the way up to the top of the farm's hill again before dinner. They watched the sky grow golden and the sun lower, but it was still too early for sunset and darkness.

There was so much to say, but it felt too soon, too momentous, so they stuck to small talk, little questions and replies sparsely spread out over the walk.

'They seem really nice, the Taylors. '

'Yeah, Harry's hilarious. I think he knew even less than me about farming when he started and look at the place now.'

'Hmmm.'

'It's a great corner of the world, isn't it?' Dave asked, trying to sound casual when they were at the top of the hill looking into the distance. He took her hand and held it. Pamela couldn't think when that had last happened in a non-hospital context and with surprise felt a surge of teariness.

They'd been through so much . . . so much. And there was *still* no baby. Just a relationship so fractured, they both wondered how much longer it could go on. Maybe they needed some time out. Time to heal . . . in a healing place . . . maybe that's what this whole farm thing was about. Making time to be together in a healing place.

She looked at the man standing next to her.

Was he not worth this? Shouldn't she risk a year or two of her time on holding them together, on giving it a go?

'Would you like to live here?' she asked in a voice which was suddenly whispery.

He looked out over the land glimmering gold all around them. Looked up and caught the dance and swoop of the swallows way, way up above them in the pale sky. He wanted this so much . . . it *hurt*. He would have to find a way of doing this alone, without her, if she said no.

Chapter Eleven

Bleep, bleep, bleep ... 6.45 a.m. ... Pamela smacked off the alarm clock and grudgingly threw back the duvet, the little blast of having-to-get-to-work-on-time adrenalin beginning to course through her veins and wake her up. It was Thursday. Only two more days to go, she reminded herself, then she'd be able to have a rest. Thank God.

Shower, dress, shake Dave out of bed, make up, tea, bowl of muesli and yoghurt eaten standing up, eyes on the kitchen clock. 7.28 a.m. She had to go. Shoe crisis at the door. She still hadn't had a chance to pick up two pairs from the repair shop. She would have to wear the high-heeled boots again, third day in a row, even though they were killing her feet.

At the tube station there had been a delay, the platform was packed and the next train was still six minutes away. 7.56 a.m. When it finally arrived, like everyone else waiting, she *had* to get on. Couldn't wait for the next one promised in four minutes' time. She scrunched in, face tucked in under someone's armpit, someone's elbow pressed into the small of her back, her bag squashed against another passenger's side, then when the doors shut, everyone was crammed even closer together. Armpit man began to blow his nose, practically into her face, with a very shredded and fragile-looking tissue. She couldn't turn her head to look away, so shut her eyes and tried not to breathe in.

8.22 a.m. At Moorgate she fought her way out of the carriage so she could change trains, a long and, in these boots, pained walk up and down stairs, escalators, corridors. She was carrying her raincoat now, sweating her make-up off before the day had even begun.

More delay. 8.31 a.m. Hell. If the next train wasn't here within five minutes, she wouldn't get to the office before nine, and Sheila liked *everyone* to be in before nine, even if, like Pamela today, they had nothing to do until 10 a.m. and had worked till 8 p.m. the night before. The train didn't come . . .

Coming out of the underground station, she took the decision at 9.05 a.m. that since she was late anyway, she'd stop and get a coffee. Might as well try and brighten the start to the day.

'Oh oh,' were Alison's first words as Pamela passed through the all-glass entrance hall and into the office. 'You didn't get the message, did you?'

'No!'

'It's been brought forward. Nine-fifteen. They're already in the conference room.'

'Crap.' Pamela rushed to her desk and pulled open her bag, knocking the last of her coffee over the pile of papers there.

'*Crap! Crap!*' She used her hand to scoop the worst of the mess off the surface and into a bin. Her mobile was bleeping at her, but she ignored it, sure it was the message about the new meeting time.

Taking the files she needed from her bag, she smoothed over her hair – with coffee, yuck – and, limping slightly with the boot pain, headed to the room. 9.17 a.m.

'Really, Pamela, didn't you get the message?' was Sheila's greeting. Her boss was already at the head of the table, spiky gunmetal grey hair, sharpest trouser suit, trademark stiff white shirt and glittering cuff bracelets. A client on either side of her, papers, drawings, plans spread out before them.

'Sharpen up,' Sheila snapped. 'And try checking your messages for once.'

Which was just outrageous! Pamela checked her messages religiously, every fifteen minutes on a workday. Just to be sure she was in touch.

She sat down in a rogue chair which was six inches lower than everyone else's, but she pretended not to notice. The Smith and Wilkinson guys were here to adjust plans for the makeover of their vast South Bank headquarters.

'The upstairs atrium isn't working for us, at the

moment,' Paul Crowe, the project manager was explaining.

They all turned to the atrium drawings: enormous glass walls, a hexagonal glass roof and as a centrepiece, indoor trees in huge marble planters. This was Pamela's touch, along with rough limestone flooring, pebbles, a wooden seating area: her idea of bringing the outdoors inside.

'There just isn't going to be the space for all this,' Paul was saying, justifying it with all the other corporate-speak words: 'no cost benefit', 'need to prioritize work space', 'maximize the office floor' . . . and so on.

Pamela tried, from her head barely above the table position, to fight her case for a few minutes: 'hugely impressive visual feature', even, 'This species of tree has been proven to counteract the emissions from the audio-visual equipment on that floor.'

But it wasn't any use. They had made up their minds. The trees were out, to be replaced by a big conference area.

'Fine, fine.' Sheila wrote notes across the margin of the plans. 'I don't give a damn about trees.'

'Oh well.' Pamela tried to hide her disappointment at the loss of such a lovely space. All of a sudden the great cluster of mature trees round the Linden Lee farmhouse came into her head.'Maybe there will be room for a tree or two in the crèche area,' she said. 'That's going to be great. I'm very excited about that.'

Sheila's eyebrows raised at this and Paul chipped in: 'Well, no, as I was telling Sheila, the crèche's out. New company policy.'

And that was that. No further explanation. Forty children they'd originally wanted to accommodate. Forty! And where did they go now? she wondered. New company policy. Bollocks!

For the rest of the meeting, she tried to muster some enthusiasm for the new colour-coded office space replacing the crèche, but her heart was far from in it. In fact, her heart was racing in some horrible over-reaction to the coffee she'd had on the way in. It couldn't have been decaf.

11.05 a.m. When the session was finally over, Pamela got back to her coffee-stained desk where her phone was bleeping at her again. Three missed calls ... Two messages. Both explaining why neither supplier was going to take responsibility for the tile colour mix-up on the Tatchell's project – grand opening, Monday. Another round of phone calls to try and get to the bottom of this.

Then Sheila was at Pamela's desk, demanding attention.

'Where are the upholstery sample books I ordered from France?'

'Erm ... I haven't seen them. I made the request last week. Nothing's arrived on your desk yet?' No, obviously not, dangerous question.

'No. I need them today, Pamela –' frightening look with that – 'I'm meeting Boyd tonight to go over the details. We need those samples. It's *the* fabric: waterproof, hard-wearing, suede effect in all the shades we need. Track them down. Have them couriered over if necessary. I need them today.'

Pointy heels clip-clipping all the way back to her office, every other head cast down, keeping clear of trouble.

12.05 p.m. Disgusting, soggy tortilla-wrap-in-a-bag lunch with Alison.

'And do you know what else I heard her say?' Alison's contribution to the Sheila-bitchfest coming right up.

'What?' They both leaned in, although they were a full ten-minute walk away (Pamela had the shooting toe pains to prove it) from the office and *her*.

'That if EC maternity leave laws come into force she's only going to employ men or "women like Pamela". You know, she meant . . .' Alison was losing heart: it had been such an awful thing to say, she was suddenly sorry to be repeating it.

Pamela just nodded, took it on the chin, stored it up in the great big book of insults Sheila had paid her over the years. One day that book would be full and she wouldn't take any more of this. One day soon.

'I have to go,' she said, glancing at her watch, 12.35 p.m., astonished at the time. 'Sadie Kingston-Jones next. The paint in her nursery is bleeding or something odd. I promised to go and look. I've got to get across town for one-ish.'

'Did you sort the sample books? The ones she needs *today*,' Alison asked.

'They insist they're arriving special delivery

this afternoon. I've told Grace. That's all I can do.'

'Yeah, short of going to France yourself,' Alison snorted.

'Yeah.'

'I don't want to cause you a big nightmare, darling.' Sadie was as pregnant, surely, as it was possible to be before exploding, protruding belly button pushing out against the stretchy shift she had on: 'But something's definitely gone wrong.'

Pamela looked around the nursery walls. The all-organic, 100 per cent solvent- and additive-free paint was streaked and patchy all over, bubbling in places.

'And you don't have any damp at all?' She wanted to clarify.

'Damp? Bloody hell, somebody's going to get sued if I do,' was Sadie's reply.

How could she wear three-inch mules in her condition? How did she do that? And in her own home, where she could slob about in Birkenstocks and no-one would know. The walk from the tube station had just about crippled Pamela. No matter what, after this meeting, she was going to buy *slippers* on the King's Road to wear for the rest of the day.

'It looks like it hasn't been mixed properly,' Pamela said, running her finger over the patches. 'The oil's separated or something. Good grief,' she let out a deep sigh. This was about the final straw. Sheila only just tolerated the nursery projects as it was. Saw them as merely a testing ground for the eco-friendly products before she flogged the ideas on to the big payers. Problems with the paint might be the death knell of Pamela's whole little niche.

'Oh darling, I'm sorry. You look really fed up. Come upstairs and have a coffee.'

'No, no ... I should head. You won't believe this but I've got to try and find an aluminium cradle for another client.' She threw her hands up. 'I know, I tried to tell her how *stupid* it was. Not to mention dangerous. But that's what she wants: a smooth, wipe-clean, aluminium cradle. To go with her black and white colour scheme! Boosts IQ or something insane.'

'What, aluminium?'

'No, black and white. Improves letter recognition – something like that. I try not to listen to her too much.' Pamela was trying to bury the raging question: why is that *mad* woman allowed to have a baby and not me?!

'Who is this we're talking about?' Sadie, sly smile, crossed arms resting on her bump.

'I can't tell you.'

'You can, go on. I won't tell Sheila about the paint.'

'No, no, don't tell Sheila about the paint –' little flash of panic – 'I'll get it sorted as soon as I can.'

'You better—' with a glance down at her bump. 'They're due in three weeks and I'm always early,' Sadie warned, then shot her a, 'Oh, don't worry, even I let them sleep in our room for a month or two.'

140

Pamela's phone began to ring. 1.41 p.m. She apologized but took the call. It was Sheila's secretary, Grace, and information which took several moments to sink in. No sign of the sample books, the factory was in Lille . . . it was on the Eurostar route . . . someone would meet her at the station this evening.

Lille?

'Lille? In *France*?' Pamela was asking in disbelief. 'Sheila wants me to go to France?'

Grace reeled off Eurostar times, had already made the reservation. If Pamela could just get herself to Waterloo as quickly as possible.

'*What?!* I've got other swatches and books we can show Boyd tonight,' she insisted. 'The French stuff is just one of the options. It'll probably arrive tomorrow and we can bike it round.'

'No,' Grace was telling her, 'Sheila is . . .' she paused to choose the word carefully, 'adamant.'

'Sheila's a mad, raving, certifiable psychotic,' was Pamela's response to this. Her heart was racing again. 'I haven't got my passport on me. I haven't got time to go and get it, if I'm supposed to make the 3.30 train.'

Grace had already thought of that, had already spoken to Dave and arranged a courier!

This was insane. But unarguable.

'I'm off to France,' she told a bemused Sadie, when the phone call was over. 'To collect a sample book for a drinks meeting tonight.'

'And I thought I was the bitch boss from hell,' Sadie said as she walked her to the door. 'But Sheila wins hands down every time. Maybe you

141

should come and work for me . . . Let me think about this.'

'Ha,' was Pamela's reply.

'Well, don't be silly darling, you haven't been sold into slavery or anything.' Sadie kissed her on the cheek and added, 'Love your boots.'

The boots. Double ha! No way was she walking one step further. Pamela hailed the first taxi she saw, only to regret it bitterly as they crawled through traffic, the minutes stacking up against her. Only half an hour to meet the courier and catch the train she was booked onto. And why wouldn't he shut up? The driver was ranting on and on about the roadworks, the new junction ahead . . . the way the lights should be synchronized, as she was held hostage. A paying hostage.

Don't be a bloody taxi driver then! she wanted to scream at him.

Pamela got to the station, found her courier, the platform, rushed through the check-in just as it was closing, hurtled across the platform, feet shrieking, almost knocking another woman over in her scramble for the door.

Settling down in her seat, she considered that. She had actually started barging people out of the way in an effort to do Sheila's bidding. What sort of lackey was she turning into? What sort of crazed stress monster was she set to become? She was 34. As Sadie had pointed out, she wasn't a slave, she didn't have to live like this. Hadn't she promised herself a change?

But she was *frightened*, she had to admit to

herself. Didn't know which thing to change first. Didn't know which direction to take. A headless chicken . . . That made her think of Ingrid. Had they really decapitated the chickens?

As the train pulled out of the station, it occurred to her that she had three hours of train travel ahead of her and not a shred to read. She looked out of the window and watched London and its trailing outskirts pass by. The countryside beyond didn't move her at all the way Norfolk had.

5.45 p.m. She got off the train and met the fabric company's rep, who insisted on buying her a *croque monsieur* and a glass of wine as she waited for the return train.

'Very important client?' he asked.

'Very impatient boss,' Pamela informed him.

'Very!' he agreed.

It was 9.46 p.m. when she pulled up outside the wine bar Sheila had chosen for this meeting. Pamela registered her exhaustion. She'd been up since 6.45 a.m., and just two sandwiches, a glass of wine, unaccustomed caffeine and a packet of crisps had kept her going all day long. But the fat samples books were tucked under her mac as she paid the taxi driver as quickly as she could, because it was pouring with rain.

Sheila spotted her first and waved her over. Boyd was there with two members of his staff. There were other books and swatches out on the table. But here she was bringing the *pièce de résistance* all the way from Lille. She almost felt proud for a moment there.

'Goodness, Pamela, you are wet. Don't you carry an umbrella?' was Sheila's greeting and then Pamela was introduced. No mention of the journey she'd just done, no word of thanks: Sheila just took the books from her and set them down with a flourish.

'This is well worth a look.' Sheila was playing it down, obviously, never ever wanted to commit to anything in front of a client, all options always open. 'Waterproof, very hard-wearing, apparently, and some great colours. I haven't seen the whole range yet.'

Boyd, a commercial property developer and one of Sheila's biggest and most regular clients, opened the first book and began to look through it. He flicked over the leaves carefully, stroking the material. When every one of the fifty or so swatches had been examined, he closed it up and said: 'No. Don't think that's quite right. I liked the first book you showed me better.'

'Yes,' Sheila immediately agreed. 'I'm not quite sure why Pamela was raving about the French stuff so much.'

'Why *I* was raving about it?' Pamela was still standing up. She hadn't been invited to sit down, no-one had offered her a seat, or a drink, or any sort of civility at all. And here it was, Pamela realized, with a great gulp of terror, the moment when the book of insults was full up. It wasn't physically possible to take one single insult more. She would have to give it back. Return to sender.

'I've just spent six hours on the Eurostar to

bring you that book, Sheila, because you couldn't wait until tomorrow morning.'

'Pamela!' Sheila turned in her chair to face her with glacial eyes, but Pamela saw that her left hand was twisting at her right cuff bangle. A scene in front of Boyd, that was just unthinkable!

'I'm sorry you've been inconvenienced,' Sheila managed, but it was too late. Way, way too late.

'Inconvenienced? Inconvenienced?!' Pamela heard herself repeat. She was shaking with fright, but knew there was still more to come: 'I have just been to France and back and yet the words "thank you" seem to be too much trouble for you.'

'Pamela, that's enough.' Sheila's voice was low now, but Boyd and his colleagues were hanging onto every word. 'You've had a long day, but you can keep your opinions to yourself. I've sacked people for less than this.'

'Well, you won't be sacking me – because I resign.' *What?! Who is this person? What is she saying? Make her stop.* 'I resign. I quit. I've had enough. I've had enough of you. I've worked for you for three years . . .' Out stumbled the words, out into the Arctic wilderness of Sheila's stare, Sheila's crossed arms, Sheila's unmistakable 'you will *never* work in this business again' look.

It was terrifying. One of the scariest things Pamela had done in her whole life, but still she went on: 'And you've treated me atrociously. You should be ashamed of yourself. I've only ever tried to do a good job for you. Tried to be the best

145

... So you can stuff your job. I'll get on fine without you.'

Through the blur of tears that was threatening, Pamela managed to turn and make for the door of the bar.

Oh my God, oh God, dear God.

Out in the street, she double-checked her purse with hands that hardly seemed to work any more. No, definitely no money left for a taxi home. She hobbled the fifteen minutes in streaming rain, in the boots of torture, to the nearest underground. 10.38 p.m. Two trains and another ten-minute walk ahead of her before she was home.

On the platform she waited; waited and looked at the posters. All promising escape, freedom, open space. A golden beach here, a mountain top there and at the end of the platform, a landscape photograph of rolling greenness, trees and a glorious sunset.

She knew a place like that, she realized, through the tears that were flowing freely now.

When she finally put her key in the front door lock, 11.26 p.m., Dave was in the hallway, had waited up, was opening the inner door for her. She flung her wet arms round him, rested her head, with soaking hair, against him and said: 'I've decided. I've finally made my decision . . . I've resigned. This flat goes on the market tomorrow and we buy Harry and Ingrid's farm.'

Dave was so stunned, so thrilled, he couldn't speak.

Chapter Twelve

'So ... what do you think?' Pamela looked in turn at each of the faces gathered round the garden table, registering the varying degrees of surprise.

'Well, that's what I call a big step.' Her mother, Helen, was the first to respond to the news. 'A drastically big step. I really didn't see that one coming.'

Pamela and Dave had just explained to her parents, her brother Ted and his partner, Liz, that they had jacked in their jobs and now planned to sell the flat and move to a small farm in Norfolk. It was the biggest news to have hit one of their informal family gatherings for ages.

She'd warned them on the phone that there was something 'big' she wanted to talk to them about and Liz had been convinced Pamela was calling them together to talk about splitting up from Dave.

'It's the strain of what they've been through,'

she'd told Ted, on the car journey to his parents' house, talking loudly over the *Percy the Park Keeper* CD and using the visor mirror to comb through her long black hair and apply lipstick: 'They're not going to make it. The last few times they've been up, it's been so obvious they're really struggling . . . so unhappy together.'

'No way,' was the response from Ted, as he glanced at the children in the back. Martha and little Jim. The children Pamela would beg, borrow, steal, just about kill to have. 'Those two will never split up, trust me on this. They're . . . they've been together *so* long. They're like . . . family.'

'So what?' said Liz. 'People split up. All kinds of people for all kinds of reasons. I'm not buying the family myth that Pamela and Dave are somehow immune. They're miserable. Why has no-one noticed this minor fact?'

But when they'd got to his parents' house, Pamela and Dave had looked better, happier than they had done in months. Pamela looked particularly well, slimmer, more relaxed, and had a tight skirt and high heels thing going on that Ted hadn't seen before.

And here they were talking about giving up the day jobs, uprooting to Norfolk. It was all very surprising.

'This is fantastic,' was Ted's response. 'Martha! Aunty Pam and Uncle Dave are moving to a farm. And you can go and stay with them all summer!' He winked at his sister, a grin cracking over his broad, handsome face.

Were there going to be lambs? Martha wanted to know. Horses? Pigs?

'Vegetables,' Pamela told her, knowing this would be a disappointment.

'Yuck!'

This provoked Liz to say, 'Martha, there are plenty of vegetables you like.'

'Yuuuergh!' came with full-on rolling eyes, sticking out tongue and dramatic falling down onto grass.

'Well, all very exciting.' This from Pamela's father, Simon, who was actually folding up his newspaper and threatening to put it down. Simon, 'Organic vegetables?' He began to roll one of his tiny cigarettelets, as he called them. 'So what do you have to do to grow those?'

Dave couldn't wait to share all his new information about manure, selective planting, crop rotation and traditional farming methods. He'd already started his organic horticulture course and the books about Green this, Manure that were stacking up on his bedside table.

'And does one flat in west London now equal a farm in Norfolk?' Simon wanted to know.

'Well ... it's a very small farm, but no, not quite. I'll be putting all my inheritance money into it as well.'

There, Pamela thought. That will show them that we mean it.

'My God.' Helen was rubbing at her temples. 'We all know what a tough, tough time the two of you are having. But are you *sure* this is the answer? Wouldn't three months off in the sun

149

be a better idea? You could both do with a long holiday.'

Nothing like a little maternal disapproval to make Pamela race to commit to an idea. 'We don't need a holiday,' she said, exasperation in her voice: 'When we get back from a holiday, nothing will have changed. And anyway, we've both resigned. We need to do something else.'

'Oh ... you've already resigned? Well, well,' her mother seemed to like this.

'Aha.' Pamela was grinning, looking forward to retelling the Sheila moment. The Monday after the *scene*, Alison had been dispatched to Pamela's home with a bag full of her belongings from the office. Inside had been a rather formal note from her ex-boss wishing her well in her career and promising 'excellent references' should she require them. She knew this was the closest she would ever get to an apology from Sheila.

'Have you looked into renting a farm, to see if you like it?' Liz suggested.

Pamela, swirling the remaining wine round her glass, said: 'I think we quite like the commitment of buying. Going for it with bells on!'

Helen, with a nod at the wine glass, asked: 'I take it you're having a break from the IVF at least?'

'Oh yes,' Pamela said and drained the wine down. 'Big break. Year off. We need a rest . . . from everything.' She looked round to catch her husband's eyes. They smiled at each other. It had been hell, no other word for it. But they were going to have some time off now, just as she'd said, from everything.

'Any more thoughts on adoption?' her father asked, one hand shading his eyes from the sunlight so he could look at her properly.

'I think,' she began after a considered pause, 'going the adoption route would be admitting to ourselves that we're not going to have our own baby. And we haven't given up the hope of that yet. We haven't been told there's *no* hope.'

'But they never tell you that, do they?' Ted's words cut across her. 'The clinics. They claim there's always a chance. They want you to keep coming back for more.'

'Ted!' A warning scowl crossed Liz's delicate features. 'You don't know enough about it.'

'We're thinking it through, really carefully,' Dave answered. 'But the main thing is to have a break.'

'Are you going to commute to London, Pam?' her mother wanted to know. 'Commuting from Norfolk will hardly give you much of a break, will it?'

'I've got two projects lined up, so I'll commute for a bit then, hopefully, take some time off, help Dave with the farm and find work up there. That's the plan.'

'I'm still trying to picture you both on a farm,' Ted said. He was sitting cross-legged on the grass beside them, rolling a ball over and over for Jim. 'I mean, Pamela needs to be within half a mile of a handbag shop at all times . . . and Dave – you're pretty good with your pot plants but I'm trying to picture you in a field.'

'I'm going to have two tractors!' Dave replied. 'One red and one silver grey. How jealous are you?! You'll be up there in a shot, begging me for a go on my tractors. Forget the latest WAP and WiFi technology, I'm going to have two diesel engines . . .'

'And a windmill,' Pamela added.

'Really? Like in *Thomas the Tank Engine*?' This appealed to Martha.

'Combine harvester?' Ted asked with a grin.

'Just wait and see.' Dave blew Ted a kiss and they both burst out laughing.

'Liz, honey, I've made the children scrambled egg, steamed carrot, green beans – everything organic –' a nod at Dave here – 'and they haven't touched a thing.'

Helen was looking at their plates, almost as full as they were when lunch had begun.

'What shall we try next?'

'Erm . . .'

'Pudding?' Helen suggested.

'Martha, Jim,' Liz called out over the garden. 'Come and have a little bit more . . . yes, just two more mouthfuls . . . then, who knows, Granny might even have pudding!'

'Yeeeeeaaaaah.'

Pamela watched the children she loved most in the world hurtle over the lawn towards the table, arms outstretched like aeroplanes, hair and clothes flapping as they ran. She looked over at Dave again. Big step . . . very big step indeed. She hoped they were going to be OK.

* * *

152

'Sometimes you have to trust your instincts,' Dave had whispered into her ear the night they had stayed at the farm. The night they had really in their hearts made the decision.

It had been very late, they had stayed up with Harry and Ingrid drinking too much wine, then even more foolishly, whisky, listening to tales from the coalface. What it had really been like to move to a farm as newcomers.

'The blisters!' Harry had warned. 'The sheer back-breaking hard labour. You realize what an easy life we have compared to our ancestors. Some nights we would come in, have our baths and be so tired, we'd have to go straight to bed, couldn't even face making anything to eat ... but the place was a mess then,' he'd added at the sight of Pamela's worried face. 'There isn't anything like that ahead of you now. You'll still find it really hard work. But have faith!' He'd reached round with the whisky bottle, topping up glasses again. 'Show some pioneering spirit.'

The evening had finally wound up when Pamela and Dave were directed to the back bedroom with its dinky, charmingly dilapidated adjoining bathroom.

After Pamela had washed her face in the lukewarm trickle of water and used the brand new toothbrush and paste Ingrid had put out for them, she'd come back into the little bedroom to see Dave propped up against the pillow with his reading glasses on, looking at a book he'd found on the side table. His hair flopped forward a little and she caught a glimpse of something she hadn't seen for a long, long time. A glimpse of the man she'd fallen in love with. There he was in bed, reading: the arty, clever guy, the man with a mission, burning up with plans, ambitions, ideas. Where had he been all this time? Maybe just ground down, by his terrible job, by London life, by the IVF – all those things manageable on their own, maybe, but together, enough to grind any-one down.

Wasn't the whole love, desire thing the weirdest thing? For weeks, months, she'd thought she couldn't bear to be in the same room as Dave: everything he did irritated the hell out of her and she'd thought only about how much she'd wanted out of this. Now ... now things seemed to be suddenly different again. He had this whole new plan, a new reason to give it another go.

He had turned to her and smiled, an unusually happy, relaxed smile. 'Are you OK?' he'd asked. 'That was a lot of booze ... for you.'

'I'm fine,' she'd smiled back and she'd gone over to sit on the edge of the bed beside him.

'How about you?' she'd asked, putting a hand on the back of his neck, feeling the warmth of him.

'I love it here,' he'd answered, meeting her gaze. 'I can't really explain it to you, but I can't think of a better thing we could do right now.' He'd gently closed the book on his knees and set it down beside him: 'I want a place of our own. Really our own. Alone. Undisturbed,' he'd added, the words tumbling out a bit. 'Somewhere to be busy, somewhere to be doing something real. I've been working on abstract figures, projections, expectations, growth forecasts for all my adult life. I think it's done my head in. I need some reality. Some earth.' He'd almost laughed.

He'd leaned his forehead in against hers and told her: 'Almost every night for months now, I've been dreaming about my uncle's farm. The one I spent all my summers on when I was growing up. All these things I'd forgotten about. They're coming back to me most nights. It's very strange . . .'

Even more confessionally he'd added: 'I'm not sure if I should be telling you this, but I'm slightly worried, Pammy, that my marbles may be on the verge of deserting me. And I need to do this to . . . save myself.'

She'd put her arms round him, rested her chin on his shoulder and rubbed up and down his back.

'Mine too,' she'd said. 'Maybe we could move here and quietly go mad together.'

He'd laughed at this and turned his head to kiss her ear. She'd kissed him back and then their mouths had clumsily found each other, her lips touched against his, then her tongue slid against his and to her surprise, within moments they were kissing with a hot desperation she no longer even associated with him.

He tasted soft, warm, minty, he put comforting arms wrapped in Harry's borrowed pyjamas around her and she closed her eyes feeling safe, feeling desperate for this connection to him . . . *wanting Dave.*

155

Wanting the man who was suddenly *throwing* her across the bed, who was pushing a lightly stubbled face into her neck, against her breasts, who wanted her. And she *wanted* him, she really did. That was the surprise of it. She pulled him inside and tensed up against him, squeezed him in further, moved up and down underneath him, giggled with him, but then closed her eyes and concentrated on coming.

'I love you,' he breathed into her ear. 'Come with me.'

And she wasn't sure if he meant coming or moving to Linden Lee.

* * *

'Is this us today then? Shall I shut the door?' Magenta, when she came to the support group, always took it upon herself to be unofficial chairwoman.

The eight women and two slightly self-conscious men in the room broke off the quiet conversations they were having and turned their attention to the loose circle of chairs in the centre of the room.

'Well, time to take the floor,' Magenta smiled brightly at them all and pulled out a chair. 'I'll start,' she said, after introducing the new and nervous-looking couple, 'because I'm loud and bossy, so that'll warm you all up.' And she went on to explain that she and Mick had now agreed one more year, two more goes and then that was absolutely, finally it: 'Because we're knackered, bankrupt, toxic. It can't go on. Otherwise it'll be divorce and he's a lawyer, so

156

he'll get the flat and all my money and I'll become one of those wizened old witches living in a squat with so many child-substitute cats, the RSPCA will be constantly at the door harassing me. It's not a good future. So, no, two more goes and then that is absolutely it. We'll book in for intensive recovery therapy. Marriage resuscitation ... marriage intensive care more like. That's what we'll need by then.'

This all delivered at jaunty breakneck speed, with much bangle-jangling, Magenta doing the truth for laughs.

And they did laugh, because it was hard to imagine this smart, successful company exec becoming a scourge of the RSPCA.

But then – Pamela looked around – everyone else was here straight from work in their razor-sharp suits, crisp blouses, briefcases on the floor; all white – apart from Donna, the only black face among them – all super-successful in every area of London life, except this one thing they were here to talk about. The fact that they couldn't make babies.

All such tryers, they'd worked and pushed for every achievement in their lives. And here they were all desperately trying for a baby.

She would look round the group week after week wondering whose turn it was next to try, to be disappointed, or to be pregnant, to miscarry, to try again. It was hard to know who actually left with a real, live baby, because people dropped out of the group for all kinds of reasons and staying in touch was sometimes too difficult.

'Has anyone heard from Fran?' Magenta wanted to know.

'She's pregnant,' Pamela told them and there was the quiet response. Excitement, jealousy, hope, foreboding all wrapped up in a complicated parcel. 'It's early days, she's very nervous ... taking it easy. She sends her love and says she'll see us soon.'

The new couple, who had looked even more nervous during Magenta's outpourings, seemed to be cheered by this, Pamela noticed, and reminded herself not to sound too pessimistic when it was her turn.

Donna was talking now. She was in the same place as Pamela, recovering from another failed attempt.

'I just wish my parents would get off my case,' she told them. 'They know we're coming here, getting medical treatment, but they can't stop giving all sorts of stupid advice, you know the thing ... my mum arriving with bizarre groceries,' then in best Caribbean mamã accent: ' "Donna, girl, I've brought you Brazil nuts, because Gary should be eating them, you know, for his sperm. And prawns. They very good too ... lots of zinc, I read it in *Best* magazine." She keeps offering to pay for us to go on holiday to Jamaica because: "You need some sun, some heat in your bones and then it will happen." It doesn't seem to matter how many times I tell them my tubes are shot to pieces, it's not physically possible for me to get pregnant unless I do IVF, they think I'm just a holiday, a bag

158

of nuts ... a mere prawn away from a baby!'

'But face it, if you have a baby, your mother will still drive you mad,' Magenta reminded her.

'Oh God, I know: "Donna, girl, I have fresh papaya for de baby, you don't want to be giving him that organic baby rubbish, it's not healthy. I read it in *heat* magazine. Papaya juice is de best." OK, I'm shutting up now. Pamela, your turn. Are you OK? Surviving?' Donna turned her warm full beam smile on her.

'Well ... surviving is the word. Hanging on in there.' Who was she telling? Many of these faces had been here with her since the beginning, knew it all, every twist and turn in the long, wretched disappointment. 'We've been tossing the decision about for weeks, and now we have, finally, decided to move out of London. We'd always thought we would ... with ...' the word 'baby' wouldn't come, neither would 'child', 'children', 'family' – every one of them suddenly too hard: 'Later, when ... you know,' she managed. She cleared her throat a little. 'But now, we've decided to go. Just for us. Change of scene, fresh start. We're buying a small farm in Norfolk.' She gave something of a laugh at this, because here in her knee-length cashmere-blend black with pinchy, pointy shoes and a mobile she still didn't like to turn off, even in this room, it sounded ridiculous. It was ridiculous. They were going completely mad.

'A farm?' Donna asked in surprise.

'Fifty acres of organic mixed-cropping farmland,'

159

she said, marvelling at her newly acquired technical language.

'When?' Donna again.

'Well, the flat's on the market, but the provisional purchase date on the farm is late September, October.'

'Are you giving up your job?' Magenta asked, in a tone that suggested Pamela must be at least slightly insane.

'I've left WLI –' slight gasps all around – 'but I'll still be in London on and off for freelance contracts. Dave is giving up totally. He's going to run the farm.' Said out loud in this room with women who knew her well looking stunned made it sound even more bonkers.

'Wow, this is pretty mega,' was Donna's verdict. 'Was this always the plan?'

'The farm? Our farm? No. Well, it wasn't mine, I'd thought big garden in the Home Counties . . . roses, fruit trees. Dave was obviously thinking on a much bigger scale. But maybe it'll make sense. God, who knows? Nothing is making a lot of sense at the moment at all.' With a thought for the new couple, she chose her words as carefully as she could. 'The IVF has been really hard, really hard. The hardest thing I've ever done – we've ever done,' she corrected herself. 'Our relationship is pretty much in the toilet.' Wasn't just about everyone else's in the room? 'So, we have to take a break and try something new. Very new. I'll have to buy wellies. Does Joseph do wellies?' she joked.

Chapter Thirteen

Rosie pulled the Isuzu up outside the boys' school. She looked at the clock on the dashboard again: only ten minutes early today, not too bad.

'Where are the boys? Where are Willy and Pete?' she asked Manda, strapped into her seat in the back, who giggled, kicked out her legs and pointed in reply.

Waiting for the school door to open was like waiting for a date, she thought guiltily, always here early, willing the clock forward ... Did she ever feel like this about Lachlan? Did she sit in the kitchen desperate for the back door to open and him to be home? Er ... no.

But the love affair with her children didn't seem to have dimmed at all. Willy and Pete, only a year and a half between them, bang, bang two in a row, because she'd wanted to have children close together who could play together, get along, be inseparable.

Then a long hiatus while the dust of mothering two small boys on a farm, where there was ample opportunity for them to break their arms, legs, even necks, every single day, had settled. Finally, she and Lachlan had decided, just one more. Although two was really enough, three would be wonderful.

So along came baby Manda. A girl! A change from boy fights, action games, daring danger stunts, she'd thought. But now Rosie knew there wasn't a hope that Manda was going to be pink, girlie, princessy and precious, the way she might secretly have liked her to be.

Manda, only 19 months old, would shake her head every morning at her tights and dresses and point firmly to her denim dungarees, stating 'Dungas.' Dresses and tights were pointless anyway, she shredded and wrecked them within hours. She had to have short hair because she was so messy, would rub her food, honey oatcakes, whatever, into it, creating the most impossible, painfully knotted tangles.

Her brothers had made her into the smallest, loudest, most stubborn tomboy in the word. If they were up a tree, Manda would be at the bottom, wailing, pointing to go up, always with a bit of chewed-up Digestive in her grubby hands, or tomatoes, pea pods, berries, things she had picked for herself from the garden, even morsels from Jessie the cat's bowl.

Rosie found her so impossibly pretty it was hard to say no to her, hard even to take her eyes from her chubby, peach-skinned, red-cheeked face framed with Lachlan's thick, dark gold hair. Just gorgeous.

Now that the summer was over, Pete had turned five and was at school all day like Willy and she missed them. Couldn't stop herself from thinking about them all the time she wasn't busy, and some of the time that she was. Teeth, she was worrying about at the moment. Willy had the jaggedy new teeth in, old teeth coming out mouth and Manda was cutting incisors, drooling all day long.

She was giving them all gallons of milk and worrying about whether or not they should have fluoride tablets because the farmhouse wasn't on the mains, but supplied by its own well.

She was strict about crisps and sweets, rationing them to twice a week. But Lachlan would sneak them stuff every day if he got a chance. Driving her wild. As usual.

But she was too busy to worry about anything for too long. Busy, busy, weren't they always so busy? It was a recent thought that in a day, she only ever got about 40 per cent of what she'd hoped to achieve done. About 40 per cent of her house was 40 per cent clean most of the time, about 40 per cent of the clothes were washed, 40 per cent of toys put away, 40 per cent of mail answered, 40 per cent of guff chased from one room to another, from one pile to another. Chasing it all about the farmhouse. Wishing there was the time or, better still, money to have the kitchen redone, or the hallway, or the children's room, or the downstairs bathroom, which had paper peeling off the back wall. And the kitchen floor beetles? Where were they coming from? How could she get rid of them? And all those other little things . . . She struggled every day to get the basics done: farm paperwork, food in the fridge, dinner made, house chaos at manageable level. How were other mothers able to polish shoes? Put on cuticle cream? Get the hand-washing done? Cleanse, tone and moisturize *twice* a day? How did they do this?

No time, no time . . . As soon as Manda was down for a nap, Rosie was in the office making calls, doing the paperwork, filling in the endless forms Lachlan relied on her to do.

They had, unofficially, somewhat unspokenly, come to a working division of labour on the farm and in their home.

Lachlan did the deals and oversaw the work in the fields, the staff, the summer student pickers. He was out for most of the day, dropping in every few hours for tea, food and a hunt round the fridge for things he could take back out with him.

She was the form-filler, phoner, cheque-writer, mail-opener, tax-checker, VAT-keeper, not to mention the shopper, washer, cleaner, cook and main childminder. But the resentment didn't spill out too often. When it did she would remind herself that he was almost always home for supper at 6.30 p.m. and then he would bath his children and help put them to bed. And he was a good dad, a devoted dad. Sometimes, just occasionally,

164

she would also remember how handsome he was. How lucky, lucky she'd been to get a husband so good to look at, even if other women did notice it too. Yes, other women ... Lachlan seemed to be one of Mother Nature's natural attractions. Rosie knew this: wasn't it what kept her glued to him? Despite the handful of incidents in their nine years of marriage which had made her wonder if he had done a little bit of straying. She'd never had any direct evidence, so she'd never confronted him. In fact, she'd always ignored the problem and it had gone away – not very grown-up, not very girl power, but there you go. It seemed to have worked.

Sometimes she blamed herself. Lachlan would no doubt have liked some more of her attention, but really she was too tired. Her last thought most nights as she switched out the light was that she really must get some sexier pyjamas, really should lose the ten pounds or so still hanging about her from the last pregnancy, really must have sex with her husband some time, should definitely arrange for them both to go on a mini break ... and then she would fall asleep. A deep, deep, dreamless sleep, broken at 6 a.m. by Manda.

The offer stood from Lachlan to get up and give Manda her milk, but Rosie could never get back to sleep anyway, so she would always go. Always a bit tired, wondering when the nights got so short, why it seemed now that she'd barely got to sleep when it was time to get up and get another day on the road again.

Today had been no different, with the added chore of cleaning out two trailers and the farm van so Harry and Ingrid could borrow them for the big move.

The school bell cut through her thoughts.

'Here they are!' she said for Manda's benefit and threw open the car door to go and get her boys from the schoolyard.

With just the four of them together in the car, it never seemed to be the problem it was when Lachlan was there too. When the children had her undivided attention, they almost always behaved, and everyone had fun. Singing ridiculous variations on nursery rhymes was the current game, which they played at top volume all the way home.

Old Macdonald had a cold, ee-i-ee-i-o,

With a cough, cough, here and a cough, cough there . . .'

'*Ring a ring of roses,*

A pocketful of bogies . . .' Pete came out with today, and brought the house down.

Chapter Fourteen

'Well, what about this then?' Alex was holding up a long black beaded skirt. 'It's lovely, a take anywhere, go with everything classic, if ever I saw one.' She rolled the waistband to see the label. 'Nice one.'

'Gorgeous,' Pamela agreed sadly. 'But I haven't been able to close the zip since the 1990s.'

'No!' was Alex's response. 'Try it. Honestly, I think you see yourself through fat specs or something.'

'Look, we're supposed to be packing, sorting stuff out,' Pamela protested. 'Not having a Trinny and Susannah moment.'

'I am not putting this in my collection unless you try it on first,' Alex insisted. She'd been brought in for flat clearout and packing day because she'd promised to sell or dispose of all the things that Pamela and Dave didn't want any more.

'All right, all right.' Pamela unzipped her skirt and let it fall to the floor.

'And you know what else I would like to know about?' Alex asked now.

'Uh huh?' cautiously.

'Ever since Barcelona, your trousers and loafers look has been ditched for skirts and heels and black is being phased out in favour of . . .' Alex made a quick rifle through the clothes in the wardrobe in front of her, 'toffee, rose . . . aqua blue . . . What is going on?'

'Oh I don't know . . . trying to get in touch with my inner Spaniard or something.' Pamela, only breathing in a little, slid the zip all the way up to the top. 'That is unbelievable.'

'See? You're NOT FAT!'

'It's the move – I'm losing weight just thinking about it. The Pickfords Diet, maybe I could market it . . . make a million.'

'Stop trying to put me off. I want to know about your Inner Spaniard. Does Dave know about your Inner Spaniard?'

'You mean is it for his benefit?' Pamela shook her head. 'No. I mean he's noticed, but it's for me. I'm 34, I really thought I would be a mum by now. And I'm not. So,' the words stumbled out, 'I feel like I've lost my bearings. I'm trying different things out. That's the only way I can explain it. The boots . . . the skirts . . . the move . . . everything. Just trying different things out. I don't know what's going to work – but won't know till I try.'

'Different man?' Alex dared to ask.

Pamela let out a sigh and sat on the edge of her marital bed, her friend never flinched from the hard questions. 'Who knows?' she said finally. 'That's not what I'm thinking at the moment. This is a fresh start. But it's also – no getting away from it – a last chance.'

'I really like Dave,' Alex threw in.

'Yeah. Me too. But that may not be enough.'

On cue, they heard the rattle of the front door. 'Fresh supplies!' Dave called from the hall.

'You better have remembered my cigarettes or that's it, I'm out of here,' Alex answered.

He put his head round the bedroom door: 'Tea bags, milk, Hob-nobs and a packet of American Spirit cigarettes. Natural chemical-free tobacco. You don't want to be smoking the other stuff.'

Pamela groaned but Alex told him he was sweet.

'How are you getting on, anyway?' he asked. 'Hope you've thrown out all my suits.'

'Not all of them!' Pamela protested.

'No, seriously.' He opened his side of the wardrobe. 'I'm not planning to work anywhere ever again where I have to wear a suit, a suffocating shirt or even worse . . . a tie.' He yanked out his tie rack, hung with the accumulated neckwear of almost a decade in management, and handed it to Alex. 'Bye-bye,' he said. 'Well no, I'll save two ties and one suit for hatchings, matchings and dispatchings.'

'Is there much call for suits at hatchings?' Pamela couldn't resist.

'Probably not. I think men are required to wear full surgical scrubs these days and, you know, those little plastic hairnets. Right . . . tea.'

Alex was impressed that this couple could occasionally crack birth gags. She also marvelled at the quantity of photos, framed and unframed, of Pamela's nephew and niece all over the place.

'Don't they make you a bit sad?' she had dared to ask her friend once, imagining Pamela scanning those faces for a glimpse of what her own child might have looked like.

'The worst bit was when Liz was pregnant with Martha,' Pamela had confided. 'We'd been trying for two years, our first IVF had failed, it was hell . . . I hated her. I couldn't bear to see her. But when Martha arrived. Oh God . . .' her eyes a little teary at the memory, 'I thought she was wonderful. And she felt as if she was a little bit mine. Suddenly there's a little person in the world who shares at least some of my genes. Both of them are just beautiful!'

She'd held out her favourite snap, of her with Martha – perfect pink lips and iridescent blue eyes – snuggled in under one arm, and baby Jim, fat enough to fill his towelling babygro right to the seams, asleep on her chest, lashes curling off a cheek so plump it rested on his shoulder.

The three of them worked through the flat, digging out all sorts of marriage debris.

'The pasta maker!' Pamela brought it from the back of the kitchen cupboard. 'Wedding present, never been out of its box, never even been fully assembled, let alone used.'

'Come to Mama.' Alex held open her bag.

'No, no.' Dave got his hands on it. 'We'll

170

have time to make our own pasta in Norfolk.'

Pamela rolled her eyes: 'Well, I won't.'

'No, you'll be too busy knitting,' Alex reminded her. All three began to laugh. Although, Pamela thought, they wouldn't if they knew all that was in the box of half-finished knits and balls of wool that Alex had brought out of the sitting room cupboards.

'What is this?' Alex had demanded, lifting the flaps and pulling out knitting needles, squares of knitting and the wool.

'I always liked the idea of knitting things for Martha and Jim,' Pamela had said, going over to close the flaps up again. 'But, you know, not a lot got finished. I'll sort it out later.'

Down in the body of the box were lots of little baby things, hats, booties, wooden rattles. Very special things she'd seen, loved and bought, telling herself they were for her brother's babies, but somehow she hadn't passed them all on. A little cache had remained with her, in the hope that one day, one day . . . she would need them.

Further down in that box were the items she had started shredding in despair one afternoon, with tiny, pointed nail scissors, until Dave had found her, prised the things from her hands and told her to stop.

At the very bottom of that box was also the wedding present book from Dave. The one she didn't like to even think about now.

'This is going to take for ever,' Pamela had moaned as they finally entered the kitchen, the last room to be done.

'As the great masters of Zen like to say: Begin ... and then continue,' were Alex's words of encouragement.

'Oh, I like that.' Dave was busy with the parcel tape, making up the new boxes. 'Beginning is always the easy part.'

'Two Zen nutters are about to go though my kitchen cupboards and take away all my belongings,' Pamela said, slightly unnerved at the size of Alex's collection.

'But look in here.' Alex was crouching down at a cupboard. 'You have basketware, half-burned candles, table mats in boxes that don't look as if they've ever been opened. You do not need all this.'

'Like your flat isn't full of a million things you don't need!' Pamela accused.

'But I sell them. This is different. Look, just pick a corner: begin and then continue,' she repeated.

Crouching down, looking through the kitchen clutter, the truth of this resonated with Pamela: beginning a marriage, in froth and flounciness, was easy; continuing was hard – harder than she'd ever imagined. Beginning her job, in her first ever designer suit, was easy; continuing under the Sheila dictatorship was hard. The first IVF attempt – easy – the seventh, bloody well almost impossible. They would begin the new life on the farm ... and continue ... see how it went. That's all they could do.

Chapter Fifteen

Pamela did a final tour, although there was no reason to. Every room of her former home was empty. Completely empty, just flooring, walls and bare windows. She looked out of her sitting room window for a few moments, across the road to the houses opposite. Touched the smooth round door handles she'd had installed, one last time. Like shaking hands with her home. A final goodbye. She wouldn't be coming back here.

She saw her hands were trembling as she closed the front door, double-locked it and dropped the keys through the letterbox, as arranged with the estate agent.

The removals men had already set off with the – big van? Small lorry? When did a van become a lorry? She was distracted for a moment by her ignorance of the technical specifications. Then she turned her head from the door she'd opened and closed almost every day for the last six years of her life.

Turned to see Dave, already in the driving seat of their Saab, smiling at her encouragingly. She walked down the path to the garden gate, swung it open with its familiar rusting creak, and crossed the pavement to the car.

Once in the seat, she buckled up her belt and they took one last look at their home together.

'Goodbye, 27b Belgrove Gardens,' Dave said. 'Hello, Linden Lee. Are you going to cry?' he asked, reaching over to touch her hand.

'No.' This was more determination to overcome the tears than a statement of fact.

He turned on the ignition, pulled out into the street and took the lefts and rights that brought them out into the great river of traffic at Hammersmith Broadway. Pamela looked out of the window at the tube station entrance, the newspaper stand, the coffee shop, the branch of Boots, all the familiar landmarks on her daily map of existence. They were driving past them, the road pulling them away, never to return. Suddenly she couldn't stop the sobs.

Dave changed lanes twice and pulled over onto a double yellow line already littered with other parked cars.

He undid his seat belt and then hers, leaned over and put an arm round her, telling her it was going to be OK. With a jolt of surprise she realized that he was trying not to cry as well.

'Why did I wear my bloody contact lenses?' Dave managed after several minutes and she felt grateful for the chance to try to laugh. To try and shrug this off. They wiped their eyes and he fiddled with his eyelids in the mirror, trying to determine whether or not the bits of plastic had swum away.

Pamela saw an anonymous little café on the corner, just yards from the car. 'Shall I go and get teas?' she asked.

'Teas would be good.' He cleared the huskiness from his throat. 'Better put sugar in them as well.'

'Sugar?' She couldn't remember when she'd last put sugar in her tea.

'British medicine for shock, isn't it? Everyone else drinks brandy, but we have weak tea with two spoonfuls of sugar.'

As she reached for the door handle, she couldn't resist telling him: 'It won't be like this in the country, you know – a café every five centimetres.'

'No. We'll have to learn how to make tea. Maybe even coffee.'

'Terrifying!' She smiled at him and he smiled back. And there it was, the glimmer of the thing that kept her hoping that maybe they would make it. She held the smile for a moment, then opened the door.

The sugary tea lasted only as far as the first snarl-up on the A205 heading east. She watched grubby off-licences, bookie shops and minicab offices pass; schoolkids kicking a drinks can between them on the pavement, the flats above shops with peeling paint, filthy blackened brick-work, dingy net curtains ... wondered if she would feel different if she didn't see all this every day. Wasn't assailed by it. The art of city living was to not really notice, not really be affected by all that you saw in one day. You couldn't take in every face you passed, every building, every advert, every beggar, so you blanked, switched off, looked away.

What would it be like to spend every day somewhere completely different?

They meandered off the motorway and had a long pub lunch, knowing that the horror of arriving to an empty, unpacked house lay ahead. Then, back in the car, a turn-off was missed and not noticed for over 30 miles, so they had to double back, adding almost an hour to the journey. At last, they made it to the small town close to the farm to collect a brown envelope full of keys in all shapes and sizes from the lawyer's office. Inside, was a note from Harry which attempted to tie some of the helpfully numbered keys up with the relevant locks:

1 – *front door*
2 – *also front door*
3 – *first door you come to after the front door.
Ingrid is a security freak*

And so on through

11 – *the potting shed (in front garden)*
12 – *the tool shed (in farmyard, next to smallest barn)*

and past

15 – God knows
16 – ditto
17 – no idea, but maybe a copy of no 12?

until he finally ended it: *Sorry. I'm sure you'll work them out after a day or two.*

By the time they were on the small, twisting road leading to the farm, the sky was already a foreboding grey and there was only an hour or so of daylight left.

But as they turned past the farm sign and into the narrow road to the farmhouse, Pamela felt the painful throb of excitement, nerves, elation . . . maybe even terror.

The house looked dark and gloomy under the heavy clouds. The removals van was there. The two men, looking sulky about the delay, had already stacked boxes at the door and unloaded all the heaviest items, including the sofa, although rain now looked like a certainty.

Surreal, seeing their sofa parked on the gravel beside this huge, grey house.

Dave went to the door with the jumble of keys, but the two he selected, a Yale key and a five-inch-long, ornate wrought iron thing, opened the locks straight away. Key number 3 sprang the lock of the inner door and then they were in.

There was only a faint light now, but they both saw a letter on the kitchen table. The kitchen table? Pamela registered. Why was that still there?

177

Dave picked the letter up and held it up close to read out. It was a cheery Harry-ish note welcoming them in, detailing a few essentials, listing neighbours' numbers and finishing with the explanation that some old belongings of the previous owners, which might hopefully be of use, had been left behind.

But Ingrid had PS-ed the note in an energetic scrawl: 'Might be of use? I doubt it. I'm sorry, I'm sorry, we ran out of time to shift that old crap. If you want to phone us up and tell us to get rid of it we will, or if you want to just phone up and shout at Harry about it, please do. The electricity was off this morning, I called the f***ers and they said it should be back on this afternoon, if not ring this no. and harass them.'

Dave felt along the walls for a light switch, pushed it down and nothing happened.

'Oh hell,' he said, with admirable restraint. 'No lights,' he explained to Pamela and the hardly delighted removals men.

Where did they want things? the men wanted to know. As if it would be obvious. Did people honestly plan this far in advance . . . box number 27 into bedroom number 3?

All boxes with a B upstairs, everything else, wherever, downstairs. That was the closest to an instruction formula she could come up with.

Dave opened the kitchen door and led his wife into the body of the house. They tripped over an old trunk in the dark hall; in the sitting room were the two chintzy sofas with the stuffing

178

gaping out of them and the matching, almost tattered curtains.

Dave was moving on to look at the next room. The dining room was empty save for the shabby green carpet, pressed squares marking where table and chairs had stood, and faded wallpaper. In the gloom the house looked even more tatty, brown and unloved than Pamela had remembered. Upstairs, they were both gripped with the thought: 'What the fuck have we done?' but were far too scared to say it to each other. And anyway, it was too early. Instead they concentrated on positive remarks: 'The kitchen's bigger than I remembered it ...', 'Lovely banister ...'

Lovely banister?

As soon as Pamela had said that, she thought how desperate it sounded.

Cold beans on bread with red wine by torchlight was the best supper they could come up with minus electricity.

Dave had suggested going into town in search of fish and chips, but Pamela was worried they would get lost in the dark and they didn't even know if there was a fish and chip shop. Neither of them had noticed on the two trips they'd made there.

'Of course there will be a chip shop!' Dave had argued.

But Pamela wanted to stay put, wanted to make their bed, unpack her washbag, towels, some kitchen things, do the very first things to tame the wild wilderness of their new home, which felt anything but homely, felt – as she huddled into a chilly bed in her pyjamas, a jumper and dressing gown – as if she was living in a dark cave.

'Don't worry,' Dave tried to reassure her as they moved in together for warmth. 'It will all look much better in the morning.'

'It couldn't really look worse, could it?' was all she could manage in reply

Chapter Sixteen

When she woke up, it was better. Early morning sunlight was stealing into the room, but despite this Pamela got out of bed and tried the light switch. The bare bulb hanging in the centre of the cracked and stained ceiling came on.

She had never before been so pleased to see a lit bulb. She could shower! She knew which box the kettle was in – and the tea bags. There was even a pint of milk, which might have survived the journey.

She felt for her shoes, jammed them on and went down the wide staircase to the kitchen. Pushing open the heavy wooden door, she walked in, disorientated for a moment, because the room was swimming in light. The late September sun streaming in the windows was jumping and dancing over the walls, filtered by the branches outside.

Going to the big kitchen windows for a look at the garden outside, she saw green, brown, the first of the autumn yellows, fields and a clear blue sky. Nothing else for as far as she could see. She focused on the few leaves scattered about the untidy lawn. The grass needed a cut, the leaves would have to be raked. Weeds. Didn't they now have 50 acres of weeding to do? She smiled back at the sunlight and for the first time didn't feel daunted at the thought; felt it might be possible, manageable.

She ran the tap and hunted for the kettle. As the water heated, she watched out of the window – a small speckled brown bird she couldn't name and tried to identify the trees but managed only a chestnut and a beech with any certainty. She realized she would be able to name all of them at a glance if they were kitchen worktops or flooring. She was an expert at interior wood: cherry, oak, ash, maple, beech, wenge, iroko . . . but looking out at leaves, bark and branches, she had no idea. She would ask Dave to tour her round the garden. She wasn't sure, but suspected he knew bird names, tree types, plants from weeds. She hoped he could tell plants from weeds. That was going to be his job now, after all.

After sniffing at the milk, she stirred it in, dumped the tea bags in the sink and carried the two mugs upstairs to the bedroom.

When she woke Dave, he looked momentarily bewildered.

'We're here,' she reminded him. 'Living the dream.' This came with a little snort.

'Tea? Thank you.' He took a mug from her.

She reminded him what this meant: 'The

electricity is back on – for now – so don't go taking your tea for granted.'

'Oh yeah . . . There's something I want to say to you, but,' he put his mug on the floor and peeled back the covers, 'I need to pee first.'

She got back into her side of the bed, sipped at her still too hot drink and wondered what Dave had to tell her.

When he got back into bed, he brought his knees up and perched his mug on top of them. 'It's our eighth wedding anniversary next week. Did you know that?' he asked.

'Um . . . well, I'm sure the date would have rung a bell, you know, as we got towards it.'

'Very romantic!'

'Do you want to do something? Go away or something?' she asked, knowing she didn't want to. A 'romantic' weekend away would probably be the final kiss of death: squabbles if they had sex, squabbles if they didn't.

'No,' he answered. 'We are away, far away, I don't think we need to go anywhere else.'

This made her smile. 'So what then?' she asked.

All serious now, he said: 'I want you to promise me you'll give us your best shot. It's a huge thing, this—' he waved one hand about, sloshing tea over the edge of his mug. 'But hold tight. I know we have a long way to go. But we'll try and make it better.'

'I want you to be happy,' he added, when she didn't say anything. 'Or at least happier than you've been. And this place is going to be the

183

answer for me. I know it. But I don't know about you.'

'Neither do I,' she said, although really, she did. A baby was the answer for her. And he knew that too. A farm was a pretty poor second.

'Will you just give it a chance? Give me and give this place a chance? Because the first months, over the winter, will probably be tough . . . lots of teething problems.'

'Dave, I've just bought the place with you,' she reminded him, 'I'm giving it a very big chance.'

This man, the one she'd vowed to take for better or worse, till death us do part, eight years ago. This man . . . she searched his face for some of the things she'd been so in love with back then. She saw the kindness and concern in his eyes, in his expression. Was that enough to stay for? A nice man? A kind person? Someone she'd thought would make a good father. That still stung in the back of her throat. *Except he didn't have the sperm!* Cruel little inner voice reminding her: *He didn't have the sperm.*

She didn't know why she was here, in this shabby bedroom in the middle of nowhere, hundreds of miles from anyone she knew. She really had no idea. Except maybe, she hoped she would have some time . . . to think things through, to decide what she wanted to do next.

'I'm here to give it my best shot.' She held up her mug: 'Is it a deal?'

They chinked mugs together and swigged back a mouthful of tea. In that moment it was impossible for them not to think back to their

184

wedding, to the clinking of tall champagne glasses, dazzling smiles, dizzying optimism that this was love and it would last a lifetime. Now, they wondered if they would make it.

'C'mon,' he broke the thoughtful silence between them. 'Let's get dressed and get outside to take a look around. I'm meeting my part-time farmhand, George later, I want to know what's in the fields so I don't sound like a complete idiot.'

'I want to shower,' she said.

'OK, shower, I'll wait for you.'

The shower, under the lukewarm drizzle from the showerhead in the wall above the bath, shrouded with a cold rubber curtain, did not take long. No-one would want to spend long in there.

'Nice shower?' Dave asked as she came down into the kitchen wearing exactly the same as she'd worn yesterday, including the pants. She would start the unpacking later.

'You'll see,' she answered.

'Are we going to go walkabouts then?' he asked.

They hadn't eaten anything, because there was only old bread left. And they had no idea in which of the boxes sensible shoes or wellies could be found, but still, going outside to walk about this new place, *their* new place, was too exciting to resist.

In the garden, they poked about in the green-house and found ripe tomatoes, which Dave put in his jacket pockets. Then, side by side, they climbed up to the top of the hill so they could look at *their* land spread out before them. For the first time Pamela took in the neighbouring farms: next door's had brownish scrub grass fields and, just visible before the curve of the hill, huge grey corrugated iron sheds. Theirs looked so green, rich brown, chocolate-boxy by comparison.

'All these fields,' Dave was explaining with a sweeping arm, 'are the ones we're going to be working on: a lot of it's in grass, regenerating, but the rest is potatoes, vegetables and some fruit.'

Dave was on the move, starting down the hill again, so Pamela followed, listening to the set-up. There were thirty customers a week who got a vegetable box delivered; there was a shop in Norwich and a stall in London which both took a selection of the very best, freshly picked stuff throughout the week with a big order on Friday, and if there was a glut, Harry had details of farmer's market traders who would flog it off.

'I hope you'll keep working for the time being anyway,' he told her, 'Till we really know how much we can make and what all our costs are. I'm putting in a small field of strawberry plants straight away but they won't be cropping at full strength for two years. Also, I wondered about doing up the small shed, you know, the one set back from the farm buildings a bit, as a little holiday cottage . . . so lots of ideas . . .'

'And George must get a wage of some sort. I don't know how much it is. He does four mornings a week, I think. Helps pick all the veg.'

'How come Harry didn't take all this business with him? He's not exactly far away.'

'Harry's new farm isn't organic,' Dave explained, a little incredulous that Pamela hadn't got this yet: 'It'll take two years to convert. But anyway he's switching to beef mainly. He's already bought himself a little herd.'

Down in the fruit and vegetable field in front of the house, Dave went to the tall raspberry canes and searching through them carefully found the very last of the season's fruit.

'Breakfast!' he said, tipping a handful of small, soft berries into her hand.

She scooped them into her mouth and found them just as deliciously sweet-sour as she was expecting.

'Mmmm . . . *Mmmm!*' she said to Dave, then when her mouth was empty: 'Pick more. So, are we going to have to come out here every morning and forage for food?'

He smiled at this: 'And every evening. I hope you like vegetable stew and vegetable soup and vegetable curry and—'

'Vegetable pie?' she added. 'Does this mean I'm going to have to get flowered skirts and start plaiting my hair?'

'That might be nice,' he answered, busy searching the plants.

'Aha, the truth is out! All this time I've wasted trying to be a slick city type and you really wanted to be married to a girl from *Little House on the Prairie.*'

He turned and they smiled at each other, might even have cracked another joke and laughed, but the roar of a red pick-up truck hurtling along the farm road towards them broke into the moment.

The truck driver saw them, gave a brief wave and then skidded the vehicle to a dust-flying stop at the entrance to the field.

'Blimey,' was Dave's comment. 'It's the Dukes of Hazzard.'

The driver's door opened and a short, wiry, messy-haired man got out and began to walk towards them with a pronounced limp.

'Hello there!' he called out.

'Hello,' they both replied.

'George,' he said, getting closer.

'Oh, you're George,' Dave said. 'I'm Dave. This is Pamela. I wasn't expecting you till later.'

'Yup.' The little man was standing beside them now, ruffling through his overgrown black hair. 'I won't be able to do the four mornings. Got a job in the supermarket, out of town. The retail park. Five days.' The words tumbled out. 'Out of the cold,' he added as an explanation. 'Better money ... Full time. Better for the leg.' He gave his left thigh a slap. 'Not been the same since the smash. Nine pins in it.'

'Oh,' was momentarily all the reply Dave could make to this.

'Can you help us out at all? Even for a bit?' Pamela asked. *Nine pins?* Wasn't that a bowling game?

George considered this request for a long moment: 'Friday mornings,' he said finally. 'Day off. I'm working Sundays. Could help you pick for the big orders on Friday.'

'That would be great,' Dave told him. 'Help get

188

us started.' He held out a hand for George to shake.

George wiped his hand carefully on his jeans before taking Dave's hand. 'Well. Got to go,' he said. Obviously not a man of many words.

'So can you make it tomorrow?' Dave asked. 'Tomorrow's Friday.' George seemed to require the additional explanation.

'Oh . . . yup. Yup. I can make it. Seven?'

'Seven in the morning?' Dave was slightly incredulous, but said, 'Yeah. That'll be fine.'

George gave them both a somehow surprisingly warm smile and turned to limp back to the pick-up.

He slammed the door, revved up into a screeching reverse and hurtled back down the road again. Obviously the nine pins hadn't made too much of an impact on his driving style.

'Well, that is a bit of a bugger, to put it mildly,' Dave said, still watching the truck disappear into the distance. 'We've got a lot of veg to pick, every day of the week except Sunday. It's going to be very hard work.'

'I'm back in town next week,' Pamela reminded him, not liking the sound of this 'we've got a lot of veg to pick'. She wanted to keep her distance; wasn't sure if she had ever picked a vegetable – maybe some pea pods in her mother's garden. She didn't think she knew what a broccoli plant looked like. Brussels sprouts, for instance, did they grow on bushes? Under the ground? No, they were green. There was some rule that green things didn't grow underground.

Chlorophyll? The vaguest snatch of biology lesson came to mind.

'I know,' Dave replied. 'Well, I'll have to see if I can manage it all on my own. If not, maybe I can find someone else to help out.'

Pamela went back to the house, leaving Dave in the field to examine how much fruit and veg there was for the big pick ahead tomorrow. She'd decided to make a trip into town for groceries, then she'd start unpacking the kitchen and move on from there.

Before she was ready to leave, she heard the crunch of a car coming up the gravelled drive and then the loud brrrring of the farmhouse doorbell. There on the doorstep was the postman, holding out an armful of packages and letters.

'Oh hello. Is this for the Taylors? I wasn't expecting anything. I'm one of the new owners.'

'Mrs Carr?' the postman asked. When she nodded, he added: 'Yup, Harry told me. No, these are for Olive up the road.'

She saw the address labels now: 'Mrs Olive Price, Linden Cottage, Linden Lee.'

'Um?' Pamela didn't understand.

'I always used to leave her post at the farmhouse. Can't get the van up the back road, it's murder on the chassis.'

'Oh . . . You want me to take it up to her?'

'Well, if you can.' The postie looked round at her and Dave's low-slung Saab dubiously.

'Yes, that'll be fine. So she's in the cottage at the

end of the road round the top of the hill,' Pamela said.

'That's the one,' the postie confirmed. 'OK, I'll be off then.' He slid the parcels into her arms. 'Be seeing you,' he added with a smile and headed to his van, waving cheerily.

She was reminded of her niece's *Postman Pat* books. Maybe it really was like that round here, everyone knew everyone, everyone was nice to everyone else. Maybe she should have offered him tea? After London, it felt a bit spooky.

She loaded the parcels into the car, deciding to call on Mrs Olive Price on the way to town. But at the start of the narrow track, she saw that the postie was right: the Saab would never get up there, the tracks had sunk deep into the earth leaving a chassis-wrecking grassy mound in the middle. She got out and, armed with the bundle, began to walk up the road.

It was a hard fifteen-minute walk, as the road sloped steeply round the hill away from their farm, but finally she came to the squat grey cottage prettily surrounded with a rosy-posy garden and immaculate lawn. She rang the doorbell and saw a woman's face appear and disappear at the window before the door was opened.

'Yes?' the fifty-something, plain-faced woman standing before her asked.

'Mrs Price?'

'Yes,' came the clipped reply. There was nothing friendly about the steely eyes or narrow lips drawn into a line.

'I'm Pamela Carr. My husband Dave and I are the new Linden Lee owners.'

'From London?' Just a little scathingly.

'Yes. Anyway, I'm just dropping off your post.' Pamela decided there wasn't much point in prolonging the conversation with Olive, who looked quite as drab as her name in navy blue Crimplene trousers, a beige turtleneck and short grey hair.

Olive took the packages being offered to her then added: 'No need to ring next time. Door's always open, just leave them in the porch.'

Then bang, the bright blue front door was shut.

It struck Pamela as strange that someone with such a lusciously, cutesy garden should be such a cow. Maybe Mr Price was the gardener.

Ah well, that dispelled the *Postman Pat* image. She set off down the hill towards her car.

It took Pamela a full twenty minutes to drive to the town. She followed signs to a back street car park, intending to spend an hour or two exploring.

She went slowly up and down each side of the high street, in and out of the Co-op, the fish shop, the chemist's, and the grocer's, where she bought fruit only, not wanting to make the mistake of bringing vegetables back to her new home.

She loaded her groceries into the car, then walked back, intending to poke about in some of the side streets, to see what else was there and maybe stop for lunch in the rather strangely

192

named Café Hacienda next door to the fish and chip shop. So Dave was right, emergency suppers would be available here. After rummaging through the tiny bookshop, and the higgledy-piggledy 'antique' shop, which seemed to sell only used gas fires and porcelain Clydesdale horses, she went into the café and picked a table beside the window, so she could watch the goings-on in the street.

The café was bizarre. Run by someone who clearly longed to own a bar in Spain, it had whitewashed walls, terracotta tiles on the floor, and on all the available surfaces Spanish souvenirs of every kind ever invented: postcards, baskets, a straw donkey, castanets, miniature bottles of liqueur, two guitars and several paintings of sad-eyed, gypsy maidens.

Pamela pulled out a chair with a raffia seat. Little ground-in bits of food clearly visible between the straws – eek! Nevertheless, the place was busy and the talk level lively and animated. She picked up the laminated menu liberally scattered with superfluous apostrophes, and surprisingly adventurous.

Toastie's:
Haloumi and tomato
Egg and ketchup
Tuna and black olive

Baked potato's:
Hawaiian baked potato's – with ham, cream cheese and pineapple

Tropical baked potato's – with cream cheese and pineapple
Cajun baked potato's – with chicken in a hot sauce

Vine leaf-wrapped parcels of one thing and another were on offer, along with taramasalata on toast and Spanish tortilla. The cake and scone collection included: *Mrs Mills spicy bun's. (Always a favourite!)*

'Hello there, what can I do you for?' A plump, middle-aged woman in a pinny was at her side with a little notebook.

'Ermm . . .' Pamela was not feeling nearly as adventurous as the menu required. 'A baked potato with cheese? Would that be OK?' This was ordering off the menu.

'Cheddar or cream cheese?' was the smiling reply.

'Cheddar, please. And I'll have a pot of tea,' Pamela added. To order the side salad was probably to risk a concoction of iceberg lettuce, shredded carrot and salad cream. Better stick to basics.

'You're a new face,' the woman said now. 'Are you visiting?'

'No, my husband and I have just moved here, we've bought a farm not far away.'

'Oh, which one?' Full of friendly interest now. *Postman Pat, Postman Pat . . .*

'Linden Lee.'

'Oh, Harry and Ingrid's place? Lovely farm, lovely couple . . . lovely children. D'you have family?'

194

The eye-wincing question. Instinctively Pamela knew that her usual 'we're still trying' answer might be a mistake here. It might lead to a half-hour conversation in which all details would be required and then passed on to most of the good citizens of the town.

'Erm, no,' she said and left it bald.

'Oh well, plenty of time for that,' the woman added, causing Pamels to wince again. 'I'm Anne, by the way. Anne Mills.'

Mrs Spicy Buns.

'I run the place with my sister-in-law, Ada. *Ada!*' she suddenly turned and shouted across the room. 'Come and meet the new woman at Linden Lee.' This had the effect of turning the entire café clientele in Pamela's direction. She smiled, embarrassed.

'What's your name,' Mrs Mills asked.

'Pamela Carr.'

'*Pamela Carr!*' Mrs Mills shouted at the clearly completely deaf Ada. Everyone looked over again.

Bloody hell.

Finally, her baked potato and tea were in front of her and she was left alone.

The potato was a tiny, shrivelled thing which had obviously met its end in the microwave. An unyielding blanket of cold, waxy orange cheese had been laid over it. Maybe she should sound the Last Post and give it a decent burial. The metal teapot burned her hand and poured out a gush of tea ominously the colour of coffee.

She sipped the tea, hacked off a rubbery

corner of potato and looked out of the window.

It was quite a sweet little high street really. She watched old ladies in buttoned-up raincoats and hats totter down the pavement, marching mothers in fleeces pushing buggies. People getting in and out of the row of cars parked on the other side of the road.

A big black 4 x 4 pulled up and began to back into a space surely far too small. She watched as the car was manoeuvred in deftly with much energetic wheel-turning by the driver. Then the door opened and out swung sturdy cord-clad legs and a pair of battered suede boots, a man with jaw-length golden hair who beeped the car doors shut with his key before he tossed it from one hand to another then pushed it into a snug back pocket. With several jaunty long strides he was out of view.

She kept on looking, hoping that maybe he would double back, have just a quick errand to do, so she could take a better look at him. Those few moments hadn't been nearly enough. She would have liked to take a proper look at the face, which from side on, had looked so ruggedly attractive. She would have liked a little longer to study the strong square shoulders beneath the farmy waxed anorak and she would most definitely have liked an action replay of the moment when he hoicked the jacket up and pushed his keys into his back pocket.

'Will there be anything else?' Ada broke Pamela's crazed reverie over a stranger's behind.

'No . . . no, no. Just the bill.'

'Not much of an eater, are you?' was Ada's pointed comment at the substantial remains of the baked potato.

'No, not feeling too hungry today.' Ada's stern look made any sort of complaint about the food quite unthinkable: 'Sorry.'

'Moving house takes it out of you. But you need to eat well, if you're planning a family.'

What? Hello?

'Ermmm.'

'Anyway, you be sure to drop in, whenever you're in town. We'll look after you – feed you up.'

As she got into her car, Pamela realized she'd been humming the Postman Pat theme tune under her breath ever since she'd left the café.

Chapter Seventeen

'How's it going?'

'Do you like it?'

'Are you *loving* it there?'

Why did everyone want to know? All the time! All these questions. Pamela only had to set foot in London, just had to pass the scrabble for the turnstiles at Liverpool Street Station for the interrogation to begin.

She was working for Sadie again, and she had more work with contacts of Sadie's lined up, so she spent much of the week in town, staying sometimes with Ted and Liz, sometimes with Alex. Her weekends were filling up with frequent visits from family and friends. Everyone quizzing her about the farm constantly.

'So, what's it *really* like out there?'

'Aren't you lonely?'

'What do you do there?'

'Are you missing London yet?'

No, not missing London, because she was

there all week, suspected that she wouldn't survive very long without coffee and wine bars, the buzz of the place where this season's bag, this year's hair, this month's noodle fusion moment, the difference between taupe and soft mouse grey *mattered*.

'How are you coping?' Sadie Kingston-Jones had asked.

'How am *I* coping?' was Pamela's rather incredulous response to Sadie, who seemed to seamlessly manage the two older children, the babies, two part-time nannies, her boutique, her husband's high-flying career, to look slim and gorgeous, and on top of all that had energy to plan further renovations to her home, which Pamela was supervising.

'Well, you look a bit raddled today,' was Sadie's excuse.

'It's Monday. Commuter hell.' Pamela didn't really want to unburden herself about the bugger of a weekend she'd just had. But Sadie wangled a few choice complaints out of her.

'Why can no-one drive out there? Round-abouts come to a standstill because no-one knows who's supposed to go first. And we have mice! There was a dead one in the bath . . . and there are bats living in the walls.'

'No! What do they do?' Sadie asked.

'I don't know yet. It's winter, they're hibernating, but apparently in the spring they fly around, scrape about in the walls all night long. *Croak*. I'm never going to sleep again.'

'Ugh! What if one gets into the house? Into your bed?'

'Aaaaargh!' Both gave a mock scream at this.

'There's nothing we can do,' Pamela told her. 'They're a protected species.' She began a fresh complaint: 'And everyone, *everyone* wears fleece out there all the time. Fleece, anoraks and hiking boots. It's like everyone's set to rush up a mountain at a moment's notice.'

'God.' The concern in Sadie's face: 'There's obviously no sex in the countryside.'

'No. None,' Pamela agreed. 'There's mating, calving ... that kind of thing. Definitely no sex.'

She didn't say that by yesterday afternoon, the close of a rainy, dull and very quiet weekend, she was so fed up with it, she'd tramped to the top of the farm's hill in a long woollen coat and un-suitable suede boots, letting both get destroyed by the mud and drizzle, and there on top, look-ing down at the view – so bewitching, bedazzling, enchanting in the summer, now just grey, muddy and bare – she'd yelled at the top of her voice: 'FUCK THIS! FUCK OFF!' But it hadn't made her feel any better.

'You should have listened to me,' Sadie was telling her. 'It's awful out there. You've been in town too long. You don't want landscape, you want designer shoes. You can't smell fresh air any more, you need clever, co-ordinating scents from Jo Malone. People live like animals out there. You have to be born and brought up to it.' She'd run perfectly oval light red fingernails round the rim of the beautiful porcelain teacup she was drinking from. 'Please tell me the bat-infested house is at least gorgeous?'

'Ah well, it has potential,' was Pamela's reply. Unfortunately, she and Dave were in an un-resolved dispute about redecorating.

She was itching to start: rip up carpets, peel all that crap from the walls, free the painted-in shutters, strip, clear, clean. But he'd gone all funny about the idea.

'Don't you think it's a bit wasteful?' he kept asking. 'I mean, there isn't anything wrong with the carpets, or the walls. The kitchen is perfectly functional . . . I like the bathroom the way it is . . . I don't want to borrow the money to do this right now. '

What was the matter with him? He'd always been the environmentalist, the recycler, the one who would walk to the bottle and paper banks on Sunday morning, but now he was becoming so sanctimonious, she couldn't bear it. Wanted only to rebel, to buy a big gas-guzzler, let off aerosol cans for the sake of it, redecorate with the most toxic paints available.

Dave made supper most nights, vegetably, super-nutritious meals which she once would have been proud to eat. But now it annoyed her. Irritated the hell out of her. And he wasn't drink-ing much, didn't even have tea any more, but hot water with lemon!

'Have you become a Mormon without me noticing?' she would tease.

His reaction was bristly: 'What's happened to

you, more like? You used to be into all this. Now look at you – you're drinking too much, eating all kinds of crap in town.'

'Well, if I'm not doing IVF, I don't care. I don't care about my diet and my bloody toxin levels and the sodding planet,' she whinged, not even meaning this, well, not really, 'I don't care.'

'Oh, I see,' was his angry reply. 'If there's nothing in it for you, you're not interested ... bugger the ethics.'

And she didn't care about his stupid vegetables either.

He would come in with bunches of leeks, carrots trailing dirt, holding them out for her to inspect with pride in his eyes.

'These are the ones I planted, aren't they beautiful?'

'Yes, lovely,' she'd agree, but this wasn't enough. She had to appraise their firmness, their smell, their taste.

'They're only leeks,' she'd snap finally. 'How many ways can you cook a leek?'

'How is Dave taking to farming life?' Ted had wanted to know. Ted sprawled over his red sofa in his funky red and black sitting room, both children finally in bed, time to open another bottle, switch on the state-of-the-art stereo, light a well-earned spliff and 'get relaxed'.

'Dave loves it,' she told him. She couldn't even begin to explain the transformation of Dave. From office bod to farmer. From man who complained endlessly about his job, to man who did nothing but his new work but loved it. He was non-stop busy from early in the morning till late at night.

When his picking stint was over, he delivered his vegetables, then came back to weed, to plant, to fix broken bits and pieces, ferry machinery to garages, oil things. After supper he went back out to his sheds again. But he didn't seem overworked or stressed out: instead he was a man with a great weight off his shoulders.

Much later in the evening, he would come in, light the fire filled with logs he had chopped, and read farming books. He was well into his organic farming course, so was busier with the reading, writing and internet research than ever before.

All week, Pamela preferred to stay in town if she could, because he didn't seem to have any time for her anyway.

'How's Liz?' she asked, to change the subject. She'd already heard all the children's news.

'Liz is good. Making my life hell as usual.' There was a jokey sincerity to this. She knew all about their legendary rows, the dents on their walls, missing crockery, even occasional grazes – testament to their clashing personalities.

Whenever she asked what they fought so savagely about, Ted could only tell her: 'Oh the usual – whose turn it is to make supper, take the rubbish out ... sweep the kitchen floor ... buy milk ... go to the post office. The absolute usual. I have no idea why it sometimes gets so intense. We never back down. There will be no compromise!' he'd laughed. 'Compromise and die!

It's quite exciting really ... but tiring. Babies should come with a warning: "May cause severe drowsiness, do not drive or operate machinery if in possession of a baby."

'And you know what else?' He was warming to his theme now: "Warning: Baby – will kill your cool." '

'No, Ted,' Pamela assured him, laughing. 'You'll always be cool.'

'No-oh. I can hear it—' he cupped a hand against his ear. 'The irresistible call of the suburbs. First it's the bigger house with the garden ... then before you know it, I'll be driving a people carrier, then going on those package holidays with kid care ... saving up for school fees. This is what they do. Small and cute to start with, they grow – they take over and infiltrate.'

'Shut up, will you? You know I'll have them in a shot if you don't want them. If you want your year trekking in Nepal, hanging out in San Fran ... whatever does it for you, sad, shallow, cool person.'

'Yes. I'm sorry, I will shut up now. How are you and Dave doing, anyway?' he asked. 'Everything OK?'

'Much calmer,' was her reply. 'He loves it. It's been so good for him.'

She thought, but didn't tell her brother, about the fact that now, after the companionable log fire evening, she and her husband went to bed in separate rooms. He had the big one at the front, where she knew he carried on reading late into the night. She had moved to a single bed in the small gabled room they'd slept in when they'd stayed overnight with Ingrid and Harry.

Tired with all the early starts to catch the 6.30 train into London, she'd suggested it, thinking it would be for a few nights. But now they had been sleeping apart for weeks.

'Are you sure you want this?' Dave had stopped her on the stairs one night. 'I'm worried. What does this really mean? Separate rooms?'

'Don't say that, I just need a rest,' she'd insisted. 'Honestly, a rest from . . . dealing with all this. I don't want to rehash all the rows. Can't we leave everything alone for a bit? Have a break?'

They both knew what she meant: the lack of a sex life hanging horribly between them every night when they shared a bed.

Now, she bathed in the rough cast iron tub, got into her narrow bed, pulled white sheets and a duvet in a white cover up over her, switched out the light, looked into the pitch darkness, velvet black around her, and fell asleep. Quite quickly.

'Calm! Everything's calm,' was Ted's response. 'What are you doing up there? Taking organic tranquillizers? Free-range Prozac? It sounds absolutely crap.'

'Ted! It's good . . . It's fine.'

'There's a difference,' he warned. 'Good? Or fine?'

'Fine. This is fine for now.'

He'd let it stand at that.

But Alex was not so easily put off.

'The truth,' she insisted over caffè lattes and too many cigarettes in the little café Pamela had chosen. 'No glossing. How is it working out?'

'I don't know. Why does everyone keep asking me? I'm so bloody exhausted. I'm not going to be able to do it for much longer. The travel is going to kill me. I'm so tired I ordered a batch of paint in chimera blue instead of Chinese blue. Big mistake, I can tell you.'

'Blue is pretty much blue. I never know why people get their knickers in such a twist about permutations of shades. Just whack it on and don't care so much.'

'Blue is not just blue. Trust me on this!' Pamela was outraged. 'Anyway, what do you mean, just whack it on? You're putting me out of a job!'

'Joke!' Alex smiled at her, 'You have to get work up there. That would be your solution. Find out if you really like it . . . stop having a foot in each camp.'

This struck Pamela as probably true – but a slightly hideous prospect. Give up London altogether?!

'I know,' she agreed reluctantly. 'Do you think I should advertise? Or hang about wallpaper shops and accost people: "You can't buy that. It will shrink your sitting room and make you feel like you're living in a bowl of porridge. Trust me, I'm a designer." '

She'd be condemned to wearing fleece and hiking boots – no, never! – eating rubberized potatoes and Cajun chicken topping with Mrs Spicy Buns . . . She'd have to somehow get over this loneliness . . . homesickness. But maybe

she'd get to know some people up there better . . .
Harry and Inrid . . . or the man in the snug cords.
Hello? Where did that thought come from?

The man in snug cords. She'd seen him again,
walking past the window of the Hacienda Café
with a blond baby girl up on his shoulders and
two waist-high boys skipping, straining at the
leash to run, beside him. The little girl's hands
were gripped round her daddy's neck, her chin
resting on his head, their identical hair obvious to
Pamela as he laughed, shared a joke with his
boys.

Pamela had looked on and felt a sharp tug at
her heart, a sigh of longing, which for a moment
had made the scene swim in front of her. And
then they were gone.

Chapter Eighteen

Surprising, really, how much she was looking forward to seeing Ingrid and Harry. The invitation to visit their new place had come at last. Ingrid had apologized for how long it had taken.

'We've been so busy settling in ... I'm sure you're the same,' she'd said on the phone. 'But now we're ready to start seeing other people again!'

It was nice to be asked, to feel there were people who knew her vaguely, who were potential friends. And in the back of her mind was the joyful recognition that she could wear her fantastic new 'I may live on a farm, but I'm still glamorous' outfit: slim long grey velvet skirt, palest blue cashmere rollneck, matching socks and turquoise suede clogs, with brass studs and the type of fine-grained nap she'd had to spend several minutes stroking. A countrified triumph, the kind of outfit that really belonged on a willowy blonde, skipping over ice floes in Finland . . .

OK, OK, it was probably all a teensy little bit impractical for day to day farm stuff, but just perfect and lovely for sociable farmhouse visits.

Dave raised an eyebrow at the ensemble.

'Would you like me to carry you to the car?' he asked.

'No. Don't be silly. I've Scotchguarded them, they're perfectly safe.'

'It's quite muddy out there,' he warned.

'I'll be fine.'

'They might want to show us around the new place.'

'The clogs are fine.' She was feeling tetchy about them now.

The Taylors' new farm was much bigger, stretched away for acres and acres beyond hills, beyond horizons. But somehow it was already taking on their own particular look. Driving up the road towards the farmhouse, Pamela and Dave saw the fields decked out in Harry's very own crisscross, cross-pollinating, crop-protecting rows of alternating plants. Everything not ploughed or planted was grass for the beef herd, which he'd already told them was in its very early stages, just twenty-five cows.

There was the nappy-chomping wormery, Pamela noted as they pulled up the drive, and Ingrid, wind-tossed in the garden with another woman, even more children and the dogs.

'Hello, hello there!' Ingrid came over to the car, giving them both an affectionate hug as they got out. 'Come and meet my friend Rosie Murray

and her many offspring. Our men are on the farm
. . . make man talk,' she joked. 'Make fertilizer
talk.'

Pamela and Rosie walked towards each other,
friendly smiles on their faces, extending hands
to shake. They exchanged the 'how are you?s',
sizing each other up. Rosie was a prettier than
usual farmer's wife, but still on the frumpy,
mumsy side, Pamela decided instantly. But she
looked very nice. Had that soft, make-up-free,
freckled face and mid-length brown bob which
could have put her anywhere between late
twenties and early forties.

Rosie's first impressions of Pamela centred on
the fact that she was so city slick and fashionable.
Her outfit was just beautiful, looked so soft and
expensive, she was obviously still working in
London and *loaded*. And didn't her hand feel all
silky soft as well? Nothing like Rosie's nappy-
changing, dog-washing, cuticle-nibbled paws.

Rosie shoved her hands self-consciously back
into the pockets of her red anorak. Practical,
waterproof, comfortable, just like her jeans, M&S
jumper and lace-up boots . . . and a world away
from this soft wool, velvet and suede vision.

'Is that your little girl?' Pamela saw Manda
standing at the bottom of a tree, pointing and
shouting at the three children already up in the
branches.

'Yes. That's Manda. My boys, Willy and Pete,
are in the tree with Kitty.'

'Oh, they're all gorgeous,' Pamela gushed,
wondering why they looked so familiar, three

children . . . *three* children? She could almost hate this woman for that alone. 'Can I go and say hello?'

Rosie was instantly won over by Pamela's so obvious soft spot for children. She hadn't worked out the husband yet, he'd shaken hands too, then gone off in search of Harry. He seemed quiet, maybe even shy.

'I love the cows,' Ingrid was telling them. 'Cows are fab, how did we manage without cows? You have to get some,' she was enthusing.

'I don't know anything about cows at all,' was Pamela's response. 'I don't even know which end the milk comes from,' she joked. 'Well, I mean, I hardly know anything about vegetables. But I could let the odd row of carrots die without feeling too bad about it. A whole cow would be a terrifying responsibility! A herd?!! Unimaginable.'

'They're so nice,' Ingrid continued. 'I never thought I'd feel so attached to them, but they are so warm and maternal, not friendly exactly, but very aware of us. I used to glaze over when people droned on about their animals, but now I understand. I'm going to become a cow bore . . . *put that down, Jake! You'll have someone's eye out!* Harry is mad for them. The children are practically jealous. Anyway, I hope you don't mind,' she added, 'but since there are so many bodies here this afternoon, we're going to shift them from the back barn to one a bit closer to the house. It'll be easier to feed them there through the winter.'

211

Pamela gave a sort of agreeing, helpful smile. Shifting cows. What would that mean? Nothing much that she'd need to get involved with, surely?

After an exhaustive tour of the garden and long explanations of plans from Ingrid, much pointing out of fields and barns in the distance, they were interrupted by Harry's head appearing up over the garden wall.

'Hello everybody, hello Pamela!' Great big smile and wave. 'You're looking well. Country air. That's what does it. Anyway, I need you all now, because it's cow time.'

Willy, Pete and Kitty all leapt down from the tree and started racing towards the garden gate, whooping. Ingrid and Rosie scooped up their youngest children and followed, so Pamela carried on behind them. Harry came round to the gate to meet them, carrying a bundle of long bamboo gardening canes.

'OK, everyone take one, then we'll put you at your spot. It'll be very easy. Lachlan and I'll shoo the cows down and you're there to make sure they don't wander into the wrong field, or onto a road or anything on the way.'

Willy and Pete were squirmy with excitement. Harry gave them two canes each with the strict warning not to hit each other, or even pretend to hit each other. 'Otherwise – straight inside.' He managed to sound very stern.

The boys seemed to treat this with some solemnity, but as they all walked towards the farmyard, Pamela didn't need to turn round to know that the swooshing and slapping sound behind her was cane swordplay.

'Boys,' Rosie warned. 'You heard what Harry said.'

Pamela had ducked into the car to get a jacket and had briefly wondered about asking Ingrid for wellies. But after Dave's teasing, she felt reluctant. Stuff him. She would cow-herd in the clogs and be damned. She'd pick a nice dry bit to stand on and she wasn't planning to really get involved with it at all anyway.

In the farmyard, Dave was talking to a tall man, back turned to them, who had dark blond hair pulled into a short ponytail . . . long legs . . . *suede boots*!

Hurtle of realization as he turned towards the approaching group: he was snug cords man, these were his three children . . . Rosie was his wife.

Pamela found herself pulling her shoulders back, running a hand through her hair as she walked over, prepared to meet him.

'This is my wife, Pamela,' Dave was saying and the man was holding out his hand. Hers slid into his.

'Lachlan Murray,' he said with an unmistakable Australian lilt. She felt his warm grip, saw how broad and strapping he was with shamelessly wide thighs.

'Hello, Lachlan.' Oh yeah. She liked the sound of her voice, slower, richer than usual. She smiled.

'Hello.' He smiled back and didn't add

anything else. Her eyes were allowed to scan his face properly now: tanned, but in that outdoorsy, grained right into the skin way, deep, green-brown eyes, all the more intensely interesting for heavy brows, hair the colour of dark honey, golden syrup, with girl-curls, caught into a band at the back. This was what surfer boys looked like when they grew up and turned into whole-some farmers. She found herself fixating on the deep scoop of flesh above his top lip. He didn't have a fine nose, wasn't even typically good-looking, but he was still quite something.

'Aren't you, Pam?' Dave was asking.

'Hmm?' was the only response she could make to this, startled to realize that Lachlan was pulling his hand out of hers because she'd held it too long.

'Looking for work up here, out of London,' Dave added.

And there goes another one, Rosie thought to herself, partly amused, partly annoyed. She was only too aware of her husband's regularly devastating effect on other women. Moving up to him now, she put a proprietorial arm casually round his waist.

Pamela saw how Rosie fitted tightly against her husband, small enough to slip her shoulders in under his arm, whereas Pamela was just a couple of inches shorter than him, met him almost eye to eye.

'Oh yes, definitely,' she said and tried to make it sound breezy, although she was anything but. She was feeling shaken. She was 34 years old but she could feel the jolt, the guilty fizz of a big, girlie crush. The kind you were supposed to grow out of when you left school.

'Lachlan was telling me they might have some work for you,' Dave added.

'Yeah,' was all Lachlan said, which was a shame, she thought.

'Well, you'll have to tell me all about it,' Pamela said into the pause, convinced that whatever the project was – even decorating their farmhouse from top to bottom in Laura Ashley – she would take it, do it, string it out for as long as possible, whatever, just so she could see him again . . . often. *Yes . . . and his lovely wife? Beautiful children. Hello? Pamela. Reality check.*

Just as Harry interrupted them with his troop rallying, canes and instructions of who was to go where, it began to rain, lightly and drizzly at first, then increasingly steadily.

Pamela was given a cane and put in front of the open gateway to a grassy hill. She didn't have to do anything, she was assured, just wave the cows on down, as it were.

She stood on her spot, thinking about Lachlan, considering only for a minute or two that she really didn't know anything about cows, couldn't even think when she had been up close to one, she'd only ever seen them over fences, at a distance.

After fifteen minutes or so of standing in the rain, waiting, the herd began to come down towards them. She was taken aback at how big they were, these dark cows. Very big, very heavy-looking. Stories she remembered from the newspapers began to flash into her mind: 'Woman trampled to death by herd of cows'; 'Man out walking dog attacked by cows' ... Good grief!

She could feel pinpricks of sweat forming in her armpits and her breath speeding up a little. There seemed to be some delay: the cows weren't moving so purposefully any more, they were milling.

Pamela was beginning to feel very anxious, breathing hard. They were close now, looking at her with great bulging eyes the size of tennis balls. Ambling towards her.

Then there was action at the back and Harry shooed them on so that they broke into a brisk trot – towards her! She was backing further and further out of the way into something the cows recognized as a lovely green grass field.

'Just wave your stick at them!' came a shout from Ingrid.

Her *stick*! The rod of bamboo now looked like a Twiglet in the face of a herd of one-tonne animals. The cows were speeding up, just as any really heavy object begins to pick up momentum once it gets going.

They were running towards her and then one of them mooed, a terrible, deep-throated groan of a moo.

Fuck me! Rasping breath, Pamela made a pathetic wave with her stick, but still they came. She realized she was going to have to run. But she'd backed into a seriously boggy bit and was rooted to the spot. Panic, PANIC. Huge effort to run.

Her cashmere-clad feet shot out of her clogs and she began to sprint across the field, convinced all twenty-five cows were belting after her.

'Heeeeeeeeeeeeeeelp!!!!!!!!'

In the grip of self-preservation, she instinctively headed for the fence.

God knows why she'd chosen a long skirt. There was absolutely no chance of climbing the fence quickly enough, so she launched herself at it, trying to jump, roll, *whatever* . . . over it, and was skewered on the barbed wire on top for a moment. Aaargh! *This is what it feels like to be a kebab.*

She yanked her whole body over, feeling the rip. The fence turned out to be on a slope so she carried on rolling, whipped in the face by long grass, scarily out of control. Finally reached the bottom at speed, where she whacked into a rusted, abandoned oil drum with a terrifyingly loud clang.

It was a moment or two before she dared to open her eyes. Yup, she was still lying there, in long grass, a bit winded, a bit stunned, but unfortunately not seriously injured, she didn't think. Much as she might wish and wish for a dramatic injury to make this worthwhile, to make sure people sympathized with her rather than fell about laughing, she seemed to be fine. Just her pride really, really hurt – she felt like a total tit. Maybe if she could just keep her eyes closed, she could pretend that none of this had happened . . . and in front of that man, that beautiful man . . . Crap.

'Pamela?'

She heard Ingrid's voice and opened her eyes reluctantly. Yes, definitely still here, still fine, still lying on her back in wet grass.

'Are you OK?' Ingrid asked, face peering down at her, full of concern. 'Does anything hurt?'

'Erm . . . yes. Everything hurts. But unfortunately, I'm fine.'

Ingrid stood up and bellowed, '*She's fine!*' over the fence. Pamela thought this was a little callous, but realized it meant everyone else could carry on tracking the cows which had now disappeared over the brow of the hill and off into the distance.

'What happened?' Ingrid turned back to her now.

Pamela thought the question a little unnecessary.

'I think I'm scared of cows,' she said, still flat out on the grass, not desperate to get up and face her audience.

'You should have told us,' Ingrid said. 'Because they *always* know and then they take the mickey.'

'But I didn't know,' Pamela said in her own defence. 'This is my first cow herding experience. And last.'

There was a little too much warmth to Ingrid's smile. Now that she knew Pamela was OK, she was desperate to laugh . . . heave, rock, positively *weep* with laughter. But with effort she pulled her face straight again and tried to sympathize. Poor Pamela.

Ingrid held out a hand to her: 'Come on, let's get you up and back to the house to dry off.'

'Dry off' was an understatement, Pamela realized, once she'd struggled to her feet and surveyed the damage. Her skirt and jumper were sodden, mud brown and the skirt had sustained a rip from side split to front in the engagement with the fence. Her frozen feet were clad only in wrecked socks so the suede clogs must still be out there in the field. Double crap.

She hobbled out from the grass and on to the dirt track.

'Oh no, your shoes.' Ingrid had just noticed Pamela's predicament. She made a quick search of the grass and climbed up the slope to look over the fence, but no luck.

'Can you manage back without them?' she asked. 'I'm sure Harry will find them.'

Pamela nodded. She didn't really like to think of the condition her clogs might be in by now.

She took the arm Ingrid offered and began the slow and stony hobble back to the farmhouse, where Ingrid made her a fortifying coffee and sat her on the kitchen's saggy sofa wrapped in a dressing gown and tartan blanket while she rinsed out her cashmere and dry-clean only velvet in the kitchen sink, then hung the clothes over the Aga rail to dry. They dripped little pools of water onto the lino floor.

Pamela was so grateful for the care and kindness, she tried to push to the very back of her mind the worry that everything that wasn't ruined would now shrink.

Ingrid, busy setting the table to feed the wet and weary cow herders due in at any moment, talked cheerily about the new place.

'If I thought fruit and veg were hard work, cows are something else . . . have to be fed and watered twice a day all winter, they'll keep us up all night calving in the spring and for the rest of the year, they break out of fields, wander off, get mastitis. It never stops – and then the tragic ending! I don't know how we'll cope.'

'Not much call for organic goldfish, though, I suppose,' Pamela commented.

'No . . . sadly!' Ingrid replied. Then they heard voices at the back door. The cow herders were back.

There was activity in the back room for some time as wellies, anoraks, hats and even several pairs of sodden trousers were stripped off both children and adults.

Pamela pulled the dressing gown and blanket tightly round her and stayed on the sofa. It wouldn't hurt to pretend she'd come off slightly worse than she actually had, she'd decided.

Dave was first through the kitchen door and came straight over to kiss her on the forehead.

'Are you OK, Pam? I didn't even hear about it until you were inside. I just waited at the shed for ages wondering why it was taking so long to get the cows down to me.'

She smiled as broadly as she could, not just for his benefit, but because Rosie, all five children and Lachlan had just come into the room.

'I'm fine,' she said in the smooth low voice that Lachlan's presence seemed to induce. 'Just sorry to cause everyone so much trouble. It's very embarrassing.'

There was a murmur of 'no no's, 'not at all's as Ingrid made them pull up chairs and sit down to the fearsome table full of tea, coffee, hot apple juice, an enormous home-made carrot cake and scones just plucked from the oven.

But Willy wasn't so polite. He and Pete came and stood beside the sofa, taking in Pamela's blanket and bedraggled hair with obvious amusement.

'Why did you roll over the fence like that?' Willy asked.

'Because I thought the cows were chasing me,' she answered.

'*Why?*' Willy asked, as if this was the most unbelievable thing he'd ever heard.

'Because they were running at me,' she replied.

'They just wanted the grass,' Willy told her. 'They were running into the grass field. Cows don't eat people, you know,' he explained, making her feel like the biggest idiot at the party. 'People eat cows,' he added and began to giggle.

It was beginning to occur to Pamela that maybe she had wildly misjudged the situation, had in fact run in terror in front of an ambling, grazing herd, not exactly a stampede. These two small boys hadn't been frightened, had they?

221

She could feel her cheeks burn.

'Willy, come and sit down,' Rosie ordered her son and he and his brother hopped up to the table.

The back door opened and slammed again and after the few necessary minutes of coat and boot changing, Harry, wild hair, face red with rain and exertion, burst into the kitchen.

'Well, I found them,' he said, holding something out in front of him. 'But they're not looking too good.'

It took Pamela several moments to realize that the filthy pieces of wood and tattered cloth that he had in his hands were in fact the remains of her turquoise clogs.

'The whole herd must have gone over them,' Harry explained, somewhat needlessly.

'Oh Pamela, we're so sorry,' said Ingrid. She came over to her husband to examine the damage.

'It's fine, honestly, my fault for wearing them,' Pamela managed. 'They weren't anything special,' she totally lied. 'Honestly.'

'Can we buy you a new pair? Where did you get them?' Ingrid offered

'No, no, really . . . don't worry about it, it's no problem at all.' Pamela felt slightly panicked, anxious that no-one in this room should know she had attempted to herd cows in outrageously expensive designer clogs.

'But they looked really smart, I quite fancy a pair,' Ingrid said now.

Oh hell.

'Never quiz Pamela about her shoes. Where they came from and how much they cost are state secrets. You'd have better luck trying to find out the Queen's bra size,' Dave chipped in and everyone laughed, including a grateful Pamela.

She gave him an appreciative smile and retreated behind her mug of coffee.

Harry dumped the shoes on the ground and sat down at the table. 'Ah!' he sighed at the spread. 'It was the clang from the oil drum that got me. My God, Pam, it was like a gun going off. No wonder the cows took off for the top of the hill.'

He began to chuckle and with that gave everyone else permission to do what they'd obviously all been aching to do since the moment they came in – laugh heartily.

Pamela smiled and joined in a little, but was dismayed at the level of laughter: long, loud hoots, snorts, attempts to stop and then even more laughter.

'The stick, the way your stick wobbled . . .' Ingrid said and there were more hoots.

'The bit where you stuck on the fence,' Rosie added. Further shrieks.

'We really shouldn't, it's a shame,' Ingrid tried. 'Your poor clogs.'

'Cow revenge,' Pamela threw in. 'I'll never wear leather again.' She was trying to take this as well as she could and chanced a look at Lachlan, who was happily mid-laugh until he met her eye and tried to pull his face straight, but a smile broke out over it again.

They held the look for a moment, and there was something a little too bold, daring and unashamed about his scrutiny that made her skin tingle. She felt conscious of the dressing gown – not how worn, tatty or unflattering it might be, oh, no – only that there was just one item of clothing separating her from him.

Driving home with Dave later on, Pamela thought the humiliating smart of the cow fiasco had almost been worth it, because all she could think about was Lachlan, Lachlan's cottages and the fact that next week she would be meeting him to view them and prepare a quote.

'So, Wednesday afternoon.' He'd shaken her hand, eyes on her again. Macho, outback, rancher type, she'd fantasized, her thoughts running away with her. 'I'll give you a call to arrange the time.'

'Great.' She'd tried to sound casual and jaunty, but saw his smile, felt his grip and already suspected that this was dangerous. Deep water.

Skaters heading out over a newly frozen lake. No good would come of it. No good would come of it at all. But irresistible. The lure of danger and freedom.

Chapter Nineteen

Pamela strode along the back road, enjoying the walk, relishing the cold, clear air, drawing it in to the very bottom of her lungs, loving the warm socks and wellingtons, her new knee-length quilted coat and snug hat. There was a bundle of mail in her gloved hand. Two days' worth of Mr and Mrs Price's Christmas mail and she was striding along to bring it to them.

Walks needed a purpose, which was obviously why so many people had dogs. The sky was still pale pink with the afterglow of sunrise. Pamela didn't think she'd ever noticed until she'd come out here, how little daylight there was in the winter. It wasn't properly light until after eight now, and gloomy again by three. Right now, just past nine in the morning, the sky was pink and white over brown, bare land, naked trees silhouetted, frozen in the cold. Her breath steamed out in front of her and she could feel the blood prickling in her cheeks and fingertips.

Such a wide horizon: she was always looking around here, to the left, to the right, out for miles around, up into the endless sky, feeling her smallness in the face of this huge view.

There had been a little thawing in her relationship with Olive Price. Olive did now occasionally open the door and say hello. There had even been talk of the weather, how Pamela was settling in and Olive's family.

The older woman's attitude had taken Pamela aback slightly.

'Four boys I've had,' she'd said dourly without any hint of pleasure or pride in the fact. 'Three's got families of their own. Only the mistake's left here now. But he's off to college in Norwich next year. Good riddance. I've done enough cooking, cleaning and laundry to last three lifetimes by my reckoning.'

'Yes,' Pamela hadn't felt she had much choice but to agree.

'You haven't got any, have you,' Olive had said.

'Children?' Pamela knew this wasn't a conversation she wanted to pursue.

'You don't know your luck,' Olive had told her. 'A lovely, quiet, grown-up, interesting life. That's what you can have. Plus, no need to stay married if you don't want to.'

'No,' she'd felt obliged to say, slightly incredulous at the way this doorstep chat was going, wondering what was coming next.

'Living on your own. That must be something.' Olive had looked at the empty landscape outside her front door, eyes reflecting the sky, then she'd added abruptly: 'Well, must get on. No time to stand gossiping.'

Gossip? Pamela had thought. Is that what she called it?

The mail had been taken from her hands, and without even a goodbye Olive had stepped back into her porch and pulled her front door shut.

The only other thing Pamela knew about Olive was what Jeff, the landlord of one of the three small pubs in town, had casually confided.

It was on their third or fourth visit on a quiet Sunday evening when Jeff had handed them their drinks with the words: 'So, what do you make of Olive the lesbian, then?'

'Olive *who*?' Pamela had said.

'Olive Price,' Jeff had prompted.

'*Mrs* Price? Who lives on the edge of the farm with her *husband* and youngest *son*?' Pamela had replied, with emphasis.

'Well that's right enough, but Simon here will back me up.'

'Oh yes,' Simon had said straight away, although until now he'd been quietly sitting and smoking at the other end of the bar. But it was that kind of pub. People were left alone if they wanted, but expected to be allowed to chime in with any conversation of interest.

Pamela and Dave now found themselves listening with unwilling fascination to these two ruddy-faced, fifty-somethings stating the case for Olive's lesbianism.

'We were at school with her,' Jeff explained.

'She had a very good friend,' Simon added.

'Very good friend . . .' Jeff was leaning in so close Pamela could smell beer on his breath. 'Lucy Tierney.'

'Lucy Tierney,' Simon repeated.

'Caught in bed together,' Jeff breathed, ruined red face flushing even redder. 'By Lucy's dad. Quite a fuss there was. The Tierneys moved away a year later.' They looked at the newcomers triumphantly, as if to say: We have our scandals here too, you know.

'At school?' Pamela had asked, wanting to get this right.

'Yup, 16 they were, and both good-looking girls,' Jeff confirmed.

Pamela desperately wanted to laugh. This was forty-year-old gossip. So what if Olive and her friend had messed about under the duvet in their girlhood? Didn't it matter at all that Olive had gone on to marry and have four children? The longevity of small town gossip was frightening. Once a 'lesbian' always a lesbian.

'Oh well, there you go then,' Dave answered, understanding perfectly that laughing out loud at this 'news' wouldn't go down well.

And then the regulars were all pitching in with an opinion, Al and his wife shaking their heads and saying they'd never thought it was true.

'But they've never been happy, have they,' someone else reminded the room. 'Utterly miserable, more like it.'

'She was quite the artist at school. Had a

scholarship to go to art school in London, but after the Lucy Tierney thing, her parents didn't want that.' Jeff, tea towel in hand vigorously drying a glass, was in full flow now. '*Artists*,' he said, as if the word was enough.

Poor old Olive, Pamela thought, sipping her drink without comment, one schoolgirl crush and her whole life had folded up in front of her. No art scholarship, no London . . . instead a hasty marriage to someone she didn't love and four sons she didn't seem to care very much about either. 'The mistake,' Pamela remembered. Hardly a charming way to describe your youngest child.

'Is this what people mean by a sense of community?' she had asked Dave in the car on the way home.

He'd laughed in response.

'People still remember gossip about you, forty or so years later. Pigeonhole you at school and never let you change,' she'd added.

'I think it's more subtle than that. Everyone knows everyone else's story. But they make allowances, they live and let live.'

After a while he'd asked her: 'Do you like it here?'

'Do you?' she'd countered.

'I love it. I love the farm, I love my vegetables, I love my customers, I even love George. He's insane, obviously, but makes life interesting.'

'You want to watch that,' she'd smiled at him. 'If Jeff and Simon hear about that . . .'

229

He'd laughed at her, then asked again: 'And you? Do you like it here?'

'Don't know yet,' she'd answered, looking out of the window into the dark. 'If I get a job up here, it might be different.' Might all be very different.

Lachlan Murray was sitting on a chair opposite her, pale blue shirt open at the neck, soft brown skin underneath. He was talking about his farm and she was trying to pay attention, trying not to let her eyes move down the shirt buttons to the worn cords pulled tight over his thigh, the knee bouncing vigorously up and down as he talked.

She felt a breeze against her leg and saw that he had moved close enough to brush his knee against hers. Then he startled her by moving a warm hand onto her bare thigh.

Looking down at herself, she saw that she was sitting on top of a table in just an exquisite silk bra. She could see the outline of her nipples pushing against the raspberry silk.

He was kissing her leg as she dipped her fingers into his soft hair. Leaning slowly back against the table, she was ready to explode with longing.

She reached out to touch his face, but instead she woke up and felt the room spin for a moment until she realized where she was and what she had been dreaming.

A glance at the bedside clock showed it was 5.20 a.m. She doubted if she'd get back to sleep again. She lay back slightly dazed with the

230

intensity of the dream. She hardly needed to call in an expert to tell her what that meant. She was stoking her crush up into some insane, border-line obsession with the married father of three she was due to meet in about five hours' time. The probably very happily married father of three – she had no reason to think otherwise – and anyway, three? Three? *Don't even go near there.*

Pamela had exhaustively complicated directions to Lachlan's farm, but still she had to pull over and hail a lone dog walker to make sure she was on the right road. The farm was tucked up in a cluster of small roads only occasionally marked with the kind of signpost she recognized from nursery books. But finally she was pulling up, as instructed, before the larger of the two cottages Lachlan was hoping to renovate. She stepped out of her car, swung the door shut and walked to the tatty green front door, registering the jangle of nerves and excitement churning up her stomach.

There was no obvious bell or knocker, so she made a fist and rapped on the wood with her knuckles. The sound of movement inside, although she knew Lachlan would be there, expecting her, was almost frightening. She was going to him, she was going to be with him, the man who'd almost had his hands in her fantasy pants just hours ago.

Except the door pulled back and there was the sobering sight of his wife, Rosie, with her knee-high daughter beside her.

'Hello,' Rosie said with a smile. 'Come in, you found us OK then? Lachlan got called to something very last minute, so he won't be able to join us.'

Pamela hoped the disappointment she felt hadn't registered too heavily on her face as she went through the 'No, not at all . . . how are you anyway,' bit.

'I'm fine . . . we're fine, aren't we, Manda?'

The little girl looked up at her mother and answered with a very solemn 'Yeah.'

Lachlan had wanted to rearrange the cottage viewing when he knew he wasn't going to make it this morning, but Rosie had insisted she would show Pamela round and he had given in quickly enough to quell her mild suspicions that he had a little crush on the city girl.

Rosie was curious to meet Pamela again, couldn't decide yet whether to dislike her because she was so smart and so obviously smitten with Lachlan, or to overlook those things and get to know her better . . . maybe even like her. But when she opened the door, Rosie thought that maybe she would dislike Pamela after all. She looked gorgeous, far too luscious to be looking round a pair of scruffy cottages: skirt, high-heeled boots, draped in a soft black coat.

'This is a great location,' Pamela smiled. 'And Manda, hi.' Despite the boots and skirt, she crouched down to say this and Rosie was changing her mind again. She was so disarmingly nice to children . . . and then hadn't she taken the whole cow thing so well?

Pamela was also on guard, trying to put Lachlan and her stupid crush to the back of her mind, trying to work Rosie out.

They toured the unloved cottage, talking politely about the renovations, the budget, the plans.

The building needed new everything: rewiring, replastering, repainting inside and out, new floors, kitchen, bathroom. But the windows were a good size, would let in plenty of light and every one framed a peaceful green view.

It would be a perfect family holiday cottage. Pamela outlined to Rosie the simple, natural look she had in mind: pale walls and wood, jute flooring, biscuit-coloured blinds.

'Holiday cottages are usually so cluttered and full of old junk,' she complained. 'Rickety secondhand furniture, Aunty's unwanted ornaments, hideous little paintings, cane things, straw baskets. Don't do any of that. OK?'

Rosie had laughed and mentally noted not to invite Pamela to the farmhouse . . . Well, not until she'd had the chance to hide all that kind of thing.

'Clean, simple, pared down. Empty wardrobes, plenty of shelves, so that the guests have space for all their stuff.'

Pamela already knew that the budget was small, way below her usual, but that she would do the job for them. Maybe work with one decorator, get a bit hands on. She could paint, she could strip and above all she knew where to get the things they needed for less. They'd have a fabulous cottage Islington families would be mowing each other down to rent out every school holiday. Then it was time to look at the second place. Rosie locked the front door with an ornate key and buckled a squirming and protesting Manda into a rugged three-wheeler buggy.

'I don't know if maybe you want to drive,' she suggested to Pamela, glancing at the high-heeled boots. 'It's not much of a road. More like a track.'

'No, no, I'll be fine,' Pamela insisted, wondering why every single farm outing seemed to cause her a footwear crisis.

Tottering and twisting her ankle, then pretending she hadn't, on the rocky rickety path, she wished for the car. And she was going to have to walk back as well.

The second cottage was hidden in its own secluded corner of the farm, surrounded by dense rhododendron bushes and a tangle of garden. It had once been whitewashed with window frames and door picked out in light blue. There were the remains of a trellised rose across the front wall.

Pamela couldn't understand why both of these homes had fallen into such a state, but didn't like to ask. If the information wasn't offered, it was safer to leave it at that.

The cottage door had to be shouldered by Rosie before it would open. Inside, it was in a much worse condition than the first one, but after a brief look round, Pamela knew it would be quicker to renovate because everything was still original and could be kept in place – the ancient old high flush loo, cast iron bath and dainty sink, the simple wooden kitchen and the open fire-places in the two rooms.

Everything was caked with grime and a dark stain on two of the ceilings suggested the roof needed some repairing, but still, the place would be habitable very quickly.

'Wow,' she enthused to Rosie, who was looking about in horror. The cattle man had moved out of here nine years ago when the herd was sold and nothing had been done to the place ever since. No money and the determination not to sell it because it was too valuable an asset. All asset and no cash. Wasn't that just farming all over? Everyone else had money, but they had assets – in waiting – not to mention a vast inheritance tax bill they would labour all their days to pay off ... when her father died.

'A love nest,' Pamela was telling her. 'That's what you need to bill this place as. Secluded, private ... log fire in the bedroom ... a totally romantic retreat. One of those big wooden beds, a sofa by the fire, it will be gorgeous.'

Rosie, walking from one filthy room to another with a tight grip on Manda, who was determined to poke in as many disgusting corners as possible, found Pamela's enthusiasm a little hard to catch on to.

'This place should be done first. I know it looks bad, but not much needs doing apart from roof repairs, new ceilings and paint – lots of paint.' Pamela was bursting with ideas ... white painted floorboards, sheepskin rugs, a teeny-tiny chandelier, '*Scandinavian luxe*', chunky candles, gingham blinds ... firelight. It was going to be beautiful.

'So, you do this one up with half of your budget, rent it out at top whack and use the money coming in to pay to do the second one properly. I'm sure it will be worth it,' she was explaining to Rosie.

'I'm aiming to put you in the top rental bracket, which has to make you more over the long term. Invest in design. That's the idea.' For a moment, she sounded almost Sheila-ish.

'Good for designers,' Rosie couldn't resist.

'Well yes, but I'm so desperate to work up here, not be trekking down to town, that you'll get me for a very good rate.' Pamela, realizing she must have this job, had to convince Rosie. 'And I'm quite good, you know. I can show you my portfolio.'

Rosie looked at Pamela carefully. Understood exactly what her reservation was: there had never been another woman she'd felt so *threatened* by. She didn't have the slightest doubt that Pamela would do a fantastic job: she saw her attention to detail in the way she was dressed. But she was only too aware of Lachlan's interest. He hadn't mentioned Pamela much but when he did, it was in a way which made Rosie suspect he'd been *thinking* about her.

'I wonder what she makes of farm life ...' he'd mused and, 'I think the cottages will be really different if she does them.'

Rosie did not want her husband to be thinking

about any woman, especially a curvaceous, childless, glamourpuss who didn't seem to have anything at all in common with her own husband. Dave had seemed so straightforward by comparison.

Pamela, wary of waiting too long for Rosie's answer, had begun to chat to Manda and now lifted her up so she could see out of the window.

'What's that?' she pointed.

'Bwudz,' Manda was pointing too.

'Bird, very good. Is that the birdie? Is he pecking?'

'Yeah,' Manda nodded.

And Rosie was disarmed again. She was making this all up. Pamela seemed like a nice person and anyway, Lachlan? She may have suspected something once or twice in the past, but really, now? He was so busy and he was almost useless at keeping secrets . . . she nearly always found out what her Christmas present from him was, because he was so careless with the evidence.

'I'll speak to Lachlan tonight,' she told Pamela, 'then we'll give you a call, let you know what we think.'

'That's great. Both cottages could be brilliant, really.' Pamela gave her a big smile, but already she was thinking about the tricky walk back in her tottery heels.

The call came later that evening, on her mobile. At the sound of Lachlan's voice, she went out of the kitchen where she was preparing supper with Dave and into the front room, where she could cradle the phone between her shoulder and her cheek and concentrate on every word.

He was matter-of-fact, telling her the plans were good, a more detailed estimate was needed, then if it was agreed, when would she like to start?

I'm pretty committed until April, maybe even May,' she warned him and liked to think there was a slightly disappointed ring to his 'Oh, I see.'

But maybe that was for financial reasons, she reminded herself.

'When I start, I'll project-manage, we'll get them done as quickly as possible. The first cottage shouldn't take much more than a month. So you'll get some summer rental if you advertise in advance. The second one . . . well, let's say mid-July. I think that's realistic. To keep to your budget, I'll do a lot of the work myself. It'll be fun, getting my hands dirty again. Like when I started out in this business.'

'Right.'

She thought he sounded happier again.

'Bit of sanding . . . bit of stripping . . .' she dared but when this was met with deep silence, she quickly added: 'Wallpaper . . . paint . . .'

'Right,' he said again, followed by: 'If you can get a full estimate over, we'll speak then,' and an abrupt goodbye.

Good grief, she thought as she clicked the phone off. Why the stripping line? Why? What was she thinking?! She probably needed to address the sex-with-Dave-situation, because

'*Look at me!*' Sex ... sexual frustration – was bubbling up in all kinds of inappropriate places.

'Mummy, when we do an N in our class, we have to do a down, back up, down and kick up.' Pete, on Rosie's lap with his reading book in one hand, was drawing carefully in the air with his other. He took primary one very seriously.

'That's right.' She scrunched him into her, feeling the bones in his ribs and spine. Always a bit skinny, a bit snotty, that was Pete. Rosie took a tissue from the supply in her pocket and made him blow his nose. His grey trousers were already bobbly at the knees because he fell in the playground a lot. She cuddled him tightly and tried to concentrate, understanding how much he relished his time with her, his slice of her busy day.

She knew what it was like to be the one in the middle, the one who had to fight for every scrap of attention because you weren't the cute youngest or the smart oldest. But over the edge of the book, she had an eye on Lachlan pacing round the kitchen, phone at his ear. He was talking to Pamela. Rosie was just checking to make sure there was nothing to be suspicious about.

Chapter Twenty

'Christmas! I don't know where to begin with telling you about Christmas! Christmas was a disaster!' Pamela said. Leaning back in her chair, she was taking this all in. A wonderful, swank hotel dining room, she and Dave all dressed up for dinner. Alex sitting opposite beside a very attractive *younger* man, who she'd introduced as 'Rob, a friend of mine.' Very interesting.

It was New Year's Eve and Alex had twisted their arm to come into London, have a glamorous night out, stay over in a hotel and enjoy themselves. 'Come on,' she'd pleaded. 'I'm worried about Dave especially. He's just going to get too wholemealy and hand-knitted out there. Bring him into town again. Remind him of all this.'

And Dave was enjoying himself, she saw.

He'd agreed to put himself into his one suit, shirt and tie. He was shaved and aftershaved. Pamela had felt an unaccustomed flash of pride in him as he'd taken her arm and walked with her into the hotel.

'My parents, my brother, his partner and their two children all came for three days at Christmas and it was hell,' Pamela was now telling Alex and Rob.

'The children were ill, sore throats, snot, all that stuff, Liz was on the verge of a nervous breakdown because she'd been working full-pelt all the way up to the 24th, had done all her shopping on the internet and half of it hadn't arrived. "Christmas, it's not a holiday, it's a bloody crisis nowadays", she kept telling me. My mother is horrified by our house, because we still haven't done any redecorating – I'll leave Dave to explain that. And then, on Christmas Day, just before lunch, the septic tank packs in.'

'The septic tank? OK, I'm not sure what that is, but I get the feeling I don't want to know.' Alex pulled a face.

'Oh come on, we're in between courses,' Pamela dared. 'My mum comes down to the kitchen and says she thinks the toilet is blocked. It's all filled up with water which won't go down and it turns out that when you live on a farm, this is very bad news indeed. Because we're not on the main sewage system . . .'

Dave took up the explanation: 'If your toilet is blocked, it means the tank everything goes into is either backed up or full.'

'That can't be good! So, what did you have to do?'

'Well, on any normal day of the week you'd be

able to call people out to unblock things or bring in a tanker to take ... er ... the tank contents away. But this was Christmas Day.'

Pamela cut in: 'Alex, you've never seen anything like it. Dave and my brother Ted took advice from Harry, the previous owner,and decided to investigate, meanwhile the rest of us have to go in the garden, which the children think is hilarious and they're all waving bare bottoms about in the freezing cold, Liz having a heart attack about pneumonia ... And my parents ... they're quite laid-back, but I could see a lot of leg crossing going on. Then finally, after about two hours or so, Dave and Ted appear at the back door and they're naked!'

'Why?!'

'We were covered in it!' Dave replied. 'We'd been digging out the tank. I can't describe how bad it was. We were in such a state, we'd both been sick and we had to strip everything off in the garage. I was going to hose myself down out there, but it was December.'

'I had to bring warm buckets of water to the back door, so they could wash their hands and *hair* before they went into the house to shower properly,' Pamela added.

'Well, that's the worst Christmas story I've heard this year,' Alex decided. 'And you have to stop now because our food is coming.'

The main course arrived and as everyone began to eat, Alex teased Dave. 'So these vegetables – not nearly as good as yours, are they?'

'No, no, I wasn't going to say anything. I'm

being very good, on best behaviour tonight, no ranting about chemical sprays and toxic slug pellets and residual poisons.'

'Oh good,' said Pamela.

'But I bet your Christmas sprouts were sensational, weren't they?' Alex nudged him.

'They were. They were perfection. You know, I think sprouts need just a touch of frost to bring out the sweetness in them. And you can only eat them freshly picked, they don't keep, get all cabbagey, that's why townies don't like them. And now . . . see . . . I'm getting carried away.'

Rob made the mistake of asking why organic food had to be so expensive, and got a mini lecture about the care and effort that went into Dave's produce.

'It should cost *more*,' he argued. 'We work so hard to grow it.' He thought of himself, frozen fingers picking veg in the mornings, out in the dark by torchlight destroying slugs by hand, working from dawn till dusk, thought of Harry getting up in the night to check on calving cows.

How many people would like a life like his in the future? How many people would be prepared to take on the work when there was never going to be any money in it, always just the scrimp and scrape to pay the mortgage?

'What about you, Rob? What do you do?' Pamela asked, hoping the man wasn't an agrochemical producer, fish farmer – something at the top of Dave's hate list.

'I'm a nurse.'

'Oh, so how did you and Alex meet?'

Rob laughed at this; it turned out he'd known Alex since primary school.

'So you can stop fishing,' Alex told her. 'He's strictly a friend.'

'But there was that time when you were in the fifth form,' Rob reminded her.

'Fifth form? ' Alex looked at him blankly. 'Oh yes . . . no, no, no I haven't forgotten that!'

Eruption of giggles, but neither would confess what it was about.

'Which trust do you work for?' Dave wanted to know, when the hilarity was over. He was keen to hear all the latest news.

'So, you had fun, didn't you?' Pamela asked as they got back to their hotel room, close to 1 a.m., woozy with New Year's champagne – although the bill had been a sobering moment.

'I did, I did have fun.' Dave was loosening his tie. 'Did you?'

'Aha.'

'Do you know what would be more fun?'

'No.' But she suspected she did.

Dave was moving towards her, putting his arms round her waist, catching her up for a full-on, mouth to mouth kiss.

Her first impulse was to pull away, but she thought she would stay in just a little bit longer and see if she liked this . . . see if it was OK. He looked good in his suit. She put her hands under the jacket, pulled the shirt out of his trousers and touched his skin.

He moved in closer to her, was making

a start on the zip at the side of her dress.

'I don't know if . . .' she began.

'Please don't . . . shh,' he said and put his mouth over hers again, then gently pulled the zip down, slipped a hand against her back and drew her in.

She let him. Let him kiss her, touch her breasts, slide her dress to the floor, move fingers down, tease her to the edge of wanting him. But by the time they were on the bed together, Dave so turned on, so desperate to please her, she was already being pulled away from him by the deep, cold undercurrent. Nothing had changed: the only things she felt at the thought of making love to him were sadness and a long-suppressed anger.

He couldn't make her pregnant. There it was bubbling over as she let him move inside, fill her up. What was the point? Why bother? She put her arms around him but clenched her hands into fists to stop herself from grabbing him, bit her lip to stop herself from shouting it out: *Why are we doing this? It's useless. It just reminds me of what I can't have.*

Afterwards, wrapped in his arms and the stark white hotel sheets, she cried, leaving him hopelessly sad for her and guilty.

Chapter Twenty-one

Dave was already in the pub, pint in front of him, busy with the newspaper when Harry arrived.

'We've got the hippies in tonight,' Jeff announced as Harry got to the bar. 'You'll be wanting a pint of *organic* beer and maybe some wacky baccy to go with it, will you?'

Harry took it in his stride: 'Oh, very funny. You're busy tonight.'

'Quiz night,' Jeff informed him. 'You and Dave going to join in?'

'Um ... not sure about that. We'll let you know.'

'So, how's it going?' Harry settled down beside Dave and they began to talk through their latest farm news.

Dave had found Harry a priceless fund of information, encouragement and, most importantly, friendship. It was a lonely business farming, and regular phone calls and pub summits with Harry kept him going through the times when nothing seemed to go right. When it rained so hard that all his seeds washed away and he had to start again, when half of his precious, new seedlings were eaten in a bugfest caused by some kind of worm which would have hatched out of the soil and flown away if he'd known to wait a week or two.

Dave listened now with sympathy to Harry's latest cow trouble, before he began to outline his big concern.

'I think Dexter Hunter is polluting the water-course,' he told Harry.

'Bloody hell,' was Harry's reaction. 'Are your streams full of stuff?'

Dave nodded.

'Bloody hell,' again.

When Dave had first moved to the farm, Harry had warned him to keep a close eye on the water. He'd explained that the drainage ditches and streams running all over the farm were the best way to make sure that his neighbours were behaving.

'The farm to the east is fine,' Harry had told him. 'Old boy, old-fashioned pig man. Lets his animals out all day, grows fields of turnips for them, has grazing for the Pony Club. He's nothing to worry about. It's the farm on your west that's the problem. The houses have all been sold off, the farmer, Dexter Hunter, lives some-where else. Mr Big in chickens and chicken shit, he is.'

Every time Dave had gone to inspect the

network of ditches and streams, the water had looked clear and untroubled. But on his last scramble down to the little valley at the bottom of the farm, he'd known immediately that something was wrong. In just three weeks or so, the stream had changed completely: where the water had rushed and tripped, it was now choked with greenery. A whole load of nitrogen, or something like it, had to be not just leaching, but absolutely flooding into it.

He told Harry how he'd waded into the water, skidding on the green, slippery stones, and walked upstream, crossing the fence into Hunter's land. 'It got even greener,' he explained. 'I passed this home-made rubbish tip. All sorts of stuff had been dumped over the banks, old machinery, broken wooden crates, potatoes, earth, old straw bales . . . a total mess, but I don't think that was causing the problem.'

Harry shook his head.

'Then I found a ditch, coming down from the fields which was really dark and murky. Stank, in fact. So, I scooted up the bank and took a look from the top. Just a ploughed field, totally ordinary apart from a deep pit in the middle of it. There were two tractors driving about at the shed, so I couldn't really snoop about.'

'You've got to sort this out,' Harry told him. 'That stream is the farm's main run-off, you can't let it get choked up or you're going to have all sorts of problems and anyway, you can't risk anything leaching into your fields that isn't supposed to be there.'

'Do I call someone in? Isn't there an environmental protection agency or something?'

'You'd be better off finding out what the hell it is first,' Harry informed him. 'Otherwise they'll roll up in a car, knock on his door and say, "Mr Hunter, stop polluting the water please," and roll off home again. They haven't got the resources to investigate a slice of mouldy bread and they can't do all that much anyway. Speak to the council as well, there might be an application for whatever the pit is. If he's dumping waste, it's against the law unless he has a licence.'

'Did you move because of him?' Dave asked.

'Well . . .' Harry took a swig from his drink. 'You know our reasons for moving, but I wasn't desperate to keep Hunter as a neighbour. That's why I've always told you to be on the lookout. Seen any tankers going up the road?' Harry asked.

'One or two.'

'He's got 20,000-odd chickens up there. He's got to put their crap somewhere. It's either going away in the tankers or he's dumping it on the farm and the tankers are bringing even more stuff up there to dump. That's what you need to try and find out.'

'And our opening category for the night: geography!' It was hard to ignore Jeff's voice booming from the bar to signal the start of the quiz. 'One for the Galloping Grandads: What's the capital of Bolivia?'

'La Paz,' came the swift reply.

'Every quiz I've seen, the Grandads have won,'

Harry told Dave. 'The Ravers put up a good fight but I think the Loons are just here for the beer . . . So, what else is happening? How's Pamela?'

'She's fine,' Dave answered. 'Busy. In London most of the week.'

'Miss her?' Harry asked.

'Too busy.' Dave gave the jokey answer because the truth was complicated. The farm, bought partly to bring them closer together again, seemed to be having the opposite effect. He was absorbed with it and she was hardly ever there. The distance between them was growing daily, creeping up. He'd thought peace, no more IVF, no more arguing would heal the wounds. But he saw now that at least when they'd been arguing, they had cared, they had wanted to change things, had raged against everything that was going wrong. Now, they seemed to have given up, they were distanced, separate, said goodnight at the top of the stairs, didn't seem to care any more.

Harry wouldn't have found out much more about his new friends, except that he began to talk about his children, told a funny story about them and ended it with: 'They're priceless, absolutely priceless. So, you two must be thinking about children? No-one moves out of town to a farm without babies on their minds.'

And Dave, who had brushed off so many variations of this question, had never spoken about it much, found himself answering: 'Actually we've moved out here to try and get babies off our minds. We've been trying to have one for seven years.'

Harry was apologetic and sympathetic, he didn't ask any details, but nevertheless, Dave began to unburden himself. Hinted at some of the strain of the IVF.

'Hell of a thing to go through,' Harry acknowledged.

'Worse for Pamela,' was Dave's verdict. 'She's not the same.' He couldn't express how lost she seemed to be, searching about for something else to believe in, something else to be, something else to channel herself into. Perhaps even jealous of how much the farm meant to him. He didn't have the child he so wanted, but there was a comfort in growing things, nurturing them. He wished he could share that comfort with her.

'Loons, if you were on "the roof of the world" where would you be?' Jeff in full quizmaster swing.

'The North Pole?'

'No . . . Shut up, Stan, I know this one, the highest mountain . . .' But Loon number two was fatally interrupted by his team-mate.

'Ben Nevis. You'd be on Ben Nevis.'

Peals of laughter all round the pub.

'Come about 8.30ish on Friday,' Ingrid had instructed. 'The Murrays are coming, so their children will sleep over. But by then we should have bribed them all to stay upstairs, either that or we'll have drugged them with an overdose of Tixylix.'

'You drink, I'll drive us home,' Pamela offered Dave on the way over. She was still in shock

251

about the cows. Dave had bought three small, barely beyond the calf stage cows, telling her his own manure supply was essential. 'Christ, but *cows*,' she'd said out in the shed taking a look at them, registering the nervousness these animals were provoking in her. 'Couldn't we just have got chickens?' But then she remembered what Ingrid had said about chickens: R-A-T-S.

'No, you drink,' Dave insisted. 'You seem much more nervous about tonight than I am. You have a few glasses of wine, it might help.'

'Thanks.' She flipped down the passenger visor to check her make-up again. Just what had given him the idea that she was nervous?! The hour-long bath, the hair fuss, the multiple outfit changes, clothes strewn all around the bedroom . . . perhaps?

And when she'd finally come down, all bare arms and satin, Dave had warned: 'I'm not sure it's that kind of dinner party,' and she'd had to rush back upstairs and make the decision all over again. Aaaargh!

'You look very nice,' he told her now. But she crossed her arms against the compliment and looked away. This wasn't for him. All this curled hair, creamy off the shoulder sweater and lipgloss was not for him. She was fidgety out of all proportion because Lachlan was going to be there. It had preoccupied her for the last few days more than she would have liked to admit, even to herself.

She was nervous of blushing, flushing, somehow

252

giving herself away . . . but knew that she almost wanted to, was daring herself to give Lachlan a clue to see how he reacted. The whole cocktail of thoughts, attraction, intentions, was so heady, she didn't think she'd felt so nervous, but so *excited*, for years. He was provoking all sorts of feelings in her that were uncomfortable, Mr Rock Solid Alpha Male and his three children. She wanted a part of him. Desired him. There wasn't any other word for it, but it was desire motivated in no small way by envy. Stupid, ridiculous, *harmful* to want him like this. But nothing seemed to block the want. In fact, she was busy blinkering all the reasons why she *shouldn't* even be thinking like this. Rosie, Dave, the children – she was tuning them all out, selfishly sharpening her desire for Lachlan. Thinking of him, imagining him . . . dreaming about him. And why? Because maybe it would be easier to just forget all this hard stuff that her life was right now and cling onto the distraction of Lachlan, the thought of sparking some sort of reckless romance.

'Here we are then, have fun,' Dave announced as he drew the car to a halt and pulled up the handbrake.

And then Harry, Ingrid and the bloody dogs were on them. No, it definitely was not that sort of dinner party. It looked as if Ingrid's only concession to glamour had been to put on clean jeans and a pair of silver earrings.

'Oh look at you,' she told Pamela with a big smile. 'You're gorgeous, you'll put us all to shame.'

253

And what was the correct reply to that? She felt caught out.

'No, no, I just . . . I didn't . . . You look really well.' That was it.

'Come in.' They were ushered to the front door, into the sitting room and there – lurch of stomach – there he was, standing up, back to the fire, beer bottle in his hand.

'Hello. It's my decorator.' He cracked a grin, came over and shook her hand, eyes on hers, but then moved on quickly to Dave and offered the explanation that Rosie would be down in a minute: 'Still settling the children.'

Harry pressed the evening's first big glass of red wine into their hands, as Rosie appeared. Rosie, who had made an ill-advised foray into dressing up which involved too tight a vest top, a big *shawl* and lipstick that didn't suit her at all. She shot glammed Pamela 'A Look' which couldn't be interpreted as particularly friendly . . . but still, the evening kicked off.

Supper in the kitchen – velvety pea green soup, then a great orange casserole dish of stew – 'our first cow,' Ingrid announced, scooping up a spoonful of the stuff and landing it on a plate. No-one apart from Pamela seemed to think that this was *horrifying*.

More wine, more wine, to swallow down the lumpy mouthfuls of casserole; talk of their crops, their children, the weather, the town. Pamela, feeling the swirl of energetic chatter whirl about her, chipped in as often as she could. But really, where was he sitting? Where Ingrid had directed, right next to her, and although she hardly dared to look round at him, unless he asked her something directly, he had all her attention. The hairs on her right arm were lifting up and leaning over to get closer to him. More wine, more wine. She heard not just every word he said, but every scrape of his spoon, every mouthful he swallowed. He couldn't breathe without her close attention.

Ingrid cleared plates noisily and with a proud 'da-naah!' brought out a mountainous meringue, cream, raspberry and spun sugar concoction, which every guest protested at, then ate up anyway, belts straining.

'So, Dave, I hear you're the competition now?' Lachlan was asking him, with a teasing smile. 'Five acres of strawberries?'

'Oh yes, well. I don't think that makes me a threat to the mighty Murray berry just yet, does it?' Dave, glancing down, embarrassed by this.

'Well, I'll be very interested to see how it goes,' Lachlan replied. 'If you can work out how to grow a respectable crop of nice-looking fruit without using any fertilizer, any weedkiller, any mould inhibitor or any insecticide, you just let me know. Because I'd be more than interested.' But it was too teasing to be a serious offer.

'Lachy,' Rosie warned, and turned to smile at Dave. 'He's been arguing with Harry for years about this stuff, but I've told him not to start with you.'

'I won't be expecting anything like the yield you get.' Dave stood his ground.

'No, if you get any berries at all, they'll be small and mouldy.'

'Not like your juicy big synthetically enhanced ones, eh, Lachlan?' Harry waded into the debate now. 'Let's face it, you're never out of those fields. Spraying them day and night with one thing and another. Gas-flashing them in their punnets.'

'Steady on now.' Lachlan leaned back in his chair, Pamela straining to keep her eyes from his lap. 'Everything I use is tried and tested.'

'Yeah, and how do they test it? Feed it to children for a decade and see if they develop anything nasty?' Dave asked, deciding that this meant so much to him, he wasn't even going to put up with a bit of dinner party banter and especially not from a man who was attracting so much attention from his wife. She'd turned in her chair, seemed hardly able to take her eyes off Lachlan.

'My children eat my fruit all summer long and so do Harry's. If we had any concerns, we wouldn't let them,' Lachlan was bristling back.

'OK, boys, that's enough.' Ingrid rushed in to restore peace. 'Harry, fill everyone's glass up again and then we'll have a game.'

Games? Pamela wondered. *Was this all going to be a bit more 1970s than she'd imagined? . . . Car keys in a basket? What was to come?*

Turned out it was Charades to start with and Harry announced the teams: 'Pamela and Lachy, Ingrid with Dave, and me and Rosie first . . . we'll show you.'

And they certainly did, with something so

complicated and obscure, Pamela didn't get it even when the answer was explained. But then, breath coming in anxious little gasps, she was about to go out of the room alone with him and have to talk about films, books, TV programmes and how to enact them. She hated Charades, loathed it, could feel heart palpitations setting in. This was far worse than anything she'd experienced as a teenager; even being asked to dance by the guy you really, really fancied had nothing on this.

'Pamela and Lachlan,' Harry announced and there was no choice. She got up and followed him uncertainly into the hallway, where he turned to face her with the kind of smile which made her think, well hello, maybe this wasn't going to be so hard after all.

'I hate this game,' she said.

'Yup.' The smile hadn't left his face: slow, sunny, lazy, knowing. 'I'd rather open a few more beers and shoot the breeze. But that's Harry.'

Shoot the breeze? She'd fallen for a countryside cowboy . . . an outback ranch-hand.

'What's your favourite TV programme?' he was asking her.

'Er . . . um . . . *Sex and the City*,' she blurted out.

'Well . . .' he began as she cringed with embarrassment, yeah, they were really going to be able to act *that* out. 'Might be fun to do, but I don't know if my wife would like it.'

She could feel a blush so red and burning spreading across her face that she thought he was going to comment on it.

'The wine has gone straight to my head,' she said, but where else does that amount ever go?

'OK.' He was straightening up, leaning off the wall. 'Let's get this over with, then we can sit back down, you with another wine, me with a beer and see if we can avoid playing anything else until Truth or Dare comes up.'

'*Truth or Dare?!*'

'That's usually interesting . . .' and he was looking straight at her, the playful smile hadn't left his lips.

'*High Noon,*' Pamela said firmly, taking the out-back cowboy in hand. 'You do "high", I'll do "noon" . . . point to my watch and so on . . . How hard can it be? Just think of the beer.'

'OK.'

Lachlan had barely reached up to demonstrate 'high' before Harry got it. *Thank God*, Pamela thought, sinking gratefully back into her chair. This had never happened to her at a dinner party before. Game playing! The horror, the horror. After dinner in London, people either drank more, took drugs or went home. What was this? At least she was drunk. Dave was trying to act out *Dancing with Wolves*, stone-cold sober with an extremely giggly Rosie. *Dancing with Wolves?* Had the man no shame?

'You settling in?' Lachlan asked quietly, turning from the Charade pantomime in front of them.

'A bit. Not sure . . . not really used to it,' she confided. 'It'll be better when I'm working here, I hope.'

'Took me a while too,' he said. 'In fact, I pretty much hate the place, hate the weather, but it's home.'

She smiled, felt she had an ally.

He'd been right: it was Truth or Dare next, and Pamela found herself, even more fuzzy with drink now, unravelling a little paper ball and reading out the words: 'If you were alone in a foreign country would you consider having an affair? And in which country?' to more blushing and hoots of laughter.

'No,' blush, blush, she said valiantly.

'But in which country?' Harry shouted.

'Spain,' her thick tongue managed.

More laughter. 'She's thought about it,' he replied to this. 'Definitely.'

Pamela looked up and met Dave's sober eye. She was so swirly with wine now, she couldn't remember if she had a reason to blush or not. It was so long ago, so far away . . . such a dreamlike haze.

Not like the burning hot distraction sitting right next to her.

The next round, hardly surprisingly, she chose 'dare' and was commanded by the terrifying scrap of paper to 'cut a lock of hair from the person on your right'.

'Oh my God,' was Lachlan's response to this. 'Not my hair, no way.'

Rosie, flush-faced with laughter, urged her on: 'As much as you can . . . cut as much as you can.'

Ingrid brought out scissors and Pamela found herself undoing the band at the back of Lachlan's neck, letting the warm curls tumble out and she was allowed, had a legitimate reason for putting her hand into them, for running a finger along the nape of his neck, watching his shoulders squeeze slightly together as she did so, to pull out the smallest strand and crop it close.

When she held the hair up for everyone to see, there was applause, a groan from Lachlan, and she laid it out of sight on the table, determined to tuck it into her bag to take away with her later.

Suddenly the background music stopped, the lights went out. The house was in total darkness.

'Oh bugger,' was Harry's response. 'That's the second time this week, they need to get to the bottom of this. Privatised electricity bollocks.'

Candles and a torch were located quickly and the party continued in low light. More wine, more wine . . . how else to explain what happened next? Harry, torch in hand, suggested Hide and Seek in the dark. The run of the house, downstairs only; the seekers had a torch. Lachlan caught hold of her hand, steered her to the sitting room and pulled her down behind the sofa with him.

As the beam of Harry and Rosie's torch lit up the wall, and the four hiders all tried to stifle giggles and be perfectly quiet, Pamela felt the electrifying effect of Lachlan's hand moving to her waist and then when she didn't push it away, under her jumper to her bare stomach and up into her bra.

The most delirious, delicious teenageness to this, groping in the dark, behind a sofa, when you really weren't supposed to . . . She thought she might have a heart attack, wondered if he would be able to feel anything other than her hammering heartbeat.

And then the torchlight hovered above them, his hand was pulled back and it was over.

'Found you!' Harry shouted out, games master gone insane, stirring them on to wilder and wilder antics, until Dave looked at his watch, pointed out the time. In just a few hours, he would have cows to feed, veg to pick. He scraped his wife up from the sofa cushions and dragged her home.

Well, that's how it must have been. Nothing seemed to be very clear in her mind after those rough, warm fingertips on her breasts. Feeling in the dark for her nipples.

Nothing was very clear at all.

Chapter Twenty-two

Sunday in the Murray household followed a fairly well-worn routine. In the morning, Lachlan, if he wasn't busy on the farm, took the children out – to the fields, to the beach, up to the woodlands, even out riding their bikes and trikes madly up and down the big shed if it was pouring with rain. While they were out, Rosie caught up with the housework – washing, ironing, hoovering, changing beds, mopping floors – but she raced through it, possessed, because if she finished early, she could lie flat, horizontal, feet up on the sofa (alone! Entirely undisturbed!) reading the Sunday papers and eating a satisfying dose of rubbish from the children's sweet box before they all returned and she had to get up, make lunch, get back on the go again.

Very odd things were in the sweet box today, the remainder of party bags prised out of their hands to stop them gorging to the point of actually puking: nuclear purple parma violets, those disgusting pink and yellow chewy lollies, an infestation of tiny white mice, liquorice chews which had been in there, untouched, for months, very poor quality chocolate money, it might actually be forged chocolate money . . . Still, she scooped up a big handful and put the haul into her sweat top pocket where she could work happily through it for the next . . . at least thirty-five minutes or so.

In the afternoon, they would go to visit her father in the nursing home he'd moved into just over a year ago. He rarely recognized them now and although she was used to it, didn't expect anything else, it still made her feel like crying, but they all kept up chirpy chat and she liked to think that the children's visits were enjoyed by the other residents even if her father didn't seem to take much in.

Before he'd got too ill, he'd lived in the farmhouse with them and she hadn't realized what a restricting presence he'd been in her life, until he'd moved out. Then, all of a sudden there had been space, freedom, to let the children run, shriek, laugh, jump on the sofa, skateboard down the hall. She and Lachlan had made love on the kitchen floor not because it was a great place – but because they could.

The house needed all sorts of redecoration and attention – carpets were worn and threadbare, the walls faded, paintwork ragged, kitchen cupboards coming off their hinges – but it wasn't theirs, might never be, so Lachlan stayed her hand, insisted the money remain in the bank . . .

for now. But it was a bore keeping a manky old house clean, letting her children grow up in this dingy, uninspired brownness. Rosie was going to rebel, was planning her rebellion. Maybe the money from the cottage rentals could be diverted . . .

Sunday evening was taken up with supper, bathtime, a lengthy bedtime with telly, hot milk, too many stories and lights finally out at 8 p.m. Then Lachlan and Rosie would crash together on the sofa drinking second, even reckless third large glasses of wine and chat, maybe watch a film. Afterwards came bedtime, and sometimes, even sex.

Rosie was conscious throughout the video watching tonight that sex was definitely on the agenda. There had been no sex for weeks, Lachlan had commented on it several times, and although he was engrossed in the film, he was massaging her feet in a way that suggested it was on his mind . . . he hadn't forgotten about her.

It wasn't that she didn't love him – she did – it wasn't that she didn't fancy him – she really did – it was just that these feelings were locked up in some part of her that she had almost forgotten how to access. She had no daily use for them. She had a daily use for tidying skills, organizational skills, negotiating skills, racing against the clock skills, caring skills, nurturing skills – but the whole realm of indulging, spoiling, seducing, being seduced, she'd forgotten. She didn't think she had any need of it any more. She didn't seem to be missing it. That was the strange thing. She didn't wake up in the morning and notice any loss. And when they had sex, it was as if she was starting about three miles behind Lachlan and never got the chance to catch up. By the end of it, she would feel warm, dreamy, glowing, just beginning to enjoy herself, while her husband would fall fast asleep in an exhausted, exhilarated puddle beside her.

She did it for him, really . . . and she was too tired to do it for him very often.

'I'm going to have a shower,' he announced as the end credits began to roll. 'What about you? Are you ready for bed?' Oh, the nuances in these questions and answers.

She gave a slightly forced yawn. 'Yup,' she said through it. 'I'll just finish the washing up.'

'Don't do that,' he coaxed. 'I'll do it later.'

'No you won't' – a little irritated now – 'I don't want to be faced with it tomorrow morning.'

He just nodded and headed out of the room to his shower. She went to the kitchen to bang and scrub pots, mood steadily disintegrating.

She waited until she could hear Lachlan coming out of the bathroom, then after a lengthy check of her children, patting covers down, pushing hair out of faces, wriggling feet back into bed, she went in to wash and brush her teeth.

When she got to the bedroom, the lights were low, he had been at the lavender oil with a heavy hand and was waiting in bed, naked, clean and warm, with an expectant smile.

'Are you wooing me?' she teased, pulling off

her thick navy sweater and unbuckling her jeans to let them fall in a heap at her feet.

She turned away from him, thinking that the sensible white pants and soft-cup, machine washable and slightly too big bra might not be exactly what he wanted to see right now. She registered her own jumble of feelings: she was tired, she didn't really want this rigmarole, which threatened to end in an uncomfortable row, and yet she wanted him to love her, to find her attractive, sexy even.

'I'm tired,' she told him again, pulling off her underwear and buttoning herself into a pair of rather shapeless floral pyjamas.

'Come here,' was his reply to this. 'I'll massage your shoulders.'

It was a loaded offer. Lachlan's massages were expected to lead to something a lot more intimate, but he was an expert massager. The thought of his heavy hands kneading out the kinks all across her neck, shoulders and back was too delicious to resist.

She went to the bed and, sliding off her top again, lay down on her front and let him begin.

He'd been a dedicated sportsman before he moved to England and settled down with her and he took massages very seriously.

First of all, oil was warmed in his hands, then he began up at the very top of her neck, long strokes, long, warm strokes, down the neck, out over her shoulders, gliding, rolling away the tension. Then tiny firm circles over and over again, bringing her blood to the surface, making her tingle with heat. A thumb on either side of her spine, he wiggled the knots and lumps out until she could feel the gaps between her discs expand. With full, flat palms he moved over the rest of her back, oiling, smoothing out.

Rosie could feel her head sink into the softness of the pillow, deep lungfuls of lavender slowing her breathing down. This was gorgeous, why didn't they do this every night? Somehow, in just a little minute, she would rouse her leaden limbs and give him a massage back. In just a little minute . . . just lower, just let him finish the small of her back . . . ahhh.

Lachlan felt her unwinding beneath his hands, saw her breathing ease into long breaths sinking down to the bottom of her chest and sighing slowly out again. She was dangerously close to sleep, poor old, worn-out Rosie.

He pulled down her pyjama bottoms and put his face against the place where her back stopped and buttocks began. He blew against it, then planted something between a slow kiss and a lick, blew on it again.

He could hear her make a murmur . . . he wasn't sure if it was protest or encouragement. He placed the slow kisses all over her buttocks, moved down the backs of her legs.

'Can I?' he asked.

'I'm tired,' came from the depths of the pillow.

'Please . . . Pleeeease . . .' he wheedled. 'I'll be quick!'

'Oh great!' Still from the pillow.

He went back to the kissing, rolled her over

onto her back and kissed her stomach, kissed her breasts, grappled playfully with her to push her hand away, so he could kiss her down there ... and when she let him, knew the game was won ... the seduction of his wife was still possible ... and so very nice ... so very satisfying.

But he was fighting the inner voice which whispered that it was just a little boring ... the same ... the inner voice urging him on to another tiny taste of recklessness.

Chapter Twenty-three

Black satin cord threaded all the way to the top of silver-edged eyelets and pulled tight, very tight into a bow. Pamela looked at the effect in the mirror: waist cinched in with the boning, white hips below, bare, propped-up breasts, spilling out on top, framed with a tight black shoulder strap. It came with suspender straps and called for sheer black stockings, high patent heels and a black leather cap . . . maybe even a whip. It was too much. Way too much.

She had come into this shop, a very upmarket but – no disguising it – kinky underwear shop, looking for she knew not what. Something to ease the burn. Or maybe express the burn.

The work on Lachlan and Rosie's cottages had started mid-May, and now Pamela had been there almost every day for over a month, busy, busy with the sander, the steamer, with a rotating team of workmen, but all the time thinking about him, needing excuses to call him, to bring him over to discuss exaggerated 'hiccups', 'problems' and decisions.

Did he like her? She had no recollection of agonizing like this over someone's every glance, every word, every frown since she was a school-girl. If she saw him for ten minutes in the morning, she would replay the conversation in her head over and over again all day, channelling the frustration into hacking away rotten carpet, jemmying out dodgy floorboards, tirelessly sand-ing windowsills.

Getting dressed for 'work' was a daily night-mare. Sexy overalls? She obsessed about how to get that right: had finally come up with a con-coction of jeans cinched in too tight with a narrow belt, slip-on trainers and a vest top that at all times showed bra. She bundled her hair on top of her head, wore vivid stay-on lipstick and consoled herself with the thought that the glow of sweat and hard work was probably as effective as make-up.

But a trip to London in search of more eso-teric decorating supplies had landed her here, behind scented silk curtains, trying on what she could only think of as highest-class hooker underwear.

A chair full of coloured silks awaited her attention. She tried them all on, carefully apprais-ing the results in the low lit, full-length mirror. A plunging cleavage here, see-through black netting there ... was a split crotch more sexy than a lace-up one? Which bras had the most alluring straps? That was all she was going to be able to lure him with – the straps of her bra, the glimpse of breast beneath her vest top.

It was a turn-on, seeing her bare nipples peek from red and apple green lace like baby raspberries in a gift box, seeing her white buttocks strapped down beneath suspenders tight enough to leave a mark. But then she was turned on all the time. Nothing made it better, nothing made it go away. She knew it was a ridiculous madness but she *had* to have him. Didn't care if it was just once, if she had to tie him up, in fact, even better if she had to tie him up. She had to have him.

The underwear made sense to her now. She'd never seen the point before. The outward expression of all this inner desire. Her way of telling him what she wanted. To be wanted, needed, craved the way she craved him. And she already knew she didn't want the kind of sex she could get at home – or make that *had once had* at home. Sweet sex, love sex, white lacy nightie sex, Dave on top, looking into her eyes, telling her how beautiful she was. No, nothing like that. When she pictured herself with Lachlan there were tensed muscles, raking nails, hard bruising bites, grimaces of pleasure way out there at the pleasure–pain dividing line.

She remembered Ted's partner, Liz, a bottle of wine down, semi-confessing to longings for wild, untamed, un-marital sex.

'Giving birth is like *really* losing your virginity,' she'd confided. 'All those strangers sticking their hands up uninvited, lying in stirrups wide open to whoever's passing, something huge, absolutely *huge* moving up and down, starting and stopping in your vagina. It's *awesome!*'

Pamela had smiled encouragingly, slightly shocked, not able to offer an opinion on this. Liz was putting a spin on childbirth she'd never heard before.

'I'm sure some women are utterly traumatized,' Liz had added. 'See it like medicalized gang rape. But after the stitches had healed, I was possessed. Had to have sex like never before and with *accessories* . . .' she'd confided, smiling, running hands though her silky black hair. 'Poor Ted, he was exhausted. A new baby and an *insatiable* partner. Very strange . . . Something definitely changed. I lost the fear – the restraint – the control most of us operate under all the time between the sheets.' She'd stood up then and made some attempt to move bottles binwards, clear the clutter of an evening spent cooking, eating, over-drinking.

'And the most important thing,' she'd added, 'about all this is that I'm slightly less frightened of having sex with just one person for the rest of my life. Because before . . . I was terrified. I mean, aren't you?'

Pamela had only needed to add a half-nod for Liz to continue.

'I was sure it was going to become as boring as eating bread and butter sandwiches for lunch every day. And I would be longing for something else and end up wrecking my entire family life just for the sake of a new flavour – but now, I don't worry about that so much.'

Yet more proof, as if Pamela had needed it, that Ted's on-off, hot-cold, shouting, *accessorized* love-making, child-filled relationship was better than hers.

Pamela-and-Dave – what an entity they'd become. PamelanDave. PamelanDave. To think of one was to think of the other, to invite one was to invite the other. 'At least you've got each other' had been the universal reaction to their joint infertility. As if she was so lucky to have found a soulmate, she shouldn't really mind that he was even less likely to have a child than she was.

She still, almost every day, despite the farm, despite the fresh start, thought about the dissolution of PamelanDave, the resurrection of Pamela, just Pamela. Hell, maybe even just Pam. Go for the full amputation. Chop the whole 'and Dave' bit off, and then some.

The black, breast-framing corset, several pairs of stockings, lace-up pants, and the red and green set were all selected and boxed up for her with crackling tissue paper and a fat black ribbon tied as tightly as corset lacing.

She handed over her credit card with the tingling recognition that she was behaving irrationally and very badly. Maybe she should tell someone about Lachlan ... dilute the intensity of this fantasy ... examine it in daylight ... listen to someone else's laughter about it. But she knew she couldn't, wouldn't and she knew why.

If she wasn't thinking about Lachlan every

273

waking moment, she would have to think about herself – about the fact that she was probably not going to have a child ... ever ... about the fact that her marriage of eight years, her relationship of thirteen years, was going to end with a divorce, with the sale of the farm, with Dave's utter devastation.

No, no. Much better to swipe the credit card, buy pornographic satin and lace, plan the seduction of the brutishly attractive farmer she was working for ... and not think about the rest.

Chapter Twenty-four

'Undercoat,' Pamela groaned. 'We're totally out of undercoat.' It was a full forty-minute drive to the nearest paint suppliers.

John, her grizzled, fifty-something co-decorator stood up and brushed himself down. They had been sanding woodwork all morning, chatting amiably. She liked him a lot, because he was good, did everything well and took pains. And in the six weeks they'd worked together, finishing the small cottage and now moving on to the bigger one, she'd learned all about John's wife, children, his early retirement from a canning factory to devote himself to 'a spot' of decorating and his two racing whippets.

'Why don't I go?' he offered. 'I forgot to bring my lunch, I'll be needing to go out and get something anyway.'

Before he left, he swept up his latest pile of sanding dust, scooped it into the bin bag, then took off his overall and folded it neatly. He was all right, John. She'd definitely use him again for other commissions in Norfolk, which she was determined to get now.

Instead of leaving her home in darkness, struggling onto the early morning train, rushing through a warren of stations, the underground, arriving at work in London already exhausted . . . she was setting off at 8.30 a.m., rolling the car through the lush greens and yellows of the hottest summer in years, noticing cottages, grazing horses, majestic old trees, all the eye-catching sights that studded the twisting B roads to Lachlan's farm.

She would arrive happy, glowing, full of life, enthusiasm for the day ahead and not just – she didn't think – because she might see *him*: he might be passing, think of some detail he wanted to check, some question he wanted to ask.

She would see either Rosie or Lachlan almost every day. One of them would call in for a progress report and now that the strawberry season was in full swing, it was more often than not Rosie and Manda who would turn up.

Pamela would hear the scrape of the cottage door opening and recognize how much she hoped it would be Lachlan. What a guilty disappointment it was to see his wife and little daughter.

Rosie kept a formality to the meetings. She would ask about the work, wouldn't stay long and always seemed a little frosty.

Whereas Lachlan, when he had time to come by, would make tea, pull up one of the two chairs and would want to chat: about the cottages, about his farm, about Dave's strawberries – he liked to know how they were getting on. He would also ask Pamela how she was settling in, how she was enjoying it. What other work plans she had.

Pamela debated with herself throughout these talks, wondering if they meant anything. Didn't he always seem to arrive just as John went out? Why was he so interested in her? Was he this interested in everyone else?

She would often look at his hand gripped round the mug and think with a jolt about the night he'd slipped it into her bra.

Once John had left to get the undercoat, Pamela got back down on her hands and knees to rub at a skirting board and was watching the grey dust of old paint spray onto the floor and over her fingers, when she heard the front door opening. No-one knocked here, she'd noticed. Must be a country thing or a farm thing: never knocking, always opening doors and shouting hello. She thought of Sadie's verdict with a smile: 'There can't be any sex in the countryside.'

'Hello?'

She felt the lurch, the squeeze on her heart of excitement. It was him. She jumped up and wiped the dust from her hands and jeans.

'Hello,' she called back. 'Come in, it's just me.'

'Hi there. Yeah. I saw John's van headed for the main road.' He came in, scrunching down, ducking to fit in through the low doorway and then expanding to full size in the room.

'He's gone to get more paint,' she explained, trying to keep some semblance of a normal conversational tone, wondering all the time if he'd meant he'd waited till he saw John's van leave before he'd come over.

There was *something* there, between them. No way was she making all this up. She saw how his gaze lingered on her face, shoulders, vest straps, how it lowered when she turned away from him. His eyes on her, making her skin feel warm, her breathing slow, her heart race.

'How are you? How's it going?' he asked, so she updated him on the latest work. They made tea in the kitchen together, elbows bumping, getting in each other's way. She had to duck under his arm to flick tea bags into the bin. Caught a whiff of clean, warm sweat, felt the dizzying wave of want. He'd always looked good to her, but now deeply tanned and blonder from all his time in the sun, he was a sensation, set off perfectly by the T-shirt, jeans and boots of his summer work wear.

They pulled the two chairs up and drank their tea together.

'First holiday-makers are going into the cottage next week,' he told her. 'And we've had lots of interest. So, good job—' he held his mug up to salute her. 'I thought it looked like a tart's bedroom in there, but that doesn't seem to have put anyone off.'

She almost coughed her tea up at him.

'A tart's bedroom!'

'It's very girlie,' he grinned.

278

'It's white and blue! There's no pink or anything!'

'But there's little chandeliers . . . fluffy things.'

'It's sheepskin, not fluffy stuff.' But she enjoyed the teasing.

'This place isn't going to be like that, though, is it?'

'No. This cottage will be macho – grey, green, plain. Think army barracks,' she joked. 'Maybe we'll have lockers and an outdoor toilet, get the visitors back to nature.'

'A dunny! Fantastic!'

'Shut up, will you,' she teased him back. 'You know nothing. I know what people want.'

'Hmmm . . . do you now?' She heard the purr in that question. She did. She dared to meet his eyes then and he didn't flinch or look away. She put a hand up to her head, tucking in a stray strand of hair, showing him a soft white armpit as she did so.

'Any thoughts about the garden?' she asked, putting her empty mug down on the floor and going over to the window. 'We should tidy the garden up, although I have to say, I like what's out there.' She looked out over the tangle of overgrown grass, dog roses and hawthorn. 'Wild.'

He was standing behind her. She'd heard him get up and come over and didn't turn to look, but knew exactly where he was because he was radiating heat at her. It was spreading through her, warming her to the very pit of her stomach.

'Wild,' he repeated.

He was looking at the pale, downy skin at the

nape of her neck punctuated with a dark mole. He wasn't going to be able to restrain himself from touching it.

She felt his fingers on her neck.

'Nice mole,' he said. He could smell her: a hint of perfume, soap, sweat. Wanted to bury his nose into her skin, touch her whiteness all over. Wanted to know if there was a red mark on her skin where her tight belt cut in, where those pink and green bra straps had dug into her soft shoulders.

'How long have you been married?' he asked, hand still on her neck.

'Eight years,' came her answer, in between gulps for breath.

'Not as long as me.' He said this lightly, his fingers moving from her neck slowly down to her shoulder, causing every hair along the way to stand on end.

Then dropping down to a whisper, he said: 'It's nice. But sometimes you must get bored?'

He didn't wait for an answer, just turned her round and she saw the look in his eyes. The want, the challenge . . . the question.

'D'you want to kiss?' he asked.

She was too surprised to speak, managed to mumble some sort of 'Ha?' sound back at him and then felt his hands under her chin, her face pulled in to his.

His mouth on hers, slight scrape of stubble, the damp of sweat across his top lip, his tongue moving into her mouth and all this time his hands holding her head tight as if he was frightened she might pull away, as if he wanted to block out the sound of any objection.

After a moment of stunned stillness, she started to kiss him back, tongue against his, pupils popping, head rushing, realizing how starved she was for him.

And then he pulled away and she opened her eyes to look at him, find out why he'd stopped.

'OK?' he asked. There was only one answer to this; one – scruples to the wind, conscience to the back door – reckless answer.

She grabbed his T-shirt and pulled him back towards her.

'Very OK. More, please.' His mouth was on hers again, his hands in the back pocket of her jeans, then pulling down the straps of her bra, moving to undo her zip. Her hands on the skin of his back, slipping in under his belt. Her foot raking down the back of his leg.

And then the unmistakable sound of tyres in the gravel outside. The slam of a car door. She and Lachlan sprang apart and rearranged themselves.

Pamela fled over to the chairs and picked the mugs up. 'Hello,' she called loudly. 'Oh John, hello, it's you.' The guilt flooding over her now had made her imagine Rosie and Manda.

'Lachlan's here –' she marvelled at her breezy voice – 'inspecting our handiwork, making sure we're not blowing the budget.'

John came into the room, four tins of paint hanging from his hands. He gave Lachlan an: 'Aye there,' as phlegmy as a cough.

'Well, that's me.' Lachlan was smoothing down his hair, re-securing the ponytail in its band. 'Good work,' he nodded at John.

John nodded back.

'I'll catch you later,' he directed at Pamela with something like a wave.

'Yeah,' she managed to reply, starting to register her shock at what had just happened.

When the door slammed behind him, she looked at John at a loss for what would be a normal thing to do. Unable to think of a single thing to say to him.

'Tea?' occurred to her only after several long moments of silence. His small grey eyes didn't miss much, she was sure.

But once John had gone home after 5 p.m., Pamela stayed on, found some jobs to do, knowing they were just an excuse to wait here, see if Lachlan would come back to her.

She was just wondering if she dared to phone Lachlan on his mobile and tell him she was still at the cottage, when the door opened and there he was, greeting her with something that sounded like far too normal a 'hello'.

'Are you finishing up?' he asked.

'Yeah.' She was aware of the electric shocks he was causing her.

'Can't you maybe stay for a bit?'

'Yeah . . . maybe,' she answered.

He walked out of the room, back to the front door, where she heard him turn the key in the lock. When he returned, his hand reached for the light switch and the single bulb in the middle of the room, lit to hold the early evening at bay, snapped out.

They were left standing in the half-light, nothing but loud bird song from the garden and the sound of her breathing breaking the silence.

'I know you want to do this,' he said.

'Do I?' she asked, but she already knew the answer, was already walking towards him.

'Come here, baby,' he said. No-one had ever called her baby before; it struck her as a bit too retro, a bit macho. Did he call his wife baby? she wondered. Or did he say 'baby' to stop himself from saying Rosie?

She didn't want to know. His arms were around her now, his face against her neck, hands pulling at her straps and her zip.

He was right: she did want to do this. She really did.

'Where?' was the single word to come from his lips.

She pointed to the bedroom. It was uncarpeted and had big damp strips of woodchip hanging from the walls but in there, flat on the floor, was the old double mattress still waiting to be thrown out.

He didn't let go of her wrist, held it tightly and when they were in the room, spun her round towards him again. Crushed against him, mouth on mouth, tongue on tongue, she dared to pull his T-shirt over his head, she bit his small brown nipples as his fingers rolled hers into hard points, she put her hands on his belt buckle and nudged it loose. His breath against her ear, strained, gasping.

He was working on her jeans zip too. Pressing his fingers against the veil of netting he met there, pushing it aside and feeling her.

Saliva ran from the corner of her mouth and dripped from her chin, but it didn't matter, nothing mattered any more apart from the desperate strip of clothes and the fall to the mattress. She was breathless, had no memory of a time before when she'd felt so ready to explode with longing.

His tongue on her neck, her finger in his mouth, his mouth touching between her legs, it all made her come, shudder and come again.

Down on the mattress, he pushed hard into her, came out again, rolled her onto her front, pulled her legs apart and pushed into her again.

His arms locked round her, he gripped her tightly and rocked against her, into her, bouncing her into the tired mattress springs. Face buried in the mildewy nylon cover, she put her hands out behind her, clasped hold of pumping muscle, hard thigh and dug her nails in.

The kiss against her shoulder was harder now, his teeth were gripping, holding her tight. Then he pulled out, came against her, his face crumpling into her neck and loosened hair. He rolled off and fell onto his back, eyes closed, breathing hard, and she envied him the complete release. Still she burned for him. Didn't think anything would take the burn away. Saw his solid, curl-haired bulk and wanted him even more . . . *more*. She'd thought that once would be enough, but saw now that, like hunger, it didn't matter how many times she would eat, she'd still be starving for him all over again.

Rolling onto her back, she felt the wet on her leg. His sperm. His super-fertile farmer sperm. For a moment, she almost considered dipping a finger in it, moving it into the right place.

But what was the point? It wouldn't do her any good, would it? Sub-fertile, pre-pre-menopausal Pamela. Then the wave of post-sex sadness threatened to wash over her, but Lachlan's arm fell across her stomach and held it back.

'You're very good,' he said, running the other hand through his hair. 'Phew.'

She felt shy of returning the compliment, so there was silence until she asked: 'Have you done this before?'

'What?' he stalled.

'You know, *this* . . . sex with someone other than your . . .' but he put a finger over her lips to stifle the word 'wife'.

'Ha, that question . . .' He rolled onto his side to face her. 'No comment,' was his reply with the same 'dare me' smirk which had landed her here in the first place. She took that to mean yes.

'Have you?' he asked.

And now she saw why it was such a hard question to answer. 'Yes' wouldn't be fair to Dave, would make her sound like the brazen hussy she really didn't think she was. 'No' might give Lachlan an inflated idea of his importance to her . . . might worry him.

Because she knew already that he wasn't important to her, couldn't be. He was sex only, could mess with her as much as she wanted him to . . . but could not mess with her head. Couldn't go anywhere near her head, her heart . . . her feelings.

'No comment,' she echoed and smiled at him. She moved to his face, kissed him slowly on the mouth, then stood up and began to get dressed. But sex only . . . she watched him pull his jeans over his broad legs . . . sex only was very interesting.

They kissed goodbye, threatening to get undressed all over again, and then made their separate ways home.

Moving, as their front doors opened, from the delirious high of secret sex to the shamefaced reality.

Lachlan was met with a stampede of children into his arms and Rosie's accusation that his phone was off *again*. Pamela found Dave at the cooker, making stew, ready to fuss over her: 'All this manual labour, you need to keep your strength up,' he'd smiled.

Both Pamela and Lachlan had insisted on needing a shower before they'd come back down to supper and their spouses.

Chapter Twenty-five

It was a full fortnight before Lachlan came back to the cottage. In that time, Pamela had worked fast, frenziedly scraping, sanding, papering, painting, thinking about him too much. Finding reasons to go in and out of the bedroom every day to look at the mattress and try to marry the reality of this room with the unreality of what had happened in it. She'd seen him now and then. Out in the fields as she'd driven past, once walking along the road with his sons, casually waving at her. She'd been alarmed at the near heart attack these sightings had caused her. But she left him alone, not wanting to make the first move, or any move at all. Maybe that was all there would be. Maybe she would have to be contented with that, hope that this almost constant, insatiable desire would eventually go away.

But then one evening, just as she'd finished cleaning up and was all set to go home, the door scraped open and Lachlan called out her name.

She wasn't sure how to greet him. No way did she want him to assume he could turn up when he pleased, lock the door and have her.

'Hi there.' She crossed her arms and squared up to him.

'Hey baby.' Yuck, yuck, he would have to stop calling her that. 'I'd have come to see you before, but I've been very busy. Season in full swing.'

'You don't need to apologize to me – I haven't been pining for you over here or anything like that.'

'No?' He was smiling, pretending to sound a little disappointed. 'It's a great evening. D'you want to come out for a walk?'

'A walk?' No! She didn't want a walk. She wanted him to drag her into that back bedroom again where they could strip off all their clothes and . . .

'I've never taken you through the fields. Never shown you the farm properly. And I'd like to. C'mon, it'll be fun.'

Little smiley smirk with that. What was he suggesting?

She switched off all the cottage lights, locked up, phoned Dave and told him she was taking John out for a drink, not liking at all how easily the lie came. Then she followed Lachlan out over the fields.

Velvety, luminous blue of a summer evening, the swoop of birds still busy in the sky, the last of the golden sunlight fading down over the higher ground ahead of them. But still warm enough for her to be walking in her vest top, him in his T-shirt.

They were climbing a long, sloping strawberry field, heading far away from the farmhouse with lights lit, Rosie waiting for her husband to come home. Pamela couldn't quite brush the thought away.

The day's picking over, the tractor and trailer were still in the field and stacked high with crates, boxes of plastic punnets. Pale pink and yellow picking baskets were piled into a heap beside, a few baskets visible in the rows where they'd been abandoned.

He was talking about varieties: which would be picked when, how he could now begin the crop in early May and continue right through till September. She wasn't really listening, just wanted to know when he was going to stop talking and kiss her.

'And over here, the polytunnels—' he was walking towards tall, head-height, plastic tunnels which ran the length of the field.

She didn't care, she really didn't. Why did he want her to follow? Why was she out here while he talked about strawberry crops and pretended nothing had happened?

'Look,' she said, peering into the long, white interior of the tunnel where strawberry plants were growing rampantly on hip-high tables, 'if this is your idea of foreplay, Lachlan, it really isn't working for me.'

He was already inside, plucking little berries, storing them in his hands.

'Whoa ... thanks for the tip,' he said and turned to face her with a smile which looked almost embarrassed. 'Come and try these—' he held out his hand. 'They're my best ones.'

She stepped into the tunnel and walked towards him, immediately aware of the clammy heat and a smell of strawberries so strong it was almost a flavour, undercut with the clean, green of their leaves.

Right up close to him, she watched him put a berry into his mouth and hoped she knew what he was going to do next.

He bit into it, then put his mouth against hers, passing the fruit to her. With a clumsy fumbling she found all the more exciting, he pulled off her vest, then her jeans but kept his clothes on. Damp, crushed berries were pushed into her bra and into her pants, where he moved them against her with his tongue. He lifted her up so she was sitting on the table in amongst the plants and rolled a strawberry with his fingers against her. Down there. Over and over, whispering into her ear: 'Please can I come inside now. I'll be very careful.'

'Not yet,' she whispered back.

He leaned against her, nudging into her, unfastening her bra, and she could feel him, swollen, pressing up underneath her.

'Not yet . . .' she said again.

His fingers melting against her, melting her down: 'But you're just about to come . . .

Wouldn't you like to come with me?' he urged.

She moved to the edge of the table so she could slide him inside: 'OK then,' she pressed the words right against his ear. 'No need to be careful.'

His grip on her buttocks, burningly tight. Her first, then him gasping, pulling her into him, wrapping arms round her, squeezing her breathlessly hard until he came too. When he let go, she fell back against the table, feeling the squash of strawberries under her bare skin.

She spread her arms out into the plants. Sex without crying . . . she could do this.

Looking up at the blank white sky of plastic above her, she asked him: 'What are we doing?'

'Playing,' was his answer.

'Playing a very dangerous game,' she replied.

'No.' He pulled her up and helped her back into her bra. 'Fun,' he said, handing her the vest top. 'We're only here for very quiet, secret fun.'

Pamela took Alex to the top of the hill above Linden Lee. Her friend complained all the way up about the steepness of the walk.

'This is far too much like exercise, I'm not liking it one bit, you know,' she whinged. 'When do we have the cigarette break?'

'At the top,' Pamela promised. 'The view is worth it, honestly.'

'If I turn around from here, I can see the view. It's not going to be any better from up there,' was Alex's response.

'Oh come on. Think of the sense of achievement.'

'Oh, arse to that.' But Alex carried on walking. More like trudging.

Another perfect summer afternoon, just a handful of soft white clouds set against the blue sky.

When they reached the top of the hill, Alex threw herself down on the grass, flat on her back and scrabbled in her pockets for cigarettes.

'Isn't it a bit wet down there?' Pamela asked.

Alex struck up a light and inhaled. 'Come on, get down here beside me, tell me what's really going on out here in your rural idyll.'

'Ha.' Pamela did as instructed: lay down on the long, spiky grass beside her friend. Impossible not to stare at the sky from here, watch the clouds chasing past, melting, forming into different shapes.

'That one looks like a man smoking a pipe – look at it.' Pamela pointed.

Alex did, but decided: 'No, more an elephant, really.'

'Oh yes. And now ... turning into a face with a huge chin. If you concentrate on clouds long enough you can make them evaporate. Apparently.'

'Depending on how many drugs you take, probably.'

'No!' Pamela protested. 'I read about it ... cloudbusting.'

'OK, so you and Dave? Do you come out here of an evening and cloudbust?'

Pamela considered the question for a few moments then confided: 'Dave and I don't do much together of an evening any more.'

'So the big plan . . . moving up here and sorting out your marriage. How is that going?'

'I can't say it's going very well.'

'Aha.' It had not been hard to guess, Alex had noticed that Pamela didn't have much to say to her husband, how she even seemed to avoid eye contact with him and now spent as much time at her work as possible.

'Has it been like this for a while?' she asked.

Pamela kept her gaze on the clouds, appearing calm and not nearly as upset about this as she had been in the past.

'I'm not exactly helping,' she answered finally. 'Not helping at all. I'm seeing someone else.' She wasn't sure if she wanted to confess this yet, invite an opinion on the slightly crazed turn her life was taking. 'Well . . . not really,' she added quickly. 'Very casually.'

'You are?' Alex couldn't keep the surprise out of her voice.

'Yeah. Nothing serious. Just sex,' Pamela said, trying to sound as offhand as she could. 'Not very nice of me, though.'

Alex leaned on an elbow and looked at her in shock.

'*Just sex?* What kind of sex? *Wild sex?*' she asked.

Pamela smiled.

'Not very nice of you at all,' Alex agreed. 'How did this happen?'

And so Pamela told her, realizing as she spoke how much she wanted to talk about Lachlan. Enthuse, unburden herself about this man who was taking up almost all her thoughts, but until now had remained a complete secret. It was a relief to confess, to confide.

'My God,' was Alex's verdict when the story had unfolded. 'You have a secret lover . . . I can't believe it. Can't believe it! You!'

'Why not me?' Pamela wanted to know.

'You're too nice,' Alex told her.

'Am not.'

'Are so.'

'I don't think sleeping with someone twice makes them your secret lover though, does it?'

'Yes, I think you'll find it does.' Alex lit a second cigarette and after a considered inhalation told Pamela: 'Well, first of all . . . I'm bloody jealous. I'll tell you that for free. *I'm* the single person here, I'm the one who should be having secret lovers and wild sex. You seem to have forgotten a minor detail: you are still married and I think you'll find that secret lovers are against the rules – will in fact cause all kinds of nasty problems.'

'Secret lover is married too. So no-one's going to find out. It's our secret. It'll be fine,' Pamela argued.

'Someone always finds out,' Alex warned her. 'And I never knew of any extra-marital affair which ended in "fine". They just don't. They end in mess, shouting, chaos, tears . . . everybody hurt. Nothing fine about it at all.'

'Oh, don't be so disapproving.'

'But you are eating between meals,' Alex insisted. 'You're hoovering up the chocolates when it's just about dinnertime and I know it's delicious but it's not good for you and someone needs to be boring and point this out.'

'What is that supposed to mean?' Pamela's smile fading now.

'If you have man trouble, another man is hardly ever the answer. And I'm saying that based on years of experience. What about Dave?' Alex asked. 'Doesn't he deserve a bit better than this. If your marriage isn't working, shouldn't you be talking to him about it?'

'That's all very easy to say . . . talk to him about it. You know what a state we were in back in London, screaming at each other all the time. Here, at least we've stopped rowing.'

'And started shagging someone else,' Alex cut across her. 'That's not better for him, is it?'

'You know, I didn't exactly expect you to be the high priestess of long-term love.' The telling off starting to rankle with Pamela.

'Me . . . no,' Alex had to admit. 'But I really like Dave and I'm willing to bet the entire contents of my van that he loves you.'

'Hmmm . . . And why am I even telling you all this when I know next to nothing about your love life?' was Pamela's rather flippant reply.

'There's no big mystery—' Alex waved a hand about, understanding clearly that she was being asked to back off. 'People came, people went. Some were very important to me, some weren't.

There hasn't been anyone important for a while. But I don't feel worried about that. Something will crop up. Always does. I'm slightly in love with my vegetable delivery man,' she said with a smile. 'I was so inspired by Dave's vegetable lecture, I signed up for this weekly scheme and every Tuesday afternoon, Andrew is delivered to my door, fresh carrots in his arms – and he wears shorts! All year round, apparently. We could do with more of that. More men in shorts. But, you know.' She looked over at Pamela, more serious now. 'I sometimes think I should just have stayed with my first love. I mean, if you're two highly developed individuals you could go through all the experiences with one person, all the different relationship stages and phases, instead of having to move on to other people to experience them. It would be so much simpler.'

'But maybe much more boring,' Pamela added.

'Well, I don't know. When you get stuck in a rut with someone, you're probably both going though the motions for each other, when really both of you want to change, and you probably just should. But it doesn't always have to be about splitting up. You could move on to another phase together.'

'I thought you didn't want a significant other?' Pamela asked now.

'Me? No.' Alex stubbed out her cigarette. 'But I'm always very sad when people mess up their big, important relationships.'

'Ah.' Pamela's head seemed to droop.

'What do you want to do?' Alex asked her.

'I don't know.'

'Maybe you have to think about that instead of getting your brains blown out by secret lover.'

'Maybe.'

'Why don't you open a shop?' Alex said after a while.

'A shop!' This was a surprise. 'What would I want a shop for?'

'You know, a farm shop. Dave's veg and his berries when they get started and many lovely, glamorous things which you and I could scour the countryside to find.'

'You think you can solve my marriage problems with a shop?' Pamela wasn't sure whether to laugh or get angry.

'No, I'm just pointing to a gaping hole in the market. I mean where do the good people of Upper-Much-Shitey-Town . . .'

'Alex!'

'Or whatever it's called . . . Where do they go when they want lovely things? An unusual lamp, an embroidered bag, a hand-knitted baby's cardigan . . .'

'They drive to Norwich and go to John Lewis,' Pamela informed her.

'John Lewis?' Alex crossed her hands in front of her. 'Aaargh John Lewis, get thee away from me.'

'What's wrong with John Lewis?' Pamela asked. 'They have some very good basics.'

'Basics? Basics? What is it with basics? I don't want basics. I want un-basics. I want things that have romance, a history, a patina. When I buy an evening bag I want to be able to think about the 15-year-old girl who had it before me ... her mother who bought it for her on the day of the big school dance ...'

'For goodness sake, you really are a big soppy romantic. That's probably why you're alone. No-one can live up to these romantic ideals. Come on, we really have to go. My bum is cold.'

'Better phone secret lover, get him to warm you up ... Take you to the Polytunnel of Love.'

'Please shut up!' Pamela shrieked. 'Why did I even imagine telling you anything about this would be a good idea?'

Chapter Twenty-six

'You can't go out tonight. You can't,' Rosie raged, out of all proportion to the situation. 'What on earth do you have to go out for tonight?'

Lachlan did not like to lie too specifically to his wife. He thought it was dangerous. But then, the whole situation was dangerous. What exactly was safe about driving around the countryside in your great big conspicuous 4 x 4 looking for a place to have sex with someone else's wife? Somebody was going to find out. Someone was going to notice . . . whisper it to someone else . . . word would get out and then everything would unravel. He *knew* this. The stakes were far too high. He had to stop this. Thought every day about when he would stop it . . . how he would tell her . . . and still he was planning to see her again.

'Look it's OK,' he was telling Rosie now. 'It's nothing I can't put off till tomorrow. I'll stay here.' But even as he said the words he felt the crush of disappointment weigh on him.

'Let me just finish up in the office,' he said, turning out of the crowded sitting room, noisy with telly, his boisterous boys and baby. He'd send her a text. Tell her 'last-minute hitch'. It had happened before.

Rosie watched him go out of the room and burned with the knowledge that he was going off to tell Pamela he couldn't see her tonight. She didn't know how she knew, she didn't have one shred of evidence and sometimes wondered if she had turned into an unreasonably jealous and paranoid wife, but the feeling of *knowing* couldn't be shaken off.

She turned over and over the idea of confronting him but if he just denied it, how would she know if he was lying or not? Her mind would never be set at rest . . . but then, what if he admitted it? What would she do? She didn't know if she had the courage to face an admission.

Better right now to half pretend to herself that there must be another explanation for her husband's absent-mindedness, complicated new reasons to be away from the house, frequent trips to the cottage for 'progress updates' and, most damning of all, his six pairs of new, white, *Lycra-enhanced* trunks.

'You've got new underwear?' she'd asked from the depths of the laundry basket, unable to keep the surprise from her voice.

'Yup,' he'd answered, not looking up from the farming paper he was reading in bed. 'Other ones were falling apart.'

So matter-of-fact. But this had never happened before. She bought his clothes, his shoes, his work boots, even.

'*I'm* going out tonight. In fact, I'm going to go now,' she told him when he came back into the room, enjoying the surprise on his face. She hardly ever went anywhere, on her own, at night.

'Where are you going?' he asked.

'Oh you know, just work stuff . . . got to see a man about a machine,' she dared him in an imitation of the vague kind of excuse he'd been making lately.

'Oh . . .' He pushed his hands into his pockets and surveyed the domestic chaos in front of him, which he would be in charge of tonight.

'Is there . . .' he began but broke off, maybe thinking better of it.

'Anything for supper?' She tried not to sound too vitriolic.

'Well,' he backtracked, 'if you haven't got anything in mind, I'll sort something out.'

'There is a pot of mince on the hob, you just need to do potatoes and veg.' She was standing up, determined to go now, wondering why she hardly ever let Lachlan do this on his own, the whole supper, bath, bedtime evening thing, and why she never went out at night.

She bent down towards the Lego world being created by her sons to say good night. They nodded, shrugged, didn't like the distraction from the intensity of the game.

'Mama—' Manda's face was at her knee, hand clutched tightly to her jeans, 'Mama.' Little insistent voice able with one word to break Rosie's heart. The baby radar had been alerted.

How had Rosie forgotten? *This* was why she never left home on her own, because it meant Manda in hysterical tears being prised from her, finger by tiny finger.

'Mummy's just nipping out, back in a minute,' she said, hating the lie.

'No,' Manda insisted. 'NO!'

'You're going to play with Daddy and the boys.' She picked her girlie up.

'NO!' came out again, roared this time, deafening.

Rosie tried to hand her daughter to Lachlan, but Manda gripped at her hair, screamed, flailed her legs.

'She'll be fine,' Lachlan said, unconvinced, catching a kick in the face. 'Oww . . .' The boys looked up to laugh at him.

'Just go. She'll be fine.'

Rosie, almost in pain now, went out of the room, pulling the door shut like a traitor. She hurried to the cloakroom, scrambled her coat, boots and bag together and fled the house.

When she'd slammed the door of the Isuzu shut behind her, she stared at the wheel blankly. Where the hell to now?

Where did you go when you were running away from your family for a night? When you were trying to run and hide from the possibility that your husband was cheating on you and your life could very possibly be about to turn to shit?

For a moment it crossed her mind to turn up on Ingrid and Harry's doorstep. But she almost blamed them. They'd sold Linden Lee, hadn't they? They'd brought *her* into their lives.

Maybe if her dad wasn't in an old people's home with senile dementia, she would go to him ... Maybe if her brothers weren't living on the other side of the world she would go to them. But they were farming in Australia, had resented working for their father so much, they'd shipped out years ago and now managed 400 head of cattle hundreds of miles from the nearest town.

'Don't worry, we'll send you back a ranch hand,' they'd promised and three months later Lachlan had arrived with a holdall, rattlesnake-proof boots and a wide-brimmed hat. Rosie, newly 22, alone in the house most of the time with her ailing father, missing her brothers desperately, frazzled with farm management, had, of course, fallen in love overnight.

'Strewth, Rosie,' her older brother had joked, his laughter echoing down the long-distance line. 'You were meant to give the guy a job, not bloody marry him!' And no, far too busy, they didn't think they would make it back for the wedding.

But they'll be back for the funeral, she couldn't help thinking now. When Dad dies, they'll be back and then will come the reckoning. The long-awaited will. The dividing up of the farm and all the heartache it would bring.

She turned the key in the ignition and fired up the engine. She would head out for the dual carriageway, blast music from the stereo, wind down the windows even, drive at 75 m.p.h., maybe even 80. See where it took her.

She only ever listened to tapes in the car, well didn't listen, let the children listen while she tuned out. The five-CD player was entirely Lachlan's thing. She didn't even know where the discs went in.

She glanced over, flicked CD one on, didn't recognize it, tried two and three, again nothing she warmed to. Unusually soft girl and guitar stuff. For Pamela? she thought with a lurch. Disc four kicked in: Lou Reed. No. All hopes pinned on the fifth and final.

Blasting electric chords and energy. For a moment she struggled to place the familiar but long-unheard music. Jimi Hendrix, of course. She pushed the volume up higher, sped on towards the main road, pressing down the accelerator, beginning to enjoy the ride.

She thought about Lachlan. He would be trying to boil potatoes and broccoli with Manda hanging like a baby monkey from his neck, desperate to poke her doll's arm into the bubbling pots. Willy and Pete, crazed with hunger by now, would probably be drop-kicking each other's toys across the kitchen, then wrestling in a murderous fury. Oh well ... She deserved an evening off.

On she sped, listening to Jimi promise that when he made love he wouldn't cause any pain.

Good grief? Was that the best he could offer?

She skipped forward to 'Crosstown Traffic'

which egged her on to hit the dual carriageway, gun down the fast lane and keep going, get out of here. At least for a night.

An hour later she was out of the county, on the motorway, wondering what she would do, when the lights of an out of town retail park beckoned her in like a landing strip.

Ikea, open till 10 p.m., the billboard informed her. Ikea? She'd heard of it, of course, but never been because she and Lachlan saved every spare penny they earned for the day when they'd have to buy their own farm. Decorating the house they lived in, which wasn't theirs and might never be, didn't seem sensible.

But she'd wanted to rebel for months. She'd had enough of living in a dull and dingy place when there was so much money in the bank. And tonight, she decided, pulling into the huge car park, she was going to start the rebellion. *Too bad, Lachlan ... If you want me to ask before I spend the savings, stop chasing every available woman who crosses your path ...* She was facing her suspicion that this had happened before. That this wasn't the first time he had cheated on her – but, *dear God*, it was going to be the last. She didn't know how ... she didn't know what was going to happen next ... but she was definitely not going to let this pass quietly, without a fuss. No way, no. She would make the most incredible fuss.

Once she was inside the glittering, cavernous showroom, Rosie found the biggest trolley she could and began to shop for the new, improved home that she and her three children, at least, were going to live in from now on. A home that would have luscious sheepskin rugs, metal lamps, wacky bedlinen, clever items of cunningly disguised storage – hell, two new sofas . . . kitchen chairs . . . She was laughing to herself at the names: Snorig this, Hemmlig that, Fartsor? Surely not? Fetid, Friskie . . .

Fresh new office equipment was piled in. No more writing desk chaos, she would have metal in-trays, a small pink filing cabinet – Lachlan would loathe that, she thought with satisfaction. She could split up with him if she had to, it was dawning on her. She used to run the farm all on her own, she could do it again, just as well as he did. The needy, needy small children phase of her life was coming to an end. Her boys were in school, Manda could go to nursery in the mornings. She could do it all, if she had to. Employ another full-time worker . . . or a home help . . . to let her get out there instead. She could do everything a farm worker could: drive a tractor, a combine harvester, manage a picking squad.

It would be very hard work and it would be lonely. That was the catch. Lachy was always around, had been around for years now . . . and she loved him. Comfortably. Was that so bad? He loved her too. She was sure of that. Loved her comfortably too. And he loved their children.

But that didn't mean that he wasn't a big, self-ish shit sometimes . . .

She didn't know what the answer was yet . . . but it would come.

* * *

306

Almost 7 p.m., but still Pamela stayed in the cottage, nursing the text message from Lachlan saying that he would try and come round, although he'd called off yesterday evening at the last minute. She cleaned up slowly, looking around every room, admiring her work. Not much left to do now: flooring, plumbing, tiling and it would all be finished. Then surely she and Lachlan would be finished too? It would come to a natural end. She wouldn't be around and it was all too obvious that this couldn't go on. What if his wife found out? It would be far worse, far messier than if Dave caught her out. Wouldn't it?

So why didn't she just tell Dave? End the marriage? Move on? She swirled her brushes in the smudged and cloudy jar of white spirit. That question again. What was she waiting for? Was life without Dave too frightening? Too unthinkable? If they had just been able to have children . . . that was what it came down to, she was sure. If they had had a family of their own, it would have been perfect. None of this would have happened.

Now every other solution seemed unworkable: stay together without a child, stay together and bring up someone else's child, or split up, have a child with someone else, help someone else bring up their own child. None of these was what she wanted.

But then you didn't always get what you wanted, did you? Usually you had to make the best of what you had. Wasn't that the art of living?

She heard the door and knew, with more excitement than she should feel, that at least one thing she wanted was here.

Lachlan's face appeared round the freshly painted sitting room door.

'Watch out, it's still wet,' she warned him, feeling a burst of happiness just at the sight of him.

'D'you want to come for a drive?' he said. 'Take your car, follow mine. We'll go . . .' he paused, considering: 'somewhere.'

Somewhere like the polytunnel, maybe. She couldn't lock up the cottage and get into her car quickly enough.

He drove fast, in and out of the bends, dips and twists. She had to put her foot down, grip her steering wheel tight and have faith to keep up with him. But still, hurtling through the dark, she knew that right now she would have followed his car through the gates of hell. Maybe that's exactly where she *was* following him.

After twenty minutes, they pulled up in a deserted, stony lay-by on the edge of a woodland trail that she remembered passing on the way to Ingrid and Harry's farm. She saw signposts and litter bins, but no sign of anyone about.

He stayed in his car, turned on the inside light and beckoned her over. As she got out, he swung open the passenger door, so she climbed up inside to him.

'Hello.' But what a loaded word it was. There in the background an almost explosive level of desire.

She closed the door shut behind her.

'So . . .'

'So . . .' he repeated. 'Want to play?'

He put his car in gear and drove out of the lay-by along the woodland trail for 100 metres or so before parking.

And they were on each other again. Fingers opening buttons, fumbling for zips, legs scrambling over seats, the gearstick, handbrake. Had to have him . . . had to have her . . .

Afterwards, she sat across his lap, kissed him and asked him questions. Some he answered, some he didn't.

'Ever think about going back to Australia?' she wanted to know.

'With the family?' he said, so naturally, so unembarrassed. Sitting with her wet and naked in his lap didn't interfere with chats about the family plans, apparently.

'Maybe,' he went on. 'The future isn't exactly obvious. We'll see what happens when Rosie's old man dies.'

'Why?' Pamela asked.

'He still owns the farm and she has two brothers, so it'll probably be left to the three of them. They'll all have to pay a whack of inheritance tax and we won't be able to buy her brothers out, so the farm will probably be sold. We'll have to buy somewhere much smaller and try to work our way up again.' He sighed and leaned his head back against the headrest, 'No farmer could just go out and buy a farm nowadays, you have to earn or inherit the money first. We're all just living hand to mouth on overpriced land. So, yeah, I might take them to Australia, it's not so bad over there.'

She made no reply to this, so he added: 'How are Dave's strawberries? Even he should get a light crop this year.'

'They're fine.' This was a conversation Pamela didn't want to have. She thought of Dave in and out of his fields trying one thing after another, picking weeds and insects off by hand when all else failed.

'Really?!' Lachlan sounded amused. 'He's going to have a crop?' Without waiting for an answer, he went on: 'Do you know what I think?' She wasn't sure she wanted to know. 'Harry is a friend, so I'd never tell him to his face. But organic farming is just bullshit – literally – only practised by amateurs. Only freaks want to eat tough little vegetables covered in caterpillars.'

She pulled back out of his arms.

'Farmers aren't going to turn the clock back,' he insisted. 'No-one wants that hard life, picking and weeding vegetables, keeping cattle for the dung, having to muck them out and feed them every day. No way. Farmers are like everyone else. They want to work nine to five, sit in machines, own more land, make a decent wage. And who can blame them? No-one in town wants to pay the price that it really costs to grow food in Britain when they can have cheap beans from Botswana.'

Pamela scrambled off his knees and back to the passenger seat, throwing a T-shirt over herself, surprised at the surge of anger she felt.

310

'What? Instead you think people prefer some puffed-up strawberry grown in a plastic tunnel, dusted weekly with anti-fungal agents and all kinds of crap?'

'Didn't hear you complaining about my strawberries the other night, baby,' he smirked.

Baby!

'Look, just leave Dave out of this, will you? And leave farming out of it as well.'

Because, apparently, it was OK for her to cheat on Dave, to slink around with Lachlan looking for quiet, countryside fuck venues, but it wasn't OK for Lachlan to take the piss out of Dave's noble, Green ideals. Well, just what sort of warped morality code was she operating under, exactly?

She certainly didn't need Lachlan to point out that not only was she cheating on her husband, but she was cheating with someone who stood for everything Dave was opposed to.

'I didn't think you gave an arse about any of it. What's converted you all of a sudden?' Lachlan asked.

'Maybe you,' was all the answer she gave him as she pulled on her jeans and stuffed her feet into her shoes, glad that her car was here and she could go.

Dave had eaten supper by himself after the message from his wife that she was working late at the cottages, then maybe going on for a drink in town. She hadn't said with whom. Maybe her current clients, Lachlan and Rosie, maybe Ingrid; maybe she was buying John a drink.

He didn't mind, he had a project of his own for tonight. He hadn't been able to find out nearly enough about what was going on at his neighbour's farm and why it was making his streams green. But he did know that once a month, tankers arrived at the farm for three or four evenings in a row and made a delivery. Tonight he was going to wait off road, then follow one of those tankers back.

He got his night's spying kit together: flask of tea, book to read, binoculars, boots, keys to the beaten-up old Land Rover he'd bought himself because Pamela was always away with the car now.

A small, high road wound from his farm up into the woodlands on top of the hill, where he'd discovered a reasonable vantage point over his neighbour's place. There were two diggers regularly at work on one of the largest fields close to the sheds on the farm. But always at night – under cover of darkness. It seemed very odd. He knew farmers were busy people who worked all hours, but whenever he'd driven up here in the daytime, he'd never seen the diggers active.

After forty minutes or so of waiting, close to 10 p.m., he saw the silvery sheen and heard the rumble of one of the tankers heading up towards his neighbour's land.

It took almost an hour before the vehicle had been relieved of its load, and even with the binoculars he hadn't been able to make much out. A hose had been attached to the tank but he couldn't see where it led. It had of course occurred to Dave, sitting in his Land Rover, binoculars clamped to his head, that this was all for nothing ... just his imagination ... his paranoia running wild. In a way he hoped it was, he didn't like the thought of some big problem next door that would be hard to solve.

As the tanker began to travel back down the farm road, he started the Land Rover up and drove down the hill to follow it as discreetly as he could. He hung back a good 500 yards until the tanker made it to the dual carriageway, then drove closer to see if there were any markings on it. Nothing that he recognized, but he tried to memorize the name and telephone numbers.

About three or four miles had passed before the tanker began to indicate left. Dave did likewise and let his car drop right back.

They turned and were on another small B road. He recognized it as the road he took to Harry and Ingrid's farm. Left at a fork in the road; on a bit further. He was glad of the dark, was sure the tanker driver knew another car was behind him but couldn't know it was the car that had been on his tail since the farm.

Passing a lay-by, Dave slowed down, craning his neck to take another look at what he thought he'd just seen there. Their car. No lights on, parked up, but he was sure it was the Saab. The tanker mystery would have to wait till another day. He felt a wave of panic about his wife. Where was she? Why was their car empty on this deserted road?

He pulled the Land Rover up, made a hasty three-point turn in the road, then roared back down to the lay-by where he jumped out and ran to look into the Saab. It was locked and when he bent down to peer inside everything looked normal ... maps and magazines in a pile on the driver's seat.

Dave stood up and looked helplessly around. Pitch darkness. He did a second sweep of the landscape and this time spotted another vehicle, only 100 metres or so away, parked in a small clump of trees down a farm track. A big black 4 x 4 dimly lit by the driver's light inside. It looked just like Lachlan Murray's Isuzu. A rush of bewilderment followed Dave's momentary relief at the recognition. Pamela and Lachlan? Out here? In the dark? What the hell was going on?

He reached for the binoculars that were still swinging from his neck, and with a very bad feeling raised them to his eyes.

Framed in the grainy circle in front of him was an image which would, against his will, be with him for a very long time. His wife, head thrown back, hair loose, breasts, bare white breasts framed with thin black straps, tipped up into the face of another man. His wife making love with another man. The other man, he could tell by the falling gold hair, was Lachlan.

He might have stood watching for as long as it took. He might have walked over to the Isuzu and tapped on the window. He might have waited crouched down beside her car to surprise her when she came back, but the headlamps of another car swung into view in the distance and he didn't want to be seen here, not by anyone.

He let go of the binoculars and fled to his Land Rover, ducking down behind the steering wheel while the other car passed at speed. Then he started the engine and drove off as quickly as he could, suddenly desperate to be nowhere near this . . . nowhere near her and *him*.

When Pamela returned home that night, she found Dave in the sitting room watching TV with an empty wine bottle beside him.

'You were thirsty,' she teased.

'Hot weather,' he answered, but not with his usual jokiness. In fact, he looked unusually serious. 'How was your drink?' he asked. 'Who did you go with?'

She didn't come into the room, but stayed by the door, one hand on her hip, one up on the door frame. He took in how pretty she looked: tight vest and jeans, visible rose-coloured bra straps, hair bundled up, and *so obvious to him now*, the post-coital pink flush and full lips.

'Lachlan, just business . . . there are a few glitches with the kitchen. Kitchen glitches . . . klitchen gitches . . .' Big smile for him. 'So we talked them through. Sorted it out.'

'Was Jeff in?' He wondered what lie she would offer him next.

'Oh, we didn't go there. Some hotel bar in town, that Lachlan knew. I wasn't paying very much attention.'

She gave a sniff at her armpit and an exaggerated grimace. 'Phew, I'm desperate for a bath.' Of course she was . . . Jesus Christ.

Once she'd gone upstairs, he drained the very last from his glass and set it down on the arm of the sofa. He thought he'd been giving her the space she needed before they could slowly put their marriage back together again. Now, he felt like an idiot – a stupid, cheated idiot. Would his marriage end? He had often asked himself that question, almost always assuring himself that no, somehow they would make it. But now he saw that he'd been wrong.

Chapter Twenty-seven

Lachlan's wife and even his children were out in the fields picking strawberries in the light rain that had finally arrived today, breaking three weeks of dry heat. There had been some sort of disagreement he knew nothing about and most of his Polish student workforce had upped and left. Buggered off to London or somewhere without even a day's notice. He was fucked. Fields full of berries waiting to go, rain lashing down to spoil them and contracts to meet. They *had* to be picked today. But here he was driving to the woodland trail car park to meet his lover.

Lover? *Lover??* How had this happened? He hadn't meant to do this. He really hadn't. He'd been tempted, given in and had meant it to be a one-off aberration. But had found, to his surprise, he had to go back for more. And now look at the possible consequences. Rosie, Jesus God, Rosie. If she ever found out . . . and the little people who depended on him, who were in the fields right now, picking his crop in the rain. What kind of a shit was he?

Pamela had phoned up and demanded to see him! Straight away, she'd insisted. No, it couldn't wait and it wouldn't take long. This was the day when he was going to have to call a halt to the insanity. But, sliding the Isuzu into fourth, accelerating into the straight stretch ahead, he realized he was nervous about how she would take it. Would she stop the work she was doing for them? Should he wait until she'd finished the cottages? Was she a bunny boiler? What was the best way to do this? Christ, why had he forgotten how awkwardly the other little 'flings' had ended? All so easy to kindle, so hard to put out.

Pamela was already there in her Saab, waiting for him. As soon as he drew up, she got out of the car and stood in the rain, a sweatshirt held over her head. Once he was parked, she swung open the passenger door and climbed in beside him. His eyes slid over her denim skirt and bare legs, wet with rain.

'OK,' he said, smiling, trying to remain calm, once the hellos were over, 'Why am I here?' The rain was getting heavier ... He had to get back. 'I'm very busy right now –' he didn't wait for her reply – 'The berries are ready to go ... two-thirds of my picking squad has just cleared off. It's a pretty difficult time.'

'I'm sure the great Lachlan Murray can get new pickers for his *super*-berries,' she snapped.

'Not straight away, no. And not today, when

318

the order is sitting out in the field, ready to rot in the rain, with some fuckhead of a buyer phoning me up every ten minutes to know when it's going to arrive. Every single strawberry in that field now and for the rest of the summer is under a contract that dictates how big it is, how sweet it is, how red it is, how bloody firm it is and when it gets picked.'

She'd never seen him angry before, this person she had kissed, licked, tasted, felt her way all around. He was still so unknown to her.

'You have no idea what it's like,' he continued. 'We are the very bottom of the food chain, I can tell you that. Just one mistake and the whole deal will be off. I'll be driving a lorryload of strawberries all around Norfolk trying to find anyone who'll take them off me. If the buyers don't want my berries because they've got in a job lot of rubbish from Eastern Europe, they'll just make something up. And we'll all be fucked.'

He was rubbing his forehead, eyes dark, deeply agitated. Pamela was here to tell him she didn't want to see him again, well, not in the way they'd been seeing each other lately. And suddenly she didn't want to do it, didn't want him to go.

'You've been doing this for years.' She put a hand on his arm. 'Everyone round here talks about what a big success you are.'

'Well, they've no idea how close to the wind we sail every year. If this summer doesn't go well, we're backs to the wall. And we all work very hard, all year long. Me, Rosie . . . even the kids are out picking today.'

There was a pause, a drawing in of breath, rain lashing down unchecked on the Isuzu's windscreen. Then they both began together:

'I think . . .'

'We can't . . .'

They stopped and looked at each other. She'd thought she'd manage to be so cool, so un-affected by this and now that the moment was here, she realized it was going to be harder than she'd imagined.

'I'm sorry,' he said. 'It's been great . . . but we can't do this any more, can we?'

There it was, out loud, lying bald and naked between them.

'No,' she answered.

'I'm sorry,' he said again. As if that made it any better.

'No, it's fine. It's what I was going to say.' She'd wanted very much to sound grown-up and together about this. He was only – not even an affair – a fling, a fuck, a casual thing. No head messing . . . remember?

But it still hurt.

She felt his arm around her shoulders and hoped she wouldn't cry.

'Pamela, it's OK.' She didn't detect any hint of upset in his voice. He was probably relieved.

'It's not,' she heard herself reply. 'I have no idea what's going on . . .' She was fumbling in her bag for tissues, about to run with tears. Hideous.

'Please think of a nice thing to say about me,' she asked him after blowing her nose. 'That would help.'

He passed her a box from the back seat and that made her cry even more. Because it was probably his children's box of tissues.

There was a Lachlan-length pause, she recognized now, as he tried to examine what he felt and summon up words to express it.

'You're a great girl,' he said finally. 'But we both have people better than us to get back to.'

Wow, she acknowledged, mid-sniff, the outback cowboy gets emotional. People better than us. Of course they were: Rosie and Dave, people better than them.

'Yup,' she said, wiping at the corner of her eyes. 'Well, I suppose this is goodbye then.' She held out her hand. But he ignored that, leaned over and kissed her mouth. One last taste of all the wildness she'd shared with him. The tunnel full of strawberries . . . she would remember that for ever.

He watched her car pull out onto the road and felt a little sorry, yes. But overriding that was how much he wanted to be back at the farm with his wife and children. Glancing at his phone, he saw that there was no signal. Crap.

Rosie was looking down the long row ahead of her. Still all that to do. Bloody hell. She and the two remaining Polish girls had picked almost half a field between them. Manda was finally asleep in the buggy underneath the rain cover and she had just angrily given in to Willy and Pete's nagging to go and play in the garden because they were bored.

Her sons had managed almost two whole rows between them before they'd begun to whinge and whine.

'Oh all right then,' she'd exploded at them. 'Don't you want to help Daddy? Daddy is very, very busy and he needs us to pick the strawberries for him today. They'll be too ripe if we leave it till tomorrow.'

The boys had hung their heads and scratched their wellies about in the earth. 'We'll just go for a bit. Then we'll come back and help you,' Pete had offered.

'Oh just go,' she'd said, then turned back to her row, not nearly as angry with them as she was with their father. Where the bloody hell *was* he when there was all this to do? Off to get some urgent machinery repaired, he'd said. The vague bubble of suspicion was threatening to surface and she was doing all she could to hold it down. Because when she let it come up, when she really thought about it, really worried about whether or not her husband was screwing Pamela Carr, it made her feel physically sick and she was too busy for that right now.

Too busy . . . too busy . . . She bent back down to the berries and felt the wet of tears as well as rain on her hands. She was too frightened to ask him about it; she was too frightened not to. She was terrified of the whole thing. What if he was? What if this whole elaborate picture she'd concocted in her head of her husband and that woman in the back of his car, in fields, even in the cottages she was renovating, what if it was true?? Rosie tried to comfort herself again with the thought that she was being ridiculous, she was making the whole thing up.

She tried to focus on the fruit, keep busy, busy with picking the fruit, filling the plastic punnets, working down the row. Another fifteen minutes passed, another row was finished and she started on the next.

She was way ahead of Ursula and Andrea. They'd been here for two months, so they wouldn't be sore and stiff right down the back of their legs tomorrow, but they would need years of practice to be as quick as her. Rosie was sure they would dream of picking berries in their sleep tonight. She wondered what they must make of it, two young, pale, leggy students from Gdansk. Had they even been to a farm before?

'*Mum!*' She was ripped from her thoughts by Willy bellowing for her in a way that stopped her heart.

He was flying down the length of the field, pelting towards her.

'*MU-UUUM!*' he roared again.

She stood up and shouted back: 'What is it?'

But he kept on running, until he threw himself against her legs and through a hail of tears sobbed out: 'It's Pete. Pete is dead.'

She dropped to her knees and gripped his upper arms, pulling him away from her legs: 'What are you talking about? What do you mean?' The words came out harshly because she was terrified. She had never seen Willy look so ashen.

'I hit him on the head ... by accident,' Willy wailed.

'What with?' She was gripping him too hard now, willing him to stop crying.

'A golf club, we were playing golf.'

'Jesus,' she leapt up. 'Where is he?'

'In the garden.' She began to run. Run and run, hearing the slap of her wellingtons against her shins, the sound of Willy crying and running behind her, not able to keep up.

She ran up the drive of the house, hammering heart threatening to leap right out of her throat. Already the accusations crowding in on her: she should never have let them go back to the garden on their own. She should have told them not to play golf without Daddy. She should never have let Lachlan buy golf clubs for them ... She should have ... shouldn't have ... The gravel flew out behind her boots as she ran towards the big lawn.

'Pete! Pete!' she heard herself screaming in a voice that didn't even sound like hers.

She didn't see him at first, was looking wildly round for a boy standing up, then realized the bundle of something she'd passed over in her first scan of the grass was her son.

Her legs wobbled so dangerously in the race to get to him, she almost stumbled and fell on top of him.

At first glance, she thought Willy was right.

Her son was lying on his back, eyes closed, motionless, the grey white of a stone with a dark, ominously trickling dent, *a dent* in his right temple.

'Pete, Pete . . . Petie.' She picked up his wrist and tried to find a pulse but her hands were shaking so much, she had no idea what she could feel. Then he made the smallest of groans and she saw a flicker of eyelid. Oh God, thank you God, thank you, he isn't dead. She had to get help.

Willy was up on the lawn now, still crying.

'Willy, shut up!' she shouted. 'It's OK. He's going to be OK.' She said this to try and convince herself.

Calm, calm – how the hell were you supposed to say calm at a time like this? Why didn't logical thoughts want to form in her mind? She took her phone out of her pocket and jabbed on the speed dial for Lachlan. She needed him first.

The connection took for ever, the rings were in slow motion, then the clink-clunk of the voice-mail coming on. She hung up and dialled Directories, all the time watching the smallest trickle of blood seep from her son's head. 'Put me through, yes, put me through!' she screamed at the operator.

The machine repair shop answered and didn't seem to have a clue what she was talking about.

'Lachlan Murray? In here today? No. Don't think so. Shall I ask around?'

'No, no, I haven't got time.'

She felt the hysteria rising in her. The nearest A & E was over an hour's drive away. She

NEEDED LACHLAN. She didn't have the car . . . how would they get there? She couldn't handle this by herself.

She dialled 999.

The age it took. Getting through to the ambulance service, describing the accident, giving all Pete's details, giving the farm's address, trying to explain to the *imbecile* on the other end of the phone that an ambulance would take too long, that the farm was too hard to find, that they would meet the ambulance on the way.

'No, I'm sorry, madam, we have to advise you to stay put with your child. We will find you. We'll send out an emergency crew right now.'

'Please stay calm,' this imbecile kept telling her. But Pete was about to die in the middle of the bloody countryside, an hour from any sort of help and her husband who had the car was out *shagging his mistress*.

She hung up.

She put her hand under Pete's neck and moved right in towards him. Her tears fell on his face.

She could hear footsteps. Other people were running up the drive now. Ursula and Andrea came into view. They ran onto the lawn to take a look at her child.

Ursula crouched down beside him and asked in her halting English: 'He is hit?'

'Yes,' Rosie whispered.

Ursula gently took his hand and felt for a pulse. At least she seemed to know what she was doing.

326

'He fainting,' she said. Then touching very gingerly near the dent, she added: 'Need hospital.'

'I know, I know, but we've no car. It's very far away for an ambulance. They'll get lost.' Her voice broke.

Ursula turned to Andrea and began to speak speedily in Polish.

'Farm van?' Ursula asked.

Christ, the farm van. Could they take Pete to hospital in the farm van? 'Can you drive?' she asked Ursula.

'No, Andrea,' was Ursula's answer.

Rosie did not need to wait to discuss the pros and cons. If they could even get to the dual carriageway, the service station, they could meet the ambulance there. Leaving Pete and Willy with the two girls, she ran faster than she'd ever thought she could, heart screaming, to the shed and fired up the big blue Transit, screeched into reverse, rammed it onto the road, over potholes, up the drive, gravel spraying all over the place.

They would lay Petie across the front seat, she would cradle him, try and keep his head as still as possible.

Ursula would have to stay here with Willy. No, Willy would want to come. No, Willy shouldn't . . . God, *Manda*. She hadn't even thought of Manda, still in the field in her buggy. Ursula would stay with Willy and Manda.

Andrea slid onto the driver's side of the long front bench. Very, very carefully, Rosie and

327

Ursula lifted Pete up onto the front seat so his head and shoulders were in his mother's lap. He uttered a gentle groan, which reassured and terrified Rosie in equal measure.

'The baby,' Rosie remembered to tell the girl at the last moment. 'The baby is in the field. She'll need a new nappy – some food. It's all in the house. Willy will show you. The door is open. My husband should be home soon.'

Ursula nodded reassuringly to everything, then slammed the door shut and they set off. Andrea drove an agonizingly slow and careful five miles an hour down the drive.

Rosie didn't take her eyes off the white face lying in her arms and began to pray that her boy was going to be OK.

They shook off the drive and the farm's road, then were on the long, twisting B road, which would meander for a full twenty minutes – longer at this speed – before they hit the dual carriageway.

Andrea's hands were gripped around the big, thin wheel. Occasionally she would grapple with the long gearstick, but mainly she stuck to driving in third, letting the van stutter as she slowed for corners.

The phone in Rosie's pocket began to ring. She unlocked the fingers clinging round Pete's shoulders and fished for it.

Lachlan's number was not flashing up.

'Hello,' she answered.

It was the imbecile ambulance woman. An ambulance was on its way, they were going to put the driver on the line for directions.

Rosie tried to summon calmness from somewhere. Yes, she was on the road, she tried to explain. She named the service station, the junction, the road number where she would meet them, but they didn't seem to want to understand.

'We need you to wait with the child, madam,' the driver kept repeating.

She was trying not to scream: 'You won't find the farm. Meet me at the service station. I'll be there in fifteen minutes. Meet me there.'

She had to hang up. Pete was groaning again.

In her mind she tried to argue that he was going to be fine, that small children were tough, recovered from all sorts of knocks and scrapes, but still came the panic thought, that he was going *to die*. She felt tears squeeze from the corners of her eyes.

Long minutes until they were finally approaching the main road. 'Left or right?' Andrea asked.

'Right,' Rosie told her, which meant crossing the dual carriageway and waiting in the central reservation for a break in the traffic on the other side.

They waited and waited. A small gob of vomit oozed out of Pete's mouth. Rosie saw the remains of the strawberries he must have eaten in the field. 'Now! Go now!' she urged the girl, who was obviously too frightened to pull out into the road.

The van juddered out in first and cranked

up painfully slowly through second and third.

But at last, she could see the service station and, thank God, an ambulance there in the forecourt.

She pointed it out to Andrea, unable to find the words.

Andrea slowed down and stuttered into the garage, manoeuvring the Transit right beside the ambulance. She turned off the ignition and jumped out to alert the crew.

A paramedic came to Rosie's door and popped it open.

Not even any form of greeting, his first words to her were: 'You should have waited with the boy. Head injuries should not be moved.'

This was too much. Rosie's grip tightened on her poor baby, she swallowed down the sob that was threatening to break from her now and, entirely uncharacteristically, told the ambulance man to fuck off.

There was a moment of silence, then everyone went all British and pretended it hadn't happened.

They fired questions at her as they eased Pete onto a stretcher, strapped him in, put blocks around his head and buckled them tight. An oxygen mask went over his face. He looked tiny on the six-foot stretcher. She ached at the sight of it.

'How old is he?' she was asked.

'Five . . . just five.'

She was helped out of the van and led towards the ambulance. Glancing back at Andrea, who was standing beside the van, Rosie scrabbled in the pocket of her jeans and found two pound coins, change from the cup of coffee she'd had during her Ikea spending spree.

'Here—' she held them out to the girl. 'Have some tea, then drive home. You'll be fine.' She managed to smile at Andrea and add a 'Thank you.'

Huddled under the rough grey blanket one of the crewmen had draped round her, she put her hand over Pete's and tried to be calm for him. She heard the siren and felt the vehicle pick up speed. Looking out of the darkened window, she could see they were hurtling along the outside lane. On the hard passenger's bench in the back, she found the ride surprisingly bumpy.

Head in her hands, Rosie sat in the small room they'd directed her into and wept, quietly and steadily, shoulders shaking, tears pooling in her palms. There was nothing else she could do. The medical staff had been as reassuring as they could, but Pete had been taken in for immediate exploratory surgery. They would know more once they'd 'had a look' – she couldn't stop picturing what that meant – but the doctor had told her Pete 'looked pretty good'. 'Very resilient, these little boys,' he'd added, giving her a smile. 'Try not to worry too much.'

She heard the swing door and glanced up – hoping it would at last be the doctor – but instead, her husband walked into the room. Her husband, the other reason she couldn't stop crying. Then his arms were around her, holding her tightly.

'He's going to be OK,' Lachlan told her. 'I know it. He's small but he's very tough.'

'Is the doctor coming?' she sobbed into his shoulder.

'Very soon, they said.'

And then, as if she'd just remembered, she pulled out of his arms abruptly: 'You were with her,' she accused him savagely, spitting the words out, 'I know it now. *You were with her!*'

He brought his wife back into his arms, folded her against him, said into her hair: 'It's not what you think, Rosie.'

But she slid out of his grip and back into the position she'd been in when he'd entered the room: head in hands, weeping. Lachlan sat down beside her, his hands gripped tightly together, not daring to reach for her again.

Long minutes passed, with just her sobs breaking the silence, until she stood up and began to walk around the room: 'I can't bear this!' she shouted at Lachlan. 'We have to find out what's happening.'

At last the door opened and the doctor she recognized was standing there, asking them in words which seemed to come out too slowly and yet tumble over her so that she could hardly take them in, if they were Mr and Mrs Murray. Rosie felt a rush of panic, the terror that Petie was dead. Instead, she was trying to take in the news that he 'had come off very lightly', was 'doing well', was set to 'make a full recovery'.

She heard it, she understood it, but the feeling of relief didn't come: she'd been so frightened, her body still felt rigid, tense as a spring.

'Can we see him?' was all she wanted to know.

'Of course,' the doctor told them. 'He's still out for the count, though.'

Chapter Twenty-eight

Pamela had gone to the cottage after her meeting with Lachlan, thought it would be best to try and get some more work done, take her mind off him. But, of course, it was stupid to go there, where she thought about him constantly, dripped tears as she wiped over surfaces, swept out the rooms, prepared them for the workmen due in on Monday.

It was late afternoon when she drove home, speeding down the farm's road, desperate not to bump into Lachlan or his wife, or anyone at all. In fact, the farm seemed unusually quiet. She turned the radio on, tried to find something pop and cheerful but ended up shouting with frustration at the useless reception. So, she drove in silence, nudging up past 50 on the twisty roads, realizing how well she knew them now: where she could speed up, where she had to slow for the biggest bends. She was turning local, just at the point when she was going to leave.

Because wasn't that the only option ahead now? She couldn't stay on at the farm with Dave. She'd cheated on him *twice* now. She hadn't slept with him for months, hadn't really talked to him for months. They weren't together any more. Just going through the motions. Maybe she wasn't really upset about Lachlan at all, maybe it was this very big thing ahead – splitting from Dave – that was really causing her pain.

Thirteen years of her life had been spent with this man. So much *past*, so many shared memories, like trees which had grown together, entwined, the boundaries blurred, not sure where one ended and the other began. She couldn't even pretend that this wouldn't really hurt. Big pieces of her were going to be cut off in the process of disentangling herself from him.

When she pulled up at the farmhouse, the rain had stopped and a pink and gold sunset was spreading out over the sky, all the windows of the house shining with it. She locked the car and walked to the back door. Open, as usual. Dave had fallen into the country habit: the back door at least was always open whether he was in or out.

She turned the handle on the second door and went into the kitchen. And there he was, but sitting down at the kitchen table, as if he was waiting for her. The big room was strangely still, no radio on filling the space, nothing on the hob to fuss over.

Just Dave, in a smart black polo neck she hadn't seen him wear since they moved up here, sitting at the kitchen table, looking up at her in a way that caused a wave of anxiety to break over her.

'Is anything wrong?' She was the first to speak.

'Maybe you should tell me.' She felt his eyes on her face, coolly appraising her reaction to these words.

'What do you mean?' She didn't move from the doorway, aware of the sharp thudding in her chest.

'We had an agreement, didn't we?' There was something a little strangled to this question. 'We came up here for a rest, a change . . . and to try and make our marriage work. Wasn't that the agreement?'

'Yes.' Pamela heard the falter in her own voice. He knew. *He knew.* How *the hell* did he know? Here it was, coming down the motorway at her, 90 miles per hour, head on, unavoidable, her very own emotional car crash.

'I don't think . . .' He paused, moved his shoulders up slightly as if to heave the words out . . . 'fucking the brains out of some local farmer was part of our agreement, was it?'

She had never seen him like this: so pale, so furious, but so terrifyingly controlled with it.

She took a step forward, meaning to put her hands on the back of the chair nearest to her, needing something to hold onto.

'Don't come anywhere near me, just stay right away.' He was almost shouting now. But there was something broken in his voice that was hurting her chest terribly.

He watched her fold down into the kitchen

chair and hoped she wasn't going to ask how he knew. He didn't think he could bear to tell her, say out loud that he had *seen* them. Seen her face as she ... He tried to turn from the thought.

'I'm so sorry,' she was telling him, 'I'm so sorry. I didn't want you to know anything about this . . .' That sounded so stupid, so obvious. 'I didn't want to hurt you. It's all over,' stumbled out. 'It's over between me and—' it felt too harsh to say Lachlan's name 'him. It's over. It wasn't anything—' she struggled for the words, the right words, knowing that every one of them was a slap in the face to this man, the one she had been with so long 'important.'

'Well, maybe not to you,' he said, something close to amazement in his voice. 'But it's pretty bloody important to me. My wife, sleeping with someone else and she tells me not to worry, it isn't anything important.'

'That's not what I said, *he's* not important to me. Of course all this—' she put a hand to her forehead. 'All this is very important.'

Hardly daring to look at her, he asked her all the things he thought he wanted to know. How had it started? How long had it been going on for? Was it really finished?

The pain of her words was like probing a fresh wound, excruciating, yet somehow necessary.

When he had heard all her halting answers, seen her twist her fingers, twist her hair, felt her awkwardness and pain, he asked the question which was so hard to answer.

'What do you want, Pamela? What do you want?'

The ghost of the real answer, the way she had always answered this question in the past – 'A baby' – was still there between them. But that wasn't what she said now.

'What do *you* want?' she asked instead, wondering if she would be spared being the first to suggest that maybe there was nothing else left. That it was time to call it a day.

'I'm so pissed off with you just now, I can't think straight,' was his answer. 'I need to get out of here. I don't want to see you.'

She could see how furious he was, but was still surprised when he added: 'I'm going to London for a week or two. Think things over.'

'*London?*' This wasn't what she'd imagined. Dave leaving her here. 'You can't,' she said. 'I'm going. I'm the one who's going back to London.'

'No, you are not.' He was glad he sounded as angry as he felt. 'I'm going – I'm going right now. I'm packed. Ted's meeting me off the last train.'

'T*ed?!*' This was even worse. He couldn't leave her and then go and stay with her brother. 'Ted is my brother.' As if this needed to be pointed out.

'He's also my friend.'

See? Entangled, entwined. Ending this would be more painful than either of them could imagine.

'How am I going to manage all this on my own?' she asked, wanting to shout too. But she didn't have the right; she knew what he was going to say next.

'You should have thought of that before you started your pathetic little affair.' There, he'd gone and said it.

Should have thought of this . . . he was right: she'd never thought of *this*. Of him leaving her in charge here.

He was on his feet now, searching the kitchen for keys, mobile phone, his wallet.

'I don't know what to do.' Even she didn't like the whiny sound in her voice.

'You'll work it out,' he snapped. 'Not much to do tomorrow, then I've arranged for George to come here on Monday, so you'll have to get up early to pick with him. He'll keep you right. I've written you out some instructions.' He pointed at several sheets of paper on the table.

Pick? Deliver the vegetables? No, no. This was a mistake. She couldn't be left in charge of the farm. She didn't have a clue. She'd tried to have as little to do with it as she could. He could not be doing this to her.

'You can't go,' she told him firmly. 'I won't stay here and look after your precious vegetables and bloody cows. I'm not doing it. I've got to finish the cottages.'

He turned to face her, really losing his temper now: 'You will do it. Because it has to be done and I'm not staying to do it. You came here with me,' he spat out. 'You bought this place with me. You said you wanted to do this. But ever since we've got here, you've run away from it, run away from me. Well, it's my bloody turn to run away now. See how you like it. You stay here and face the bloody facts, Pamela. Take a good look at this place and decide what you want. And even if you do want to stay here with me, I don't know yet if I'll have you. You're a nightmare right now ... I can't cope with you any more. I know it's hard, I know it's the worst thing that could have happened to us ...' She knew he wasn't talking about Lachlan, knew he was about to open up the pain they had managed to leave alone for months now. 'Not having children ...' there was a break in his voice – 'But at some point you are going to have to accept it. Really face up to it and move on. Move forward. Move somewhere – and not into some messed up "not important" affair with a married man. You prat.' He raked a hand through his hair and looked around the room: 'I thought this place was the answer. I thought you would get some peace, rest ... a change ... a chance to get better. Instead you've gone even more bonkers than you were before. I mean, what are you thinking? What is going on? I thought you were starting to settle in, but maybe you want to move back to London? Do you want a divorce? I've no idea ... You don't talk to me any more. I've no idea what's going on.'

'You've cut me out too,' was the first thing she threw back at him. 'You're working even longer hours here than you did in town. Every spare moment is spent reading about all sorts of bizarre stuff.' She went to the kitchen bookcase, hauled out a selection of titles and held them out to him: *Five Acre Independence*, *Greener Than Green* and the rest.

'You're convinced there's some plot afoot to poison your land. Don't you think you're going more than a little bit bonkers out here yourself?' she added.

He folded his arms across his chest, glancing at his wristwatch as he did so.

'Well, thank you, Pamela. That's given me plenty to think about. Now, I have to leave this enlightening conversation and catch a train.'

'You're not taking the car, are you?'

'You'll need the Land Rover,' he shot back, 'for the deliveries.'

The reality of the days ahead of her while he was away was just beginning to sink in: 'For God's sake, Dave . . .'

'Goodbye, Pamela.' He picked up the two bags she now saw had been at the back door throughout the row and headed out, managing with his elbow to slam the door shut behind him.

'Are the cows OK?' it occurred to her to shout after him.

'Yes,' he shouted back. 'They'll need water later.'

'I'm not doing this,' she shouted at him.

'You bloody are,' came back at her.

She sat at the table for a full twenty minutes, staring into space, thoughts chasing madly round her head, before it occurred to her to open a bottle of wine and cope with this in the first instance in the time-honoured tradition of drinking too much. She would phone Alex, tell her what had happened, persuade her to come up and stay.

Should she tell her parents? Ted would know ... would he tell them? She decided she didn't want to talk to her family yet, didn't want to face explaining this yet.

Halfway into her second glass of wine, she thought she'd better water the cows. She pulled on boots at the back door, but there was no need for a jacket; despite the showers earlier, it was a warm night, smelled of drying rain, reminded her of Barcelona. Ha! Maybe she should have just stayed there. Then she wouldn't be out in the dark middle of nowhere with a seriously pissed off husband, heartache for an Aussie farmer – a married-father-of-*three* Aussie farmer – and days of vegetable picking ahead of her.

But without the farm, where would she be really? Working for Sheila, probably, enduring the daily hell of life at WLI. And wasn't Norfolk beginning to grow on her just a little? Wasn't it sneaking up on her how much she liked to wake up to the quiet, the green? The drive through the countryside, instead of the rush from one side of town to the other? The friendliness offered by most of the people she'd met here? It was only the farm and the house she hadn't settled into ... part of the endlessly postponed decision about whether she was going to stay with her husband or leave him. He was right: she had run away from it, run away from him.

All this was rattling about her head as she went out to the shed to get the water buckets for Dave's three small, shy cows. They weren't even

cows, they were 'heifers', 'steers', whatever –
something that meant they were boys.

Beside a tap on the side of the wall were the
huge buckets. She filled them up and heaved
them into the back of the Land Rover. The cows
lapped at the water with pinky blue tongues.
From the safety of the other side of the fence, she
thought they looked quite sweet. But she would
double-check the fence and the gate very carefully. There was no way she was doing any cow
herding on her own while Dave was away.

Her mobile was out by her side for the rest of
the evening. She shouldn't have, of course, she
shouldn't have. But it had been too hard to resist,
so she had finally sent Lachlan a little, tiny text.

OK now. How u?

Now, she was pretending not to notice that
there had been no reply . . . not for two further
glasses of wine.

Alex was out. Pamela left brief 'call me back'
messages on both her phones and sank into the
quiet evening ahead of her.

Just as she'd decided she really should go to
bed, her phone bleeped at her and she knew at
once who it was.

Pete in hospital but going to be OK. Good u OK.
Pls txt for biz only. Lx.

She spent a long time scrolling the words up and
down the screen, taking them all in. Pete was in

hospital? She wondered what had happened to him in the hours since she'd seen Lachlan.

And then the brutally blunt 'Pls txt for biz only'. Maybe Rosie had been at his phone? Maybe she knew all about them? Pamela wondered if she would ever find out what Rosie knew. If she and Lachlan would ever be close enough to have the conversation.

Lx.

The first and, no doubt, the last time he would sign off with a kiss. She thought of their few snatched private moments – velvet skin, lean muscles, arms clasped round her, Lachlan moving inside her. Gone. Leading to nothing. Wild slices of time they might both think about now and again, otherwise, absolutely no proof that anything had happened at all ... Well, except that her husband had somehow found out ... might divorce her for this.

Chapter Twenty-nine

All through the first night Pete spent in hospital, Rosie had stayed by his bed and tried to keep awake so that she would be there when he came round. Over and over again she imagined the TV perfect moment when she would see the first flutter of his eyelashes, when he would open his eyes and say, 'Mummy.' But when Pete did wake up, she had finally fallen into a doze and was roused by the sound of him being sick. Never had she been so glad to see child-puke.

'Feel sick,' he'd announced and promptly thrown up all over the bed again.

In the days that followed, it was obvious that Pete was going to make a complete recovery and Rosie could feel at least one great knot of tension inside her gradually loosening. But she stayed on at the hospital for the three days and nights of scanty sleep it took before they would let Pete come home.

She wanted to be with her little boy. But also,

she didn't want to be at home, facing Lachlan, until she was ready. She nursed her fury for him. In the grey hours of the night in the chair beside Pete's bed, she tried to cope with the pain of his betrayal, and wondered where she was to go from here.

Lachlan came at visiting time without the other children, spoke mainly to Pete, made nothing but small talk to his wife because this wasn't the place to have the blow-up with bells on that they both knew was coming.

When Pete came home, they drove back from the hospital in the Isuzu, all five of them together: Lachlan, Rosie and their three children, the nurses smiling at them, looking to outsiders like such a happy family.

Back at home, Willy and Manda were touchingly sweet to their brother. Pete, drained by the excitement of the journey and his return, was ordered to lie and rest under a blanket on the sofa. There, Willy triumphantly brought him the golf club which had caused the damage.

'Here, you can keep this,' he told Pete. 'This is the club I hit you with – by mistake,' he added quickly. 'Look, I think that brown stuff is your blood.'

They both spent some time examining it with fascination, scraping out the grooves on the head, trying to decide what was dirt and what was blood. Finally, Pete tucked it in under the cover beside him.

Manda, sensing that the occasion required

346

gift-giving, got her favourite dog out from her cot and trailed it down the stairs for Pete to tuck in beside him. 'Dwog,' she told her brother, trailing drool onto his chest, one of her cheeks a hot red as back teeth made a painful breakthrough. Then she clambered back onto Rosie's knee, overjoyed to have her mother back, determined not to let this woman out of her sight ever again.

Lachlan offered to make supper and all evening, while the children were awake, their parents were polite, almost unusually civil to each other. Rosie watched him smiling and joking with his children and wondered if he had any idea how angry she was with him. Just wait, she thought, just wait! She had been suspicious in the past, but this was the first time she *knew*. And she was determined to make sure that it was never, ever going to happen to her again.

They put the children to bed early and the sight of the three of them cuddled up in their beds – Willy protesting through yawns that he wasn't tired – took some of her anger away. They were all there, safe and sound: Pete with a fresh dressing over his stitches, almost asleep already, so happy to be back home.

Lachlan put an arm round her waist as they left the room and squeezed, felt it too, the relief that they were all here . . . all OK now.

'I've got stuff to do upstairs,' she told him in the corridor outside the children's room.

'I'll do the kitchen then come up and help you,' he offered. She nodded in reply but was seething again. Oh, he would come and help, would he?

As if a sudden interest in domestic chores could redeem him.

When he came up to the bedroom to join her, she was folding washing on the bed and he picked some of the clothes up and began to help, annoying her with his clumsy, botched attempts. His things were all odd shapes which wouldn't fit into their piles in the drawer now.

'I've just looked in on them,' he told her. 'They're all asleep. All fine.'

She didn't make much of an answer to this, wondering what he might try to talk about next.

He chose Pete, repeated what they both knew about his recovery and the doctors' instructions for his care. Then he moved on to the picking squad and how he'd managed to find some replacement foreign students.

'OK,' she interrupted him finally, feeling the surge of adrenalin hit her veins, 'I don't want to listen to any more of this. It doesn't matter what you try to talk about . . . I'm not going to forget what's happened.'

He made no reply to this, just leaned back on the bed.

She remained standing, heart hammering – too bad – she was going to get it all off her chest. She was going to say all the things she wanted to.

'How long have you been seeing her?' she demanded first of all. 'And don't even think about lying to me.'

'For a few weeks, just now and then . . .' There wasn't much he could do to soften this

348

blow. 'It's over now, Rosie. Totally over. I'm sorry.'

'Well, I'm not having this.'

For a moment, he thought she was going to cry, but then saw her blink, swallow and cross her arms. 'I'm not having this,' she repeated. 'And you know what, I'm beginning to think you've done this before, haven't you?'

He shook his head, not trusting himself to speak, frightened a denial would just give more away. But she took the shaking head and silence as an admission of guilt.

'And with such a townie,' she added, *beyond* furious with every single aspect of what he'd done, even that. 'With some dressed-up, high-heeled townie. I didn't even think she was your type.'

He shook his head again and made no reply.

'Well, I've obviously been wrong all these years. I should have worn skirts, low-cut tops. Maybe then, you'd have been faithful to me.'

'Rosie, please, stop this. You're way over the top. It was a mistake. A big mistake. It really didn't mean anything.'

She couldn't believe what she was hearing. There would be no big apology, he wasn't pleading with her to take him back, the way she'd imagined. He was actually daring to get angry with her, suggesting that somehow she was making too much fuss. Ha! He hadn't even begun to understand what a fuss she was going to make.

'It didn't mean anything?' she spat back at

him.'Well, what a big stupid arse you are. You would end our marriage over nothing, would you? For nothing?'

She had his full attention now.

'Because that's what's going to happen, Lachlan. I'm not staying married to some pompous shit who thinks he can screw around and get away with it. How stupid do you think I am?'

Her fear was falling away from her, she could hear all her rehearsed words spilling out . . . and then some. She would let him know just how this felt.

'You have to go. *Now. Tonight.* I've packed your bags for you.'

To his astonishment, she walked round to his side of the bed and dumped a suitcase and a bulging holdall at his feet.

'You can come back for your other things later on, but that should do for now,' she told him.

'What are you doing?' he asked her. 'I don't want to move out.'

'Oh sorry,' she fired back. 'Did you think you could stay? Did you think I wouldn't mind? "Don't worry, it's all over, let's pretend it didn't happen"? You haven't even had the sense to apologize properly. Stupid, stupid man.'

'I'm sorry,' he said, but it sounded as if it was coming through gritted teeth.

'No,' she kicked his holdall towards the bedroom door. 'You're going. And you know what: you're sacked. I'm sacking you. I'm the legal executor of this farm and you're not my manager any more. So take your bags and get out of my life. Go on, you can go back to Adelaide for all I care. I mean it. I really mean it.'

He couldn't believe what he was hearing. He had never seen her like this: hands on hips, cheeks red, eyes flashing, roaring at him.

'What are you talking about?' he countered. 'What about the children?' Of course he was aware that as her husband, their father, he must have some rights, but didn't dare to mention them right now. Not with her in this nuclear rage.

'The children?! It wasn't them you were thinking of on your little secret meetings with her, was it?' she thundered back at him. 'I hold all the cards here. You should have thought of that too. It's my father's farm, my father's house, it's me you work for. I'll get custody of the children . . . You should have thought of all this.'

Before he could make any reply, she added: 'I've taken money out of the savings account so I can start doing up this hole of a house, no matter what you think. And the rest of it is frozen, so you can't disappear with it. I've spoken to Alan.'

Rosie had already spoken to their solicitor?! When? From the hospital? Lachlan was stunned. For the very first time in his married life, it was occurring to him that he had taken Rosie for granted, taken everything for granted. Always thought she would be here to come back to, that she would never dare go it alone. Now, he was seriously beginning to wonder if he was wrong as the whirlwind of a cheated wife hit him with terrifying force.

'Rosie, I don't want to leave you,' he tried.

'We'll talk about this. But not tonight. You're very tired. You've been in the hospital for days . . . it's been hell.'

'Don't talk to me about what's been hell,' she threw back and he heard the break in her voice, the crack of pain in the anger. Shit.

'You can go to the cottage,' Rosie told him, as if she was awarding a big concession. 'The one that isn't finished yet. You can sit in there and think about her day and night. But don't you *dare* even consider seeing her there again. *On my land!*' This barked out with the ferocity of a landowner staring down the barrels of a shotgun.

'I'm not going anywhere,' he said, still sitting, legs up, across their bed. 'This is crazy. We are both going to get some sleep and talk about this in the morning.'

Rosie went out of the room without another word and he listened to her footsteps heading down the stairs, along the lino towards the kitchen, but then the distinctive drawn-out creak of the office door being swung open and shut.

Several long minutes passed, then came the creak of the door again and the footsteps returning.

Why had she gone into the office? he wondered.

Her footsteps were near the top of the stairs, turning towards the bedroom, as he guessed – with a jolt of shock – what she might have got down from the carefully locked box on top of the big wood and glass bookcase in the office.

'Get out,' Rosie commanded, walking into the

352

room and levelling her father's antique, but nevertheless extremely accurate, double-barrelled 12-bore Holland & Holland shotgun at her husband.

Fuck!!

'Whoa, Rosie.' Lachlan rolled straight off the other side of the bed and stood up to face her, just five and a half feet of king-sized marital mattress between them. Her finger was on the fucking trigger! The visible shake in her hands was terrifying. The bloody thing could go off without her even trying.

'Never, ever tell her that I knew about the two of you,' Rosie was saying from behind the gun. He was shaking his head vehemently. 'I don't ever want her sympathy ... And anyway, this isn't about her. This is about us.'

He was nodding now: 'Rosie, baby, put the gun down, OK. You're very tired, you're very upset.'

'Upset!' she shouted back at him.

'And you have every right to be.' His eyes fixed on her trembling trigger finger, he added: 'Hon, I love you. I want to be here with you and our kids. I don't want to be in the cottage, I don't want to be anywhere else. Just here with you.'

Funny, she was thinking, how it took a shotgun to inspire Lachlan to romantic declarations.

'Get out,' she repeated.

'Rosie ...' he was daring to come round from the bed towards her. 'Put the gun down, baby, this isn't the outback. You can't chase me out of our home with a gun.'

'Ha! I'll say you were going to beat me up. Me, the cheated wife, with the three little children. You, the ranch hand who married me for the inheritance, then went out and put it about. Who do you think the jury's going to have sympathy for?' She was still shouting but starting to cry too. 'I should just fire away.'

She was insane. She had gone nuts. No farmhouse anywhere in the world should keep a gun, even locked in a gunbox. Look at her! She was a wronged woman armed with a double-barrelled gun.

'Did you marry me for the farm?' she demanded now, tears streaming down her face.

'Of course not.' The gun was level with his chest, focusing his thoughts remarkably. 'I love you. I've loved you since the moment I met you.'

'Take your bags,' was her response.

'Steady, baby,' he said in the flat, neutral voice he'd learned, way back, to use on nervy horses, calving cows. 'I'm going. OK? Point the gun at the floor now. You don't need to put it down, just point it at the floor. We don't want an accident.'

'It won't be an accident, I can tell you that. I am so angry with you. So angry. You have no idea.'

He was beginning to get the idea.

'I'm going to pick up my bags and walk to the front door.' He was moving slowly, using the calm, steady voice. 'I'll get the key down for the cottage and my coat, then I'm going. I won't come back tonight, I promise. So once I'm out, put the gun away. Properly. In the box. We can't have the kids coming across it . . . or coming across you like this.'

His words seemed to sober her a little. She lowered the gun, moved her finger away from the trigger, he saw.

'Are you going to be OK?' he asked, all of a sudden wondering if it was a good idea to leave her here like this.

'I'll be fine,' she said. 'Once you've gone.' The heat seemed to have gone out of her a little.

He picked up the things he needed and let himself out as quickly as he could.

At the sound of the front door closing, she began to walk down the stairs towards the office. She heard the car start up. He was driving down to the cottage, maybe just to let her know. He was definitely going.

As the engine noise moved away, she sat down at her father's desk and began to dismantle his gun, unloading the cartridges and putting them back in the box. Because it had been loaded, maybe that had been a reckless touch. But it had worked very well.

She began to shake first with tears and then with laughter. She had frightened the life out of him and he had deserved every moment of it. But still, poor Lachlan! He'd had to cope with several very big frights in the past week: his wife finding him out, his son seriously injured while he was with his lover, her threatening him with a gun. Poor, poor Lachlan! She almost felt sorry for him. She definitely felt amused. Oh God! And the worst thing – she was almost certain that she still loved him. Wondered where she would find the strength to carry out all the things she'd threatened.

She ran the soft felt cloth over the gun and thought of her dad. Her on the back of her big horse for the first time: Blaze, prancing, twitching and nervous, Rosie not much better because he seemed so much bigger than her pony. Her father giving her a leg up, the calm in his voice as he patted the horse. Just like the voice Lachlan had used on her.

'Don't worry –' her dad with his hand on the reins – 'he's more frightened than you. You just let him know who's boss, girl. But be gentle. Let him know gently.'

Her Dad teaching her how to use this gun. Lining up tin cans on top of a stack of bales, explaining how she would have to move her shoulder with each shot. The first time, it had sprung back and kicked her hard. But she wanted to be brave for him. Not let him see how much it had hurt. Wanted to be like her big brother Ewan, so she'd gritted her teeth and pulled the trigger again. Blam! Cans still there, bits of straw flying. Bloody gun kicking her again. She'd reloaded and tried over and over until the squeeze-trigger-shoulder-twist-and-roll move became smooth and practised.

She was a grown-up, she told herself, closing the polished walnut lid on the gun, turning the brass key in the lock. She had three small children to consider. She had to keep it together. If she was to take Lachlan back, he would have to be very, very sorry and she would have to be sure this wasn't going to happen again. Her eyes were blurred with tears and tiredness; she had spent the best part of four days awake, terrified for her son, tormented by her husband. Lachlan was right about one thing – she had to get some sleep. Maybe none of this would seem so bad in the morning.

And anyway, she had to put a wash on. Life could spin off into all kinds of dramas, roller-coasters, tears and tantrums, but still the housework had to be done.

Chapter Thirty

Pamela was getting set to pull out of the farm road in the Land Rover. It was only the fourth time she'd driven it and it felt like an old banger: grinding gears, a stiff steering wheel, unyielding pedals. Bolt upright in the driver's seat, she was concentrating hard on the drive.

Left, right . . . no-one about, she pulled out and ground her way up into third and then with a diesely roar into fourth. Still the thing was only moving at 35 m.p.h.

She was three days into looking after the farm, and to her surprise, it wasn't so bad. It really wasn't. In fact, creeping up over her was the suspicion that she was quite enjoying it.

She liked the early sunny mornings, the sparkle of sunlight and dew on the thousands of tiny cobwebs all over the vegetable plants, chatting amiably with George about what he'd seen on telly last night, as they crawled through fleece and netting to get to the crop, watering the three silly cows, delivering the baskets of veg everywhere.

She had even caught herself whistling. *Whistling?!*

A glance in the rearview mirror and she could see a black 4 x 4 in the distance, coming up behind her, weaving in and out of the landscape's dips, turns and hills.

As it came closer she saw that it was a big farm Isuzu, just like Lachlan's, and for a moment she had the flutter that maybe it was him, wanting to see her again . . . wanting to tell her . . . *oh what, exactly?*

Then she saw that it was Lachlan's Isuzu, coming up fast behind her, closing the gap, driving right up, too fast. Pamela accelerated, worried now that Lachlan was about to crash into her car. What was going on?

The Isuzu was right behind her, bumper to bumper, and its horn began to blast. What was this?

She put her foot down harder, scanned the mirror for some clue and realized that it wasn't Lachlan at the wheel, it was his wife, waving at her, blasting the horn, gunning the Isuzu down the narrow road. Oh hell! She couldn't slow down for this woman, the Isuzu was too close behind her, they would crash unless Pamela sped up and got out of her way. She pressed further down, knowing this road was too twisty to do fast, and that anyway, her clapped-out Land Rover was no match for Rosie's car.

The veg was sliding around in the back now,

slipping from side to side at the corners. Christ! Here was the sharp left, her right shoulder slapped against the window and she held on, feeling her muscles strain against the steering wheel.

What the hell did Rosie want to do? Run her off the road? She turned and looked through the back window and saw Rosie, unsmiling determination across her face. Maybe that was her plan – she was going to nudge Pamela off the road . . . She'd be found in a burning shell at the bottom of a cliff. *Don't be ridiculous!* She was not joining in with this. There were no cliffs on this road: the worst Rosie could do was run her through a fence and into a field. On the next stretch of open road, Pamela indicated that she was turning left into an open gate and began to slow the Land Rover down. She braced herself for the smack of the Isuzu into her rear, but it didn't come, Rosie must have seen what she was trying to do and braked.

Pamela parked 10 metres or so into the field and switched her engine off. She did not have a good feeling about this. The Isuzu was banked up on a verge, engine still running, and here was Rosie jumping out, stomping over in her direction. Angry, angry face. Arms crossed, heading towards her.

Pamela couldn't decide whether or not to get out of her car. There was a sense of safety in staying in the cab, she could even turn the key, have the engine running for a quick escape. But she had a horrible mental picture of Rosie opening the door and dragging her out by the hair. Maybe she should get out of her car herself . . . with some dignity.

'Rosie, hello,' Pamela tried as an opening gambit, deciding that was more civil than 'Rosie, are you trying to kill me, you stupid cow?'

Rosie began to shout at her, which came as a surprise, although Pamela now suspected that this woman knew she'd been sleeping with her husband. As Rosie got closer, her words began to make more sense and Pamela realized Rosie wasn't screaming about her and Lachlan – or anything related to that.

She was ranting about the cottages.

'And why the bloody hell aren't they finished yet? I thought we had an agreement. A time frame. You're totally behind. We've got people booked into the big one in two weeks' time. And the sisal stuff? Who OKed sisal for the floors?'

Pamela had dealt with all kinds of client complaints in the past, but being bawled out in the middle of a field by the wife of her lover? This was bizarrely new.

Rosie was almost up beside Pamela now. She saw with surprise that Pamela wasn't really as dazzling as she'd built up in her head. That she wasn't wearing high-heeled boots with her tits out, the way she'd imagined. Pamela was looking confused and even a little frightened, in the kind of jeans-and-T-shirt outfit that Rosie herself had on.

She was shouting nonsense. Even she knew that. She was shouting none of the things she really wanted to shout.

'It can't be cleaned,' she was saying. 'Haven't you thought about that? How will we deal with red wine stains? People who bring pets?' Raging about nothing, when really she wanted to shout: *He bought new pants to wear for you! In nine years of marriage, he's never bought new pants to wear for me. It's so unfair! He was with you when our son got hit. Do you know that? He was with you when I was in the ambulance with Pete.*

Instead, she was spouting all sorts of stuff about sisal, carpet tiles and linoleum.

'It has to be washable. Has to be. I'm not budging on that,' Rosie heard herself say.

'Well, I'm sure the order can be cancelled. We could take a look at the floorboards, see if they could be cleaned up.' Pamela sounded calm and professional, which annoyed Rosie even more.

'Who thought sisal would be a good idea?' she fumed.

'I OKed it with Lachlan.' Pamela winced at his name.

'You OKed it with Lachlan!' Rosie had a new head of rage. Almost incoherent, she was thinking only *Was that during one of your little trysts? In MY cottage? In OUR car, maybe?* – wanting to slap this woman in front of her. Hands gripping the tops of her crossed arms to stop herself.

'Lachlan is not in charge of everything. I have a say in this too,' Rosie managed. 'The cottages belong to my dad. Can't you understand? This is not all about Lachlan.'

Although Pamela knew now that it was *all* about Lachlan, knew that Rosie knew. Flooring was an essential element in any room, one of the defining factors, but even so, in over a decade of decorating she'd never seen anyone get as murderously upset as this about it.

'Just when are you planning to finish?' Rosie demanded.

'The kitchen and bathroom go in next week. We'll be ready for the rental in two weeks' time. I'll cancel the sisal and we'll get something else in. It can be sorted, I want you to be happy with the end result.' She risked a smile.

Both women were now desperate for this conversation to be over. They'd had some kind of madly distorted picture of each other in their minds lately. But Pamela saw now that Rosie was still, bar the shouting, a nice person, much prettier than she'd remembered. *Much better than us*, as Lachlan had said. Rosie, for the first time, got a sense of Pamela's insecurity and maybe her loneliness out here, saw how normal she was. She had dirt under her short nails . . . hardly the painted harlot, the urban sophisticate she'd imagined.

'I'll be at the big cottage on Monday afternoon. Why don't you come round and we'll talk about the floors? I'll bring samples, photos, that kind of thing,' Pamela was soothing.

'Yes . . . that's fine.'

For a moment, Rosie hesitated, as if she was about to say something else. Pamela realized how much she didn't want Rosie to say anything,

363

to indicate that she knew. Nothing would ever recover if Rosie said something now.

'I'll see you on Monday,' Pamela said, filling the space, wanting to move on to the goodbyes.

'Yes. See you then.'

And Rosie turned and walked towards her Isuzu, as if it was quite the most normal thing in the world to drive your husband's lover off the road and shout at her about decorating before making an appointment to see her again.

'Am I glad to see you! You have no idea!' Pamela, flinging her arms around Alex who'd stumbled off the 9 p.m., dazed with the boredom of hours on the train after a busy day's work.

'So, quite a lot going on in your life then?' Alex hoisted her bag over her shoulder and put an arm though her friend's.

'Oh, just the usual,' Pamela tried to joke about it. 'Me and secret lover have split up, my husband's found out and left me . . . the secret lover's wife is stalking me in her 4 x 4 . . . It's just another day in the sex-free countryside.'

They climbed into the Land Rover and Pamela headed it in the direction of the pub. 'No booze left in the house,' she explained.

'That bad, huh?' Alex asked.

'No . . . no, I haven't been drinking too much . . . not really, I just haven't got any left, because . . . with something between a laugh and a sob, 'Dave buys the wine.'

'How are you doing?' Alex wanted to know.

'I'm totally bonkers,' was Pamela's reply. 'No

idea what is going to happen next. Tell you one thing though, it's taken my mind off babies. I haven't noticed a pregnant woman for weeks, I've moved right out of the nursery decorating schemes in my head, I haven't thought about my fantasy baby for a long time. That is something. Really something.'

'OK, well let's accentuate the positive. Woman with life in meltdown forgets other worries . . . Do you think you and Dave are really going to split up?'

'Looks like it.'

Alex was filled in with the full details of Dave's departure.

'Will you have to sell the farm?' she asked after she had listened to it all.

'I suppose so. I don't know . . . We're not exactly talking at the moment. We haven't spoken since he left – so that's a week now. He must be absolutely frantic to know how I'm getting on . . . whether I've messed up all his orders yet . . . killed the cows. I can't believe he hasn't phoned . . . you know, about the farm at least.'

'How have you been getting on with that?' Alex asked.

'Quite well!' Pamela turned to give her a smile. 'Which is a surprise. And you know what?' her voice dropped to a mock whisper. 'I quite like it.'

'So the London sophisticate has at last gone native,' Alex threw in. 'Would you stay up here, you know, on your own?' She hesitated to use the word 'divorce', it was far too soon.

'I don't know.'

'Time to think about all that.'

'Hmmm.'

Walking into the pub, neither woman could ignore the ruffle they were causing. All ten or so heads were turned in their direction and blatant staring was going on.

Alex rather proudly thought it was because she looked so London: spiky red hair, her finest pair of vintage NHS men's glasses, bright pink lipstick. Pamela suspected the entire town knew about her and Lachlan. Had Rosie taken out an ad in the local paper or, worse, let someone in the Hacienda know?

'Evening, ladies,' Jeff boomed at them from the bar.

'Yikes,' Alex said under her breath. This was a bit too much like gatecrashing a party.

Pamela had barely got the drinks order out before Jeff wanted to know: 'So what do you think about Olive, then?'

Oh for God's sake, he was obsessed. Why did he want to talk about her poor old neighbour again?

'What do you mean?' Pamela didn't make this sound very friendly.

'Haven't you heard?' He was positively licking his lips in anticipation. 'You won't have seen her for a few days, then.'

'No.' Pamela had been up at the house just two days ago, but for the third visit in a row, Olive hadn't come to the door to speak to her, so she'd just left the mail in the lobby. She hadn't given it much thought. Olive was fickle with her friendliness. Some days she stayed indoors, didn't even say hello, on other days she wanted to talk about all sorts of things and had even, just the once, asked Pamela in and given her a cup of tea in the most gloomily pristine living room Pamela had ever experienced. She'd been frightened to sit down and crease the sofa cushions.

'Well now . . .' Jeff, leaning heavily on an elbow, was settling in for the long haul, even though Pamela didn't want to sit up at the bar. She wanted a quiet table with her friend to herself, but there didn't seem to be any choice. Both women dutifully pulled up an imitation tapestry barstool and listened.

'She's upped and left. Packed her bags, note on the table for Fraser telling him she'd stayed to bring up the boys and now that the youngest was old enough, she was off . . . said she didn't care for him any more, didn't know if she ever had much . . . and she was tired of staring at the same old hilltop view, so she was off to London—' at this he nodded in Pamela's direction. 'Seems she'd been talking to you,' he added.

'No . . . no.' Pamela took a swig from her bottle of beer, slightly panicked. Another marriage crisis could not be pinned on her, definitely not. 'Nothing to do with me,' she said. 'I can't even remember us talking about London much.' Although she did now, with a lurch, remember Olive asking her if she'd had a cleaner in London and how much did cleaners cost there.

'And . . .' Jeff's beery breath washing over them both . . . 'turns out she had an investment account. Been putting some of the housekeeping away every week and she left with plenty of money in her pocket.'

Grubby old sozzled Simon, sitting beside Pamela, whistled for effect.

'Well, that'll only last a couple of weeks or so in London,' Alex chimed in, not sure she'd ever had so much fun in a pub before.

'You from London?' Simon asked, leaning across to her.

'Yes,' Alex ventured.

'Terrible place, isn't it?' Simon replied, certain he would get her agreement on this.

'Er . . . no. That's why I live there.'

'Oh, it's not for me . . . no, no, no. When I was in the army . . .'

'Well, it's obviously the place for Olive,' Jeff mercifully cut across what might have been a long and painful reminiscence.

'Well, well,' was Pamela's measured response. 'Where's she going to live?'

'No-one knows. She said in her note she would look for a place and work as a cleaner. "I've done it all my life, be nice to get paid for it," that's what she wrote. Fraser is devastated,' Jeff added. 'Been in here almost every night with his son for supper. Doesn't have the first clue how to look after the two of them.'

'Bout time he learned, then,' came a voice from one of the tables.

This seemed to throw the debate open to the floor and opinions were tossed about. Most quite admiring of Olive's dramatic action.

'Fraser was always a boring old git.'

'She's well rid of him.'

'Good for Olive. Who wants to look at the same miserable old face for the rest of their days?'

Chairs were turned and pulled closer at this.

'Well, that's the thing about staying with the same person for life.' This from the man Pamela knew as Al, who was almost always in with his wife, but not tonight. 'It can be very good or very bad. When I see Jane's face,' he went on, 'I see her the way she was when we married twenty-seven years ago. Just beautiful. When I look at another woman her age, I just see an old woman.'

The room was a little hushed for a moment with the romance of this. Pamela and Alex exchanged a look.

'We should go,' Alex said, draining the last of her beer. 'We have lots to talk about.'

Once they were outside in the car park, Alex teased her: 'You're terrible. You're causing havoc out here.'

'Oh for goodness sake, Olive can't be my fault. No way. If they were miserable together, of course she should have left – probably years ago. Good luck to her.' She thought of the sitting room. 'She'll be an excellent cleaner. And who knows? Maybe she'll finally go to art school . . . get back in touch with her – alleged – inner lesbian! Go, Olive!'

'And there won't be any staying up late tonight,' Pamela warned her friend, once the Land Rover was back on the road again. 'We're up early in the morning to pick vegetables.'

'Come and visit me in my rural idyll, you say – actually I've just been brought here as cheap labour.'

'I found Dave's farm diary,' Pamela confessed.

'Have you been reading it?' Alex asked, then added, 'Why am I asking? Obviously, you've been reading it . . . or you wouldn't be mentioning it with such a guilty look on your face, would you?'

'Yes . . . but it's not what you think, it's not that kind of diary.' Although there had been one entry she wasn't going to tell Alex about. 'It's about what's planted where and when and all that, but there are also pages of notes about the farm next door to ours. He's worried we're being polluted by it and he's been out at night logging the comings and goings of tankers on the road.'

That was how he'd found out about her:

9.45 p.m. Tanker left Bridge Farm, decided to follow. Three miles or so up dual carriageway west, turn off to H&I's farm. Didn't follow tanker to final destination because saw our car.

All was clear from those words. Her husband had seen the Saab, had almost certainly pulled up and seen her together with Lachlan. The thought sent a cold shiver down her spine, gave her a pain in her chest.

'What kind of tankers?' Alex wanted to know.

'I don't know, I'm not sure he ever got close enough to find out.'

'Maybe we should go up there and take a little look around,' Alex suggested.

'I don't know about that.'

'Oh, why not? We could go up tonight, poke about in the dark a bit, hope no-one sees us. What's the worst that could happen?'

'We could get shot!' Pamela pointed out.

'No! We'll just pretend we're silly Londoners who've got lost – or we'll say we're from the telly, location scouting for "How Clean Is Your Farm?"' They both laughed at this.

'All right, all right,' Pamela agreed. 'Just a little look though, not that I have any idea what we're supposed to be looking for.'

Chapter Thirty-one

After stopping at the farmhouse to park the Land Rover and change into boots, they walked up the road to Bridge Farm in the dark. Pamela had a torch in her pocket but they'd decided not to use it until absolutely necessary and now that their eyes were adjusting, it didn't seem too hard.

Pamela knew she would never have dared to do this on her own: tall black trees looming over them, whooshing in the light wind ... freaking her out.

'If anything darts out at us – you know, a bird or rabbit or something – I'm going to faint,' she confided in a loud whisper.

'Don't be stupid. We'll be fine.'

They tramped on, hands in pockets, chins down. As they came nearer to the farm, they saw lights on in the farmhouse but there was no sign of tankers, deliveries or any other kind of activity going on outside.

'If we cut in through this field, we can skirt

round the back of the house and get to the other side of those big sheds. Have a good old poke about behind them,' was Alex's suggestion.

'Right.' Pamela wasn't exactly brimful of enthusiasm at this. She was wearing wellies and a light anorak but still . . . a big, unknown field . . . in the pitch dark.

'C'mon then.' Alex pulled her by the arm and plunged them both through the open gate and into a field which felt soft and boggy underfoot, clods of earth sticking to their boots, weighing them down.

As soon as they were 20 metres or so in, they began to notice the smell – rotting, manure-y. The kind of smell that caught in the back of your throat and didn't budge, getting stronger and stronger.

'God, what died?' Alex said, wading on through the mud, an arm over her nose and mouth.

'It's getting worse, Alex, I don't like this at all.'

'Neither do I, but we've got this far . . .'

There was the outline of a parked digger, left overnight in the field, not far away from them. They both felt that whatever was causing the stink must be very close now. Pamela was straining her eyes to see what they were walking through. It didn't feel right, it was too lumpy and uneven, with unyielding bits. It didn't feel like earth, but in the blackness she couldn't make it out. She hated the fact that she was scared. What a wuss. If they ran into a cow now, that would probably finish her off.

'Shite!' With a surprised cry and squelching, squooshing sound, Alex fell down. A pained 'Owww. Bugger' followed. 'Don't come over here,' she said next, still wincing. 'The ground is really boggy, I'm up to my knees in it and I've hit something really sharp.'

'Bloody hell.' Pamela, fumbling in her pocket for the torch, didn't care who caught them now. Alex needed to see properly.

'Oh arse, I'm stuck,' Alex said. 'And I'm bleeding. What is this stuff?'

Pamela switched on the beam and directed it at her friend. The pale shaft of light revealed an extremely unpleasant sight.

They were in a field littered with shredded chicken corpses. Not very well shredded either – there were visible legs, wings, heads with eyes and beaks, claws and rotting bits of breast lying out on the open earth. Swinging the torch about, Pamela could see they were close to the edge of a deep hole which had been gouged out of the earth by the digger.

Stepping closer to it, she shone her light in and looked down. It was about 10 feet deep and filled with far more chicken bodies.

'Oh God!' was her response, 'We're in a chicken dump.'

Alex, struggling to get up out of the mud, added grimly: 'Chicken Armageddon, more like.'

Pamela turned towards her, wanting to help, but Alex warned her off. 'Don't worry, I'm getting there, you don't want to get stuck in this as well.'

'Where are you hurt?' Pamela asked as Alex made it over to her.

'Here—' she held up her forearm, where a small puncture wound was bleeding, blood trickling down to her elbow. 'I've been attacked by a dead chicken.'

Pamela couldn't laugh at this. It was too horrible.

'Let's go and look in the sheds.' Alex was undeterred, up for the full adventure now.

'I just want to get out of here,' Pamela told her.

'Chicken!' Alex said, which did make them laugh. 'Come on.'

They kept the torch on and waded through the field, giving the pit a wide berth and scrabbling over two fences to get to the back of the enormous grey sheds.

The lights were on inside the sheds, but it was quiet and they were sure there wasn't anyone around. The problem was how to look into these buildings. There were no windows, just ventilation grilles which began well above head height.

'Do you think you could give me a leg up? If you did it at the corner there, I could hold onto the drainpipe and maybe climb up and look in through that grille.' Alex was turning out to be just the kind of reckless adventurer Pamela really didn't want to have on her hands right now.

But reluctantly, she went to the corner, made her hands into a stirrup for Alex's slimy, muddy boot and boosted her up the drainpipe, then stood underneath so she could push Alex's legs up a bit further.

There was a moment of scuffling when mud and dirt rained down on Pamela's head and then she could see that Alex had managed to press her face against the grille.

She stayed there for a minute or two, then let herself fall back down to the ground.

'OK, you have to see this. Come on—' and Alex was bending down, offering Pamela her gripped hands as a step up.

'Oh hell,' Pamela sighed, but put her boot into her friend's hands. In a very ungainly struggle, which included stepping on Alex's head, Pamela clambered up, fearing the drainpipe was going to come loose on her. But finally she managed to get her face to the small holes punched into the shed's metal wall.

It took her eyes a moment to adjust and work out what she was looking at. Under long strip lights, the flesh-coloured floor of the shed seemed to be writhing, wriggling, alive.

And then she saw that it was. A sea of chickens, crammed in together in their thousands, many featherless and the ones closest to her even bloody. Moving, shuffling, pecking away relentlessly at the floor, at the long feeding troughs, at each other. And she saw the little darts of brown weaving between them, moving at the troughs . . . rats. RATS. She felt a horrified shudder pass up her body. She wondered how many rats had been in the field, been in the pit . . . had just scuttled out of view at the sound of their approach.

With a stifled cry, she slithered clumsily on the drainpipe, let go and fell to the ground, landing heavily on her back.

'Ouf.'

Alex pulled her up to her feet with the words: 'Not nice, is it?'

'No, it's not nice at all.' Pamela heard the wobble in her voice. 'Please can we get out of here now, and not through the field?'

'Yeah. Time to go.'

They walked round the shed into the farm's courtyard and, as quietly as they could, set off down the road back to Linden Lee, talking in fierce whispers about what they'd seen.

'So, how was it?'

Alex knew Pamela had just spent the best part of half an hour on the phone to Dave and she was frantic to know how it had gone, full of concern for her friends. She had once been certain that Pamela would finally leave Dave and that it would be the best thing for her to do, but now that she knew them both well, she wasn't so sure. No longer knew what was going to make them happier . . . or, at least, cause them less pain.

'It was OK,' Pamela told her, pulling a chair out from the kitchen table and sitting down. 'He knew all about the chicken dump. Said the farmer needs a licence to do that and he doesn't have one, so it's being investigated . . . the water in the streams being monitored and so on.'

Dave had sounded surprised to hear from her. Surprised that she had so much farm news for him and even more surprised that she'd been up to tour the chicken place.

'How is he?' Pamela had asked Ted, who had answered the phone.

'He's OK. Pretty upset with you, though – to say the least,' had been Ted's reply.

'What do I do now?' she'd asked her brother, longing for some sort of advice.

'How should I know, Pammy?' he'd said. 'Maybe you need to come down and talk to him.'

'I don't want to know about the farm stuff!' Alex waved Pamela's preamble away. 'I want to know about Dave. How is he? What's happening? What did you say about ... you know ... the important stuff?'

'Er, well ... not a lot ... is the answer,' and Pamela outlined the brief, more than awkward conversation that had followed the farming talk.

'So it doesn't sound like he's going to come back. Well, not yet anyway,' was Alex's verdict.

'He says he's looking into some things. I'm not sure what that means ... maybe he's looking for a job?' It had just occurred to Pamela. 'Somewhere else to live?' But she couldn't imagine it. All the suits and ties he'd thrown out, determined not to go back. As soon as Dave had moved to Linden Lee, it was obvious that he loved it. He'd told her more than once that he could imagine being there for the rest of his life, which, OK, had panicked her then, but she couldn't believe he was now thinking of leaving. Although maybe what she'd done was going to force his hand ...

'What do *you* think?' Alex asked her for the hundredth time this weekend. 'What do you want to do?'

Pamela thought for a long time, twisting the rings on her fourth finger round and round, before she finally answered: 'It's taken me this long to find out that I really, *really* like it here . . . and I miss him. I miss him terribly, every little thing about him.'

There it was, out loud, the thing she'd never expected to feel this strongly, that she missed him in the morning, she missed him all day long and in the evening, she kept looking up to the other end of the sofa and missing him some more. His poetry in praise of vegetables, his strange wholemealy cooking, his latest plan to curb the snail population, tea the way he made it, his smell, his face, his voice. She missed it all.

Alex smoothed crumbs from the tabletop in front of her, opened her cigarette packet, then changed her mind and closed it again, before telling her friend: 'OK. So you have to get him back, then.'

'Ha! I don't think that's going to be so easy.' Pamela could feel the tear about to slide out of her left eye and quickly pressed it away.

'We should probably have some food,' Alex tried to rally her. 'Anyone for chicken?!'

'Bleurgh!!!'

In the hectic fortnight that followed, Pamela worked very hard to keep Linden Lee in business, their customers in vegetables, and also to

379

finish off the Murrays' cottage in time for the first holiday-makers.

She got up early to do the daily pick and delivery round, then divided the rest of her time between cottage jobs and problems and on to working late at the farm, watering cows and crops – checking with George and Harry that she wasn't messing up – but even so, she was never busy enough not to notice that Dave didn't phone, didn't want to be in touch or even let her know what he was planning to do next. She'd tried to reach him several times but he hadn't responded to her messages. And Ted, a reluctant go-between, had told her to leave it for a while.

When the cottage was at last finished, Pamela toured Rosie round, then walked to the farm-house with her because Rosie wanted to settle the final payment straight away.

'I'm really pleased with them,' Rosie told her. 'They've turned out even better than I was hoping. It's a shame I can't afford to get you to do the farmhouse.'

Pamela smiled politely at this, suspecting nothing was further from the truth. Rosie probably never wanted to see her again, was straining to be nice.

'But,' Rosie added, 'I've made a bit of a start on it myself, shamelessly pinching some of your cottage ideas.'

'That's OK. I pinched them all from somewhere else myself,' Pamela replied, part of her desperate to know where Lachlan was ... how he was doing ... if her involvement with him had caused major ructions with his wife or not. Part hoping she wouldn't have to see him again for a long time.

They made it to the house and Pamela saw Lachlan's jacket hanging up on the coat rack behind the door. Pulse suddenly racing at the thought that he might be in.

But Rosie, maybe seeing Pamela clock the jacket, said: 'Lachlan's sorry he'll miss you. He's picking the children up from school and taking them out somewhere. Giving me a bit of a break.' Rosie tucked in a little smile at this. Giving nothing away.

'So, you're starting with the hall?' Pamela asked. The long corridor was covered in a patterned wallpaper which had been over-painted in white.

'Yes. Egg yolk yellow, that's the plan. It shouldn't look too bad with the carpet.' Rosie pointed at the brown, battered old weave beneath them. 'No funds to change that just yet.'

'It'll be fine,' Pamela assured her. 'Yellow and brown, very warm, rich.' She would have offered to look around and listen to Rosie's other ideas, but Rosie didn't suggest it, so neither did Pamela. Maybe the last thing Rosie wanted was Pamela even standing inside her home.

So they went into the scruffy kitchen and concluded business quickly.

Once Pamela had Rosie's cheque in her bag, there was no reason to linger. She stood up from the table to take her leave.

'How are you enjoying farm life?' Rosie asked. 'Do you think you and Dave will stay?'

It seemed an intensely personal question in the circumstances and Pamela struggled with the answer: 'Ummm . . . yes . . . It's very different. I'm still settling in – I feel very new to it. Dave loves it, though . . . I think.' She couldn't help putting in the doubt at the end. What did she know now about what Dave thought? Would they stay on? She had absolutely no idea.

Back at home after the meeting with Rosie, she'd thought she wanted the comfort of tea, but rifling through the varieties in the cupboard she didn't feel as if she could face any of them. She was so tired and so wound up – to the point of feeling physically sick. She had felt like this for over a week now. No wonder, she'd thought at first, all this bloody stress. But then over the past few days she'd worried, in the back of her mind, if maybe it wasn't the beginning of something more sinister, so she'd decided to try and speak to the IVF doctor who had treated her last.

She'd left several messages for him and now, just towards 5 p.m., the house phone was ringing and it was Dr Rosen, finally calling her back.

As charming as ever, he asked how the move was going and wanted to know if she and Dave were planning to come back to London for further treatment. Pamela answered the questions, then began to outline her current symptoms and her fear that her pre-menopause was kicking in.

'I have dizzy spells,' she confided. 'I've skipped two periods, I feel sick and a bit strange, not at all myself. I think I need a check-up. I'm worried that this is it. The end of the road and I won't be able to try again.'

The doctor asked further questions and listened carefully to her. 'Something seems to be up,' was his verdict. 'It could be a number of things . . . or it could be nothing. Like you say, you should come in and have a check-up. Those are of course typical early pregnancy symptoms,' he added, followed swiftly by, 'Although I suppose in you and your husband's case that's very unlikely. Still –' authoritative doctor voice – 'we'd want to check that out.'

'*Pregnancy??!!*' she repeated. He couldn't have said anything more surprising to her. '*Pregnancy?*' she asked once again. 'Hello. This is me, we're talking about, the woman whose body has rejected the finest embryos medical science could provide. No, definitely not pregnant.'

But even as she said the words, she could feel the conviction draining from her. In her and Dave's case it was very unlikely, yes, but what about . . . her and *Lachlan!?* In her mind, suddenly, he was there, his mouth pressed right up against her ear, gasping . . . Pregnant? *Pregnant?*

What if . . . somehow . . . by some miracle, Lachlan had succeeded where medical science had failed?

'How would I know?' she asked her doctor, almost dazed with the idea . . . with the problems . . . with the possible . . .

383

'Just take a pregnancy test!' She heard the bemusement in his voice. 'If it's negative, make an appointment to see me and we'll check you out. If it's positive, well ... maybe it's your husband who should come in for a check-up!'

Then he added, 'Look, I don't want to give you false hope, Pamela, it is unlikely, but then again we don't have all the answers. I've come across all kinds of inexplicable pregnancies which have happened when couples weren't trying.'

Not *trying*? Well, she and Dave certainly hadn't been trying, but wasn't it possible, just maybe, way in the back of her mind, that she'd thought it was worth a try with Lachlan? – *No need to be careful* – That she'd known there was always the remotest, slightest of chances? Wasn't a huge part of his attraction that he had to be one of the most fertile men she could have picked for herself? But it hadn't really been like that! She checked herself. He had wooed her, seduced her ... she hadn't coldly picked him out as possible genetic material!

As soon as Pamela put the phone down, she *had* to have a pregnancy test. It was ten past five. If she raced to town, there was a chance of catching the chemist's, which she knew closed at 5.30. She grabbed her bag and keys and rushed out of the house, into the Landy and down the road as fast as she dared.

The blinds were being pulled down in the shop as she got there, but she knocked on the door and the woman inside opened up.

'Something urgent?' the woman asked Pamela.

'Yes, if it's OK. It won't take a minute.' Putting aside the thought of how this might be quite the talk at the Hacienda for days to come, she said, 'I need a pregnancy test.'

'An over the counter one? Or the pharmacist's own? They take 24 hours and I'd need you to come back in the morning,' the woman said. Still standing in the doorway, she hadn't let Pamela into the shop yet.

'An over the counter one, please. Please can I get it now? It's very important.'

She was ushered in and directed to the shelf.

'I'll take these two, please.' She handed the boxes to the assistant.

'They have two tests inside,' the assistant explained.

'Well, even so. I want to be on the safe side.'

The woman nodded and took her money without asking Pamela any of the things she'd been bracing herself for: *Is this your first? Have you been trying long? Are you hoping for good news?*

'Thanks. Sorry to keep you,' Pamela said, bundling the packets into her handbag, thinking only of getting home as quickly as she could.

No minute in her whole life had ever taken as long as the minute needed for the test result to develop. She turned the indicator over in her hands with her eyes closed, holding her breath. Finally, she allowed herself to look and saw that it was positive.

Positive. Two straight lines.

She gasped with the shock of it, then did the only thing she could think of in the enormity of the moment – opened another test, to do it again.

Then another . . . then once again . . .

Until all four had indicated the same result. Pregnant. Absolutely, positively pregnant.

In the past, she'd always imagined that the positive pregnancy test moment would be one of the happiest in her life – but then she could never have imagined circumstances like this.

She could feel the rush of dizziness, the ominous sway of the room, so sat quickly down on the lid of the toilet to steady herself.

This was terrible but wonderful, awful but glorious, a disaster . . . a miracle! She was pregnant! But by Lachlan. She might have a baby! But Dave would never forgive her.

The flood of tears loosened in her now. 'This is so *unfair*!' she sobbed into her hands. Seven years of trying with Dave. *Seven years!*

It had only taken Lachlan about seven minutes.

So unfair! So unfair. Not how it was supposed to be at all. This was like a horrible fairy tale, where someone is granted their one and only dearest wish, their heart's desire, only to make a total balls-up of it.

Chapter Thirty-two

Sunday morning, a full 36 hours later . . . Pamela woke up to full-beam August sunshine glowing through the faded green curtains. Surfacing from sleep, she remembered where she was, why she was alone and then, with a rush of reality, the pregnancy. Definitely real, very real, she hadn't dreamed it, this was happening . . . she acknowledged the accompanying merry-go-round of feelings: high, low, up, down, happy, terrified.

No denying how different she felt, almost weightless, full of energy, slightly manic even. The low-level grind of depression she had lived with for so long now, so long she had almost stopped noticing it, had magically lifted and although there were unimaginably big problems ahead, she knew she could . . . she *would* meet them head on.

Her brother's voice, his favourite phrase, was in her head: 'Live for the moment, Pammy, what else is there?' For once, that was what she was going to try and do. No regrets for what had happened, no projecting forward to how it was going to be ... she was going to try and calm down, concentrate on today.

Wrapping her dressing gown around her, she went down to the kitchen, enjoying the lurch of nausea brought on by the smell of tea bags, the secret thrill of what that meant.

Already the sunshine and warmth of the day were calling her out of the kitchen, so she set up a breakfast tray and took it to the garden with a chair. In the spring, Dave had thrown a packet of wild flower seeds over the lawn, deciding that he had no time to mow the grass, so he would let it grow up tall and wild all summer long. Now it was scattered with white, yellow and blue flowers, pale poppies, which let sunlight stream through their petals: all alive with bees.

The twin thoughts stole uninvited into her mind that this would be the perfect place to bring up a child and that Dave would still – no matter if he was in love with her or not – make a wonderful father. She considered them carefully, then tried to put them away, out of her head. It felt too soon to begin to think about all that. She was still trying to adjust to pregnancy, to being here, in the place she'd tried so long to get to.

And anyway, she had plans for today. It was Sunday, no vegetables to pick, so she was going to open windows and doors wide, throw the house open to the sunshine and start decorating.

The farmhouse had been dull, gloomy and

unloved for too long. Today she would at least make a start on the process of transformation.

And she wasn't going to do anything that Dave wouldn't approve of either. In this house, all the ideas she'd experimented with in her nurseries were finally going to come together. The doors, window frames and woodwork would all be gently peeled back so they could be sanded and lavishly oiled. The walls taken back to plaster, repaired, then painted with breathable non-toxic paints. This house was going to be full of wood . . . sisal . . . pure wool . . . untreated cork. There would be reclaimed wooden shelving . . . antique wardrobes . . . faded mirrors . . . recycled curtains sewn together . . . She had all sorts of ideas. Was buzzing with ideas, desperate to start.

Once she was in her work clothes, she brought ladders, scrapers and the wallpaper steamer into the sitting room, pushed all the furniture into the middle of the room, covered it in dust sheets, plugged in the radio and began.

Gradually, layers of wallpaper peeled off and slid onto the floor all around her, layers of house history. This room had once been green and flowery, before that, dark blue and flowery, pale pink and right at the bottom, a faded orangey-yellow. She worked slowly, wanting to do it perfectly, as if she had all the time in the world. The conviction growing in her with every section of bare wall she revealed, was that this was the house she wanted to be in for a very long time to come: *the family home*.

Late in the afternoon, when she'd sat down to

rest and examine the damage she'd inflicted on the room so far, all of a sudden out of the radio, a Dave song came at her.

Acoustic guitar, clever chords filling the room. She knew this song – what was it again?

Lloyd Cole. The student bedsit days, Dave with a tape recorder at the foot of his messed bed blasting this song out over and over again, even though she would hit him with pillows and beg him to stop or at least move on to the next track. Dave, her husband, stroking her face, looking into her eyes, making her tea, pouring her wine . . . trying, always trying, to kiss it better. There was no denying how much she missed him. Three weeks exactly he'd been away, the longest they'd ever been apart.

Having a baby without him just wasn't in the plans. That was the problem. Every fantasy she'd ever had about having a baby was about having one, somehow, with Dave.

When the song was over, she felt the prickle of tears behind her eyes but picked up her scraper and set back to work, soon so absorbed in what she was doing, she didn't hear the tyres on the gravel, nor the back door catching in the breeze and closing with a slam. So it was something of a shock to turn mid-scrape, still singing along with the radio, and find Dave standing in the doorway.

'Hello!' they both said at the same time, the new and unfamiliar awkwardness between them apparent immediately.

She came down from her ladder and went over

to the radio to turn the volume down because going over to kiss him, the way she would always, unthinkingly, have done before, seemed impossible now.

'Hello,' she repeated, standing up to look at him properly. 'This is a bit of a surprise.'

'So is all this—' he gestured at the room.

'Well, I thought it was about time I started . . . and it's all going to be totally ethical. You don't need to worry. Biodegradable, non-toxic – and it does need redecorating, one way or another . . . I mean . . .' she stammered to a standstill. It was just a little bit early to be kicking off the divorce/sell the farm discussion.

'No, you're right,' he agreed. 'It needs work. It all needs work.'

'So . . . how are you?' she asked, but she could see already that he looked well. Looked good, in fact. It was obvious he'd had a rest, been well cared for. He'd even put on a little weight and was wearing a new shirt, something Ted must have helped him to pick out.

'I'm OK,' was all he said. 'How about you?'

'Fine . . . fine.' The gap between 'fine' and how she really was seemed so insurmountable, she wondered how she would ever tell him. How would she even begin?

'D'you want some tea or something?' she asked instead. 'I'll finish this corner and come through.'

'I've brought wine, shall we open that?' Wine for a serious, maybe difficult, discussion. She could see the logic. But she was planning never to drink again. Well, not until . . .

'You have wine, but I need builder's tea – it's thirsty work.' Her jokey excuse seemed to ease the tension between them.

'I've already had a look around . . . at the cows and in a few of the fields. You've been doing a pretty good job,' he told her with a smile now.

She could only smile back and confess: 'I've really enjoyed it. I didn't expect to, but I have . . . farming in my high heels.'

Just as he turned to go out of the room, he added: 'You were singing . . . I haven't heard that for ages.'

Across the kitchen table they began talking, first of all about Ted, Liz and their children, and then with far more difficulty about themselves and what to do next.

The smiles and friendliness Dave had shown when he'd first arrived back were all gone now and he was very serious . . . talking in a calm, detached way about selling the farm, *dividing their assets . . . splitting up.*

What else had she expected? she kept asking herself, trying to stay calm, trying to breathe through her rising panic: some impossibly romantic reunion? He didn't want to be with her any more . . . and this before he even knew she was pregnant with someone else's baby.

'What are you going to do?' she wanted to know, 'once we've sold . . .' she didn't want to finish the sentence.

'Carry on farming,' he answered. 'I'll definitely carry on farming . . . I might be able to scrape together the money to buy a big enough place somewhere else, or I might go abroad and do it.'

'Where?' Her horror at this idea. She thought she could just about cope so long as they could remain friends, stay closely in touch, but now he was thinking about moving right out of her life, out of the country.

'I've been looking into Eastern Europe ... land's much cheaper ... the climate's good.' He kept his eyes on his wine glass, didn't look at her.

She couldn't understand where this plan had come from, he'd never seriously talked about going abroad before: 'Is this what you really want?' she asked.

He lifted his glass and took a drink before answering: 'I'm trying to make the best of this – do some things I maybe wouldn't have done if we'd . . .' he broke off.

She didn't know what to say, could only think how stupid, how pointless and sad it was to discover that you really loved a place and really loved a person just when you'd messed it all up and had to leave.

'Divorce is sometimes the happy ending – or at least a happy new beginning,' Dave said, reaching over to touch her hand. 'Well, so Ted kept telling me.'

Ted?! Oh he did, did he? She would smack him the next time she saw him.

'You look really upset,' he said now. 'But you've been telling me for ages we can't go on like this . . . and you were the one who . . .'

She nodded, blinking hard.

'Is this what you want?' she asked again, just to be sure.

'I think so . . . No great rush. I'm sure you'll need to sort out what you're going to do next, where you want to go. Have you thought about that?'

'No,' she swallowed back the sob at this. 'No, not yet.'

'Well, as I said, no rush.'

He finished off the wine in his glass and looked as if he was about to get up, draw this talk to a close for now, so she knew she had to stop him. Tell him the two most important things, however hard it might be.

'Dave—' she put her hand on his forearm to keep him seated and took a breath to steady herself: 'I'm really sorry. I'm truly sorry for hurting you. You didn't deserve that . . . Not at all.'

He gave a little nod, acknowledging the apology. And now she was going to have to hurt him much more. Oh dear God . . . how was she going to do it? What were the best words for this? No, there were no good words for this at all.

'I'm not sure how to tell you this . . .' Her hand squeezed into his forearm; his eyes intently on her face now.

'I really don't want to tell you this . . .' she stalled, 'but it's . . .' Her heartbeat hurt, it physically hurt, her eyes scanned his face, then moved back down to the table again, wishing he could somehow guess, say it aloud for her, just *know* without the excruciating pain of her having to tell him.

'Dave—' just above a whisper, 'I'm pregnant.'

For a moment it was as if she hadn't said anything at all. Her eyes fixed on his face saw it was unchanged, unmoved . . . Maybe she would have to say it again, he hadn't heard . . . hadn't taken it in . . .

'The . . . fling . . . thing . . .' she added reluctantly, totally unnecessarily. 'I'm pregnant.'

'Oh no,' came from him now. 'No, no.' The pain in those words.

His hands went up to his face and he began to rub his eyes as if he wasn't able to believe what was in front of him.

'Not that . . . *no!*' He stood up and looked at her wildly. 'How do you expect me to cope with that?' His voice was a strangled shout now: 'What am I supposed to do with that? Just what am I supposed to do?'

She had no idea how to reply to this, but he didn't wait to hear anyway, just hurled himself furiously out of the kitchen door, then out of the back door, out of the house, so she wouldn't see any more how upset he was.

Bloody hell. Bloody, bloody awful hell.

She didn't deserve to sit at the table and cry, the way she wanted to. This was her fault, all hers, and she would have to go, she saw now. He couldn't bear for her to be here any longer. So she would have to pack a suitcase straight away and go to her parents. The farm would go on the market and she would have to find somewhere new to live, a new job – and pregnant? How was that going to work? Too bad, she told herself . . . this was her problem.

She went to the bedroom and got her suitcase out from under the bed, hands shaking as she piled her clothes in. She'd never done this before, in all their years together, she'd never had to pack her things and storm off to her parents' house. But now she had finally done the unforgivable.

As she was loading her bags into the boot of the car, she heard Dave's footsteps on the gravel behind her.

She turned to face him and he stopped in his tracks, realizing what she was doing. They looked at each other, a long look. Long, long look. This was really it, she suspected, heart full of fear. This could turn out to be the day when she left him, only planning to be away for a while, but actually never to come back. It had escalated so quickly to this. How had she managed to spend the day decorating?! Dreaming about how the house could be, how their life could be together . . . and by evening, be leaving?

'Dave . . .'

He crossed his arms and seemed to look past her, into the distance.

'I think I should go . . . I don't think you want me here any more, so I'm going to stay with my parents for . . .' For what? A bit? A while? For ever?

'Fine,' he cut in. 'You do that, because no, I definitely don't want to see you.'

'OK, well . . .' She struggled to shut the boot, didn't seem to have the strength to get it to close.

'Goodbye, then.' They didn't make any movement towards each other, the 10 metres or so
between them wide as a sea. 'I'll phone you,' she
added, not sure if she could do this, really go,
when every part of her wanted to stay with him,
comfort him, somehow help him through this.

'If you have to,' he said and turned abruptly
away from her, heading to the house without a
backward glance.

By the end of the farm road, she wondered if it
was safe to drive while crying this hard.

Chapter Thirty-three

Pamela worried all the way down the motorway what to tell her parents, how much to reveal and how she would do it. But once she'd arrived at their home, her mother and father made it easy for her. Prepared by mobile for her arrival and aware that something was very wrong, they ushered her into the house and led her to the sofa.

They went through the hellos, the weather and the motorway traffic small talk, offered her a drink, then her mother decided it was time to get the real conversation under way.

'So, what's happened, honey?' Helen wanted to know. 'Can you tell us?'

Pamela saw the concern in both of her parents' faces.

'I'm sorry I'm here,' she told them. 'It feels so stupid, so teenagey to be coming home to you with my problems.'

'Don't be silly,' Helen reassured her.

'But I might need to stay for a bit, if that's OK . . . and you have the best spare room,' she smiled at them.

'So?' her dad's eyebrows raised at her: 'What's the story?'

'Well, er . . .' There didn't seem to be any way to give it to them, other than straight, 'I've been having an affair.' Bombshell number one. 'It wasn't serious and it's over now,' she added quickly. 'But . . .' Deep breath, 'I'm pregnant . . .' Bombshell number two, 'And, well . . . it's not exactly surprising, but Dave wants a divorce.'

She watched as their faces changed, almost in slow motion, with the news. Her father looked purely surprised, her mother seemed to be struggling to know how to react.

So, she came over and sat down on the sofa beside Pamela. Already in her dressing gown, Helen put a silky-sleeved arm around her.

'Bit tricky, isn't it?' Pamela said into her mother's bathed and body-lotioned shoulder.

'Well yes . . . but I can't help thinking that at least part of this is . . . wonderful,' Helen said finally and kissed her daughter on the forehead.

'I know,' Pamela whispered, feeling the surge of relief. 'I'm glad you understand that.'

'So, do you want to tell us a bit more? How did this all happen?' her father said, still looking stunned over on the other side of the room.

She nodded at him: 'I think maybe I do need a drink first. Does anyone want a cup of tea?'

Simon shook his head: 'I think I'll go for something a little stronger.'

'Me too,' from Helen.

Drinks were organized in the kitchen and once they were settled down round the table there, Pamela told them all they needed to know. She appreciated how calmly they listened. They didn't panic, make disapproving noises or rush in with a judgement at the end.

When she'd finished her story, Helen was the first to speak. 'So, you've had this all out with Dave, have you?' she asked.

Pamela nodded in reply.

'And you think divorce is going to be the next step?' Helen asked as if there might be another option, when really, didn't Pamela deserve a divorce? What else could happen now?

'I'm not sure I've got any choice in the matter,' she managed, feeling that the tears she'd held at bay throughout this conversation were not far away now.

'Oh honey,' her mother soothed. 'You're going to stay with us for a little, though, aren't you? Let us help you sort things out.'

Pamela held out her hands, one for her dad to hold, one for her mother: 'Is that OK?' she asked, moved by the offer, their sympathy and under-standing. 'You're both really cool. Do you know that? I hope my baby . . .' But she couldn't finish the sentence.

'How pregnant are you, honey?' her mother asked.

'I don't even know . . .' bubble of tears at this. 'Maybe two months or so . . . I need to see a doctor.'

* * *

For several days, Pamela allowed herself to wallow. She wore her pyjamas all day long, cried through whole boxes of mansize tissues and watched almost everything on the TV, as if life lessons of some sort could be drawn from re-runs of *Cagney and Lacey* and *Murder She Wrote*.

In the evening, her parents were home, making her supper to 'keep her strength up', trying to support her.

'So everyone's devastated,' she overheard her mother on the phone to Ted. 'Dave's devastated, Pam's devastated. You're upset . . . we're upset . . . I'm not sure where we go from here.'

'We drink just a little bit too much wine – for a few days at least,' was her father's suggestion over dinner one evening. He even insisted Pamela have a little glass of red 'for medicinal purposes'.

'I'm very glad you're not *too* shocked by all this,' she confided to him.

'We're older than you, Pammy,' he reminded her with a smile. 'We're in our sixties . . . and we did the Sixties. There's not a lot we haven't heard before. And you know what? I've been wondering for years when you were finally going to break out and go a bit wild.'

'Simon!' Helen ticked him off.

'Really?' Pamela was surprised by this. 'I always thought the two of you were really keen for me to settle down and marry Dave.'

'Well, yes,' her mother answered. 'That too. But maybe you should have been a bit wilder first . . .'

401

'Dad should have given me a better allowance then,' she managed to joke.

'I met Aunty Peg in town today,' Helen told them. 'But you'll be very impressed with me, I didn't say anything about Pam. It seems a shame, though. She'd have loved it.' She twirled spaghetti round her fork and smiled. 'Because, you know, you've had an affair with the local landowner, you've fallen pregnant, your husband has sent you from the farm in disgrace ... it's a real live historical romance ... bodice-ripper territory, the kind of thing she gets from the library in bulk.'

'Helen!' It was her husband's turn to tell her off now. 'It's far too early for jokes.'

But Pamela was smiling and threw in: 'I'd just like to say, no bodices were technically ripped.'

Her mother rewarded her with a pat on the arm. 'That's my girl, everything has to be funny from at least one angle. Has to be. How else do we cope?'

The following night, Helen curled up on the sofa beside her daughter and began to massage her feet and just chat about nothing in particular until she managed to spark the conversation that Pamela had wanted to have for days.

'Can I ask you something very personal?' Pamela dared.

'Probably ...' Helen encouraged with a smile and a slightly too vigorous thumb circle into the ball of her daughter's foot.

'Ouch ... How do you manage to stay in love

402

for thirty-eight years and make it seem easy?'

Her mother surprised her by bursting into laughter at this: 'You're asking *me*?'

'Of course I'm asking you. I don't know anyone else who's been married this happily for this long.'

'Oh boy ...' still laughing a little. 'Well, I'm flattered you ask, honey, really I am. But I want to be serious with you, give you the answers you deserve ...' So she thought for several minutes before replying, 'First of all, two major things I have which you don't.'

'Yeah?' Pamela was hardly able to contain her curiosity. Two major things? No wonder she didn't have a hope.

'Children and religion,' was her mother's answer. 'We had the two of you to care for, worry about, distract us, from pretty early on – and I was brought up a Catholic. I don't know what holds any marriage together quite as strongly as those two elements.'

'Er ... well ...' Pamela was somewhat taken aback. 'I was expecting you to say love. You know, the famous Helen and Simon Zing Thing.'

'Oh yes, well ... love, of course.' Her mother waved her hands about effusively, bringing the massage to an abrupt halt. 'But maybe not the kind you're thinking of – swoony, heart-racing, can't keep your hands off each other sort of thing. That goes—' she started to laugh again. 'No, that's not fair. It comes and goes, comes back again, cools off ... returns. It depends on all sorts of things: how fat or thin I am, how many chores your father's done round the house lately ... how much money he's earned, you know – complicated things!'

'But you've always done the big, romantic lovers act,' Pamela reminded her.

'I don't think it hurts to pretend, does it? If you pretend you're something, you're that bit closer to being it, aren't you?'

'So what kind of love are we talking about?' Pamela wanted to know.

'Unconditional, of course.'

'Ooh. The big one.'

'I love you and Ted *unconditionally*. No matter what you do. And I've never seen anyone else's children and wished I could have them instead! I try to feel like that about Simon too.'

'That's very sweet,' Pamela told her.

'And because your parents love you like that, you're probably programmed to go off into the world and look for it again. Won't be happy till you find it ... were happy because you did find it with someone.' She picked up Pamela's foot and began the kneading again, adding gently, eyes down, 'I always thought you and Dave made each other very happy, until the infertility problem took over.'

'Yup. We did,' Pamela agreed and for a moment thought she would have to reach over for the mansize box again. But it passed.

'And so,' Pamela went on, 'how do you keep attacks of the other kind of love at bay? The swoony, can't keep your hands off each other stuff?'

404

'You don't – can't!' Helen laughed. 'I fall in love with someone else at least once a decade. But I try not to do too much about it.'

Well, this was a revelation.

'You don't!' Pamela insisted.

'Everybody does. They're lying if they tell you otherwise.' Ouch. Ouch. Vicious thumb circles.

'Who've you been in love with?' her daughter was longing to know.

'I definitely can't tell you that.' Helen let go of the foot she was working on and took a sip of the drink by her side.

'Yes, you can,' Pamela insisted, 'I'm your daughter . . . your 35-year-old daughter, who is up the duff by her married lover, you can tell me anything.'

Helen replied with a laugh, but then, finally halting the foot massage so she could concentrate, she confessed, still smiling: 'The big romance of my married life – I really don't know if I should tell you this, darling – oh, what the hell, it was so long ago . . . was Father Brian.'

'Father Brian?! The priest!'

'Oh, he was *beautiful*,' her mother replied. 'And such a sensitive soul.'

'Did you have an affair?' Pamela, wide-eyed now, was racking her brain for an image of Father Brian.

'No. No, well . . . I was obsessed. I was going to church three times a week. I couldn't get him out of my head. You know what these things are like, I imagine—' pointed look. 'There was a bit of heated kissing in the vestry.'

405

'NO!'

'Oh yes, then the next thing I knew, Father Brian was "on holiday", then transferred to a parish in Scotland.'

'He got found out?!'

'No, I don't think he did. He was such a tortured soul, I think he confessed – of course – so the Church stepped in to give him an easy getaway.'

Pamela, stunned, finally asked: 'So I'm sworn to secrecy then, am I?'

'What do you mean?'

'Dad?'

'Oh no. No, of course not, Simon knows. We often have a good old laugh about that one.'

'So how many other ones are there?!' Pamela asked.

'About once a decade . . . Simon too . . . so that's about eight between us, I suppose. Best not to do too much about it because they go away – you get over them. But then, I'm beginning to think people get over everything . . . eventually.' She reached down for her drink once again. 'However . . . unconditional love, that's what the world needs more of. But hey, I was at Woodstock.' Helen flicked a peace sign at her.

'Of course you were.' Pamela gave an eye roll. This was a famous family legend.

'Will I get over Dave?' she asked her mother then.

'If you want to, honey.'

'What if I don't want to?'

'Then it'll take a little longer. But you know

406

what?' she looked at her daughter very seriously now. 'You should probably get in your car, head on up there and at least tell him you don't want to get over him.'

'Ha! I don't think he wants to hear from me, ever again.'

'I think you're wrong there, Ted says he's absolutely heartbroken. But anyway, you won't know till you try, will you?'

'Mum, I'm pregnant with someone else's baby!'

'Oh so what . . .' Helen dared. 'It's not the nineteenth century, no-one expects you to go off and shoot yourself. And anyway, you were doing donor sperm stuff before you left London, is there such a big difference?'

'I think you'll find there is. Penis versus pipette. Believe me, it's a little different.'

But Helen wasn't backing down: 'This is modern life, Pamela. People can get used to anything if they want to.'

'You think we should get back together again, don't you?' She sounded her mother out.

'Can you stop worrying about what I want? Please. All I want is to point out to you, that you and Dave often talked about moving to the country, together, when you had children. Maybe if you both stopped making such a big drama out of this you could finally get what you wanted . . . Did you ever think of it that way?'

No, she hadn't thought of it that way – and how did she even begin to make Dave think of it that way?

She dared to ask her mother's advice once again.

'Big declarations,' was what Helen recommended. 'Big declarations are always good. If you leave now, you'll be there by . . .'

'One in the morning! No, I have to sleep on this.'

'Bah!' her mother scoffed. 'Not exactly the Woodstock way, is it?'

'I have to phone a friend. I need to ask someone else about this.'

'No, you don't. Make up your own mind!' Helen scolded.

It was after midnight and she was on the motorway. This was insane. Yet another of the many, many insane things her mother had made her do. Let's see. Top of the list was still dressing up in pink PVC as Barbie for Hallowe'en, before anyone in Britain knew who Barbie was . . . before anyone in Britain knew what Hallowe'en was! Then came nudist beach holidays in Lanzarote when she was a *teenager*!

Followed by the enforced addition of a *bride's* speech at her wedding, not to mention a mother of the bride's speech . . .

Suggesting she paint her first sitting room bright red . . .

No, it wasn't any use, she couldn't be angry with her mother for any of them any more. They were funny! Helen was wild, daring, glad to be alive. Had always tried to impart this feeling to her careful, easily embarrassed, stuffy little daughter. Well, that's how Pamela saw it now.

* * *

1.25 a.m. The farmhouse at Linden Lee was in total darkness. She rolled up the drive and parked the Saab beside Dave's Land Rover. Fumbling her key into the back door, she couldn't decide whether to creep in or be noisy, to wake and forewarn him. Whatever she did, it was bonkers. All bonkers. What difference did it make whether she turned up here in the middle of the night or the middle of the day? He was still not going to be pleased to see her.

She reached for the kitchen light and switched it on. The room was in a state. Dave had obviously carried on with the wallpaper stripping: maybe thinking of the sale . . . maybe just keeping busy.

She put her handbag down and, hand on the kitchen door, hesitated. Did she really want to go and wake him now? Maybe she would just creep upstairs, but instead of disturbing him, go to her little back room, see him in the morning . . .

Quietly, quietly on the stairs, but once she was at the top, she thought she would maybe just take a look in his room, check on him. She pushed the door ajar slightly, but had forgotten how horribly it creaked. So before she could decide whether she wanted to speak to him or not, Dave was sitting bolt upright in bed, gasping with fright.

'It's OK, it's just me . . . I'm so sorry. I didn't mean to frighten you.'

'Pamela?' The surprise in his voice. 'What are you doing here?' He clicked on the sidelight. 'Are you trying to burgle me?'

'No, no ... I'm here ... I'm sorry ...' All the words she'd thought about in the car, she'd hoped she might be able to say, seemed to be drying up, disappearing out of sight. 'I'm just here because ... because I'm losing the plot. I shouldn't be here ... Why don't I let you get back to sleep? And I'll see you in the morning.'

'No ... it's OK. I'm wide awake now,' although he looked anything but. 'Sit down—' he gestured to a chair beside the bed. 'You look tired.'

She settled into the seat, then took him in properly: hair on end, stubbly, in a white T-shirt: 'So do you,' she told him, 'And you've got all thin again.'

He asked about her parents, about her stay with them. She was careful with her answers, really not sure how to play this at all.

'What have you been reading?' she asked, looking at the bedside table, for want of something to say that wasn't anywhere near the momentous things she really needed to tell him. Not yet.

'Oh, usual stuff,' he said with a shrug.

But there on the bedside table was something she hadn't seen for years. The leather-bound sketch book he'd given her as a wedding present, filled with drawings, paintings, poems, stories about their past, present and the future they'd hoped for back then.

'Oh,' she said, picking it up, 'I haven't looked at this for ages.'

'Me neither ... It's nice. My best work.' Another casual shrug.

Pamela held it in her hands and slowly turned the pages over. How could she have forgotten about this? Here were cartoons of them at art school, pages of sketches of her face, her naked 21-year-old body, a careful watercolour of how he pictured their wedding day. Then onwards to drawings of a house and garden, the two of them with twin babies he'd named Pamid and Davela. Next was: 'Pamid's first journey on the Space Shuttle' and 'Davela's inaugural speech as the first Green prime minister of Britain'.

She couldn't help the tears at this, but tried to hide them from him, holding the book awkwardly in front of her face.

The closing pages, before her now, he'd written out and illustrated so long ago: a double-page drawing and story with the title: 'The Perfect End'. The words spiralled round a drawing of an old couple, which he'd managed to make look convincingly like them, watching the sunset from the garden of a clifftop cottage.

They were so young back then when they married. She had often thought they had been too young, wonderfully naïve, hadn't known much about anything at all. But now she wondered if maybe they had known it *all* then. And over the years, had almost forgotten the really important things.

'Sorry,' she put the book down and wiped at her eyes frantically. 'You must think I've gone totally mad, turning up here like this . . . weeping . . .'

'It's OK,' he answered, 'I've no idea what's

going on either.' He ran a hand through his hair. 'I really miss you,' he risked. 'I miss you very much.'

'Me too.'

Long, long silence.

'How are you?' he asked finally. 'How's the ... how's it going?'

She knew what he meant: 'Fine. It's going well. I'm going for a scan next week. But it's about 11 weeks now, so fingers crossed.'

'That's ... great,' he said, entirely unconvincingly. 'Does *he* know?'

For a moment, Pamela had no idea what Dave was talking about. He? Oh ... *him*. She had completely forgotten about him.

'No! No – he'd be horrified. He's with his wife, their children ... I think. It was by mistake ... this ... to put it mildly.'

'It hasn't turned out the way we planned,' he said, with a nod to the wedding present book.

'No.' Pamela pressed her finger underneath her nose, determined not to cry again. 'But it hardly ever does, does it?'

'I suppose not—' hand ruffling through hair again. He looked at a loss for further words.

And all the things she wanted to say to him, ask him, all choked up in her throat. She was going to lose him if she didn't say something soon. But it was so hard.

'Sometimes you have to make the best of things as they are,' she began. 'Look ...' Both hands over her face now, as if it might be easier if she couldn't see him, 'I came here to say

412

something . . . to tell you . . . I just want to tell you this and if you think it's insane, fine, but I just want to say–' voice wobbling dangerously – 'All I can imagine doing, all I want to do is to live here with you and share this baby with you. I've been thinking and thinking about it . . . it's all I can think about . . . and that's the best plan I can come up with. Nothing else would be as good as that.'

She didn't dare to come out from behind her hands.

Silence . . . silence. He wasn't making any reply.

Finally, she stood up: 'I just needed you to know that.' Then, hands off her face, she turned and began to walk quickly out of the room.

Just as she got to the door, she heard Dave say: 'Thank you.' But she didn't dare to go back to him for that. She fled to her back bedroom.

Chapter Thirty-four

'Everything looks fine . . . That's baby's head, this is the spine . . .' The scan operator pointed to the magical black and white image spinning, twirling across the screen in front of them.

Pamela had already been weighed, blood-tested, examined, had done the questionnaire, had her bag stuffed with more leaflets: pregnancy leaflets, breastfeeding leaflets, delivery leaflets, weaning baby on to solids leaflets. And here was the moment, when she saw the baby bud for the second time. The bud had grown, 22 weeks now, it looked like a proper baby with fingers and toes, complicated vertebrae which shone sharply, intricately white on the screen. It was a miracle.

The operator could sense the emotion in the tiny, darkened room. Both the patient and her partner were wiping away tears.

'I'll print off a picture for you, then leave you to get . . . um . . . dressed,' she offered, although Pamela only had her coat and shoes off.

As soon as the operator had shut the door on them, Dave leaned in from his chair so that his head touched hers. His nose pressed against her temple and their tears ran into each other's.

Pamela remembered this position – on the examination couch, his hands tight round hers, their heads touching together – from all the IVF attempts. Through egg collection, egg re-insertion. Hoping, hoping all the time that they would get here, to a baby bud dancing and wheeling in front of them.

'Clever girl,' he whispered against her ear.

She vaguely recalled some warning from an IVF handbook that a baby didn't solve all the problems. Partnerships under strain became even more strained by pregnancy, strained sometimes to breaking point by the arrival of a baby.

But she knew, as surely as the two dear hands gripping onto hers, that it wasn't going to happen to them. In weeks spent apart, weeks spent together, in long, long talks, uncomfortable fights and late-night reconciliations, they'd finally decided how to move forward. They were making peace and coming to terms with this.

The details didn't matter any more: this was going to be their baby. The baby they had longed for, prayed for, dreamed of for so long.

'Are you OK?' he asked.

'Yeah,' she nodded, tears still streaming, 'I'll be fine.'

He helped her to her feet where she clasped her arms round him.

'Do you really think it won't matter, that

this baby isn't mine?' Dave asked into her hair.

'We've talked about all this,' Pamela answered.'This baby will be yours from the moment it's born. OK? And I'm going to name it after you, to mark that.'

He held her tight, deeply moved, until it occurred to him: 'What if it's a girl?!'

'I'll think of something.'

The thin sheet of paper with the scan image stayed in Pamela's hands all the way home. She tried to picture the face, guess how this child was going to look. Boy? Or girl? As if she cared!

She was tempted to start the baby bargaining in her head: 'Please, please let this pregnancy go OK. Please let everything be OK and I'll be the best mummy ever, I'll never . . .'

But she let it go, saw now that you had to let some things be.

'Harry will probably let you have his worm box,' Dave was telling her. 'You know, to compost the nappies.'

'Oh no!' was her response. 'I couldn't face that. Please don't make me do that!'

'Well, we'd better buy a job lot of the reusable ones, then.'

'Are these my options? Worms or washing?!'

' 'Fraid so.'

As Dave swung the car left, they saw a big silver Merc racing down the road towards them.

'It's him,' Dave said. 'It's the Bridge Farm boss,' and he decided that this was as good a time as any to kick things off.

He flashed his car lights, slowed down and held steady in the middle of the road. Both cars drew to a stop.

'What are you doing?' Pamela was feeling nervous.

'I have to speak to him about it.'

'Do you?' It wouldn't have been her choice of action. Couldn't Dave just write him a letter or something?

Dave swung open his door and got out. Dexter Hunter did too: a stocky, grey-haired man in cords and a green anorak who didn't look too pleased at this hold-up. He was standing by his car, squared up, hands in his pockets, waiting for Dave.

'Mr Hunter?' Dave asked.

The man nodded: 'You'll be the people who bought Linden Lee.'

'I'm Dave Carr.' Neither of them offered a hand at this. 'I'd just like you to know that if you bother to apply for a waste licence, we'll be protesting against it.'

'What happens on my farm is none of your business,' Mr Hunter shot back.

'If you pollute our water and our land, it certainly is our business. You know what we're trying to do here.'

This didn't go down well. 'Bloody townies,' Mr Hunter began. 'You come out here, expect us to keep the countryside like a park. We have to make a living, you know.'

'What kind of an argument is that?' Dave demanded.

'I've got 20,000 chickens up there, their shit has to go somewhere. Just keep out of my business and I'll keep out of yours,' Mr Hunter replied, pointing a finger.

'But you don't seem to be able to keep out of our business, do you?' Dave countered. 'We don't want your crap in our fields, or in our water, or in our air. My wife is pregnant, Mr Hunter, we're not bringing our baby up next to some toxic tip.'

'Better move then, Mr Carr. Better move to some part of the countryside where no-one farms . . . better move to a park, or something belonging to the National bloody Trust.'

He turned to open his car door but before he could climb aboard, Dave got in a stern: 'We've reported you before and we'll report you again. Just try to keep to the rules, Mr Hunter.'

Dexter Hunter slammed his door and revved off, bumping up over the grass verge to pass their car.

'He's totally out of order,' Dave said as he got back into the driver's seat. 'And he knows it. He thinks he can get away with murder.' With almost a smile on his face, he added: 'We're going to be the most annoying neighbours he's ever had.'

'Are we?' Pamela asked. He had just said, out loud, to another person, 'our fields . . . our land . . . our business . . . *our baby* . . .' All things they were only just beginning to talk about . . . very tentatively . . . carefully.

'Yes,' was all Dave said.

But she needed a little more than that: 'Are we really going to do this?' she asked him. 'Live here together? Have the baby? Give it all a go?' She held her breath for the answer.

'Yes,' he said again. 'I haven't got any better plans.' He glanced over and smiled. But it still wasn't enough for her.

'You definitely don't want to sell up and go off on your own to . . . Poland or something?' she asked.

He took his hand from the steering wheel and put it over hers, slowing the car so that he could look at her properly, without driving into the ditch: 'No,' he said, squeezing her hand gently, eyes meeting hers very seriously; he added, 'I don't speak Polish very well.'

That was enough.

Chapter Thirty-five

The oh so long awaited Davina Helen Alexandra Carr, nine full days overdue, finally slithered into the world at 5.15 p.m. on 4 May, allowing Pamela at last to fall back from the kneeling position she'd delivered in and release her grip on Dave. She'd clung to his shoulders, hung from his neck and ground his T-shirt between her teeth for the last two and a half hours of a long, exhausting labour. But he hadn't dared to utter the slightest complaint about the pain she'd caused him. Especially as she had waved away even the gas-and-air, determined to do this drug-free.

Pamela – frightened of cows, of bats, of rats, hell, of chickens, pigs, goats, horses, low-flying pigeons, spiders, wasps, bees, beetles, bits of fluff which looked like beetles ... Deep down inside, Pamela had found the bravery that was there all along. She had just needed this baby to set it alight. To be brave for.

As she fell back against the bed and took the

small, damp, blood-streaked body into her arms, looked down into the puffy face, half-opened underwater eyes, Pamela was sure there would never be another more perfect moment than this in all her life.

Dave seemed fine, seemed good. He beamed, kissed his wife, took the pictures, cut the cord, cracked jokes with the midwives . . . until it was time to phone Pamela's parents.

And then he found himself breathless with tears on the line, watching his money tick down on the ward payphone as he stood helpless, unable to get the words out.

'Dave? Dave? Are they OK?' he heard Helen's voice. 'Are they both OK?'

Finally: 'Yes . . . Perfect . . . It's just . . .' Nothing else would come.

'Girl or boy?' she asked.

'Girl . . .' he squeezed out with the edge of his voice. They had a baby girl. He was a father. It was beyond . . . beyond everything.

'It's OK, honey!' He heard the joy in Helen's voice. 'That's wonderful. Wonderful! You call us back later, we'll tell Ted. Love to you both . . . *all* . . .' she corrected herself, overwhelmed with the news. 'Love to you all!'

Chapter Thirty-six

'Isn't this fantastic? It's just brilliant!' Magenta, the sharp and sassy former leader of Pamela's IVF group, looked around from her seat at the big table set out in the June sunshine of the Linden Lee garden. Two small children were pelting through the overgrown meadow of lawn, and the two babies were sleeping, one in a carrycot, one in Dave's arms.

Alex was dishing out spoonfuls of the farm's small, sweet strawberries and Pamela was daubing thick cream on top.

'No, stop!' Magenta insisted.

'You're in the country, you have to have cream!' Pamela carried on.

'Oh, who cares, I look crap anyway. I'm never going to look anything other than crap. I have three children!' Irrepressible laugh at this.

'You don't look crap,' Pamela assured her.

'I do and so do you, by the way. But it's brilliant!'

Pamela smiled full beam back. She knew exactly what her friend meant. There they both were, unwashed hair scraped into ponytails, no make-up, clothes from the bottom of the laundry basket, faces ringed with tiredness, but this was *motherhood* and they wouldn't swap one moment of it for anything else. Thought almost every day of how long they'd waited for this, of their other friends still waiting ... still hoping.

Magenta had phoned, just weeks before the arrival of Davina, with news of her own.

'I'm going to get a baby too!' she had shrieked down the line. 'But he comes with a brother and sister already attached! Isn't this amazing! It's a three for one deal. Instant family!'

Many months into the laborious adoption process, Magenta and Mick had been granted more children than they'd ever dared to hope for. So now, Magenta was at the farm, visiting the Linden Lee baby and proudly showing off her own new arrivals. Pamela was delighted to see her, because here was someone who knew, who really knew what this was like.

'I'm loving every second of it,' Magenta had confided. 'Every second ... cooking teeny little meals, washing mini clothes, going to the park, even being woken up three times a night. I love it, I'm never going back to my job and I swore I would ... but no way.'

'I'm obsessed with her,' Pamela confessed. 'With everything ... I love her tiny little nappies and her car seat and her babygros and just saying

"I'm off with *the baby* . . ." "I'm going to check on t*he baby*".'

'Oh, yes, watching them sleep . . . I would pay to do that, you know,' Magenta added. 'Watch the children sleep.'

'She's just so sweet,' Pamela sighed.

'You are both demented!' Alex reminded them and they were happy to nod in agreement.

'We are going to get the full tour after lunch, aren't we?' Magenta asked now.

'Yup,' Dave confirmed. 'As soon as Eeny wakes up.' He brushed the tip of his nose against the silky baby head asleep on his chest.

'I can take her,' Pamela offered. 'You can go round the fields with them and I'll meet you at the shop.'

'No,' Alex swooped down and scooped the baby up, rearranging her without any protest against her own chest. 'She's coming to Aunty Alex now, she's had enough of her two soppy parents.'

Pamela and Dave's eyes met over the table, just for a shared, smiling moment. It was true: they would have to watch, they were in danger of becoming the most loving, most spoiling parents on the planet. Alex would have to keep them right.

'The tour, then,' Dave offered when all the plates were scraped clean, every last strawberry and smudge of cream gone. 'Are we all set?'

'Can we do the shop first? Please?' Magenta wanted to know. 'I'm just not sure how much interest I have in fields full of manure.'

Pamela couldn't help but recognize her old self in that remark. She now found fields full of manure endlessly fascinating, totally absorbing . . . but she directed the little party in the direction of the renovated barn.

Somehow throughout the postnatal haze, she, Dave and Alex had kept the idea for the shop moving forward, all three of them working like demons to bring it to fruition.

The barn had been re-roofed, whitewashed inside and scrubbed out. They'd set up rows and rows of shelves, tables and display baskets. Alex had found them an old cashier's desk and till. Now, the day before the big opening, there were hand-painted road signs to guide visitors and all the treasures which the shop was going to sell alongside the farm's vegetables and strawberries had been priced and set out.

Such treasures Alex and Pamela had *sourced*! Alex had done every antique stall, secondhand shop and car boot sale for miles around and Pamela had, both online and by word of mouth, tapped into Norfolk's craft-y mainline. She was now inundated with the amazing, the charming and the simply quirky. Everything had to be eco-friendly, recycled, home-made, in some way ethical . . . that was Dave's proviso.

So now they had a barn full of crocheted baby blankets, patchwork throws, rustic earthenware, hand-painted ceramics, home-glazed tiles, knitted dollies, rag rugs, antique vases, handbags, shawls . . . there was too much to display. Pamela was going to sell stuff through

Sadie's boutique as well and Alex was already thinking about a second shop of her own in London called ... 'Finisterre's' of course, they loved that!

They had decorated the place inside and out with flowers in tubs, pots and hanging baskets; they'd staked out a car park, taken out adverts, Alex had even stood in the high street handing out flyers.

'Wow! Where did you get that incredible painting?' was the first thing Magenta asked as she stepped into the barn. 'I want one of those.'

'Oh that,' Pamela said casually, slipping her arm round her husband's waist, trying to hide the smile as she looked up at the huge, wild, orange-yellow-red-green-sludgy-corn-coloured-chunky-crunchy abstract creation which filled the whole wall behind the till. 'We did that.'

'How many people do you think will come tomorrow?' Dave asked her in bed that night, slightly nervous at the scale of this venture.

'God knows. It's Saturday, first berries of the season, we're offering food, shopping ... free wine ... Maybe hundreds – thousands! Who knows?' Pamela couldn't keep the smile from her face. 'You'd better pick a lot of stuff. Get out there at six, maybe even five. And Eeny's told me she wants to go out with you ...'

'No way!' from Dave. 'I have work to do.'

Work?! Tomorrow he would step out into the pale pink morning and head for the sloping field filled with tiny red strawberries no bigger than your thumbnail but which exploded like bombs of sweetness in your mouth. *Work?!* No. This was life. This was really living.

'Do you really think we can turn the town green?' he asked his wife.

'Of course I do . . . I have every faith in you,' she replied, moving over to lie right next to him, sliding her hand round his neck, thinking how good he looked now that his hair was longer, that little bit wilder, his face already tanned from being outside so much. 'Think of Dexter Hunter,' she added, kissing him on the mouth.

Mr Hunter had been fined ('not nearly enough', according to Dave) for dumping waste without a permit and polluting the watercourse. His recent application for a waste licence had been refused.

'Anything can happen eventually . . .' Pamela told her husband, a little dreamily. 'That's what makes life so interesting.'

She was just about to tell him how extra-ordinary her trip to town had been that morning. She and Alex attracting all kinds of glances in their first outfits of the summer: Pamela's jiggling breastfeeding cleavage bouncing behind the pram, Alex fag in hand, vest top, Capri pants and wedgy cork sandals which showed off toes varnished in a variety of colours.

Pamela had seen *them* coming from 400 metres away, although they hadn't seen her. In the past, she might have ducked into a shop, crossed the road, or done whatever she could to avoid the confrontation, but now she took deep breaths, carried on walking purposefully and linked arms with Alex to brace herself.

'Hello, hello there,' she'd sung out because Lachlan and Rosie, too preoccupied with the gang of three wandering along beside them, still hadn't seen her.

'How are you all doing? This is my friend Alex and my baby, Davina. She's awake at the moment, I think,' she'd carried on, smiling at Rosie, looking at Lachlan, amazed at how calm she was now that it was here, the moment she'd so dreaded.

Rosie had called her children together, then leaned down into the pram. The sight had taken her breath away. Such a small baby, how did she always forget how small they were? And so different from all hers, with its doll-like delicate face, pale blue eyes and dark shock of hair.

This wasn't Lachlan's child. She could lay all her doubts to rest: she was absolutely certain of it.

'She's so small,' Rosie said. 'Gorgeous.'

'But big for a preemie. She was a whole month early but she's four weeks now and really coming on.' Out so smoothly came the script she and Dave had agreed. Had told everyone apart from the very small circle who knew.

Pamela had wondered if Rosie and Lachlan had ever asked themselves the question on hearing about her pregnancy. And now she was giving them the get-out clause.

'She's very special,' Pamela had added. 'We spent seven years trying, it drove me just about insane . . . she's an IVF baby.'

In Rosie's face she could see the beginning of an understanding. A woman crazy with wanting a baby, out of her mind on prescription hormones, maybe wouldn't seem such a big love rival now. And could definitely be blamed. Pamela hoped Rosie hadn't been too hard on Lachlan.

In Lachlan's face, she couldn't read anything at all. Whatever had been there that had so fascinated her, had now gone, totally disappeared. Probably all the baby-bonding hormones in her system, but still, the relief!

'Ingrid said you're opening a farm shop,' Lachlan had ventured.

'Yes, from tomorrow, every day. You'll have to come along. We'll be open all summer, maybe longer if it goes well.'

'We will. Well . . . congratulations, on the baby – on the shop,' and there was a warmth to Rosie's smile which had made Pamela think that maybe if she lived here long enough, she would be Rosie's friend. Because given enough time, everything can heal . . . She suddenly had a mental picture of them leaving the Hacienda together, in raincoats and headscarves, pushing matching tartan grocery trolleys.

'Was that him?' Alex had whispered into her ear after they'd said their goodbyes and moved on down the pavement.

Pamela gave the tiniest of nods, to which

429

Alex responded: 'Dish of the day ... and did you see his gorgeous children. What a breeder!'

'Will you tell Eeny one day?' Alex had wondered.

'I don't know yet,' was the honest reply. 'That's Dave's call.'

When the day finally arrived, it was not as hard as Rosie had expected.

'Bye, bye!' Manda even waved, safe in Ingrid's arms, desperate to go play with dogs, see the cows, try to climb trees with her big brothers and Ingrid's Kitty and Jake.

'They'll be fine. We'll all be fine,' Ingrid assured her, kissing her on both cheeks, in her Swedish kind of way: 'I've got all the meals in the freezer, we've got the beds out upstairs and a full plan of activities. For goodness sake –' she unhooked Rosie's arm from round her waist – 'it's only two nights. Go away! Enjoy yourselves. Phone as often as you like. But have fun, because I will when you return the favour.'

So finally, after another round of goodbye kisses, Rosie, girlishly pretty in a light blue summer dress, climbed up into the passenger's seat of the Isuzu and shut the door.

Lachlan didn't start up the engine straight away. He took a long look at her first and asked if she was OK.

'Yes, I'm fine ... I'll be fine,' Rosie told him.

'There's something for you in the glove box,' he said.

She popped the button to find a can of ready-mixed gin and tonic in there along with a plastic glass.

'I thought it might help,' he explained.

She laughed at him and brought the glass out, seeing a small bundle of tissue paper inside it.

She picked it out and was about to scrunch it into the ashtray, when she felt something hard inside.

'Is this . . . ?'

'Open it,' he instructed, turning the key in the ignition and sliding the car into gear.

She unfolded the paper to find a pair of diamond and pearl stud earrings. Written in felt-tip pen inside the paper were the words: 'I love you, Mrs Murray.'

'Oh,' she said, 'I didn't think . . . I haven't got you . . .'

'Tenth wedding anniversaries are pearl, apparently,' he said, words coming out awkwardly. 'But you're my diamond always, Rosie.'

He was learning, despite what his mother had told him, that love means *constantly* having to say you're sorry.

Rosie grinned at him, kissed him on the cheek and the Isuzu pulled off with a terrible, rattling, clanking commotion in its wake.

'What the *hell* is that?' he asked. 'Sounds like the exhaust's gone.'

She began to laugh. 'Keep going, it's fine. I'll show you later.'

So, they carried on out of Ingrid and Harry's farm road and on to the two-day country house holiday – arranged entirely by Lachlan – with ten tin cans tied to the back bumper beneath a large handwritten note Rosie had taped on, bearing the words:

STILL MARRIED (JUST)

THE END